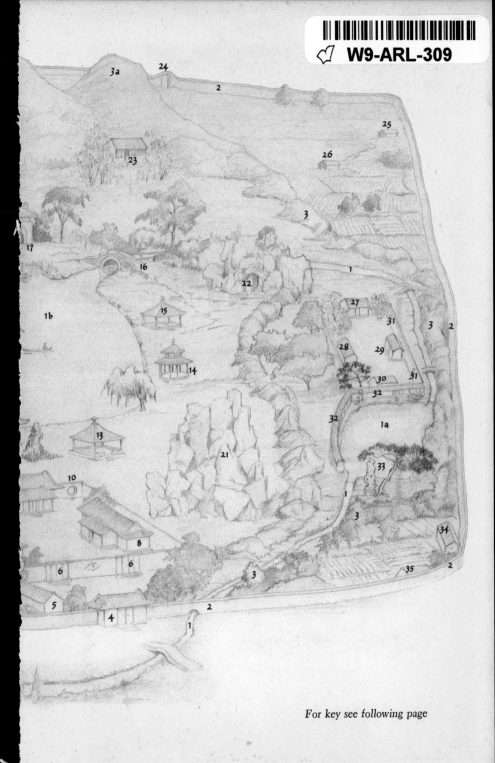

For key see following page

The River Garden of Pure Repose

CENTRAL SECTION

1 Water System
  1a Pool of the Rock and Pine
  1b The Happy Sea
  1c The Pool for Reflecting
    the Clouds
2–2–2 The enclosing walls
3–3–3 The system of artificial hills
      3a, b, c The Celestial Peaks
      3d Stone seats and table
4 The Main Gate
5 The Gatehouse
6 The Turquoise Gates to the Court
  for Inviting the Pleasures
7 Tranquil Heart

8 Quiet Mind
9 Hall for Inviting the Pleasures
10–10 Moon Gates
11 The Water Mirror Pavilion
12 The Plum Blossom T'ing-Tse
13 The Orchid T'ing-Tse
14 The Lute House
15 The Chess T'ing-Tse
16 The Moon Bridge
17 The Temple to the Flowers
18 The T'ing-Tse for Awaiting
  the Moon
19 The Porch of the Fan
20 The Island of the Bat

EAST SECTION

21 The Garden Rockery
22 The Grotto
23 The Joy of Bamboos
24 The Rear Gate
25 Tool House
26 Coolie Quarters
27 The Nameless Room
28 The Cool Room
29 Room for a Little Nap
30 The Chai of the Three Friends
31–31 The Vase Gates
32 The Gallery for Placing
  the Hand upon the Pine
33 The Mi Fei Rock
34 Kitchen
35 Servants' Quarters

WEST SECTION

36 The Fox Fairy Temple
37 The Studio of Clear Sounds
38 The Library of Four Delights
39 The T'ing-Tse for Looking to the
  Snow Mountains
40 The Gate to the Court
  of Retirement
41–41 The Gallery of the Lantern
  Windows
42 The Shadow of Pine
43 The Fragrance of Bamboo
44 The Hall Where All Past
  Wishes Come True

The RIVER GARDEN
of PURE REPOSE

The RIVER GARDEN of PURE REPOSE

GRACE M. BOYNTON

McGRAW-HILL BOOK COMPANY, INC.

New York Toronto London

THE RIVER GARDEN OF PURE REPOSE

To my godchild and namesake
Grace Li-En Lew
I dedicate this book

The RIVER GARDEN
of PURE REPOSE

God lies in wait for us with nothing so much as love. Love is like a fisherman's hook. Without the hook he could never catch a fish, but once the hook is taken, even though the fish twists hither and yon, still the fisherman is sure of him. And so, too, I speak of love: he who is held by it is held by the strongest of bonds, and yet the stress is pleasant. Moreover, he can sweetly bear all that happens to him. When one has found this bond, he looks for no other.

Meister Eckhart (1260–1328)

Translated by Raymond Bernard Blakney

History of THE WANG FAMILY

and their

RIVER GARDEN OF PURE REPOSE

as incorporated in the novel

c. 1650   The WANG ANCESTOR leaves the city of PEKING out of loyalty
to the dethroned MING DYNASTY and follows that house into exile.

1650–1760   THE WANGS, after wandering, become merchants in Canton,
and grow rich in trade with the West. They own many estates but
finally settle in the garden property they have acquired in Szechuan.
When they take possession, the garden has already come into
existence. Its WALLS, HILLS, and WATER SYSTEM have been built.
It also has

> THE COURT OF RETIREMENT, which includes THE HALL
>   WHERE ALL PAST WISHES COME TRUE
> THE WATER MIRROR PAVILION
> THE GROTTO

The GROTTO is a very ancient site and may have been used as a
shrine or hermitage before there was any garden. Soon after the
WANGS take up residence, a MING PRINCE seeks asylum with them
and while he is there he gives the garden its name and writes the
pien, or name board, for the gate.

1760–1800   THE WANG FAMILY continues to prosper and uses its increasing wealth to build

> THE COURT FOR INVITING THE PLEASURES
> THE ISLAND OF THE BAT
> THE TEMPLE TO THE FLOWERS
> THE MOON BRIDGE
> THE GARDEN ROCKERY

They set up on the ISLAND OF THE BAT a fine life-sized statue of
KUAN YIN, GODDESS OF MERCY, who appears seated upon her lotus
pedestal. At this time the family acquires THE MEI FEI ROCK.

1800–1870   Trade is now a matter of past history for the WANGS, who
have become landed gentry. WANG WEN-HAO becomes a convert to
Christianity and makes changes in the garden. He destroys the

family tablets in THE HALL WHERE ALL PAST WISHES COME TRUE. He removes the images of THE FLOWER MAIDEN and her ATTEND-ANTS from THE TEMPLE TO THE FLOWERS; he takes the KUAN YIN away from the ISLAND OF THE BAT and conceals her in THE GROTTO. However he adds

> THE COURT OF THE THREE FRIENDS, including THE CHAI
> and its GALLERY
> THE LIBRARY OF FOUR DELIGHTS
> THE LUTE HOUSE

1870–1890 WANG CH'ENG-HSIN, a second-generation Christian, is cut off from any Christian community and is less zealous than his father, WANG WEN-HAO. This son is of a gentle and scholarly disposition. When it is time for his marriage the family wishes to do honor to his highly connected bride, and for her they build

> THE PORCH OF THE FAN

Years later, in order to entertain his artist friend WU MEI-SUN, a descendent of a famous painter of the YUAN DYNASTY, WANG CH'ENG-HSIN builds

> THE STUDIO OF CLEAR SOUNDS
> THE CHESS T'ING-TSE

In the STUDIO OF CLEAR SOUNDS, WU MEI-SUN produces the series of paintings which constitute the ALBUM called THE BAMBOO MASTERPIECE, which is a family treasure.
For the accommodation of a concubine there is also built

> THE JOY OF BAMBOOS

1890–1910 WANG TSUNG-TAO, son of WANG CH'ENG-HSIN, has less money than his forebears and when his turn to deal with the garden arrives he adds four small structures. These are

> THE PLUM BLOSSOM T'ING-TSE
> THE ORCHID T'ING-TSE
> THE T'ING-TSE FOR AWAITING THE MOON
> THE T'ING-TSE FOR LOOKING TO THE SNOW MOUTAINS

1910–—— WANG WEI-CHOU, who is a modern-minded medical student, has no money to spend in his garden. During his absence SHANG MA, the wife of the gateman SHANG SHIH, becomes possessed by a fox-spirit, and in order to exorcise this spirit SHANG SHIH secretly builds a miniature shrine, THE FOX FAIRY TEMPLE. This is placed in an out-of-the way corner, and is the final addition to the structures in the WANG FAMILY RIVER GARDEN OF PURE REPOSE.

Chapter One

Wilfreda Grayson finished her letter. The thin sheet made of flimsy fiber caught in the point of her pen which was much worn; the ink would not flow freely, and when it did, the soft paper spread it in blots as often as in writing. The stamp would cost so much that she thought she would not buy her usual handful of peanuts when she went out on the street. It was an ordinary refugee letter written to tell an ordinary refugee story. Jane was not going to live long. Wilfreda read carefully:

Dear Bishop Chambers,

A fairly decent journey. The truck lost two wheels, one after the other, but we didn't turn over. One is grateful to arrive anywhere in China—especially West China—still intact.

Went at once to Jane. She greeted me with her own smile and talked of you. She knows her time is short, and her one desire is that nobody shall be troubled on her account. She understands she may have days, and perhaps months, of freedom from suffering, but that each ordeal brings her nearer to the end. She is just now weak from an attack which seems to have spent itself.

What do you think of my remaining? That is my answer to your question whether anything can be done for her. She is not one of our Mission, of course, but the Friends have no one else here, and while all the overworked people in this hospital do their best, Jane must lack attention if I leave her. The community is hospitable but it is crowded with refugees. The most that can be managed is to give Jane a room to herself. I think it was originally a supply closet, but it has a window so it could be pressed into service. Here she lies, and my traveling cot has been set up at the foot of the best bed the hospital

1

could find for her—trestles with planks, but free from vermin. There is no place to put anything away. Every article needed for her care is piled on one narrow shelf and the clutter is unavoidable. You know her love of beauty—curiously combined with her "plain" tradition. When she is well enough, she asks for her studies of Chinese gardens, they tell me, and adds a note here or makes a comment there. You remember, such studies are her hobby. She has worked with Chinese scholarfolk and with Dr. Barry Manners, a Sinologue. So she does what she can to forget her surroundings, or rather, as she would say, to accept them thankfully, since everyone is extremely good to her. But there is no such thing as quiet or comfort, nor can she have much attention if I am not here. Let me know whether I may stay.

W.G.

Wilfreda slipped the sheet into its flimsy envelope and addressed it to the Right Reverend Michael Chambers, Bishop of Ho Si. Subordinates and friends addressed him as "R Square," but Wilfreda, a junior member of her Mission, had never ventured to adopt that informality. She was aware, however, that hers was not a usual sort of bishop. He made his headquarters near the fighting, and held his services in a bombed-out medicine shop among the despairing and dispossessed. His concern over Jane was another case in point. It was not the affair of an English bishop to look after an American Quaker. But R Square, upon hearing of Jane's illness, had sent Wilfreda to investigate and report.

Pushing her stool back from the table where she had made a place to write in the shadow of bottles and jugs, Wilfreda rose as quietly as she could. She picked up the light—a saucer of crude pottery in which burned a thick wick fed by evil-smelling rapeseed oil—and held it over the figure stretched in the shadow behind her. The face was turned away but the breathing was quiet. Jane's last attack had left her weak, but she was now out of pain. Wilfreda opened the door and went out into the corridor.

A nurse loomed up in the yellowish darkness created by the lamps which were placed at infrequent intervals in the passage. She spoke in Chinese.

"Miss Grayson? There is someone who wants to see Miss Breasted. Will you go down?"

In the waiting room below, Wilfreda found a tall, grave-faced man in Chinese army uniform. He was standing as she came in, and he turned to her with a movement which she noted was graceful and courteous. He spoke in formal, meticulous English.

"You are here with Miss Breasted, they tell me. My name is Wang Wei-Chou. I am a colonel in the Medical Corps of the Army of Resistance. Years ago, in the north, I was Miss Breasted's student. I know her as 'Teacher Jane.'"

"I am Wilfreda Grayson of the Anglican Mission. I am sorry Miss Breasted is too ill to see her friends."

Wang Wei-Chou smiled.

"You are besieged with us, I am sure."

The door opened and another figure joined them. It was the hospital superintendent, a bustling little man in a white coat, whose voice sounded kindly, tired, and hurried.

"Well, well, Wilson Wang! High time you came back to Huai Yuen. Doing great things, we hear; we know about you. We're proud of you."

They shook hands as he went on talking.

"I see you have met Miss Grayson. Anglican Mission. Taking care of one of our refugees, Miss Jane Breasted. You wanted to see me about her?"

The formality of Colonel Wang's manner was in contrast to the bustle of the other.

"I have a request to make of Miss Breasted, with your permission, Dr. Hartshorn."

"A request, eh? She's pretty weak. Not seeing anyone but the nurses," said the superintendent.

"Dr. Hartshorn, I was on the surgical team which operated on Miss Breasted in Nanking before the Japanese took over. I have some knowledge of her medical history. My request—"

"Is Dr. Hartshorn here?" a voice interrupted.

The door opened and the little man in white ran out of the room. A glare of light fell through the window and a heavy car came grinding over the road outside. The light and the noise of the wheels and the engine were followed by footsteps, voices, and then groans.

"An ambulance," said the Chinese, glancing out.

"I'm afraid it has awakened Miss Breasted. They come in constantly and she sleeps very badly," remarked Wilfreda.

"I have thought of it. I also know how crowded and uncomfortable a hospital in West China must be in wartime. You know we Chinese take the student-teacher relationship very seriously. I have come to make sure she is moved to better quarters."

"Better quarters, eh?" said Dr. Hartshorn, popping back into the room as suddenly as he had left it. "You want to move Miss Breasted, do you? How would she feel about that?" he said to Wilfreda.

"I am sure she feels that she is very fortunate to be where she is," the Englishwoman answered.

"We do what we can," said the superintendent. "But conditions are against us. We're full up—except for the bugs. There seems always to be room for more of them—and I know I shouldn't be frivolous about 'em. What do you have in mind, Wilson?"

"You remember, sir, there is a garden not too far away from here which belongs to my family. For two years now it has been empty except for an old scholar who was my childhood tutor and who has come as a refugee from the north. And, of course, there are the servants. But there is plenty of room."

"So there is; so there is. Good idea, Wilson. You always did have sound ideas. Miss Breasted doesn't need constant hospital care. Crowding, dirt, noise, confusion, all exhausting, eh, Miss Grayson?"

"I am counting upon your persuasion to convince my old teacher that this is the wise arrangement for her," said the Chinese to Wilfreda. "May I beg you to say to her that I hope you and she will make the place your home indefinitely, while I am absent with the army?"

"Couldn't be better. I can get a breath of air and country when I go out for the periodical examination," said Dr. Hartshorn. "Do you good, Miss Grayson. Do us all good. Now, that's settled."

Wang Wei-Chou took a step toward Wilfreda.

"I should like to have arrangements made in the garden before we move Teacher Jane. Could you go out with me—tomorrow at ten?"

Dr. Hartshorn answered for her. "Of course she can. I'll have someone else on duty with Miss Breasted while she's gone. Glad to have seen you, my boy. Come around to Mrs. Hartshorn for a meal before you go back to your army. Must know more about what you are doing."

The Chinese bowed to Wilfreda, shook hands with the superintendent, and was gone before the Englishwoman had spoken. She turned to Dr. Hartshorn dazedly.

"Are you sure Miss Breasted will agree?"

"Doctor's orders," was the brisk reply. "In this case, two doctors. That's a fine boy. Old Szechuan gentry—no better stock in the world. Known him all his life. Spoiled as a kid. Too much money. Too important at home. But he has brains and the will to use them. Studied in Peking, and Europe; went to Nanking later—where he got to know your patient, you see. When the war came, he joined up. Not many of his sort did. Now he uses his garden for two of his teachers. You'll love the place."

Wilfreda found herself talked down the corridor and out the door into the entrance court, with no pause for remarks from her. She passed on through the tall hospital gates to the narrow track of muddy street, and picked her way through rills of water to the post office where she mailed her letter. She hurried back without stopping at the shop where the smell of hot roasted peanuts reminded her of the persistent drawing sensation in her stomach. In the little second-floor room, she found the patient stirring.

"Pain, dear one?"

"Oh no," the voice came faintly. "But Brother Ass is full of nerves tonight. He twitches and twitches and turns and turns, and he has no sense at all. St. Francis was right to call his body 'Brother Ass.' A body is a ridiculous creature."

The words were spoken lightly but with physical effort.

"Can I do anything for Brother Ass?"

"Distract his mind," said Jane. "Although of late he hasn't had any. He hasn't even allowed me to read my letters. Could you get them out for me, Freda?"

"Where are they?"

"In the straw basket hanging on the wall. I use that for my letter file because of the rats. They run all over the place, you know. They'll eat the soap and the candle if you don't turn a basin over them before you go to bed. I don't much mind except when they run across my face."

The speech was too long for her available strength, and her voice sank at the end into a whisper. Wilfreda took the basket from its peg and drew her stool near the vegetable-oil lamp.

"How shall I choose from all these?"

"As they come," murmured Jane.

The nurse picked up a stiff, square envelope.

"This is good thick paper," she said. "It was never made in West China. It is from Major Robert Trent, U.S. Air Force in Chungking."

An uneasy movement on the plank bed indicated that Brother Ass was claiming attention. Wilfreda opened the envelope and read aloud:

Dear Jane Breasted,

My mother was a Friend, and a distant connection of yours, so I could claim to call you cousin, although you've never seen me, nor, I suppose, heard much about me. I use your first name and I'm hoping you'll use mine. I have just reached Chungking and enclose some home-side messages I have brought for you.

Are you interested in other news from God's country? If you will ask me questions, I may be able to supplement what you have heard, although of course I write through censorship. I have a great desire to hear from you. I am new in China, and very much bewildered by my surroundings. If you will undertake to help me to an understanding of all this strangeness I shall be most grateful. And I will answer any questions you care to ask me about myself.

Sincerely yours,

Robert Trent

P.S. I have discovered that Daisy Fairchild, a young subordinate of mine, knew you well in North China.

"He appeals to a poor source of information," commented Jane, and she brought out the words draggingly. "Now—I—could only—give—him the ideas of Brother Ass who is not to be—relied upon."

Freda laid down the letter and decided to delay discussion of the wishes of Colonel Wang until the next morning.

"I think that's enough, isn't it?" she suggested gently.

"I can't seem to pay attention," was the weary answer.

settled Jane for the night, stretched out in the dusty sleeping bag on her own cot. In spite of fatigue, she was up every two hours for the routine of nursing care, and in the intervals she kept an ear out of her

Wilfreda put the letters back in the basket, and when she had sleep and was aware that the night passed in dry wakefulness and twitching distress for her patient. It seemed an extraordinary piece of good fortune that a change in arrangements could be made—that is, if Colonel Wang's garden proved to be a place where one could manage the nursing. Wilfreda hoped the Bishop would let her stay on for a bit.

Chapter Two

Promptly to his hour, Wang Wei-Chou presented himself with two rickshas, and Wilfreda was notified of his arrival. She found him not less impressive than the night before as she scrutinized him in full daylight, and saw the cut and quality of his uniform which proclaimed prosperity in almost offensive contrast to the poverty of wartime Szechuan. But the lines in his face, the spareness in his body reminded her that he had been sharing in the hardships of the war, and his gravity bore witness to the responsibilities he carried. She found it possible to forgive his conspicuous tailoring in spite of her consciousness of her own travel-worn clothes, rough in material, shapeless in fit, and nondescript in color. He asked her at once whether she had spoken to Jane about the move to his garden.

"I told her this morning. She can hardly believe it. She accepts your kindness like a happy child."

"She is very weak and very much worn?"

"So much so that she finds it too taxing even to listen to the reading of her mail. She asked me to open a letter for her last night, but she could not pay attention for more than a few moments. I decided to wait until this morning to tell her about your invitation. When I explained it, the tears rose in her eyes, and she did not speak immediately."

He was listening intently. "But then what did she say?"

"When she could, she whispered, 'Please thank him.' A little later, she pulled me by the sleeve, and when I leaned over her, she said, 'Do you think we can go soon?' "

"It shall be as soon as possible. Please sit on the ricksha."

As she got in, she was interested that this was the first slip she had

8

noticed in his English. But she at once transferred her attention to the little vehicle which was a startling contrast to the Huai Yuen examples of the same conveyances. Its black-lacquer body was speckless as were its brass fittings and lamps. The rug, folded over the seat, was fine in quality, and it was immaculate. The puller was dressed in whole, clean clothing, and looked sleek and well fed compared to the gaunt people in the streets. He took up the shafts when she was in her seat, and trotted away with her. Her companion followed in a broken-down contraption which he had hired at the gates.

They went through rough streets between low, dilapidated buildings standing on the edges of rubble where bombs had fallen. They passed through a breach in the ancient wall, which had been made to give the city crowds a chance to get out when the Japanese planes came over, and entered a section devoted to the manufacture of dusters and fans and other articles made out of chicken feathers, thousands of which were laid out to dry at the edge of the road. They filled the air with a vague but disagreeable stench, and once free of them, Wilfreda drew a long breath. It was a mild, gray day, and the river, very low in its bed, was to her left, the long city wall to her right. Presently the crowds and the smells were gone. She found herself in a countryside of level fields, bordered by streams of gray-green water. Here and there she saw temples and walled compounds; but the fields made a misty plain to a dim horizon which veiled the foothills of the Snow Mountains to the west; and it was to the foothills, she found, that they were bound. The runner paced fleetly along down the wide, dusty road which stood high above the surrounding country. Its holes and ruts were continuous. Wayfarers passed in dust and rags and shouting; primitive carts were dragged along by men with ropes over their shoulders; rattling trucks and bulging buses creaked and plunged like vessels in a heavy sea. After more than an hour of this main highway, the rickshas turned off on a narrow track which wound around the first projections of stony rises in the plain. At last the road came to dim-gray walls which lifted under the shadows of immense trees, and Wilfreda's runner stopped before a roofed gate built of heavy, dark timbers. She looked up at the lacquered board hanging above her, on which four Chinese characters were traced in gold.

"How would you translate?" asked Wang Wei-Chou as he came to help her out of her ricksha.

She stepped down, and then stood still, concentrating and reading with her lips as well as with her eyes.

"The River Garden of Pure Repose," she suggested.

Her host was pleased.

"I see you are accomplished in Chinese," he said. "The name was given to the place by one of the Ming pretenders, who, wandering as a fugitive, was sheltered here by an ancestor of mine. You observe the reason for the name," and he pointed to a channel of flowing water which came from the west and entered a water gate a little farther to the east than the spot where they were standing. Wilfreda noticed that they must cross a low footbridge of hewn stone in order to approach the entrance, and as they went forward, Wang added, "Of course the name given by the refugee prince is not very commonly used. The people always call the place the 'Wang Family Garden'— the 'Wang Chia Yuan.'"

He beat upon the double leaves of the gate and called aloud: "Shang Shih."

There was a sound of shuffling feet within, and as Wilfreda waited for the unbarring of the gate, she looked again at the name of the garden. Repose for a weary body, purity for a pilgrim spirit—it seemed a strange and perfect refuge to discover in time of war.

They were admitted by a stooped old man with a kindly, intelligent face pitted with scars. He bowed to his master and stood aside for the men to bring in the rickshas. Then the leaves were swung shut, and Wilfreda found herself in a gloom cast by two spreading trees overhead. Underfoot was gray stone flagging, and in her ears the sound of running water.

A low, dark house with a fiber thatch crouched at the left of the covered space inside the gate; the pullers had put down their shafts and were taking out their pipes and tobacco. A small, dark woman, wearing blue homespun linen and a white cloth turbanwise on her head, came out of the door and, with Shang Shih, bowed before Wang Wei-Chou.

"Here are Shang Shih, the gateman, and Shang Ma, his wife," said her host to Wilfreda, and he then spoke to the servants in rapid

Szechuanese, which was sufficiently different from the Mandarin which she had been taught to be quite unintelligible to the English-woman. While the talk went on, she looked eagerly about her, for during her ten years in China she had never before been in a place of this sort.

She was a little disappointed that she was not able to see more. The area surrounded by the outer walls was large, but this rather narrow entrance space was blocked to the north by lower inner walls. These were pierced by two side doorways, each closed with four leaves of greenish blue dimmed with damp and age. Between them, the wall was ornamented with a stone carving in a delicate peony pattern, over which luxuriant creeper hung its long stems. For the rest, the flagged path branched and led east and west along this screening wall toward ground which rose unevenly and was planted with trees and a tangle of other growing things. The great girth and lofty branches of the trees made her feel like a child in a fairy tale.

Wang Wei-Chou was ready to go on. He turned to her apologetically.

"I ask your pardon for keeping you. We go this way."

He turned east and then went north around the corner of the inner wall. Wilfreda caught a glimpse in the distance of a summer house, with slender columns supporting an airy peaked roof, but she had hardly had a chance to look at it before her attention was caught by something which seemed an utter contrast to the elegance of the little garden structure. Directly opposite, on the east side of the path, was an extraordinary collection of stone shapes—she could scarcely recognize them as the objects she knew as rocks. They were porous in substance, and somehow startling in their manifold forms. Their colors ranged through shades of gray and tawny earth hues; they were piled together with no apparent reason in their arrangement. She stopped at a point where the rocks rose several feet above her head, and her guide turned inquiringly as she lost step with him.

"Oh," said Wilfreda, "please excuse me, but I have never seen anything like this. What . . . what in the world is it?"

"Ornamental garden rock," the other explained. "We Chinese use a great deal of it. I understand foreigners do not like it."

The old gateman, who had followed his master and the guest, came up to them now and Wilfreda saw him point upward with his chin. Upon a ledge and before an opening high in the pile of stones there was a small clay bowl. She was quite sure she caught what the old man said, since he spoke emphatically after his master had addressed a question to him.

"The Golden Ones have not come this year. You should burn incense before you leave the garden."

Her host gave no outward sign of his reception of this admonition, and Wilfreda had a feeling that he was a little annoyed; but she did not like to ask questions. She decided, as she followed on, that the bowl was like those she had often seen before roadside shrines. Perhaps the rock pile was something like those shrines. Then, were the Golden Ones garden deities? Jane would probably know. The path, still in deep shade, was narrow, so that it was difficult to keep at Wang's side.

"I suppose," she said to him, "the servants have been asking for news of your family. Where are they now?"

"There are only my mother and my eight-year-old son," was the reply. "Before the American Air Force moved into this district, there was a good deal of banditry, and my mother did not consider it safe. She has gone to another family estate, a great distance from here, where she will remain until the war is over. But I hope," he added, "that you and Teacher Jane will not feel nervous. Everything is now under very strict control."

As he spoke, they came out of the shade and Wilfreda caught her breath in delight over the prospect before her. There was a sheet of water with a little island in it. There were trees leaning from the deeply indented shore, which sent long, green shadows into the still, gray depths. Immediately at her left she saw a structure, oblong in shape and of fine proportions, planned for the enjoyment of the garden scene. It had a low, dipping roof, carried on smooth, dark pillars; it had wide steps on three sides leading up to its pleasant shelter. It had, on the water side, a seat with a curving back running the length of the pavilion which was built into the water so that ripples lapped its stone foundation. On the bench, occupying himself with a fish pole when Wilfreda first caught sight of him, was an elderly Chinese in a robe of faded-blue silk.

"There is my old tutor, Master Yuan," said Wang Wei-Chou as Shang Shih went forward to announce the newcomers.

Wilfreda had never before encountered a fisherman wearing silk, and she took in as many details of the sportsman as she could before he had come near enough to make her scrutiny a piece of bad manners. He was very thin and hollow-chested; he had a few gray strings of beard straying out of his upper lip and chin. When he became aware of the new arrivals, he moved toward them with dignity and deliberation, and then he and Wang Wei-Chou stood bowing to each other, uttering courteous expressions of pleasure and the proper inquiries concerning health and prosperity until all the requirements of politeness had been met. The bows of the younger man were much deeper than those of the old scholar, and Wilfreda felt in the formality a genuine reverence for his former teacher on the part of her host. He presented Wilfreda, explaining his errand, and the old man bowed ceremoniously but without looking in her direction. He expressed the hope that Jane's health would improve, but it seemed to the nurse that he was addressing the garden in general rather than herself in particular. She experienced the sensation of being suddenly invisible and murmured a subdued reply which elicited another polite bow. It was then possible for the host to suggest that he must complete his arrangements for the reception of the invalid, but that he would call at the Library of Four Delights before returning to Huai Yuen. Upon this, Master Yuan bowed again, and his pupil bent low several times, after which the old man returned to the bench where he had put down his fish pole, and the others continued along the strand of the little lake.

"Do you mind my asking," said Wilfreda, "about one thing I caught as you were talking? You and Master Yuan used Mandarin so it was easier to follow than when you were speaking Szechuanese."

"Of course we speak Mandarin," said Wang Wei-Chou. "My parents invited him to take charge of my education because he was a distinguished scholar from the capital, and they wanted my Pekingese to be good. What is it that interested you?"

"You spoke of a 'Library of Four Delights'; I wondered what they are?"

"Breezes in spring, flowers in summer, moon in autumn, and snow in winter. All proper garden libraries are supposed to be placed so that they have these pleasures."

"Oh," said Wilfreda. "And I want to know something else. Do you put on silk when you are going fishing?"

Wang laughed.

"I don't," he said. "But a Chinese scholar is a Chinese scholar. I'm only an unrefined soldier—a very different matter. Master Yuan doesn't go fishing for fish, you know."

"Doesn't he? Then for what?"

"To enjoy the garden scene—or get an idea for a poem or a letter— or an entry in his journal, maybe. And, of course, he might, incidentally, catch a fish. Teacher Jane understands all such matters, and if Master Yuan takes a fancy to you ladies, he will tell you quantities of things about this particular garden much better than I can."

Wilfreda was longing to ask about other buildings of which she had had glimpses, each one set apart in its special nook, all looking fragile and fantastic like bits out of fleeting dreams. But Wang Wei-Chou was walking more rapidly than before; keeping pace with him, she promised herself many leisurely hours beside the lake when she and Jane had actually taken up residence. Now she was guided along the east bank, until they came to the point where a narrow stream flowed into the main basin. This was spanned by an arched bridge. Instead of crossing it, her companion followed a path which led around a spur of the hillocks into a secluded part, shut away from the water by the rises of ground and the density of trees. Presently she saw low-lying roofs, and damp-greened walls ahead of her, and then they came to a vase-shaped gate and stepped into a little paved court-yard planted with pine and bamboo. In one corner, a single branch of a flowering plum, the Chinese *meihua*, stretched faintly pink against the gray-tiled roof and filled the air with its cold spring perfume. To the north, south, east, and west stood separate rooms, little rooms with deep eaves and paper-backed lattice, all joined into a unit by the wall which framed each corner.

"Where are we now?" Wilfreda asked.

"We call this the 'Chai of the Three Friends'—the 'San Yu Chai,' " said Wang. "I sent word to Shang Shih to sweep out and have all ready for you."

"I don't know that word '*chai*'; is it the same as '*yuan*,' for court?"

"I see," said the other smiling, "that this matter of names is important to you, as it is to us Chinese. '*Chai*' means, literally, a place for abstinence and meditation; I suppose you might translate it 'study,' although that's very far from giving its complete idea. It does mean the whole courtyard, but often we apply it to that main room to the south here where, I suppose, you will eat and spend your days."

"But the three friends?" said Wilfreda, looking around.

"The traditional friends you meet in art: the pine, the plum, and the bamboo, to which I now introduce you in reality," and he swept his hand in a circle which included them all.

"How beautifully quiet."

"Yes. It is the most secluded of the houses and it is within reach of the servants. Shang Ma doesn't stay at the gatehouse. Her quarters are just beyond the hills you see around the little water basin in front of the Chai. By the way," he broke off, "I hope Shang Ma won't bother you ladies."

"Bother us?"

"I think I should just mention what my mother wrote before she left. It seems Shang Ma occasionally has a . . . a . . . delusion. It's nothing violent, at all, just hysteria, brought on by bad war experience, I suppose."

"What sort of delusion?"

"Well, she thinks she's a fox."

Wilfreda remembered prevalent superstitions about human beings who become possessed by fox spirits which are very unpredictable in their behavior, and felt immensely interested as Wang continued:

"She goes off into a sort of trance and says all sorts of things appropriate to foxes, but she comes out, if you leave her alone—and if she doesn't get excited. She's never done any harm during her seizures, but I understand Shang Shih is badly frightened by them. However, they don't happen often, and otherwise you will find her very helpful. She will cook and clean; the garden coolies will go out to buy food for you in the villages. Of course, some arrangements here are primitive, but with the servants, I hope it won't prove too difficult for you."

"Difficult! Nothing could be more perfect. I'm sure Shang Ma's fox spirit won't trouble either of us."

"I am afraid our accommodation is not entirely suited to a sick foreigner," said the Chinese. "But please list whatever you find lacking, after you have been in the rooms, and my coolies will bring the things out from Huai Yuen."

He handed Wilfreda a notebook and pencil which he produced from his pocket, and swung wide the door of the room to the north.

"This will be best for Teacher Jane. There are no beds, as you see, but I have approached some acquaintances for army cots, which you should find comfortable. Shang Shih knows how to set them up, with their frames for nets. Do you have nets?"

"Yes, both of us."

Freda had taken a hasty look inside the door and was scribbling down items needed.

"If you will excuse me now, I must go to pay my respects to Master Yuan, and attend to a few other matters. I will not be long. Perhaps you will be glad of a chance to concentrate on your list."

He went away, and Wilfreda wandered about the court and looked in at the doors which were all standing open. She felt the freshness of the uncluttered rooms, which had evidently just been put in perfect order. The floors were of stone; the white plaster walls reached to open rafters. There were chests of dark wood, and wardrobes of homely solid shapes with hinges and locks set in perfect rounds of plain brass. Slender-legged tables were flanked by straight-backed chairs; the patterns in the lattices differed in each room and gave a touch of delicacy to the prevailing austerity.

Wilfreda sank down upon the stone step to the west room which she intended for her own use, and felt the soft grayness of the day and the green silence of the court creating an utter peacefulness within her. Living here would be primitive, as Wang Wei-Chou had pointed out. It would mean hard work for her even though she could count on some help. Water must be carried in and carried out again. Laundry would be a problem. All food must be cooked on a charcoal brazier and taken to Jane, who must not be subjected to the fumes of the open stoves. It would probably tax her ingenuity to deal with sanitation. She added disinfectants to her list, which now included dishes, basins, pails, a chair with cushions for Jane—and then she paused, wondering how she would contrive to pay for what she had already put down. Inflation prices were cruelly impossible. Then she recalled a supply of sulfa drugs which Michael Chambers had sent with her in case it might be of use to Jane, and decided that the hospital might barter what she needed for the drug. She wondered how many tablets of sulfa she would have to pay for ten bars of laundry soap. A refugee world was not without its resources.

She put the notebook away and walked across the Chai, which was to be the living-dining room, to the covered gallery built across its south windows and extending an arm on the west side of the pool, which gave the whole arrangement an air of the greatest privacy. It would serve the added purpose of space for promenades in the wet weather which was so persistent in Szechuan. It fronted on a little scene, prepared especially for those who indulged in abstinence and meditation, consisting of the pool, edged with natural stones and surrounded with cupping hills which shut the Chai into its isolation and silence. On the other side of the pool immediately opposite the door from which she had emerged, Wilfreda noticed a great rock shape starting up from the ground in a whorl of gray-hollowed mass, thinned in places to rounded openings made by water action in some forgotten past. It was not only strange in its effect but it was positively disquieting, Wilfreda felt. Why, in that retreat of peace, should such a startling form be introduced? She found a place to sit and ponder the object, trying to think what it resembled and coming to the conclusion that it was like nothing at all, which was what made it so uncomfortable.

As she watched the rock, her thoughts reverted to the refugee world in which both she and Jane had been immersed, and from which it seemed incredible that they were now to be released. She thought of her own hospital, crowded with the sick who had broken down under the hardships of terrible journeys away from the greater Japanese terror—the dysentery, the ulcers, the malaria, the other fevers; she remembered the children brought in from the bombings burned and maimed. She thought of those who had gone frantic with their fears and sufferings. . . . She shivered and tried to break the train of associations. She hoped that the rock was not going to get on her nerves.

And now it was the suffering of the overtaxed hospital staff she thought of—the weary arms, the aching backs, the burning feet, the minds so tired they could not keep the power of grasp and memory to deal with the remorseless demands of the long hours on duty. . . . Then the night of the attack. Her hospital without light . . . the hustling of litters into the basements . . . the obstetrical case they had to manage with only their electric torches . . . the grind and roar of the planes. And then the end of everything in one crash, and a depth of blackness.

She had been in Michael Chambers' cot when she came to herself. She remembered how her eyes had opened on the wooden cross on the mat-shed wall, and how the Bishop had come quietly in and sat by her. He told her what had happened. There was no hospital left. Plans would be made to reopen, but it would take time. And then his plan for her. She had lost consciousness from shock, but they hoped nothing much was wrong. She had hastily tried at this point to get up and prove herself unhurt, but the Bishop had forbidden it. He said a Red Cross unit was coming to take the place of his exhausted staff, and he was sending her north to Jane, for her own sake as well as for that of the sick Quaker.

And so she had come from the war world of weariness and violence to find Jane facing the end. Now, the two of them had a door open into peace. It was unbelievable that the serene beauty of this place could exist on the same planet with wartime China. Was it right for any two people to be delivered from the hardness of the common lot? But Wilfreda put this question from her. For Jane, the garden would mean not deliverance but only respite. And whatever respite was possible, Jane should have.

When Wang Wei-Chou returned, he found Wilfreda pacing the gallery and disinclined to talk. She followed him back through the garden paths without question or comment. But as they passed the rock pile, she raised her eyes and noticed that two sticks of incense were smoking in the little clay bowl on the ledge.

Lao Ch'i and Lao Pa brought Jane to the River Garden. They carried her on a bamboo stretcher which had a blue-cotton awning to hide her from the public eye. Wang Wei-Chou walked by her side the whole way, and had the stretcher set down at intervals that he might see how she was bearing the journey. Wilfreda was in the rear with rickshas loaded with her purchases, under the superintendence of Shang Shih who was faithfully carrying out his master's directions with regard to the "Shih Mu," as he phrased "Teacher Mother." At the gate, Shang Ma opened to them, and as the stretcher went forward into the green paths, Wilfreda saw two yellow butterflies, unusual in size and in intensity of color, that made her think of crusted gold. The gorgeous pair went playing about Jane's stretcher, hovering over it, sometimes lighting upon it, and going along with it with flourishes of shining wings. She spoke to the old servant.

"Shang Shih, do you see those yellow butterflies? What do you call them?"

The old man looked intently and seemed to experience satisfaction and relief.

"We call them 'The Golden Ones.' They come, every year."

"Do you have many Golden Ones?"

"We have only these two."

On the stretcher, Jane raised herself for a moment to look out into the freshness and silence.

"Ah," she said softly as she sank down again. "This is right. This is a green-gray Chinese garden. I shall be better here."

To Shang Ma the gateman gave his views upon the new arrival.

"The Golden Ones have returned. They followed the Shih Mu and even rested upon her curtains. It is certain that good fortune has entered our gates with her. It must be that she is a *sheng jen*—a holy person."

Chapter Three

The morning after he had brought Jane to the River Garden, Wang
Wei-Chou arrived at the door in the wall of the courtyard of the San
Yu Chai, and paused before asking to be admitted. Inside he could
hear Shang Ma in conversation with Wilfreda.

"And what is the age of the Shih Mu? Forty-seven? Even though
she is so thin and weak, she doesn't look it. Are her parents living?
Oh, they have left this world. Ayah! Brothers and sisters, how many?
None? The Shih Mu is alone, then, for she is not married; is that so?
I have heard about the customs of foreigners. When a girl reaches a
certain age, her mother says to her, 'Shall I find you a mother-in-law—
or will you be a missionary?' And so the Shih Mu became a missionary.
A pity, a great pity."

Jane's host knocked, and when Shang Ma opened to him, he dismissed her. She departed to recount to Shang Shih the information
she had gleaned during breakfast of the first morning, and her master
entered the court.

"Do you find you can talk with the servants without difficulty?"
he asked Wilfreda as she came to meet him.

"They seem to understand my poor Mandarin," she said. "At least,
well enough to provide the simple things I ask for. And, if they don't
talk too fast, and stick to limited topics, I get enough for all practical
purposes. In time, I shall learn to understand more."

"Szechuanese is a form of Mandarin," said Wang. "I hoped you
would find you could manage. If you are ever in difficulties, Master
Yuan will help you out."

He saw Jane on her cot under the pine which was growing before
her door. Faint sunlight was filtering through clouds, and little touches

of it lay like golden straws on the blue blanket in which she was wrapped. She greeted him happily.

"Good morning, Wei-Chou. You see, I am already living out-of-doors. I begged to be moved to the veranda of the Chai, but Wilfreda allows me to go only outside my own room for this first day."

"It is better not to do too much," her friend said, appealing to the doctor for approval. He bowed, and noted that the nurse as well as the patient seemed the better for the removal from Huai Yuen. Wilfreda had lost the abstraction and the tenseness he had observed in her during their first visit. She had been sitting on a stool at Jane's side, and a bowl and a feeding tube were on the flagstones under the cot. She gathered them up and left her place to the newcomer while she carried the dishes to Shang Ma's kitchen.

"You had a good night?" he asked, sitting down and placing a finger on Jane's pulse.

"Deep, quiet sleep, thanks to you—the greatest gift you ever gave anyone, I do believe."

"Not to be compared to the debt a student owes his teacher," said the young Chinese. "I shall go away happy that you are a little better already." And he laid down her wrist.

The content in Jane's eyes clouded a little.

"Going away? You are going away?"

"This morning I join Dr. Hartshorn as he comes out in the hospital jeep. He will drive me to the air base, which you know is nearby, whence I have a chance to fly to Chungking. Then he will come back to see you."

"When will you come again?"

"It is not possible to say."

Jane sighed.

"I suppose it is inevitable. My consolation is that your part in this war is the relief of the suffering. You see you have already relieved it for me."

"I wish I could keep all suffering away from you, Teacher Jane."

He spoke with such feeling that she looked up at him with a brightness in her face which he would long remember.

"Thank you for that good wish. But you and I know what lies before Brother Ass. The thing to remember is that he is not of the first importance. I hope you don't confuse Brother Ass with me, myself."

The other hesitated before he answered. She had banished pretense, and he must be honest, too.

"I am a doctor," he reminded her. "Brother Ass is my business."

Jane smiled.

"But . . . 'I am not contained between my hat and my boots,'" she quoted. "Didn't I teach you that?"

"You are still teaching it," he answered. "And I am still trying to learn."

She put her hand on his arm and spoke almost shyly.

"I can't tell you how it touches me to have you come back to me so kindly, so generously—after these many years."

"I have never been away from you."

He saw the tears in her eyes and she saw his fear that he had overtaxed her strength. As he made a movement to rise, she detained him.

"Before you go," she said, "one question more. Do you know anything about Willow?"

The name brought memories to them both of the young beauty, the indomitable will, the passion of rebellion in one of the most powerful natures either had ever known. For the man, the memories held the bittersweet of early love soon over. For Jane, they held the questing of an affection which brooded and did not waver.

"Willow?" said Wang Wei-Chou. "I have never seen her since we were your students in the north . . . it must be eleven years ago. You probably know more about her than I do."

"I did hear from her at long intervals until I came to West China," Jane answered. "She was always in political hot water, and once was in jail. I have heard rumors that she is here in Szechuan, still an underground Communist agent. You haven't any word at all?"

He shook his head.

"After graduation we went different ways. We never agreed in the least, you know, in spite of. . . ." He stopped and then went on. "I was already committed to working in medicine for the people; I was going into Public Health after I got my M.D. But of course her philosophy scorned anything short of revolution, and I wanted to try the middle way. Also, I am—as her father and, incidentally, all her ancestors were—a landlord, which to her is wickedness. We said good-by, and have never kept in touch."

"I knew that," said Jane. "From asking her about you. But I thought perhaps you might hear rumors from other University folk more than I do. We are scattered all over West China."

He made no reply, and she added, "If anything should come to your ears, you will let me know?" He bowed. "And one thing more. If she should ever come to me here—if she should seek asylum with me—what shall I do?"

At this he smiled.

"My dear Teacher Jane," he said, "when I brought you to the garden, I knew that you could not be expected to remain in it alone. There is space here, and I foresee that it will be in use. I shall give Shang Shih orders that he is to admit anyone who visits you and to consider your wishes as my own. And now I think you have talked enough."

She did not protest, but as he rose she held his sleeve and, looking up at him, said quietly, "Try to come to me once again if you can, before Brother Ass collapses. Always remember my gratitude. You are very dear to me."

He bent over her and took both hands in his as he made his reply. "I am your son."

When the sound of his steps had died away, Jane lay still and closed her eyes. She was utterly content. The effort which the brief talk had cost her did not leave her with a sense of exhaustion but rather with a perfect satisfaction in the quiet which closed around her. Hours passed before she stirred again, but she was not asleep. Her senses made a harmony of the sun's warmth on her body, of the pure air on her face, of the freshness of plants, and the winging of birds. Her spirit rejoiced in the compassion which had wrapped her around, the manifestation to her of the divine mercy which sustained her through human means. Words dropped away from her mind, but with her whole consciousness she drank in that mercy and gave back pure praise. The sun climbed high; the shadow of the pine boughs grew warmer; she breathed through golden hours.

Wilfreda had waited outside the gate for Wang Wei-Chou, and

when he appeared, she walked with him toward the entrance to the garden. There was an exchange of questions, and each confirmed the other in finding Jane already benefited.

"But it's temporary," said Wang. "And it is clear that she knows that."

"Oh yes, she knows," said Wilfreda. "How long, should you think . . . ?"

"Dr. Hartshorn believes not more than three months," was the reply.

When he was gone, Wilfreda returned to Jane. She looked in upon her from the inner door of the south room, and observing her deep repose, decided not to disturb her. In order to be on hand when Dr. Hartshorn would arrive from the airfield, she went back to the garden entrance, and when Shang Shih appeared to await her orders, she looked at the turquoise gates inquisitively.

"May I go in there?" she asked.

"It is permitted," said the old servant. "There is a place where the Hu Shih may sit and wait."

He opened the nearer of the twin gates, and Wilfreda passed into a spacious court with buildings larger and more formal than anything she had seen in the garden. Each had its nameboard, and she amused herself with attempting to read their characters. A hall opposite her on the north had a lofty roof and stood on a stone plinth over which its spreading eaves cast deep shadow. This was "Inviting the Pleasures." Shang Shih maneuvered its oblong lock, and the tall doors heavy with carving swung open. Inside were great empty spaces with ceremonial chairs set on either side of ponderous tables.

"The Hu Shih may await the Tai Fu here," the old man suggested, using his formal terms for "nurse" and "doctor" as he addressed Wilfreda in the third person.

She nodded, but as Shang Shih shuffled away, she continued her examination of the buildings. The rooms standing to the east and west were less imposing than the main hall, but their graceful proportions and fine ornament continued the impression of elegance and ordered living. Wilfreda felt her interest rather overwhelmed by the multitude of unfamiliar forms of architecture and detail surrounding her, and was grateful to observe that the names of the buildings were in simple characters which she knew. "Tranquil Heart" stood to the west and confronted "Quiet Mind" on the east. After idling about outside, she went into the Hall for Inviting the Pleasures, and sat in the straight-backed chair by the heavy table opposite the open doors, wondering what pleasures had accepted the invitation of the place. It did not suggest those of great hilarity.

Dr. Hartshorn found her there when Shang Shih ushered him in from his jeep. He carried a wicker basket and at once set about unpacking a lunch.

"They gave me some coffee and sandwiches at the airfield," he announced, displaying a Thermos bottle. "Brought some along for you. How are you two women going to manage about food, anyway?"

He cast a shrewd glance at Wilfreda's thin shoulders and at the sharp point of her elbow in its cotton sleeve. Szechuan produced plenty of everything necessary for a proper diet. But missions were having a hard time getting funds to their people, and when money did come, the inflation reduced its purchasing power. Everyone was getting thin, Chinese and foreigners alike. Two isolated women might be in difficulties.

"Oh, we'll manage. . . ." Wilfreda spoke absently. Then she changed the subject. "Did Dr. Wang get away as he expected?"

"Yes. He's well known. Colonel was glad to have a talk with him."

Wilfreda looked eagerly at the hot coffee poured for her into the cap of the Thermos bottle and gratefully accepted a sandwich as she remarked, "You have known Dr. Wang a long time, I believe?"

"All his life. His family was the first to have any truck with our Mission. Old Szechuan gentry . . . slow to get over distrust and suspicion of outsiders. They were Christian long before I came."

"Christian?" Wilfreda was surprised.

"Why not? There've been Christians in China for more than a hundred years. The Wangs have kept the faith for three generations. They combine it with a lot of Chinese customs. I saw the boy married in this very hall. There was a reverent ceremony; but then there were three days of firecrackers, theatricals, and teasing the bride—the whole clan came and enjoyed itself. Had the time of their lives."

"Oh." Wilfreda looked about. "So this hall is for family festivals. That accounts for it."

"For what?" The doctor's mouth was full.

"For the name, 'Inviting the Pleasures.' How long ago was that wedding?"

She took another stout sandwich, and Hartshorn placed some stuffed eggs on her side of the table.

"Let me see. A good ten years ago—maybe more. It was when he came back from the north where he did his university work. Soon afterward, he went away again for his medical training."

"And the bride remained here, I suppose. I think Dr. Wang mentioned that now there is only his son? And his old mother?"

"His wife died when the child was born," said Hartshorn. "She was a delicate little thing. Odd the old mother hasn't made him marry again. One grandson wouldn't be according to her notion of things."

Wilfreda took a sip of coffee, and as she savored it lingeringly, the doctor noted hollows in her cheeks under the prominent bones. The girl had probably never been much to look at, but there was a shine in her dark eyes and a sensitive line about her lips that the inroads of life in West China had not erased. Still, as a man, he could not help but remark that the good looks the Lord was supposed to supply to young women were sinking beneath the neutral surface with which he was all too familiar in the missionary world. Wilfreda was big and dark and getting gaunt. . . .

"It's very good of Dr. Wang to let us take possession as he does," she was remarking.

The little doctor blinked as he tried to suppress the inner reflection that it would be refreshing if the worthy women about him could manage to be a trifle more attractive. He answered Wilfreda after an instant's pause.

"Wang Wei-Chou can still do things in the grand manner."

He stared out into the court before he continued. "But it can't go on. You are seeing something out of the past, and it won't survive our generation. But now," he shifted the topic abruptly, "what about your eating? You can't bake, I suppose? No bread?"

"We can slice Chinese *mant'ou* and toast it." Wilfreda finished her sandwich with an attempt at being casual. "Jane isn't hungry. She likes her cabbage soup and her rice gruel. She craves oranges, and I can get those. As for me, fortunately I can eat dough strings and vegetables."

Hartshorn sat looking at her as she finished her coffee, and on his face was an intent scowl. When she put down the cap of the Thermos, he jumped up and brought a package of paper money tied up with string out of his raincoat pocket.

"Here's what's left of Jane's last remittance," he said. "When she went into the hospital, I took charge of her affairs. I've done the best I could and the hospital bill can wait, but not the drug account. She's had to have expensive sedatives."

Wilfreda took the money and counted it.

"How long must this last?" she asked.

"That's the difficulty. Nobody knows," was the answer. "Of course," he added, "if and when it's all gone, we'll manage to carry her, somehow. Her Mission will make it good eventually, we know. But we're all living on uncertainties. I needn't tell you that," he broke off.

"No, of course. Don't worry," said Wilfreda. "We'll manage."

"You won't feel you can buy meat and eggs, I'm afraid," said Hartshorn. "And there's no milk and no sweets to be had. You won't get enough."

"Who does?" was the simple answer.

Hartshorn pursed his lips and blew out his cheeks, which was his way of sighing.

"Mind, I'll be keeping an eye on you. I won't depend on what you two tell me. And now, we'll go and check the patient."

As the doctor made his examination of Jane, he entertained her with accounts of the air base he had just visited.

"Extraordinary sight. Got a landing field and a runway in operation, but lots of coolies swarm around doing things with their wicker baskets. They've built the whole place; the cargo planes over the Hump can't fly in much machinery. Personnel and supplies take a lot of doing. The losses are terrible—makes me sick to think of them. The buildings on the field are just little huts of mud and straw. If the Japs bomb them, they can be put back in a jiffy. I suppose you don't worry about being bombed?"

Jane smiled.

"Don't you think," she said, "that as things are, a bomb which was a businesslike affair might even be a good idea? No, I'm not worrying."

The doctor went on with his account.

"The big boys are in now."

"The big boys? Are our men particularly big?" Jane wanted to know.

"Bless you, they are. But I meant the new bombers, the B-29s. They're the big boys and they are sitting around in one camouflage or another all over the field. It's a noisy, ugly nightmare of a place, not like this garden of yours—where there doesn't seem to be a war. Well, young woman, you are in better shape than I've found you for some time. See that you continue to behave yourself. And just as a reward of merit, here's a letter for you."

Jane held it out to Wilfreda.

"From Stephen Purcell," she said. "Such a nice boy and such a vile penman."

"Read it to her," said the doctor. "It's probably good medicine," and nodding, he took his departure.

Wilfreda settled down on the stool by Jane's cot and glanced over the remarks of the "vile penman," and as Jane watched her, she began to smile.

"He doesn't waste any ink upon formalities, does he?" she observed, "Here he starts off in the middle of things."

And she began to read:

Chez Bishop's Palace (two mat-sheds, villainously untidy and hellishly hot)

And what does thee know? That damn girl hasn't written me for six months, and she promised me a letter every two weeks. I wish to the good Lord I could forget her, and I have tried, but it's no use. Nobody and nothing but Daisy will do for me, and what does thee think are my chances? Tell me the truth—thee knew her in childhood. Thee was intimate with her mother. Wasn't she sort of an Ibsen character—completely frustrated? That's what she sounds like. What a miserable existence she had—Daisy, I mean—dragged around the world by a missionary parent so full of programs and committees she couldn't take time for the kid. And then said mother crushed under tragedy . . . husband dying suddenly and only D. left from the wreck; mother dry-eyed, never indulging her grief so it ate her alive. I've thought many times of that childhood thee once painted for me. No wonder D. is hard now. Anyhow, she's got me to stand by her even though she doesn't show much sign of wanting me; and she's got thee, Jane. I know she cares about thee as much as she allows herself to care about anybody.

She's afraid of love—any kind of love; she knows it can give you hell and she isn't having any. That's why I'll stand for anything she does. God knows it's a stiff assignment.

Jane, is there any chance at all? Does thee think she's off me because I'm a conscientious objector? That's the one way in which I won't change, even for her. I want to find out what thee really thinks about us two, and I'll be driving up over the road before long. Does thee remember how we talked the first night I met thee and found out thee was D.'s Aunt Jane? That was before this war; that was in another existence. . . .

And how is thee? I hear, from the Bishop, ailing. Thee has been doing too much and eating too little, like everyone in China these days. Only, thee had no reserves of strength to start with. Ninety pounds on the bathroom scales are not sufficient foundation for austerity. See here, how about letting me supply a little cash? Thee knows I have more than is good for me.

I won't be leaving this here Bishop's Palace before thee could get a letter to me. If thee has ink, prepare to shed some now via air-mail to

Ever thine,

Stephen

P.S. R Square sends greetings. What a prince he is.

Wilfreda looked up as she came to the end and found Jane had risen on her elbow as she lay in her cot, and was listening with smiling attention.

"Here, here," the nurse said gently. "Lie down again. You can follow quite as well on your back as on your elbow, and it takes less doing."

Jane relaxed obediently.

"I see, Freda, that you enjoy the style of this correspondent more than you enjoyed Major Robert Trent."

"And I see that you have much more energy than you had that night. You have no trouble in paying attention to this."

"Stephen always does me good. I can't think why Daisy blows hot and then cold."

"She sounds like a little baggage," said Wilfreda, putting the letter in its envelope, "and Stephen is the salt of the earth, I suppose. A Quaker?"

"Oh yes, for generations. His family came with William Penn. As for Daisy, I've loved her all her life—at least whenever I haven't been furious with her. It's the way she affects most people." Jane sighed and then immediately chuckled.

"The thing that interests me most," her nurse remarked, "is the suggestion that your friend Stephen has more money than is good for him."

"Of course. The Quakers work hard, live frugally, and before they know it they are in the situation of those who find it hard to enter the Kingdom of Heaven. Isn't it a paradox? But why are you interested that Stephen has more money than is good for him?"

"Because," said Wilfreda thoughtfully, "you have distinctly less. But we'll talk of Stephen and his riches and his ladylove another time. You've had enough for today, haven't you?"

Jane nodded, then pointed to the stone step of her room, low and roughhewn and green with moss.

"See," she said, "in the crack? There's a violet. And she has her eye on me!"

Chapter Four

Li Pei-Ni was putting on his tie. He was a gorgeous creature for the dingy room in which he stood. It was cracked from bombing, and dirty from lack of care. The window was simply an opening into the murk of Chungking, with no screen, glass, or paper lattice. The furnishing consisted of a wooden bed frame laced with string, on which a single heavy quilt lay in disorder. Underneath this bed were two suitcases which were made of stout materials. Each had two locks. A small mirror was propped against the wall on a shelf which held a comb and a scent bottle, but no soap or arrangements for washing were visible.

The occupant of this apartment wore Western clothes. His coat and trousers matched; his suspenders, which were fastened over his shirt, were of pink and lavender silk elastic, and were occasionally allowed to reveal themselves. His shoes were new and heavy enough to clump importantly. His tie, a ready-made bowknot, which fastened behind, was blue with white dots, and on the hand adjusting it was a large green jade ring and a bracelet watch. These possessions were proof of prosperity.

Li took a final look into the narrow mirror. He approved his square jaw, and passed his hand over his black hair, which had reddish glints and a slight wave in it. He preened himself to get a good view of his natty neck. Then he made his arrangements to go out. He stuffed the quilt into one of the cases, locked it, and chained it to a staple in the single solid timber in the room, since the remainder of the wall surface was mud daubed on woven bamboo. He picked up his hat, dusty and stained but one which could be worn at a jaunty angle, and went out, snapping two locks of American make upon his flimsy door. Such precautions were usual in the Chungking of those days. To lose his one quilt or any of his clothing would be a major disaster, and thieving was inveterate.

He had not eaten that morning, and as he passed down the street to his usual food shop, he stopped to buy a copy of the newspaper he read each day. He did not choose a restaurant or a foreign-style café, but patronized a sort of shed entirely open to the street where the cooking was done in plain sight. He sat down on a two-inch bench at a rickety table near the stove in which a shallow pan set over a charcoal fire was sending up a cloud of steam from noodles boiling with a few scraps of pork and a selection of green vegetables. A shop boy several degrees dirtier than the average citizen brought him a dish of shreds of salted turnip and a pair of wooden chopsticks, after shouting his order to the cook at the stove. Li took notice that the other customers were two ricksha coolies seated at a distance. He opened his paper and began to read.

The shop boy brought a dark-gray bowl filled with slippery lengths of coarse dough strings, received his money, and shouted out the amount of the tip. Li began to eat without ceasing to read. Presently he opened his page to its complete size and found, as he had expected, a strip of paper slipped between the sheets with a few characters written on it. His eyes sharpened at the sight of two names written in English. The message was brief:

Proceed to Huai Yuen and take over forwarding of reports from air base. Establish relations with a missionary, Jane Breasted, and pick up information relative to her cousin Robert Trent, just arrived in OSS in Chungking. If possible, get B. to recommend you to T. for a job.

Li bent over his bowl and drew in the hot food with audible gurgling and hissing, and at the same time swallowed the thin strip of paper, which went down without difficulty. He finished his breakfast and called for some tea. Then he lighted a cigarette, and appeared to devote himself to the business of leisurely digestion. As he watched the curling smoke, he entered another time and place.

Before the Japanese invasion. Many years before. A bright little house in Harbin, melting pot of many racial strains from east and west. A bright little house in Harbin, with the sun strong on bare, painted floors. Two small boys playing noisily all day, and when bedtime came, listening to their mother's stories. She was slender and energetic, with yellow braids around her head, and fresh color, and brave blue eyes. She told her boys about her home in Scotland, about her poverty there, and how she had a cousin, an engineer, on the river steamers of the Sungari, who got her a chance to "come out East" as nursemaid to a British merchant family. Fine people they were, and she earned a good wage and was well content. But then they left the Far East and she kept house for the engineer cousin. That was lonely. He was always away, and she needed company. So it was she met their Korean father, and married him, and the two of them were born. One boy looked like Scotland, and one like Korea. They had happy days with their brisk little mother, and with their gentle-mannered father when he was at home. But Li had only dim recollections of the father whose business obliged him to travel.

The two boys were still small when he died. The house was sold, and hard times began. The mother became the breadwinner. She was housekeeper to an irascible fellow countryman of dubious reputation, who was increasingly in need of nursing as well as of housekeeping. He permitted the boys to live with their mother, and for that reason she bore with his temper and his demands, but life was no longer pleasant for any of them. Then the hard lot of the Eurasian began for Pei-Ni and his brother. They went to a mission school where there were pupils of many races, but among them all there never seemed to be friends for Benny and Bobbie. At home, the old Scotchman swore and growled at the woman who worked for him, and put more and more nursing on her, so that finally in a school squabble, another boy shouted the inevitable gossip at her sons. Benny could still see his elder brother's face, white as a sheet, fixed as ice when those words hurtled into his ears. The boys were sixteen and fourteen, of an age to feel. They never told their mother what they had heard, but they began to beg her to leave the old reprobate she served. Her reply never changed: "We cannot leave yet. We have no money and no place to go. You must get your schooling, and we must wait until you can earn."

But the waiting was too long for the elder son. Benny remembered the summer when his brother grew stranger and stranger. Then one day, he went bathing in the river. It was an accident that he was drowned, they told his mother, but Benny knew. And he thought his mother knew, too. That was when he was fifteen, and he vowed it should be his last year at school. It was the first year for "Teacher Jane." He remembered her wanting to be called that—it had made her different from the others. She had seemed drawn to the boy who looked like an Oriental but talked English with a slight Scotch accent. She wanted to know Benny's mother. She seemed quite unaware that no other white women went to see the Scotchman's housekeeper.

And so it happened that when his mother fell ill, and knew her last hour appoaching, she asked for Jane. When the funeral was over, the old Scotchman sent for Benny and put his situation bluntly.

"You'll not be staying longer in my house," he announced. "And I've a final word for you. Your mother was a good woman, but her marriage was her mistake, and you'll be to suffer for it. There's but one way for such as you. Get money, if you can. There's no other power or protection for you, and so you'll find it."

Many years ago. The few months he had known Jane had been almost forgotten in the welter of experiences since. The struggle to find employment, the dislike for his mixed blood. The sharpening of wits to make a try at different jobs, all menial, all humiliating, but also the discovery that he was clever, able, capable of more than one method of making his way. Then the flooding in of the Japanese. Well . . . Benny had seen his chance and had made himself useful. He was treated contemptuously and he was set hard and evil tasks, but when he was found to be intelligent, he was paid more than anyone had ever paid him, and Benny had long ago decided that he could not afford to be particular. He took his money, and studied cunning ways to get it—at least some of it—out of Japanese hands. They liked to control the wages they paid out, and Benny obediently opened an account in one of their banks, which he knew he could touch only so long as his masters were pleased with him. He managed, however, not to put all his savings there. Slowly, steadily, he was getting ahead. Someday he would end his bondage. Someday he would get away, perhaps to Australia, or New Zealand, and court respectability and know security at last.

In the meantime, the war offered certain opportunities to young men who were not particular. Benny traveled to North China ahead of the Japanese invasion in the summer of 1937. When the great movement of Chinese fleeing from occupied territory began, Benny went with the refugees, under orders to carry out, in Free China, instructions given by the Japanese Secret Intelligence.

And now, he was set to make use of Jane Breasted, who had been good to his mother. Well, no harm could be intended to her. Benny shrugged, dropped the butt of his cigarette under the table, and went to take a bus to Huai Yuen.

Chapter Five

From the Journal of Wilfreda Grayson

Jane and I have been a week in the Wang Family Garden, and we are at this five-o'clock-afternoon moment sitting together in the covered gallery of the Room for Abstinence and Meditation by the Pool of the Rock and Pine. This is the second time Jane has been up in her chair, and she is busy, with her writing pad on her knee, composing a reply to the letter from Major Robert Trent which I read to her the night I arrived at the Huai Yuen Hospital. I keep my eye on her as I scribble in this record, which for some reason I go on with even though in this out-of-the-way place there is nothing eventful to put in it. But I've not yet noted down the impressions which flood in upon me in this old garden, not that I'm busy with the esthetic much of the time. I have a good bit to do as nurse and housekeeper, laundrywoman, and general link with the outside world.

I think I have our schedule fairly well organized for the present. Because of my nurse habits, I am up early. Jane sleeps extraordinarily well since we came, and as we have the blessed privacy of rooms to ourselves, I can get my own toilet attended to without disturbing her, although I am so near her, that through the open doors and windows I can be aware of her every movement. I roll out from under my net, run a comb through my hair—which I have kept short after one awful struggle with vermin in it when I first got to this unhygienic part of the world—and then I tiptoe out to the pine and rock pool. Chinese, I know, wouldn't ever bathe in cold water out-of-doors, and the pool was never before subjected to such a use; but it is fed by mountain water, and it has such complete seclusion in its little cup of hills that I can't resist my own barbaric longings. I slip out of my

36

raincoat and into the freshness while the early light is still in the tops of the trees, and a smart toweling makes me feel equal to the oppression of the atmosphere. The fact is that on the Szechuan plain one seems to be breathing feathers instead of air—so thick and dead is the substance one draws into one's lungs. However—as I was saying—

I creep back to the Cool Room, which is the name of my house on the east side of the court where the westering sun cannot shine in during the two months in summer, and after pulling on slacks and a shirt, I pick up soiled clothes and go off to Shang Ma's washing stones. There isn't a washtub within miles of us, but these stones placed in the stream just as it emerges from the hills around the pool are not a bad substitute. I squat down (this is something I'm not yet used to and it lames me), put a garment on a flat surface just above the flowing water, rub a little soap on the same, and after dipping, proceed to whack away with a stick until the water runs clear from the fabric. It is laborious but the best I can do at present. Shang Ma is horrified and hints that a cousin of hers would do the whacking for a consideration, but we can't afford that, and I tell Shang Ma I prefer to do it—without mentioning why.

Once I get through this job, I look to see if Jane is awake. If she isn't, I get a walk in the garden to a high spot where I can look out at the Snow Mountains, if they are visible, which they usually are not. I carry my prayer book and read the Psalms for the day, and wonder why Jane never seems to follow any routine in such matters. Not that it is any of my business. . . .

When I return from the hilltop, it is broad day, though seldom clear sunshine. I tidy Jane for the morning meal, which is oranges, millet porridge, and tea (what I would give for a little variety in diet for her and for me!), and then her routine takes up a good bit of time. When it is finished, she must rest, and I must see about food supplies and messages to the outside. There is always something to consult Shang Shih about. Lunch consists of a bowl of rice and vegetables cooked with rapeseed oil, and a cup of cabbage soup. A long rest in the afternoon is followed by such reading, writing, and chatting as we feel inclined to do, and that brings us to supper—a piece of steamed bread with a cup of tea for me, and, for Jane, a cup of cocoa. (I have had to sell her typewriter to buy a few tins of supplementary food like this, and I haven't yet confessed it to her. Maybe she will not want the machine again, but she doesn't use me as her amanuensis any more, and if she demands it, I'll have to confess.) However, she does share her letters with me, and one has come in from a Dr. Barry Manners, a curious sort of person to appear in a theater of war. He is such a sensitive plant that I got the impression he is actually a hypochondriac, and since he proposes to visit Jane, I really took alarm. But she says he is a great Sinologue and a very old friend, and also a most charming person, and the limitation of her vitality in the face of his demands doesn't seem to trouble her a bit.

Dr. Barry Manners to Jane Breasted

You will be surprised to learn that I have arrived here in a capacity connected with our Embassy, which I am not at liberty to discuss; and this, in spite of the fact that I am very far from robust. The hardships of refugee conditions may well prove more than I can bear, and I must be careful to conserve my strength and take frequent vacations. I am therefore hoping that I may fly to Huai Yuen from time to time, and get away from this supremely distasteful Chungking, which is a bustle of modernity in imitation of the West, with all its fever and fret but with very little of its efficiency. However, I am as well situated as I could expect. I have a house which I share with one other, and a competent staff of servants. The bombing seems unlikely to recur, so I am told, and if there is an alarm I can take my work into a shelter only a few paces away from my desk. But in spite of these circumstances, there is a great deal which I find very wearing, and I appeal to you, my dear Jane, to enter into a little conspiracy and discover for me what might be termed, in bandit parlance, a "hide-out."

Have you been able to continue our investigations of Chinese gardens here in the west? Will you have some spot to show me to compare with the places we studied in the north? Always we found those Peking pleasure-grounds full of nostalgic echoes from the south. Now, we ourselves are in the land to which Chinese scholars and officials used to be sent as exiles from emperor and court and all they held dear. My sympathy for them is poignantly renewed. I find myself wearying for the mellow beauty of Ch'ien Lung's capital, and the joys of the connoisseur which you and I shared together there.

And what are you doing? Let me have a line to say where I shall find you in Huai Yuen and whether you can provide for me there.

B.M.

Jane Breasted to Barry Manners

. . . In Chungking, and wanting to come to Huai Yuen . . . . My dear Barry, nothing could be more perfect because I have your hide-out all ready for you. It happens that I am quartered in a garden with plenty of space, and the sooner you come to occupy the Hall for Inviting the Pleasures, the better I shall like it. There will be so much for us to go into together here, just as there was in Peking palaces and gardens in the good days gone by. The owner of this place, who is an old student of mine, has given me privileges, including that of offering hospitality. And to crown my satisfaction, Wang Wei-Chou's former tutor, Master Yuan, who took the highest degree in one of the last imperial examinations, is making his home in the garden study. He, of course, will have the answers to all our questions.

As for me, I am in the Chai, where I feel the benedictions of the scholarly traditions you have taught me to understand a little. I have been thinking how you once said that scholarship in the West smells of the lamp, but that the scholar-poet in China knows only the air of Nature herself. Surely the family which built this garden had such men. They understood the art of providing for the refreshment which you seek and which I have been enjoying for some time.

There is a long gallery where I spend many hours if it rains, and it is here that I am writing to you in happy anticipation of your coming. You will be charmed with the intimacy of its small scale; its roof is low, its pavement of old flags. It fronts on a scene which is designed to hold a great ornamental rock, as remarkable as any you and I ever found in Peking. It never ceases to fascinate my eyes and intrigue my thought. My nurse, Wilfreda Grayson (oh, I forgot to mention that I have been on the sick list, but am now on the mend)—well, Wilfreda, who is new to these things which you and I have studied for years, feels a quality in it that makes her uneasy, but for me the uneasiness is the urge to grasp its inner significance. It looks like a thunderhead caught in permanent form. As it stands motionless it seems always to be rising, it is so alive in the rhythm of its balance and mass. It is at once fixed and fluid. I cannot tell you how it affects me.

I have been trying to remember your explanations of the concept of the Tao. Did you say that it is an intuitive grasping after the inner essence of things? I believe that if I have ever experienced that grasp it has been in concentration upon this object, which escapes from all the patterns of form I know and yet speaks to my instincts with such power.

Well, well! I have gone too far, I fear, in trying to tell you about me and my rock, but I hope the result will be that you will find my excitement contagious and will be all agog to see for yourself. And so, when may I expect you? You know I will take care to leave you perfectly free. You may be sure that no one will intrude upon your privacy while you are here. Bring a servant and some supplies. I do want you to be comfortable.

J.B.

Jane Breasted to Robert Trent

And so you want me to call you Robert, and write to you, and are willing to answer any questions about yourself which I may choose to ask! My dear cousin, indefinitely removed, aren't you a little rash? Suppose I inquired whether you are bald and have a thick neck? And then suppose you demanded of me whether I have wrinkles and wear spectacles? You must agree that such a beginning would spoil everything! Let us leave some matters to conjecture. . . . As for regular letters, you will be busy and I may be prevented at times from using my pen. We'll write when it's so's we can, as we always say in New England. Since I am Jane to you, you shall be Robert to me.

You demand to be instructed about China. Now her civilization . . . but I have a better idea. There is a great friend of mine in Chungking who is deeply learned and can discourse on things Chinese much better than I can. He is Dr. Barry Manners, and he's attached to the Embassy. Go see him.

I should have replied to you sooner, but I've been occupied in moving to a new place. I'm in the Wang Family Garden and I am sending you the address in Chinese. We are not far from the new air base, and late in the afternoon I often hear the thunder of the planes going . . . somewhere. So I know there is a war on; I am not allowed to forget it.

Give my greetings to Daisy Fairchild. She has not seen me for years, so you can't check up on the wrinkles and glasses through her.

J.B.

P.S. Would you like to tell me how often you read your Bible?

From the Journal of Wilfreda Grayson

(In the summer-house t'ing-tse, "Looking to the Snow Mountains")

It's early in the morning, and for a wonder I think the day is going to be clear. The plain is full of mist, but it is glistening white instead of the usual gray and the heights of the Snow Mountains show above it. Some trick of the atmosphere makes them seem so lofty and so near that I have an awed sense of being overpowered—of fearing they are about to fall upon me. It's not a pleasant sensation.

We have been nearly two weeks now in the garden and Jane is a different person from her hospital self. We pursued the even tenor of our ways until yesterday, when there was a slight interruption. During the siesta hour, Shang Shih called me out and said there was a young Chinese asking for Jane—said he used to be her student, and wanted to see her. I went along to the Mirror Pavilion, and found a Eurasian there. He was well dressed in Western clothes, in fact rather gaudy as to his tie and socks and a big piece of jade he wore on one forefinger. He looked distinctly disappointed to see me, and when I explained that Jane was recovering from an illness and was not able to receive her friends, he seemed so concerned that I could not quite decide why he was upset. He hasn't seen her in years—he knew her in her Harbin days—but would hardly take no for his answer. I was not going to have Jane dissipate her new-found strength, especially with the prospect of Stephen Purcell turning up before long, so I dismissed the young man, but told him frankly I was doing so without her knowledge. He asked if he might come back later, and I agreed that he might try in another ten days, but said I couldn't promise him an interview even then.

But I am really worried that we shall have a spate of visitors who cannot be sent off so easily. All the people who write to her seem determined to come and see her. Major Trent speaks of flying across from the capital, which takes only forty-five minutes, and Dr. Manners is definitely planning it. He wants to see this garden, for Jane has sent him an account of it. Of course she gives these people no hint of her real situation and talks as if she had a normal life span before her. I marvel that she can care about such things as the affairs of other folk, and Chinese garden architecture, forsooth! After she had read me her reply to Dr. Manners' letter, she looked at me and laughed.

"You are puzzled," she accused me. "You are saying to yourself, Jane is on the brink of eternity—so for heaven's sake, why Chinese rock work—now aren't you?"

"Yes"—I admitted it.

"My dear," Jane reached her hand to me. "Do you know why you are a comfort to me? In many ways, of course; but the great thing is that I may speak freely with you about the end of Brother Ass. He is on the brink of death and subsequent corruption; but you know as I do that I myself am in for no such things. I stand on no brink at all. I am at home—here or hereafter."

Tears were in the eyes of us both. But Jane having asserted that I comprehend her, I do so increasingly, if blunderingly. I have heard that the true mystic is usually silent about his inner life. This seems to apply to her. I am glad she says she can speak freely to me, but even so, she has very little to say about herself.

Robert Trent to Jane Breasted

You do write a letter which makes a poor fellow brush up his wits and wish he had a little more Bible. Only, dear Jane, there is one thing we have to get straight right now. I may be getting bald (only getting), but my neck isn't red, and I wear size fifteen collar. And I don't give a damn how many wrinkles you've got, and I bet the twinkles in your eyes make up for spectacles, if any.

Now, if you don't write regularly, I'll find a half day somehow and fly over to your garden to check up on you.

I'd like it if you'd tell me how you put in your time. How does a person live in a garden, anyway? According to my poor knowledge (there's a Chinese touch for you), a man lives in a house where he has a garden about which he makes himself a nuisance—wanting to tell you how many bugs he picked off the tomato vines, etc. But gardens of any kind are a long way from life in Chungking, and even tomato bugs would be a welcome change from the things I have to think and talk about. So go to it, Jane, and while telling me about your garden, I expect you'll betray a good bit about yourself.

R.T.

Jane Breasted to Robert Trent

You are pretty well used to handing out assignments, aren't you? You say to a fellow human being, do this—and he doeth it. Also, you can make yourself very agreeable when you try—that was a nice speech about the twinkles and the spectacles. However, I shall keep you in the dark upon these points, in spite of your candor re the size of your collar!

This morning I feel like telling you how I put in my time; and I defy you to make any inferences of a personal nature about me from what I am to say, because I occupy myself with appreciating this Chinese garden which is not at all like the kind that grows tomatoes. I haven't been here very long and shall probably not remain after the summer is over. My regular job is teaching, but just now I'm having vacation and enjoying my hobby, which is the study of Chinese garden art. And if you would welcome the subject of tomato bugs as a change from your war job, I am wondering how you will respond to this one? And I know you'll think I sound like a teacher— which won't be strange because that's what I am!

A Chinese garden begins by being a flat space entirely surrounded by walls. Then the owner engages a lot of coolies and sets them to work scooping out water basins according to the plan he has in mind. The earth which is thrown up in the digging is formed into artificial hills which enclose the water basins like the sides of a cup, and when they are in place, the garden is ready for the little ornamental and purposeful buildings which the owner wants scattered about in it. He also starts his planting, which is trees and shrubs rather than flowers, and at the end of something like twenty years, he begins to bring into existence the series of landscape effects or views which he originally proposed to himself. He is an artist who works in actual earth and water and building materials and he creates hills and valleys, lakes and islands, which are Nature in miniature, scaled down from the real thing, but so perfectly done that you can't tell where Nature has been at work and where Art has taken over. The buildings are of varied forms and uses, but all of them have a common function. They are to provide a roof from which Nature can be contemplated and enjoyed. Some are called "libraries," some "studies," some are dwelling houses, some are *t'ing-tses*, which means "places to gather and wait." These are the most common and have just the roof carried on supports, with all sides open to the air—we might call them "summer houses." Furthermore, no garden is complete without the literary element which pervades all Chinese civilization. Each view and each building has a name written on a *pien*, a nameboard, and hung up for all to see. Sometimes one finds bits of verse, or even long passages from literature, written in the spaces of walls or on stones set up especially to carry them, and these give one a clue to the learning and taste of the owner and the mood he wished to evoke by the particular scene. There are all sorts of moods, including the humorous and the fearful along with the idyllic. The Chinese consider you might tire of being in a learned (or uplifted or romantic) state and would welcome a touch of the eerie to give you a thrill or a stroke of humor to make you smile. There are sometimes special surroundings for getting intoxicated or playing with ladies—but I won't enlarge upon those. I shouldn't omit to mention masses of porous rock which are set up by themselves as ornament (and more than ornament). These have a lore of their own, but I won't start on that either. And when a man begins to live in the garden, he always tries to put into words some of the feelings and impressions he has arranged for himself to receive. If the garden is any good as a work of art, the maker is able to write poetry about it, and he invites his friends and those who follow him in his garden to write also. This morning I went up to a high place from which I could look out over the Szechuan plain and see, in the west, the Snow Mountains. I wrote a garden poem myself . . . shall I put it down for you?

> Untroubled is the pool below me
> The snowy heights unsullied in the west.
> But northward, on the far edge of the air
> Floats a bombing plane.

But this is such a garden poem as was never written in China before.

J.B.

Robert Trent to Jane Breasted

I feel somewhat dazed by your hobby. Tomato bugs I can grasp, but not Chinese natural-artificial gardens. If you weren't living in one, I'd probably not be much interested. It's got a poetical name (and I discover it's so near the base that there's no sense in sending my letters by mail when they can go by air and take only forty-five minutes instead of two days). Pure Repose is far removed from me, and I'm not ready to join in contemplating Nature with or without a roof. There's the honest fact! Your poem bears witness there's a war. It (the poem) hits me where I live. I'm no critic but I get your suggestion that natural things are quiet and good and a bombing plane is neither. I wish we didn't need the plane, but I'm not a Quaker, and I'm convinced we do.

And I'm convinced of something else. I gather from your letter (in spite of your being sure there was no personal information to be had) that you are an extra-special kind of human being. And I suspect something else. Daisy Fairchild has said a word or two about you and this is my suspicion: you must be an angel.

R.T.

Jane Breasted to Robert Trent

Dear, dear, you should cultivate caution in letter writing and above all you should not be suspicious. Angel, indeed! It simply is not done. "Poor mortal longingness" obtains for me as for anybody else, but it never got me far from the dust of this earth. (Do you ever read Walter de la Mare?)

This does not mean I don't like compliments; on the contrary, I adore them, so please go on saying anything charming that occurs to you and I'll take great pains to keep you in the dark as to how mistaken you are . . . that is, just so you leave angel out of it.

J.B.

P.S. Did you ever know an angel aged forty-seven?

Robert Trent to Jane Breasted

All right, all right, I withdraw angel. And who is Walter de la Mare? No, I don't read him. I haven't finished yet with the Bible.

R.T.

Chapter Six

Jack Fernald was going nuts.

That was the way he put it to himself as he stood outside his tent on the isolated air base in the foothills of the Snow Mountains of West China. In India, he and his mates had been keen to get on to China. Now, in China, they all wished they hadn't been rushed out of India so fast. There, at least, they had been able to get to places with somebody in them. Also, in India, everybody had been busy.

Now they were sitting under the Himalayas with no missions to fly as yet, and no place to go when they got leave. The morale of the whole bunch was cracking up. They were so low on Japs to kill they were damn near starting in on each other.

A coolie servant appeared at the door of the next tent, with his arms full of GI washing. Jack watched him padding off down the row of shelters toward the service quarters, and his thoughts took another turn.

He was mighty leery of slopeys. Wished the Chinese government hadn't supposed American pilots wanted to be treated like wealthy playboys on a big-game hunt. No security possible with the place lousy full of those silent eyes. Made you too comfortable and lazy to have everything done for you. Comfortable! God, what a word to use about this dump. The physical work was done, but you were ready to claw at your own flesh. . . . The slopeys worked hard all right, but they were a bunch of chiselers and wouldn't be sorry to see the GIs rubbed out—that was what he'd decided about them. And the Japs had found out the B-29s were in. They probably knew the fighter protection hadn't arrived yet. One spunky little bastard had flown over with all his lights on, to make us think he was not an enemy plane . . . the nerve of him. Got away, too, because we weren't ready. And now, all he, Jack, had to do was to think about the damn Japs and the stories about what happens when you get shot down behind their lines.

He was going to get killed.

That was it—that was what was in the back of his mind—of everybody's mind. They were all thinking about that, but they wouldn't say it. And he was going nuts first. He was getting queer. His head was bursting—all mixed up. He couldn't talk to a soul; he couldn't take it any longer.

Fernald began walking down the field in the opposite direction from that which the coolie had taken. The road which had been built from Huai Yuen to the field entered the base at a point in plain sight, and he could see the sentry on duty. His head was whirling, his ideas jumped in and out of consciousness like jack rabbits—but one train of thought persisted.

He was getting out of here. He was going AWOL. They might try to stop him, but he didn't care. He was going to get killed. Might as well be now, as under Jap torture. Yes, he was a coward, so what? He was going nuts, he was going AWOL. He was going to get killed.

He was starting off into the landscape. Somebody was shouting at him. Somebody came up behind him. He wheeled about and spoke.

"Look you. I'm going to be by myself. I have to get to a place where I don't see GI, hear GI, smell GI. And that means you, buddy. If you bother me I'll shoot you first and myself afterward. Now, get going."

Somebody else seemed to arrive. He heard voices.

"Let him go." "He won't get far. The medics will handle him." "He's been queer for a week."

So he walked off into space.

He didn't notice much outside his own head at first. But by and by things quieted down a little. He was striding along a path off the main road that led to the base. It skirted the fields of rape all in bloom like great squares of gold pasted on the gray countryside. There was gray sky and no sun; there was green cultivation in hollows and on terraces between outcrops of gray rock and low rises of ground; and there were streams of water between all the fields. He stopped and watched the water whenever he came to it; it was just sliding along, and the sound was a help to the buzzing in his ears.

He did not notice where he went, nor how long he walked. If he saw people, he kept away from them, but there were only a few peasants laboring face downward to the earth. Then he found his path was running beside a big high wall, and on the inner side of the path there was a ditch of water—the smooth-flowing water. Inside the wall he became aware of tremendous tall trees. He noticed their shade because it seemed queer to find so many all at once.

He walked on. He went around corners of the wall—three of them —three sides of a rectangle. He wondered why the place was so big. He began to think how he could get inside that wall—up into those trees. The medics, he figured, would have a hard time catching him if they had to shin up such big trees.

He came to a door, and stopped. It seemed an unused door. It was double-leaved, with cracks in it so that he could make out a big bar going right across it, inside. There was a stone lintel, and the top of the wall was not out of arm's reach from that projection. Soon he was astride, looking over on the other side.

There wasn't much to see, except some irregular rises of ground that went along in a wavy line inside the straight line of the wall. It struck Fernald as queer. You don't get hills to follow walls in everyday life. The big trees grew on them, and on the ground lower down, too, and presently he saw a footpath on the top of the aqueduct-looking thing, so he got himself over on the path, and walked along there. He was becoming curious. He was forgetting the base, even forgetting he was going nuts. It seemed, instead, that he was going places.

The ups and downs he walked on were never more than fifteen feet high, and mostly about ten or twelve. The trees and growing things were thick, but the path was clear. So somebody must use it. Soon he found steps cut in the slope and faced with bricks. They led down to a wider path below; he descended and followed that. It took him to a flat bridge of rough gray stone, standing over a current of the smooth gray water, which in its turn made a parallel to the line of hills, and to the outside wall. The hills stood and the waters flowed just the way the walls went—it beat Jack to think why. Then he came to another wall. This was on the other side of the stream, and only as high as his head. He could jump the channel, and when he saw an opening in the wall he did. He had to stoop a little as he went through.

He found himself standing under a roof carried on pillars—so much he could take in. There was a house, or a sort of room, mostly paper-backed lattice, to his right. To his left was more roof carried on pillars, and space and greenness, and a wet light. He didn't notice more because a voice then said:

"Hello there."

The voice was quiet but he started violently. Then he saw a big chair with its back spread out like a full moon, and in it, done up in something blue, was a small pointed face looking at him.

"Hello there," said the voice again.

Fernald stared and stammered "hello," but he couldn't say anything more for a moment. He could only look. And the face in the chair looked at him. At last he remembered something about manners and brought out:

"I'm sorry."

For some reason this made him feel better, and like himself.

"Sorry? For what?" asked the quiet voice.

"I didn't know anyone was here," said Fernald.

"No," said the voice. "Of course not. I haven't been here very long myself."

Then the eyes shut, the face went dreadfully white, and he saw that it was in pain.

"Can I do anything? Shall I go away?" He found himself backing toward the low door through which he had come in.

But the face in the chair opened its eyes again, and said:

"Don't go. Sit down."

It pointed with its chin toward a flat rock in the ground nearby, and Fernald sat down. He saw now that there was a little pool in front of the house, partly surrounded by the roofed gallery. The pool, the house, and the gallery lay in a circle of miniature hills, and there were dwarf pine trees, and bamboos, and fruit trees in blossom all about him; at the other end of the picture was a strange-shaped rock under the shadow of an umbrella-shaped pine. The air was spring-warm, and gentle in its grayness.

Soon the face in the chair spoke again.

"The pain is gone now."

Fernald turned his eyes cautiously toward the face—a woman's face, he came to understand.

"It was mighty bad, wasn't it?"

"Yes. It comes, but it goes again. I wouldn't have spoken about it, but you saw. Perhaps you and I are in the same boat?"

Fernald wondered what she could mean. She was gray-haired and a woman. He found himself blurting out, "How can we be in the same boat?"

"We are both facing death, aren't we?"

He turned his eyes away, muttering, "How did you know?"

"How did you know when my pain came on me? When it is bad, pain shows. I have one kind. You have another."

His face began to twitch.

"We can't talk about this to people who are not in our place," the voice went on. "But I see by your uniform that you are a pilot; you see that I am ill and can't recover. We both face death, and we can speak of it to each other."

He never afterward could quite sort out what happened to him next. He knew there came a sound of a tearing sob, and all the confusion and anguish seethed up within him to a great bursting point. He found himself down beside the chair with his head in the folds of the blanket, and time stopped.

When he could think again, there was relief. The confusion was gone. The tight stretch of the nerves was released. The strings of his eyeballs did not pull. And she was smiling.

"That's better," she said. "What's your name? Mine's Jane."

He mumbled his name and tried to rise to his feet, but she put her hand on his shoulder.

"Don't get up," she said. "Turn around, and lean your head back and be quiet.

He obeyed her. She had arranged matters so that he did not need to meet her eyes, and he sat staring out into quiet spaces and at smooth water which stood still and received the long green shadows of the trees upon its banks. That water was not sliding as it slid outside of this place—this unbelievable place he had somehow gotten into. He could not tell how long they sat together there, but finally he turned his head and looked up at Jane. He found her gazing into distance, and her lips, though not smiling, seemed about to smile. As he moved, she brought her eyes to dwell upon him, and he felt a lingering, seeking quality in her look.

"How did you get into the garden?" she wanted to know.

"Is that what this is?"

"Of course. It is a Chinese garden, and a very beautiful one. Don't you think so?"

"It's all right by me, whatever it is," Jack said. "I came in over the wall. I suppose I shouldn't."

"You weren't quite yourself."

"I was going nuts. And then I found you . . . and when you spoke . . . I went to pieces. But now I'm okay. I don't know what's happened to me. I can't figure it out."

He uttered the short sentences with pauses between each one, and at the end shook his head.

"You might talk a little," Jane suggested. "It's one good way to figure things out."

"Talk? What's the good of talking?"

"It seemed to do some good a few minutes ago."

He thought this over.

"Yes," he said. "I was all mixed up. I was going nuts. Now I'm okay, but what's to stop me going haywire again when I get back to the base?"

He put his head between his hands broodingly.

"I don't think you'll 'go nuts' any more," she said.

"You don't? A fat lot. . . ." He stopped.

"Yes. To other people you could say 'a fat lot you know about it.' But you can't say that to me. I do know."

He pulled himself out of his brooding and looked at her.

"Say, you told me you can't get well. Are you sure?"

"As sure as my doctors and my best friends are. They think it may be about three months now."

"And you think so yourself?"

"I think so myself."

"But you're so quiet . . . so perfectly quiet, that's what you are."

He kept repeating it.

She said nothing, and again he felt the lingering quality in her gaze.

"It's your quietness that has got into me."

He continued to turn this over in his mind. Then he looked up again. "Say . . . what's the matter with you?"

She told him, and he drew a sharp breath.

"God! I've heard of that. They say it's awful: it's the worst . . . can't they do anything about it?"

"Oh yes, they can do a great deal. I shall have help. But in three months I expect I shan't need help any more. And it's all right."

"It's all right," he repeated. "You don't go nuts. You just sit still and say it's all right."

She was silent again, and short sentences with pauses between occurred.

"You haven't got a chance . . . you've got to go that way . . . hell, what have I got to crab about? At least I've got a chance."

"And you have youth, and strength, and courage."

"Courage? You say that after seeing me as scared as a lost kid in the dark? I sure gave myself away. But you aren't scared."

"No," said Jane. "And neither are you, really. I know you won't go nuts again. You said yourself you are clear now. Think. There is a difference, isn't there?"

He reflected and nodded slowly.

"You said it, Jane. There is a difference. It's your not being scared that's getting into me. If you're not, I don't have to be."

"You don't have to be. At the base, or anywhere else."

There was silence again, and he noticed that Jane relaxed in her chair as if something had been settled. Presently he was looking anxious.

"You told me your name. You're Jane. But . . . but . . . who in hell are you anyway?" He stopped suddenly. There was a dimple playing at the corner of Jane's mouth.

"Oh," he said in dismay. "I bet you're . . ."

The next thing he heard was laughter.

"One of those damn missionaries," said Jane. "Yes, I am."

Jack looked at her reproachfully. "I hope you don't think I mind," he said earnestly. "I wouldn't hold anything against you, you know."

Jane produced a handkerchief and touched her lips, but for the moment speech failed her. Jack got to his feet. "I'm afraid I should be going," he suggested.

But this woman was full of surprises. She stopped laughing and made a little face at him—a rather impish face which left him grinning uncertainly.

"Sit down," she commanded, and he sat.

"Did you think I would proceed to preach you a sermon?"

"I suppose so," said Jack. "But I'll say you've got a right to do anything you choose with me. Only you certainly are the most . . . the most surprising person I ever met."

"Don't worry," said Jane. "I'm not a preaching missionary. I find there are some things that don't go into words; and I belong to the Quakers who have a great fondness for silence."

At this point, an old slopey came shuffling into the veranda, and after Jane had listened to what he said, she turned to Fernald. He could see that the old Chinese was scandalized at the sight of him.

"Your friends are here, looking for you."

Jack remembered that there were such things as medics and AWOL regulations in the world, but as he got slowly to his feet he felt able to cope with them.

"Jane," he began, "I don't know what to say. But there's two things I've got to ask. What's your last name? And may I come again?"

"My name is Breasted," said Jane. "And don't you forget it. Will the authorities at the base encourage you to come?"

"They damn well better," was the fervent response. The old Chinese cleared his throat as if to summon the parting guest to the path outside the door where he stood, and Jack, after a swift glance, strode over and shut it in his face. Then he came back to stand before the big chair.

"Jane," he said. "Do you mind if I kiss you?"

"Not at all," said Jane demurely. "But I'm afraid Shang Shih would."

"Who is Shang Shih?"

"The gateman who is patiently waiting for you. And Jack, if you do come again, you'd better let him open the gate for you."

"Oh," said Jack cheerfully. "To hell with Shang Shih," and leaning over, he kissed her hands and then her cheek. "I'll be back," said he, "just as soon as I can fix it up; in a few days if I have luck."

"You'll be having luck," said Jane, "from now on."

He left her and followed Shang Shih along the garden paths. At the grotto he encountered Wilfreda, who threw him a glance of surprise as she passed, and who reflected during the account which Jane subsequently gave her that she had never seen a more magnificent-looking young fellow. The next morning when she picked up the soiled linen, she found three of Jane's handkerchiefs rolled into little hard balls.

That boy was too much for her, she said to herself. But she made no remarks about the telltale handkerchiefs.

Chapter Seven

"Are you there, Jane? May I come up?"

Jack stood at the base of a minuscule mountain on the west side of the lake and peered at the outline of a small *t'ing-tse* perched fifteen feet above the path. He could see a rustic prop or two, the peak of a roof rising above the jungle growth of green things on the slope, and he caught just a patch of blue low down which he took to be Jane's Chinese robe. Her voice answered him, and when he had climbed up, he came upon her sitting on the steps of the platform on which the shelter was erected. She had her fountain pen, and an old-fashioned portfolio was open on her knee. As she closed it, a piece of paper fluttered to the young man's feet.

"Better sit down, before you pick it up," she advised. "You do have such a long way to go in bending over."

He took the place opposite her on the steps and returned the slip of paper, saying as he did so, "Miss Grayson told me where to find you. You get a chance to look outside the walls, here, don't you?" And he surveyed the foothills with their bumpy green surfaces and the gray stony outcrops which stretched away to the west and the north.

"We ought to be able to see the high range," said Jane. "That's what this *t'ing-tse* was built for. Its name says 'Looking to the Snow Mountains.' But today the air is so dense that they are completely hidden. You seldom catch a glimpse of them, except after rain."

"I don't want to," Jack answered. "Anybody who flies the Hump will do something besides sit and look at it in his spare time."

"I came for another reason myself. It's almost five o'clock, isn't it?"

"Just." Jack looked at his watch.

A sudden thunder arose somewhere among the green bumps to the north, and then, lifting over them, five winged shapes slanted up, catching sunlight which did not reach to the plain. They flew in formation with one in the lead. They hummed away to the east.

"It's our only reminder of the war in this garden," said Jane, "that coming and going."

Jack was scowling at the step.

"I've been grounded for a week. The medic let me come over here today instead of being around when they took off."

"But you are better?"

"I'll be perfectly all right when I'm flying again. Tell me about yourself. Has that awful pain come back?"

"Oh," said Jane. "I'm glad you brought it up. I couldn't say all I wanted to the other day."

"When I thought it over," Jack remarked, "I realized you didn't say much, especially about yourself. Only what I made you."

He looked at her and, finding her tranquil gaze fixed on the distance, felt again the comfort of being unobserved.

"Well, then, here's some more about myself. But I have to begin with you. Your life at the air base must be kept secret, of course. When you are going out on missions, you won't be able to tell me. When you come back, you won't give me the details of the flight."

"No," admitted Jack. "I won't. Security is our headache. We have to be strict."

Jane nodded.

"I understand. And so, it would be unfriendly of me to try to find out from you about such matters when you are here. I must take them for granted, and leave your main job alone, no matter how much I am concerned for you."

"I'm afraid that's what you must do."

"And I will. But I have my security problem, too, and you must do for me what I do for you. Only my doctor and my nurse . . . and you . . . know my situation. Please remember, if you meet other people here that it is top secret."

"Okay."

"And more than that," went on Jane, "my routine—what happens in my days when you come and perhaps don't see me—or in my nights—when you are on mission—you must not ask about. More than you know now, you need not know, and I ask you to leave it."

Jack was silent.

"It's a queer thing we've got between us," he said finally.

"There's one detail I think you can tell me," Jane remarked after a pause. "Did you give a full account of last Saturday to your medical officer?"

Jack began a slow grin.

"Say, there was one mixed-up medic. He couldn't figure me out. I didn't tell him much. I just said I met you and we talked a little bit, and now I wasn't haywire; he could see that it was so. He wanted to know what we talked about, and I told him I couldn't remember it all—that it wasn't what you said so much—that I just came out of my tail spin. He had to let it go at that. And he grounded me for a week," Jack concluded with returning sulkiness.

"He's let you come to see me. We'll put that down to his credit. And now you've come, we shouldn't waste time. There's a great deal I want to know that has nothing to do with air bases and the war."

"There is? I can't seem to think of much else."

"For instance, what do you do when you're not in the war?"

"Oh that. I'm a mechanical engineer, and I had a good job in Oshkosh, Wisconsin, before Pearl Harbor."

"Is that your home?"

"Yes. I've lived there since I was five, except for the years at the U. of Wisconsin . . . until 1941."

"Do you get letters from home?"

"My kid sister and I are the family," Jack explained. "Dad died when I was seven, and my mother—" He stopped.

"Don't talk about anything you'd rather not," said Jane quickly.

"I suppose I shouldn't mind telling you, but I wouldn't want the medics to get hold of it. She's . . . not quite right. I had to put her in a place where they take care of mental cases. You see, she was lonely after my father died. She's sensitive and high-strung. She was brought up back East, and she'd traveled a lot. She spoke French and Italian and she loved music and pictures, and knew about them more than most folks in Oshkosh. . . ."

"Did your father like those things?"

"Well," said Jack. "Here I am, spilling the whole family history.

Dad was the son of an immigrant, a man who came from Europe with nothing. He got into lumber in Michigan in the early days, and made money. He brought Dad up to have everything; sent him to Yale, and let him do what he wanted. I guess Dad didn't miss much. When he met my mother, those two went clean crazy about each other at first sight, and Grandad let them marry and just play around. I guess Dad liked all the things Mother liked, but he didn't know as much about them. Grandad died all of a sudden, and pretty soon Dad found out there wasn't as much money as he supposed. He brought us to Oshkosh where Grandad had been living, and where he could pick up the pieces of what was left. My kid sister was born there. But before Dad got far earning any cash himself, he took pneumonia . . . and died. He had made Doc Farnum, a friend of his, trustee for Mother and us kids; there was enough so we could get along and be educated. Mother was always hiding away from people after Dad died. She was wrapped up in him . . . got to be more so when he was gone. But she didn't begin to be queer until I was in high school. Even now, she isn't the dangerous kind. Only, she's so withdrawn . . . sometimes doesn't talk or eat. She's gone away into a dream." His voice trailed into silence.

"So, it's your sister and Dr. Farnum who keep in touch with you."

"There isn't very much touch. I wish you could understand what my mother is like . . . I haven't given you the right idea if you think of her as just a . . . a . . . nut. Even now, she's one of the loveliest persons to look at. I've never seen a girl so . . . so exquisite."

He looked up, caught Jane's eye, and smiled. " 'Girl' . . . that word interests you, Jane?"

"If you don't mind."

"There've been girls, of course. Seems sometimes like they won't let a fellow alone. I get letters from Oshkosh. But I'm a poor correspondent."

Jane sat with folded hands and eyes on the horizon where the earth mass and heavy air made a line of finality. It was some moments before her companion spoke again.

"I guess I want too much. When I was a kid, my mother talked to me about herself and Dad. It was queer to talk like that to a child, but she hadn't anybody else. I've never seen anything like what she had

. . . or what she gave . . . coming my way. Now, it's on the cards I never will."

Jane stirred.

"You can't tell," she said. "Your future is not in your hands."

He did not seem to hear her. He was following his own thought.

"I guess you haven't had it yourself, Jane."

"No," Jane said. "I haven't had it myself."

She looked at the somber face half turned from hers and took from her portfolio the slip of paper which Jack had rescued upon his arrival.

"You picked this up," she said. "I was working over it when you came."

She leaned nearer and touched his arm. "It's a translation of a folk song, about a homesick boy," she said. "I expect the coolies at the base sing it. Have you heard the air?" And she hummed it until he turned unwillingly.

"Can't say I have. Chinese music is all discord and percussion racket so far as I know."

He was still far absent from her.

"You are thinking of theater music. There are other kinds. The folk songs are often hauntingly sweet, like this one. I shall never forget when I first heard it."

She had more attention now.

"Tell me about it. It's your turn to talk."

"When I first came to West China," said Jane, "I lived in the Taoist Temple of a village a good way from here, with the School of Religion students who had come up river with me. After some months, we went through a bombing raid that pretty well knocked down the temple and wounded seven of my students. There were not enough of us to look after those in bed very satisfactorily, so, I got tired. Once as I was lying down, I heard one of my girls singing this. It is about war, and an old home—of another place and time, I suppose. The girl's voice was so fresh and young, and the sorrow of the song so weary and old that the feeling of the two sides of experience came sharp into me— and remain with me. When I asked later, she said the song was called 'Five Forks River.' And this is the way it goes."

Jane began to sing softly:

My home is on the Five Forks River
On the Five Forks River is my home;
The hills stand tall behind it.
The soy bean grows in the loam.
The ninth month, the ninth month
And the eighth day:
That was the season of sorrow
When I was driven away.
My old parents lie dead in the ashes;
I wander the roads alone.
My home was on the Five Forks River.
Now . . . where is my home?

She had won back his attention. He was looking at her quizzically.

"Where is my home?" he echoed. "That's the question of the whole world, just now. Jane, you are a whole box of tricks. You start off doing psychiatric stuff, then you admit to being a missionary, and now you're a poet. What are you going to pull on me next?"

"I'm not a poet," she made an eager disclaimer. "Although I do like 'words set in delightful proportion' which is the best description of poetry I know. And I like 'Five Forks River' as I've dressed it up in English. I'm vain of my little translation."

"I know. I feel that way when I've done something better than usual in sketching. I think I'll be coming to draw in this garden of yours while I'm grounded."

"You didn't mention that you draw."

"My mother liked me to fool with paints and crayon when I was a kid. I studied a little at the U. Never had time afterward to do much with it." Jack was shy, but the cloud was gone from him.

"The garden provides plenty of subjects for sketching."

She pointed to a cluster of tiled surfaces on a slope below them, which Jack made out to be the roof of something, although it was nothing like any roof or any structure that he had ever seen before.

"What do you call that?" he asked. He was obediently following Jane's lead away from the personal.

"It's a garden house built in the shape of a fan. The Chinese call it a 'hsuan,' which is sometimes translated 'porch,' and it does have a triangular terrace in front of it. But there are rooms—three of them —and the roof which is the most complicated thing in the garden.

The place has a family story connected with it, which goes with the picturesqueness."

Jack did not show much interest in the suggestion of a story, but Jane, on the watch against the return of the somber face, launched into it without being asked.

"Shang Ma, the gateman's wife, tells me this sort of thing. The story is touching and not so very far back. It is the romance of the grandfather of the present owner."

"May I smoke?" Jack inquired at this point.

He lit his cigarette and leaned back against his pillar in greater relaxation, watching the smoke rising into the green shadow of the umbrella pine above him.

"I don't know how much you understand about the customs of great Chinese families. The pattern of life in their long past was one of the heights which human behavior has achieved. The Wangs of Szechuan go back to an ancestor who followed the Ming pretender in his flight from Peking, after the Ming emperor had hanged himself. The Wangs drifted, and finally began again here, in this plain near the mountains of Tibet. It's remote; and yet it is one of the ancient centers of civilization."

"If anything in these parts can be called civilized," murmured Jack.

"My dear boy, civilization is not a matter of sewing machines and railroads," said Jane. "But we'll quarrel about that another time. The Wangs have always been important people and their brides have always been taken from families of distinction. The Wang of whom I speak had the given name Ch'eng-Hsin, and he was betrothed—"

"I've heard"—Jack was trying valiantly to take an interest—"that in China, names all mean something. Did this one have a meaning?"

"It did. It means 'continuation of the faith,' and it was given him because Wang Wen-Hao, who was his father, had become a Christian and wanted his son to follow in his footsteps."

"We're forgetting the bride," suggested Jack.

"And the Fan Hsuan, which was what set me off on this story. The bride was from the family of a Cheng Tu official, and the Wangs wished to do her particular honor. They determined to add a building to their garden which should be a perfect compliment to her and a great credit to them. They asked an artist scholar who was living here then—his name was Wu Mei-Sun—"

"And what did that mean?" said Jack obligingly.

"I see that you know how to indulge a talkative woman," said Jane. "You give me a perfect chance to show off all I've been learning. Wu Mei-Sun was the descendant of a great painter of the Yuan dynasty, who chose as his signature to his paintings the plum blossom, called the 'meihua.' So this Wu chose to be Wu Mei-Sun, the son of the plum blossom."

"Son of a plum blossom," murmured Jack. "Can you beat it for a man's name! So what did he do about the building for the bride?"

"He knew about the great gardens of past dynasties, and from his suggestions they built the Fan Hsuan. It has symbolical meaning. The fan is supposed to waft favoring breezes or influences into the life of the married pair."

"Did the bride like it?"

"She never saw it. Just when it was finished, and only a month before the wedding chair was to go for her, she died. But there is another chapter to the story. Ch'eng-Hsin had lost his heart to a young relative who had been brought up in his mother's care. The two lovers had never dreamed of upsetting the family arrangements. They had wept and, I suppose, tried to keep their secret. But the parents were watching, the girl was sent off to live at a distance, and the young man was told he could have a decent time to get over his fancy before he must welcome his bride. When the news of the death of his betrothed came, he did nothing in a hurry. But finally he put it to his father that since plans had miscarried, he now would take his own way, and refuse to accept any bride but his beloved. In this case, no agreements had to be broken, and the red chair was finally sent for her. Wang Ch'eng-Hsin insisted upon receiving her in the beautiful Fan Hsuan which was built for the great lady. She made a devoted wife and daughter-in-law, and had many sons. At last she took her place as the head of the family, and Shang Ma can remember her—a wise and gentle old lady, whose favorite place to stay was the rooms to which she came when she was first married."

Jack did not comment for some time, but sat smoking lazily, and Jane finally asked if he had liked her story.

"I was thinking," he said. "I expect they . . . the people who got married . . . I expect they had it."

"It?" Jane was a little puzzled.

"They had what I was talking about," Jack explained. "What I guess I'll never have."

"Oh," said Jane. "Yes, they did. And they didn't suppose they ever would."

Chapter Eight

"This chair," said Jane, "cost me five hundred dollars two years ago. How much do you think we could get for it now?"

Wilfreda looked at her friend who was enjoying her afternoon hour out of bed. She was established in a low wicker chair, the back of which was a wide curve against which Jane in her blanket looked not unlike the body of a peacock against the spread of the tail. She had always called it her "peacock chair," with the comment that it was reminiscent of moulting with its battered edges and the blues and browns of its woven pattern dulled by time and dust.

"What makes you think of selling?" the nurse asked.

"Because we need some extra cash, don't we? I can see your forehead pucker into a knot every time Shang Ma comes to you for the vegetable money. Of course the inflation goes on grinding higher and higher."

"Don't bother about it," was the hasty reply. "Let me think what to do. We can't spare your chair."

"I could do without it."

"No, you couldn't. You are too weak to sit long on stools with no backs, or to perch on the chairs which are high and stiff. Besides, you enjoy the big back of this one, and it has a comfortable 'give' to it. We will not part with the peacock chair."

"It was sheer worldliness which made me buy it," Jane confided. "Two years ago, five hundred dollars was about one dollar in American money, which might not seem a very steep price for a bit of comfort. But I didn't buy it for comfort, but for style! I got it because I wanted to sit in it and make believe I wasn't a refugee where everything I handled and used was broken and nondescript and colorless

64

and ugly. It was supposed to remove me from the tedious make-do of my existence. And of course this was perfectly absurd of me, and I found it was always in the way until we came here. However, if you don't sell this, we must think of something else."

"I don't see that you have anything to spare."

"Take my underwear," Jane suggested after a moment of reflection. "Good wool commands a price in the chilly months in Szechuan, even if it is worn and darned. Mine was Dr. Eleazar Humphry's best! When he was obliged to leave for the States, I made all the other single ladies very mad by getting him to sell to me. But he was rather stout, although not much taller than I, and I've had quite a time taking the things in, you know, to make them fit, and they've always prevented me having anything like a *spirituelle* figure in winter. So take them. Brother Ass won't be needing his winter things again, you know."

"It isn't the season for selling wool," said Freda. "But I will go into Huai Yuen before long, and I'll visit the hock shop."

Jane leaned back contentedly. She found the appearance of the little court from a sitting position something to be freshly enjoyed. In her cot she had been aware chiefly of the warm green shadow flowing over her from the trees under which she lay. Now she could savor more detail than had been possible in her horizontal hours. The pebbled path under her feet, the lattice patterns under the downsweep of the gray-tiled roofs provided a background of grateful neutrality for the vivid hues of the green foliage. The planting had been done by a cunning hand. The smoothness of the plum leaves, the brilliance of the young-bladed bamboo, and the dark masses of the evergreen had been placed for contrast and variety. The quietness spread before her eyes like the quietness which floated in at her ears and reached deep into her being. She was soothed into renewed strength.

She realized that her bodily powers were quickened by her delights. Each sense impression was sharp and brought keen satisfaction. The feel of her foot on the little gray stones of the path was the new pleasure of that day. It seemed her illness had created a sensitivity in her flesh which could respond to the benedictions of smell and sound and sight to a greater degree than ever before. This had been the case on her first days of sitting up in her chair, and now she was able to go about outside the San Yu Chai. She was busy with plans for adventure.

"Freda," she began, "did you ever come across Master Yuan again, after the day you met him with Wang Wei-Chou?"

"Never," was the answer. "I've often wondered why he doesn't come to inquire about you."

"Oh, that would not be good manners."

Freda looked puzzled. "I've had very little to do with old-style gentry since I came to China. I realize that I don't know much about their ways. But why wouldn't Colonel Wang's old tutor be friendly to you?"

"It isn't a case for friendliness. In China, in the old days, a well-bred woman asked only one courtesy from a man, that of being left completely to herself. If she was modest, she could not endure the suggestion of having the slightest interest in anyone outside the family circle. Therefore, Master Yuan keeps to his side of the garden and presumes that I wish to keep to mine."

"But you don't?"

"No. I'm not a refined Chinese lady. I'm a Westerner who wishes to talk with Master Yuan about a thousand things. So I shall be bold-faced and send him a note. Could you bring me writing materials, Freda?"

"I never learned to write Chinese," sighed the nurse as she fetched Jane's portfolio, and watched her friend take out paper ruled in small squares.

Jane's dimple showed for a moment. "Master Yuan will hardly regard me as literate. My handwriting is laborious and uneven like a child's. My style will be utterly plebeian; my writing materials beneath contempt. But he will be able to make out what I mean."

She used her fountain pen and filled a few squares on her paper with very stout, definite-looking characters. She folded it and inscribed the scholar's name on the outside.

"When Shang Shih goes over with his evening rice, he can take this to Master Yuan and bring the answer. And when you see it, you will be able to judge a little of the vulgarity of my efforts."

"When are you asking him to come?"

Jane appeared shocked.

"Freda, you horrify me. Of course, I'm not asking him to come."

The other looked suspiciously at the note in her hand.

"You'd better tell me what you did say. I don't want you overdoing."

"Don't be tiresome. I asked Master Yuan whether there would be some time in the course of the next week or two when he would allow me to call upon him."

"Now Jane! At least he can walk easily and you can't."

"Modify your statement, my dear. He can walk, very true, but he wouldn't want to walk across the garden to call upon me. He would be embarrassed; he wouldn't know what to do about a lady in an invalid state. As for me, let us say that just at present I don't walk very much. However, by the time he is ready to receive me, I shall be able to get to him . . . you'll see."

Freda made a gesture of mingled amusement and despair, but she dispatched the note by Shang Shih. When the reply came, Jane displayed it with pride of showmanship.

"Now observe, Freda. Here is an envelope of proper scholar stationery. It is thin, slightly browned paper; it has a suggestion of fragility and age. My name is written in graceful but careless strokes. The brush and the ink must be of superior quality. Now, I open, and draw out the message itself, folded, you see, rather intricately. There are many ways of folding letter papers, and one can convey either compliment or insult by the means."

"Which is this?"

"Well," said Jane, "I've never been able to take in such refinements in detail. I've heard them talked about, but that's all. We will hope there is no subtle rebuke intended in these creases."

"What does he say?"

Jane's brow was wrinkled.

"It's lucky I know to start with what he's likely to say. He uses an elaborate literary style, and his character, although it isn't exactly the running kind, is certainly very free . . . let's see . . . let's see."

She studied the note.

"Um . . . um . . . yes; he will be glad to see me whenever I wish to come. He is always in the library. A word to Shang Shih will be sufficient."

"Doesn't sound like an exact translation."

"No," said Jane. "I can't read it all. And I don't approve of these literal flowery translations which are always being produced as amusing. Courtesy, which has grown up through generations of cultivated living, isn't funny. It is a gross kind of behavior to treat it as if it were."

"That," said Freda, "is the best excuse for ignorance I've ever heard. It would be vulgar to translate—wonderful, Jane!"

The two burst into laughter, and Jane put her note away, saying, "I promise not to walk over to the Library of Four Delights until you give me leave. I believe that will be sooner than you think."

Jane's days of sitting up in the chair had been followed by promenades in the gallery beside the Pool of the Rock and Pine, and soon she was able to go to the Water Mirror Pavilion and back. Her first serious exertion had been the climb of a few steps to the *t'ing-tse*, Looking to the Snow Mountains, where Jack Fernald had found her. Wilfreda marveled at the increase of energy, and longed to believe the improvement was permanent. She put the inevitable out of her thoughts for the time being, and she wondered if Jane were not doing the same, as gaiety took the place of patience and all reference to Brother Ass was sheer drollery. Freda was of the opinion that it would not do for so cloistered a soul as Master Yuan to be confronted with two women at once, and Jane was inclined to agree that her initial call would go off better if she presented herself alone. It was finally agreed that the next time Wilfreda went to Huai Yuen, Jane should walk over very slowly, stopping to rest at the Water Mirror Pavilion, and spend a morning hour in beginning her acquaintance with the old scholar. Shang Ma was to be taken along as a precaution.

The shopping and hocking excursion required that Wilfreda set off very early. She was on her way before sunrise, anticipating her walk through open country and on the great road before it became too traveled for a pedestrian. She could save ricksha fare by going on foot into the city; it would take her about three hours and would bring her to the shops just as business began. Coming back, there would be things to carry, and she would ride. She started when the light was filling the tops of the trees, and she had her knitting bag full of bulges; but what she was about to pawn she would not confide to Jane.

"Leave it to me," said Wilfreda.

The morning turned out to have shafts of misty sunlight for Jane's encouragement, and by ten o'clock, she was on her way with Shang Ma. The serving woman was full of the importance of being in charge of the Shih Mu and also full of the desire to talk, and Jane deflected her from the subject of herself by asking for an account of Master Yuan.

"Ah," said Shang Ma. "He is a man whose learning must be very deep. He passed the imperial examinations when he was only eighteen. I have heard there are no more examinations in Peking, and that is a pity. It must account for the disorder of our times. Well, Master Yuan was born in a village not far from here, and went all the long journey from Szechuan to the northern capital for the gathering of the stars."

Jane was puzzled. . . . The gathering of the stars . . . ? Oh, the coming together of the scholars, of course; she had heard the phrase but had never known it was current among the people. Shang Ma was prattling on.

"I am told Master Yuan married and was a magistrate somewhere in the north. But in the time of Sun Wen, he returned to Szechuan and lived in poverty in his village. Our young master was very clever and required a tutor who had deep learning. So Wang Ta Jen, our old master, invited him to come and live in our family."

They had been skirting the shore of the lake, and now they were in front of the Water Mirror Pavilion; Jane sank down on the broad seat in the shade and motioned Shang Ma to a place beside her.

"And so he has been here ever since?" she asked.

"No. When our Hsiao Yeh went to the north to enter the University, Master Yuan went also. He has a son in Peking. But do not speak of that son."

"Why not?" Jane knew this was important.

"The Wang family has never known the shame that has come upon Yuan Hsü-Feng," said Shang Ma, using the scholar's full name for the first time. "And may we never know it." She spoke under her breath.

"The son of Master Yuan is a traitor. The old man does not know that we have heard it," she added quickly. "In former days, he could have kept it secret. But now many people come down the north road and it has been told to us. The son of Scholar Yuan is a puppet serving the dwarf monkeys. It was four years ago that his father returned. Since the day he came, he has never left the garden. . . . Is the Shih Mu refreshed so soon?"

The son a traitor. . . . Jane lost the thread of Shang Ma's talk as they walked on, passing south of the Water Mirror Pavilion and coming to a section of the garden which was new to Jane. The path led them along the outlet of the Happy Sea, narrowed to a channel between low hills which screened this section from the central scene. The waterway then turned north and widened in an irregular oblong. Jane deserted her inner thoughts for the outer world, and looked about her.

She was walking along the west bank and immediately opposite was an unwalled dwelling with three rooms. The middle *chien*, projecting from the others, was carried on piles and stood over flowing water so that its windows opened on the rippling flood. As Jane looked, she caught the blue flash of kingfisher wings, and a bird plummeted from the overhanging willows into the gray shallows.

"What is that place?" she asked Shang Ma, putting aside the painful revelation she had just heard.

"That is the Studio of Clear Sounds. It is for the entertainment of guests. But I remember that when our young master returned from the north after his first studies were finished, he shut himself up there for many days and was very sad. He played the flute and would not eat. I was young and curious then," Shang Ma giggled apologetically, "and I used to creep up among the bamboos to listen. Once our old master came to talk to the Hsiao Yeh about his wedding. The Hsiao Yeh did not wish to marry. He was lovesick about somebody in the north. There was such a quarrel that I was frightened and ran away. But then, the Hsiao Yeh did marry, and his son was born, and his sadness was cured, for after the wedding, I never heard the flute again."

"Clear Sounds. . . ." Had Wei-Chou named the house on account of his flute music Jane wondered. She thought of Willow in the spring days when the stormy revolutionist had been gentle for a little while with her young lover. But all that was long past. The "clear sounds" were the bird calls and the running of the water which would never cease, while the sorrow in the flute had gone the way of all transient human things.

While Shang Ma chattered, Jane had been lingering opposite the first building she saw; but her destination was further on, near a rustic bridge which spanned the watercourse under leaning trees and ended the little view. The Library of Four Delights stood to the west and north, out of earshot, but not out of sight of Clear Sounds. At first it was only a curved roof, lifting in the midst of sheltering trees, and outlined against a screen of the curious rockwork. But as Jane came nearer, she saw its ample proportions under its deep eaves, with all the windows open to the summer air. Its distinguishing feature was a stone terrace, broad and square and surrounded by a lotus-carved balustrade, on which the readers of books could refresh themselves with garden breezes.

Master Yuan was expecting her. His dark figure appeared on the path near the Library, where he stood bowing to receive her. Jane halted several steps away to bow in return, and was then ushered into the house while she apologized for intruding, and was made ceremoniously welcome. She was seated opposite the open door, in a blackwood chair, the exact mate of the one in which Master Yuan took his place. Shang Ma put cups of tea on the square, black table between them, and then retired outside the door, where her kettle was steaming on the little trivet placed in the midst of glowing charcoal in the brass pan which served as a stove.

Jane knew she could not enter directly upon the subjects which had brought her to the Library, and she fervently hoped she acquitted herself without too many blunders while the introductory politenesses were going on. She took in the appearance of the apartment where they were sitting. It had a desk drawn near a window, and cases along the walls for the books, which were protected by their covers secured with ivory pegs in silken loops. Before she left, she knew it would be proper for her to make a tour of the room and admire the bronze curios, the porcelain jars, the bits of jade carving which were placed in their respective niches in cabinets prepared to exhibit such treasures. But to begin with, she should drink tea and make general observations with as much repose as she, being from the uneasy West, could manage.

Their host and former student, Wang Wei-Chou, was the bond between them and could be the subject of their first exchange of remarks. Jane mentioned his brilliance in science, and Master Yuan said that in Chinese the young man had applied himself industriously but had gone to Western schools before he could be considered accomplished. Jane observed that Chinese studies were now being pursued in the West; she referred to the collections of Chinese books at the Sorbonne, the British Museum, the Library of Congress, and spoke of her friend Barry Manners who had left a diplomatic career in order to delve more deeply into the lore of the Far East. But here she was aware of a certain stiffness behind the urbanity of the reply. "Foreigners meddling with Chinese studies—it's a species of sacrilege," thought Jane. And she shifted the subject to the garden. Could Master Yuan tell her something about the family history of the Wangs and their ownership of this place? Did it go back many generations?

The scholar bowed and replied with a quotation from the classics. Jane caught the style but entirely missed the sense, and looked at the old man for the first time.

"Please, Master Yuan," she said, "this miserable person is a foolish woman from the outside with no literary education. If Master Yuan would speak to her as to a child, it is more possible that this unworthy one would understand."

That the master agreed entirely with Jane's account of herself was clear even while he made a polite rejoinder; but then he did descend to a level of communication which she could follow. He did not use the expression "Teacher Mother" which the servants had adopted as her title. He called her, instead, "Precious Teacher," using her Chinese surname which meant precious, and employing a term for "teacher" which was courteous but carried no connotation of especial respect. The Precious Teacher had undoubtedly a knowledge of Chinese history and remembered the flight of the Ming rulers before the Ch'ing conquerors?

The Precious Teacher had no deep knowledge at all, but had heard of the Ming dynasty and its sad end.

"The ancestor of Wang Wei-Chou," said Master Yuan, "through

loyalty"—Jane quivered at the firmness with which the word "*chung*" was pronounced—"followed the Ming emperor to the south."

Jane asked his name, and saw Master Yuan hesitate.

"His name is not known," he said finally. "Through a misfortune the family tablets were burned, and no records of the remote past are left. After vicissitudes without number, an ancestor settled in Canton and became a Hong merchant at the time when trade was opening between China and the West, and great fortunes were being made. The Wang family became rich and purchased land in many places. It was in the reign of Ch'ien Lung that they became owners here. Such was the beauty of this place that they preferred it to all their other lands. It was also rather remote from the Ch'ing power, although China was then nominally united."

"Were they still adherents of the Ming pretenders?" Jane inquired.

"They were faithful. The last Ming emperor, Yu Lung, was murdered by the Yunanese Wu San-Kwei in the reign of K'ang Hsi, but there were still princes of the blood hiding and wandering from place to place. The *pien* which hangs over our gate was written by one of them when he was a refugee within these walls."

"The name of the garden was given by the prince himself?" Jane asked.

"As the story has come down to us, we learn that on the tenth day of the fifth month in the twentieth year of the reign of Ch'ien Lung at the hour of the Dragon, a traveler sought entrance at this gate. He was a young man, attended only by a rough country boy who drove his donkey, and he was very weary. The servant who opened the gate was not inclined to let him in, but the young man drew a seal from his sleeve and bade him show it to his master. Great was the servant's surprise and confusion when he had done so. His master hurried to the gate and there prostrated himself before the shabby young man and his donkey. The guest was brought within and remained for some time. Before he went away he bestowed the name of 'Pure Repose' upon the garden, and wrote the characters for the *pien*, which the family has cherished ever since."

"I remember," Jane murmured, "that once I read a passage which says that the fortune of a garden is closely connected with the merit of its builder. If he possesses lasting integrity, it will stand through the ages, though it may occasionally suffer neglect. If the contrary is true, the garden will eventually be left in ruin, although it may prosper for a time."

"The ancestral integrity of the Wang family has been great," replied the Chinese. "And it has not been lacking in the descendants. The grandfather of Wang Wei-Chou, Wang Ch'eng-Hsin, had such integrity. When he was a young man, he passed the imperial examination and entered official life with high hopes. But he served in evil times. He gave up his post when he discovered that he could not remain both a magistrate and an honest man. When he returned without distinction to this garden, he was visited by Wu Mei-Sun, an artist, who was his friend."

This account of integrity was given with an undertone of severity, which Jane wished she need not have understood. But the stern aspect was relaxed at the mention of the artist.

"He was not one of our great painters, of course," said Master Yuan, "but he was descended from Wu Chen, who was the best painter of bamboos in the Yuan dynasty, and he tried to follow in his ancestor's footsteps. He did a series of views of this garden showing the joys of the retired life. It is called 'The Bamboo Masterpiece of Wu Mei-Sun' and is a famous possession of the family."

Jane did not remember that Wei-Chou had ever mentioned either his illustrious grandfather or his collection of paintings. He had moved far away from such matters into a world of science, which perhaps had crowded out the world into which he was born. She had known him intimately, but she had known him as a scientific modern rather than as an heir of the great past. She was recalled from her musing by a movement of her host. He rose, went to a table near at hand where an album of pictures was lying open. He brought it to her saying, "These paintings in my collection are also from the hand of Wu Mei-Sun."

There were eight landscapes bound in book leaves with covers of worn brocade. Each picture was in a different style of brushwork, although all were from the same hand, and on each leaf were the red seals of the collectors who had owned the paintings before Master Yuan. The old man talked about his treasures and their history, and as he talked, Jane became aware that she was in the presence of a dedicated soul. He had made his escape from the world of violence, and from it he had rescued a few belongings. He had made the exhausting and terrifying journey; he had become a pensioner upon the bounty of his old student in order that he might keep alive in his own person the tradition, the culture which he embodied. It was his duty to go on being Yuan the Scholar in the face of Japanese atrocities and American B-29s. Provinces were overrun and new weapons of destruction were planted in the shadow of the Himalayas, but the Scholar Yuan continued to practice calligraphy, write occasional poetry, and examine paintings and ink slabs as his highest duty. Now he made a startling remark.

"You have some understanding of these paintings. Can you, perhaps, suggest how they might be sold?"

She was shocked by the sudden intrusion of his necessity. Only actual want could separate the lover from his beloved—the connoisseur from his treasures. She was careful not to change expression and to keep her eyes on the picture before her. It showed a river with two tiny figures ascending a mountain track leading up from water level. The way led to a fairylike temple perched in a gorge among lofty peaks. There were thousands of feet of height and miles of winding path suggested to her eye; the grandeur and indestructibility of Nature and the irrelevance and insignificance of man were borne in upon the mind. The whole was managed on a slip of silk, six inches by five, in the monochrome of Chinese ink.

"This should be in the hands of a lover of Chinese art," Jane finally said. "Would Yuan Hsien Sheng regret if it passed to a foreigner?"

The old man gazed wistfully at his album, but he did not hesitate.

"If one of your honorable friends is interested in such trifles, this might be added to his collection."

Jane thought of Stephen Purcell, and wondered if she could induce him to become a customer. But now she was obliged to close the book and rise to take her leave.

"It is very beautiful," was all she could think of to say, and the courtesies of leave-taking put an end to embarrassment for the time being.

As she started back to her own quarters, Jane was conscious that she had done enough for that day. Shang Ma had lingered to wash and put away the teacups, and was not at hand when she felt the exhaustion which had been the most insistent symptom in her final breakdown. She thought of stopping to wait for the woman's appearance, but there was no convenient seat.

Nonsense, she said to herself. I can certainly get back to the Chai, and once there I have nothing to do but to lie still.

At this moment she saw Shang Shih turn the corner of the path, evidently in search of her. He gave her a visiting card with a line scribbled on it:

Dear Teacher Jane: Do you remember Benny, in Harbin, in Truth Hall days?

Benny—of course, she must see him. She looked at her watch. It was nearly twelve. Wilfreda had been expecting to return by the middle of the day. Perhaps she would soon be here, to help entertain the unexpected guest. Where had he come from? What could they scrape up to offer him to eat? She quickened her steps and, with Shang Shih preceding her, came within sight of the Water Mirror Pavilion.

The Eurasian had been standing by the balustrade looking out over the lake to the island which hid the northern shore, and as he heard her step, he swung about and came toward her.

"You do remember me?" he asked as he took her hand.

"You are much heavier and very much more elegant," she told him. "But of course I remember you. Let us sit down while you tell me where you have been and what you have been doing."

"Oh, refugeeing, just like everybody else," said Benny as he took his place beside her.

"I hope you've not had as hard a time as most," said Jane. "So many of my friends have turned up with hollow cheeks and the little points of white in their hair which show they have been hungry."

"I haven't either of those marks, have I?"

He submitted to her gaze with good grace and made himself meet her eyes fairly. "I suppose I've had the usual experience. Sometimes it's been hard; sometimes, not so bad."

"Tell me what you've been doing."

He adhered strictly to facts in dealing with matters which might conceivably come to Jane's ears through other channels. In the account of the years when he had been out of her orbit, he invented freely and gave her a moving history containing the elements which would appeal to the interest and compassion of his missionary friend. He described his poverty and his struggles to better himself as a country schoolteacher, his adventures and successes as a newspaper-man, and he concluded with a thrilling escape from the Japanese and an arduous journey into Free China. He was quite carried away with his own inventions and paused, fearing that he was being too glib. But it seemed to him that Jane's attention wandered a little and that her shoulders were sagging unnecessarily—surely not the effect he had been working for.

She came up with an encouraging question, after a moment of si-lence.

"So you are on a special assignment from your Chungking paper now. Are you staying long in Huai Yuen?"

"A week or two. Then I may not be needed any longer, and I'll have to look for another job."

Jane leaned her head against the pillar behind her and wished that Wilfreda would come. Benny's voice seemed very far away.

"I heard you were here. I remembered how good you were to Mother and Bobby and me. I thought you wouldn't mind if I looked you up."

"I'm glad you have."

She could keep on saying short sentences like that one for some time.

"You know, Teacher Jane, I was hoping you might help me get work."

There was quite a pause before he got an answer to this.

"Perhaps we can talk about that when you come again."

There was a quick step behind him and Benny rose as another woman came into the Pavilion.

"Freda," said Teacher Jane in a very small voice, "this is Benny Li . . . an old student of mine . . . who will stay to lunch."

Benny scarcely understood how it was that he found himself stroll-ing along the path to the west of the lake, while the two women vanished somewhere behind the low hills to the east. The person called Freda had slipped her arm under Teacher Jane's drooping shoulders and moved off with her, at the same time waving Benny toward the opposite end of the Pavilion. She made no explanation, but remarked over her shoulder that she would be back, and it was very plain that Teacher Jane wouldn't. Benny continued in the direction in which he started, reflecting that he should have been more observant . . . something must be wrong. He had drawn a blank in his first attempt to introduce the subject of her cousin, Major Trent, but she had assumed he would be coming to see her again. That was something.

He reached a point where the path left the edge of the lake and ran along the wall of a building which stood separate from the garden scene in an indentation of the shore. For a short distance he was shut in by the wall on the east and the artificial hills to the west, so that he felt free from observation. He plunged his hand into the pocket of his coat and brought out a roll of printed matter, about as thick and as long as a pencil, which had ordinary second-class postage. It was the daily newspaper which always contained his orders, and he looked at it with great disfavor before he ripped off its wrapping and hunted for the piece of rice paper. He glanced at it only a moment and swore softly as he disposed of the message. He had received a sharp reprimand for delay in setting up the broadcast service to Tokyo. American Intelligence had been so active that all former channels were now impossible, and he was at his wit's end to think what to do next. As he followed the path around the lake, he began to wonder whether this garden might not be a possibility for a few broadcasts. He must cultivate enthusiasm for Chinese garden art, he thought.

When he reached the Water Mirror, he found Wilfreda there.

"I'm sorry," the nurse said. "And Miss Breasted is very distressed. But she has been ill and is not yet quite strong."

"I should have realized that she was tired," Benny replied. "At first she seemed as I remembered her . . . only older. But now I see that she was putting up a brave front; really she is . . . pretty brittle, isn't she? And may break, someday?"

Wilfreda was surprised. The visitor did not seem a sensitive type, and yet he was displaying more understanding than was desirable.

"She hopes you will stay to lunch," she said, evading further discussion of the brittleness of Jane.

"Thanks, but not this time."

He turned toward the gate, and Wilfreda fell into step with him.

"Do you think I might come out again?"

"It's not certain you would see her, I'm afraid."

Benny glanced around.

"I could come on the chance of it. And this is a wonderful place to visit, isn't it?"

"It really is. Miss Breasted would like you to enjoy it whenever you can spare time to make the trip from the city."

"Please tell her I shall come again."

Shang Shih closed the gate upon Benny and went off to Shang Ma's kitchen for the old scholar's noonday meal. He opened a deep wicker basket and lifted from its compartment a pewter bowl which was made in the shape of a lotus flower. It was lined with crackleware porcelain, and in it he placed a frugal portion of rather inferior rice. The basket was provided with padding, covered with faded silk, in which were spaces exactly shaped to keep hot the four shallow plates, formed like lotus leaves, which made up a complete service for a Chinese meal. The gateman put a spoonful of cabbage, prepared with one or two dried shrimps for flavor, in one of these, and then poured into a slender winepot, nestled in its place beside a bud wine bowl, a mere thimbleful of hot wine. Shang Ma was out of the kitchen, looking after the two women, but Shang Shih knew she had prepared nothing else for the old scholar. Over the two poor portions of food he adjusted the little covers with knobs of white jade; the wine jug went into its place, the wicker cover was fastened down, and the gateman went out of the service courtyard to the Library of Four Delights where his master's old tutor was starving out the war. When he had arrived in Szechuan, he had had money with him. But the war had gone on too long. Shang Shih had noted that the food given out to be cooked had grown less and less in quantity, and when he carried out orders to purchase supplies, he was directed to get poorer and poorer quality. Still, he supposed there must be some further resources.

He presented himself in the Library and set his basket on the floor. Master Yuan was sitting before the square "eight fairy" table at the inner end of the room, and the pewter dishes and winepot were placed before him.

"Venerable Teacher, please eat."

The servant retired respectfully outside the door, to remain until the meal should be finished. He waited long, for today Scholar Yuan ate very slowly. He savored each grain of rice and each morsel of cabbage. He poured out the wine, a tiny portion at a time, and took it drop by drop. In spite of a delicate appetite and careful management, he was at the end of his last purchase of grain, and his money was exhausted. His approach to the subject of selling his album had brought no help. What was he to do?

"Shang Shih," he called.

The servant appeared at once.

"This is the last of the rice I have measured for you?"

"The last, Venerable Teacher."

"You may clear the table."

Shang Shih fitted the dishes and the wine jug into their compartments in the basket and said, "What will the Venerable Teacher eat this evening?"

"This evening, I shall not eat."

The gateman departed, his faithful head concerned for Scholar Yuan. The latter sat very still for a long time. The next day he must break his habit of seclusion, venture into Huai Yuen, and find some way to turn one of his treasures into food. It was a more horrifying thought for the old man than the prospect of battle to a young soldier. What should he try to sell? And where could he find a purchaser? How should he know whether he was receiving fair treatment? How long could he eat from the sacrifice of one treasure? The war had gone on too long . . . too long. . . .

Chapter Nine

"You are Miss Grayson, aren't you?"

The driver leaned out as Wilfreda came to the side of the truck which had just stopped at the gate, and she was aware of his dark, deep-set eyes and the frankness of his smile, in spite of the grime which covered his face.

"I'm Stephen Purcell," he went on, opening the door and climbing down to her. "Don't dream of shaking hands. I'm a mass of dirt. But I've got a letter for you from R Square, and I can tell you straight off that he says to stay with Jane until he sends for you. How is she?"

"Much improved since she came to the garden, though she still must rest a great deal. She is eager to see you."

"But not like this." Stephen seemed to tower above Wilfreda as he stood beside her in his rumpled uniform. "I must tidy up before going to her. I got her note saying there was a place for me to stay out here, as soon as I pulled into the Section Hostel at Huai Yuen, so I came along at once."

"Jane is delighted. Everything is ready for you, if you'll come in."

Wilfreda moved toward the gate but the newcomer stood looking about.

"I don't like leaving the truck outside," he said. "Jane told me the place was immense, but I don't see any way to drive in. This gate's got a roof—very pretty, but much too low for my cab."

"I think there's another gate somewhere in the back. I'll ask."

Wilfreda turned to Shang Shih. The gateman had been making his own observations as the conversation went on, and had been uncertain how to regard the new arrival. Proper guests did not drive evil-smelling, noisy motors; proper guests at the Wang Family Garden

had never arrived with sleeves rolled up on hairy arms, and hands
blackened with grease. The Hu Shih, who washed clothes like an
ordinary servant, had been hard to classify; but he had accepted her
as one above, and she was not treating this person as menial. Moreover, Shang Shih had been duly notified by the Shih Mu that someone
was coming who must be domiciled in the Studio of Clear Sounds.
Now this outlandish creature was addressing him—did he suppose he
was talking Chinese? The Hu Shih, whose language was queer enough,
but who was sometimes comprehensible, was talking, too. Another
gate? What did they want with another gate? Big enough for that
noisy, dirty truck? The driver was slipping money, much money, into
his hand. Shang Shih looked at the amount of the tip, and the status
of the newcomer became indubitable. He was a guest—most decidedly
a guest. Shang Shih was even able to understand him better. Yes,
there was another gate. Lao Pa should be sent to unbar it immediately.

"Let me go in the cab with you," said Wilfreda. "Then I can guide
you through the garden after you have parked the truck."

She added a word to Shang Shih, climbed up over the wheel, and
directed Stephen to follow the track around the wall.

"Must be something like ten square acres," he remarked as he
drove.

"We've been here almost four weeks, and I haven't explored the
whole of it yet. I have the general layout in my head now, but there
are out-of-the-way bits still to visit. I've wanted Jane to be cautious
about presuming on her strength, so she has seen less than I. She wants
you to take her for a stroll after tea, but you won't let her go too far or
talk too much, will you?"

"We'll obey any orders you give us," Stephen assured her. "Can you
tell me what's the matter with her? R Square wasn't very communica-
tive. Said something about overwork—a general breakdown. Jane
has never struck me as being nervous, which is what most people
usually mean by a breakdown."

"No," Freda agreed. "Still, you see, there was overwork, of course
. . . and the climate is notoriously trying . . . and malnutrition."

Stephen pulled up before a gate, and turned in his seat.

"Did you say malnutrition?"

"It's common enough in West China, isn't it?"

"Miss Grayson," said Stephen with emphasis, "overwork is something people like you and Jane can't seem to help; the Szechuan climate is something the Lord Himself can't seem to help; but malnutrition is something I can help. If Jane needs food, I propose to see that she gets it. Perhaps you will be so kind as to tell me what should be done."

He was profoundly embarrassed to see the water standing in Wilfreda's eyes. To his relief, the gate was at that moment opened, so that the driving in engaged his full attention. He followed the track inside the walls, around rises of ground deep in tangled growth, into an open space, where low buildings stood opposite sheds in which farming tools were kept.

"This ought to be safe enough. The coolies evidently sleep here. Be sure to keep the gate barred at night," he added in Chinese to Lao Pa, putting the encouraging tip into the servant's hand. "Do you think he understood that?" he appealed to Wilfreda.

"He's smiling very intelligently, and his duty is to look after the garden, so I shouldn't think you need worry. Do you always use money like that? It's rather breath-taking."

"It depends on circumstances," said Stephen. "I learned early in my days in China that it's well to be on good terms with the dependents and underlings of yamens and great houses. You never know when you may need a friend. Where are you taking me?"

Wilfreda had been leading him down a path through a bamboo grove where the trees grew far above Stephen's head, and the ground was yellow with their fallen leaves. They came out now on the north side of the hump-backed bridge. Shang Shih was waiting.

"He'll take you to the other side of the lake, beyond the ridge of hills you see over there," explained Wilfreda, pointing out the way. "You are to be in the house the Wang family always used for their guests. When you are ready, Shang Shih will bring you to us. Tea will be waiting."

"I won't be any longer than I can help," Stephen promised, and followed his guide.

"What did you think of him?" Jane demanded when Wilfreda got back to her. "Isn't he an unusually nice truck driver?"

"That's understatement," said Wilfreda. "I like your Stephen so much that I am more annoyed than ever with his Daisy. He will want to talk to you about her, so I am going off to read the letters he's brought me. There's one from the Bishop. It says I am to stay."

Jane stretched out her hands with a gesture of thankfulness and the two were silent a moment. Then Wilfreda went away, and Jane leaned back to wait for Stephen.

Her thoughts reverted to the years in Peking when she had lived in the same courtyard with Miriam Fairchild. Her first sight of Daisy's mother she had never forgotten. She closed her eyes now, and was again at the entrance of the palace where an emperor had once given audience. She was in the gateway of a spacious court, surrounded by tall, sloping roofs and stately colonnades. Coming toward her in the brilliant sunlight was a slender, black-clad woman with bronze braids wreathing a small head carried high. . . . Yes, she had sensed something at once splendid and pitiful about her. . . . A courteous welcome, and then the threading of a maze of passages and courts; then, here once more before her eyes was the familiar image of an octagonal opening in a wall; inside, a court, small, shaded by old cypress trees, and bright with autumn chrysanthemums; and the buildings, small but vivid, with vermilion lattices picked out with gold and with paintings of flowers and birds under the eaves in peacock blue and bamboo green, all incredibly festive, Jane had felt. She had stood open-eyed, she remembered, hearing Miriam say, "The place used to be a ducal palace, you know . . . the fresh paint is gay, isn't it?" Then came the eruption of a small figure, all knobby brown knees and flying brown curls, which threw itself upon Miriam.

"Mama, I want you to—"

"Darling, here's a new auntie who's come to live with us. Miss Breasted, this is Daisy. Darling, where's Fu Ma?"

"Mama, I want you to—"

"Darling, I can't stop now. I must go back to the office, you know. Good-by, darling."

And there was that picture before her again . . . the small figure in the octagonal gate, waving disconsolately at the one which was hurrying away and quavering out, "Good-by, Mama. I just want you to—"

There were other recollections of the same sort. Jane had soon realized that she had been assigned the room in the court with the Fairchilds because no other was available. But with all the unavoidable intimacy, she found Miriam holding her at arm's length, and had the sensations of an intruder. Night after night, she was awakened by slow, smothered sobbing behind Miriam's locked door, but no word ever passed between them concerning that searing grief. Daisy's mother immersed herself in the task of building up a new and rapidly expanding institution in which Chinese women could receive a university education. She was at the beck and call of committees and conferences, classes and meetings, from morning till night. Daisy was otherwise provided for. Other mothers, other teachers, and her amah, kept her small routine going. At the end of the day, her own mother tried to share the child's supper hour.

"Daisy, darling," would come the call from outside the octagonal gate, and then Miriam would come hurrying into the small room where a stove was glowing, and Daisy, in her padded blue Chinese robe and generous bib, was already busy with her bowl and spoon while Jane read to her. On such evenings, Jane always slipped away. But there were others when the hour passed, and the mother was delayed. Daisy would snuggle into Jane's arms for her story, but at the same time she listened for the call and the step. As she was tucked into her bed, she would say, "Aunt Jane, would you hold my hand a little while?" and the fingers would curl so tightly around hers that it was only when sleep was deep that Jane would open them and release herself.

Sometimes Jane had ventured a protest. "Miriam, what kept you tonight?" she would say, when the mother, exhausted and chilled, finally appeared. The answer was always a variation of the same thing, "Jane, don't. I couldn't help it. We've this building program to carry through, and I had to go over all the specifications for our administration offices with Mr. Martin. He came late. We've only just finished." —"But Daisy . . ." And then the cry, "After all, I have to earn her living, don't I? I must be father and mother in one. We must get along with what time I can squeeze out from a thousand other demands." With the impatient words, Jane remembered the suffering eyes. . . .

. . . "In a brown study, Jane?"

She was looking up at Stephen, and now it was teatime in West China.

"I was remembering Daisy's childhood," she confessed. "Sit down. Sit down. Has thee heard anything from her?"

As she gave him a bowl of tea she was amazed to see his big hand actually unsteady. There was an odd note in his voice as he said,

"I—I've seen her."

"Thee has! Thee came by way of Chungking and saw her. And so thee has direct news of her for me."

"I have—direct news. In fact, I have a message for thee from her, which she told me to be sure not to forget."

Jane looked up. Daisy had not written to her for years. It was at the time of Miriam's death that their last exchange of letters had taken place. Therefore her acquaintance with Stephen meant a new connection with Daisy, who was now sending a message. She waited. Stephen did not go on.

"Well," said Jane. "And has thee forgotten?"

He looked at her, and then she knew.

"You two—?"

Stephen's smile was positively enormous.

"Don't take too much for granted. What I was to tell thee is this: If, by the end of the war, she hasn't married anyone else, she will probably take me—she adds, if I'm still in favor of such an arrangement—but that part of the message is superfluous."

"Oh." And Jane sniffed.

"Does thee consider an 'oh' and a sniff a sufficient congratulation, Jane?"

"Does thee consider thee is in a position for congratulations?" Jane countered.

"Of course," said Stephen, passing his bowl for more tea. "This is much more than anything I could ever get out of her before. It's a distinct advance on our last conversation four years ago in Washington."

"That was when R Square was visiting the States and raising funds for the Chinese cooperatives? And he persuaded thee to come out to the Service Section already set up by the English Friends? How did Daisy take that?"

"She had been driving me nearly out of my wits. I'd got to the point where I wasn't taking any more, and R Square had put it to me to make a clean break and come out here. So Daisy dismissed me—or I dismissed her. Anyhow, we were all washed up."

"But thee hasn't remained washed up?" Jane prompted.

"No. I've told thee all about me—four years in West China, and can't forget her. Now, we meet. And—she hasn't forgotten me."

He had been looking away from Jane, but now he met her eyes.

"But that isn't the whole of the message."

"Oh? What else?"

"She's coming to see thee."

"Oh, she is. I feel that I may sniff again. How does she know she's invited?"

Stephen seemed puzzled.

"Does she have to have a formal invitation? She didn't think of that."

Jane's dimple appeared, and she studied Stephen's face.

"When is she coming? While thee is here?"

"Not this time. I'll have to be in Chungking again shortly and we—er—rather—thought—it would be when I come back again—if it would be all right to have me again?" he ended rather anxiously.

Jane laughed outright.

"Stephen, thee is really a humble soul. Hasn't thee gathered that thee is as welcome, if not more so, than thy young tormentress? And if she comes, she is to behave herself. No driving of worthy young men out of their wits under my auspices!"

His anxiety persisted. "Jane, thee doesn't mean thee wouldn't understand? But it is through thee and thy stories of her childhood that I see her—as she is—not as she wants people to think she is."

"Oh," said Jane candidly, "I am being naughty about Daisy. She really tries my patience to the breaking point. Thee must remember I knew her as a sixteen-year-old girl, and it is through thy eyes that I know her now—as much as I do know her. But, if she will try to be good, I will try to be understanding when we meet."

"Now, how about congratulating me properly."

"Ah," said Jane. "Thee is not in the position of a promised husband according to what thee tells me. It's more as a—as a—dependable factor in an uncertain world, isn't it? I do congratulate thee upon being taken for what thee certainly is."

"If thee knew," said Stephen seriously, "the way the top brass buzz around that young woman; if thee knew the career she had in India, thee would wonder, as I do, why she casts a thought in the direction of a CO who drives trucks and is nobody—or rather worse than nobody—in the world she lives in."

"Should I wonder at her for that? I don't think so." Jane shook her head. "But Daisy, I grant thee, is unpredictable."

"Quite. And thee should add, 'utterly adorable.' "

"Like her mother before her," remarked Jane. "Stephen, shall we go out into the garden? If thee has finished thy tea?"

"Take my arm," said the young man as they passed the door of the court. "Take my arm, so that I can tell when thee tires and bring thee back as Wilfreda Grayson told me to. Jane, is thee sure thee isn't a ghost, or something? I can hardly feel touch of thee. Now, that's better. Lean so. What was thee saying about Daisy's mother?"

"Only that she was charming, too."

"It's hard to believe. I would never have thought that a woman who spent her time in committees could deserve the word. Still, Daisy, I suppose does even less alluring jobs."

"Exactly what are her jobs?" Jane wanted to know.

"Espionage and sabotage are what her outfit is for. I don't know, of course, very much about her doings. Ostensibly she sits in an office and deals with papers. But I gather her real activities are connected with her nights out."

"Did she ever tell thee about the time she ran away to a dance at the Peking Hotel and about the charm of her mother on that occasion?"

"Go on, go on. I have driven all the way from Kweiyang, ostensibly to carry medical supplies for the suffering Chinese, but actually to see Daisy when and if I can, and to spend all the rest of the time hearing and talking about her. Thee wants to go north, does thee? Once around the lake will be enough, I expect."

"I've not been all the way around yet," Jane told him. "I want to see what lies north of the island. Here is the marble chess table with its seats. Let us rest here and look at that little arch with rose walls making a splash of color in the water."

"Is thee comfortable on that drum-shaped thing?" Stephen asked as Jane seated herself and leaned toward him over the table which was scored with the lines for a complicated Chinese game. "While thee looks at thy arch, I will keep my back to it, so that I can pay close attention to a story about Daisy's running away, which is somehow to prove that her mother was a charming woman."

"It was when Daisy was only sixteen," Jane began. "She was a little witch, of course, and we had a difficult time with the young men in the legations. There was a great dearth of suitable young women to amuse them, and they flocked around the teen-agers and wanted to force the social pace. Teen-age Daisy threatened to get quite out of hand."

"Out of hand by missionary notions, I suppose," commented Stephen. "But did it matter, really?"

"One evening," continued Jane, "it was June, nine o'clock, moon-light . . . Miriam came to my room distracted. Daisy was supposed to be studying for college entrance examinations next day. But she had slipped off, leaving a note which I still remember. It said, 'I'm sixteen, and I'm going to have a good time; and there's nothing you can do about it, Mother.'"

"She didn't tell where she'd gone?"

"Oh that was easy to find out. The coolie grapevine works all the time, and Miriam learned that she was at the Peking Hotel with a man much older than the young crowd, a heavy drinker . . . a person we didn't like and didn't trust."

"I see. Enter the villain," said Stephen. "But what could the mother do? I should think Daisy was right that she was successfully defied. A missionary parent arriving on a hotel dance floor in a heat of righteous indignation would simply cut a ridiculous figure, and get nowhere."

"I don't think Miriam Fairchild was ever ridiculous in her life," said Jane reflectively. "No. She was born with a dignity that people felt, as well as with this charm we are talking about. I made her dress in the one evening thing she possessed. It was a black chiffon which a tourist woman had left behind when she didn't pay the board money she owed us before disappearing without notice. I got Miriam to look her best, with her bronze-brown hair piled high to give that superb air she could adopt when she chose. I telephoned Barry Manners, who was First Secretary then and a great friend of ours. I told him what was going on and he was very amused and came around at once to escort Miriam to the hotel. He told me afterward that she was the most stunning woman in the room. Although she went out very little, she was well known in Peking, and her arrival in the ballroom created quite a bit of interest. Barry lent intelligent support. He got a group of the rather more important people at his table. Daisy went dancing by, uneasy but very nonchalant of course. Miriam only nodded and smiled at her, but kept an eye on the villain of the piece who presently made a move to leave, probably for one of the night clubs. Then she and Barry just joined Daisy's party. Miriam put an arm around her daughter, said it was time to go home, and went. . . . You see she was charming. She charmed even Daisy herself."

"And from what thee tells me," Stephen eyed Jane, "the whole disgraceful plot of dressing up Mama like a worldly female, and ruining a gal's date originated in thy fertile brain. Isn't thee ashamed to tell it?"

"Daisy took her examinations next day," concluded Jane. "And then I took her off to the hills until it was time for her to sail for America. That was the last I've seen of her with any intimacy. Thee knows she came back to China after her college years to be with her mother, but by that time, I was in Nanking. Daisy is twenty-eight now, but I think of her as sixteen."

"She's never told me in much detail about her Peking days," said Stephen. "But she did say thee was always helping her out when she got into trouble. I know she is still fond of thee."

"Shall we go on?" Jane rose. "The arch is very pretty, but I wonder why it stands alone over there. . . . I wonder what it is for."

"I don't," said Stephen as they went on. "I don't wonder in the least. I'm thinking about having Daisy to myself in this lovely place. Take my arm again, Jane. Thee is too much of an independent woman. Just try to be a clinging vine, for this afternoon anyhow."

They walked on slowly, and when they reached the arch they found it marked the bottom of a flight of steps which led to a higher level cut into the side of the hills. Jane stood with face uplifted to the green stillness above her.

"Thee wants to go up there, doesn't thee? That is not allowed according to Wilfreda Grayson, but since thee wishes it. . . ." Stephen stooped, lifted her in his arms and walked with her to the top, where he set her down.

"Very kind of thee," she thanked him. She stood looking over the tops of the trees on the island, to the Water Mirror Pavilion, and the roofs of the Hall of Inviting the Pleasures. Then she turned in the other direction. "And now it is clear about the meaning of the rose arch. It marks the entrance to the temple."

"Temple?"

Stephen looked across a space of old cracked pavement at the roof and walls of a small building. The oval windows on either side of the doorway were filled with an intricate stone grille, but the door was empty and stood vacantly yawning upon a dim interior. When he approached with Jane, he looked into a recess where a sculptured pediment ran the length of the chamber. There were no images, and the altar table had been removed, although the mark of it remained in the floor.

"It's dusty looking, isn't it?" commented the young man. "Where are the images? There ought to be images, oughtn't there?"

"I suppose they were taken away at the same time the tablets in the ancestral hall were burned. Master Yuan was telling me . . . and that reminds me. . . ." Jane looked questioningly up at him.

"Come, we'll sit at the top of the steps for a bit. Reminds thee of what?" Stephen wanted to know.

"Stephen, does thee have some extra money just now? I mean, money it would be quite convenient to spare . . . money thee wouldn't get back again, thee understands."

"Unfortunately, I have."

"Well then, I should like some of it."

"Jane, thee comes to the point very sensibly. How much does thee want, and when does thee want it?"

"I want it at once, please," was the brisk answer. "But . . . I don't know how much."

Stephen looked at her in great amusement. "I haven't the Bank of China in my pocket, Jane. If thee doesn't know how much, I infer thee has rather a large sum in mind. I might need some time to get it."

"Of course," said Jane. "It's very stupid of me to ask before I've thought how much the album is worth."

"Album?"

"Yes. Master Yuan has an album which he must sell, and I thought I would get thee to buy it. I know thee doesn't need an album of Chinese landscape painting, but Master Yuan has to buy food, so if thee has some money to spare, it will solve my problem."

"I see," said Stephen. "Or rather, I don't, quite. Who is Master Yuan, and why is his financial embarrassment thy problem?"

"Did thee notice the house across the pool from thy Studio of Clear Sounds?" Jane asked. "Master Yuan lives there. He is an old-style Chinese scholar, and . . . and . . . he's facing destitution, I'm afraid. He wants to sell this album I speak of. I'm sure he wouldn't part with it if it wasn't really necessary. So, if thee would be willing . . . ?"

"When thee can think up a price, I shall be charmed," Stephen assured her. "But thee must keep the whole transaction in thy hands. I have heard no recent market quotations on albums of Chinese paintings and thee must look after that. Now, let us speak of something else. I'd like to bring Daisy up here. She used to talk to me about her favorite temples in the Western Hills. What kind of a temple was this, anyhow? The Chinese don't have temples to anyone like Venus, do they?"

"No they don't," said Jane dimpling. "They'd be scandalized at such an idea. This is the Hua Shen Miao, the Temple to the Flowers."

"Appropriate to a garden, certainly," said Stephen. "What sort of a flower was worshiped here?"

"There was a goddess," said Jane, "and her attendants. Master Yuan will know all about it. I think, Stephen, if thee can spare sixty dollars of American money that will buy food for months, and probably it will be much more than Master Yuan expects for his album."

"We seem to be back to worldly matters," said Stephen. "Can thee go down the steps by thyself, Jane? Yes, and of course, thee shall have sixty dollars as soon as I can get the equivalent in Chinese National Currency."

Chapter Ten

"Dr. Manners has arrived."

Wilfreda brought the news to Jane at twilight when the garden was full of indefinite shadows, and the pools glimmered uncertainly beside the paths and under the trees.

"Oh, he has?"

"The jeep drove up to the gate just now. I left Dr. Hartshorn talking with him. I saw no more of him than that he was tall."

"Barry is tall," Jane agreed. She made no move, and Wilfreda was puzzled. Her friend had been all anticipation over this arrival, but now she appeared indifferent.

"Aren't you going to meet him?"

"My dear, I shouldn't dream of it."

"Perhaps you gave Shang Shih orders to bring him to you here? If not, I can go back and show him the way."

Jane caught at Wilfreda's skirt as the latter turned to go.

"Don't stir a step, Freda. I must warn you that the thing Barry dreads above all else is any invasion of his privacy. He will establish himself in our Court for Inviting the Pleasures, and from this moment, until he leaves the garden, you and I must shun the place. Neither should we be impatient. We probably won't see him until tomorrow, or even the day after."

"But he is your guest. Hasn't he come here to see you?"

Wilfreda's face was such a study that Jane could not help laughing.

"Well, yes; but he has also come to rest and enjoy the garden and to make connections with Master Yuan whose acquaintance he covets. I should say that seeing me is the last, rather than the first, object of his visit."

"Why Jane, I supposed he was a great friend of yours."

"So he is. And the reason we are such friends is that I have always understood his need to arrange his life exactly as he sees fit. I leave him completely free to do as he chooses."

"And you don't expect to see him very soon or very much?"

"At his pleasure," said Jane sweetly.

Shang Shih's shuffle upon the pebble path was audible at this point, and he appeared in order to deliver a note to Jane, who read it by the light of her glimmering candle lantern.

"Listen to this, Freda. Barry says:

My dear Jane,

I have arrived in your enchanting garden and find the quarters you have had prepared for me all that I could ask. You will be glad to know that I made the journey without incident, but travel by air always exhausts me, and I am conscious of considerable fatigue. I learn from your Dr. Hartshorn that you are not too vigorous yourself, and so I suggest that we postpone our first meeting until we can both command more resilience than at the moment. If you have an atomizer and some Dobell's Solution, will you send them by your gateman? I find that my servant has omitted to include my malted milk in the supplies and I should be glad of that and also some sherry wine, if convenient. If you ever need a nightcap, Jane, sherry in malted milk is excellent.

B.M.

Wilfreda's indignation left her speechless, and Jane prompted action.

"I think you do have an atomizer, Freda?"

The nurse went into her room and returned with the article in request.

"That's good," said Jane. "He probably won't have any use for it, but he will just feel better if it's on hand."

"But we have no Dobell's Solution, of course. And to demand such luxuries as malted milk and sherry of you, Jane is . . . is . . . incredible."

Wilfreda was so upset that Jane came out of her amusement and tried to soothe her.

"Barry doesn't know we are poor. He doesn't even realize we have no PX upon which to draw. We'll send the atomizer and a note, and you'll see when you meet him that our lack of sherry and malted milk doesn't matter in the least. He's an impractical and lovable soul."

While Wilfreda fumed, Jane penned a message, which restored her nurse's good humor when she was asked to read it:

Dear Barry,

We haven't much of anything on hand, but if you listen to our cicadas they will make you just as sleepy as sherry in malted milk. Rest well.

J.

The Englishwoman's curiosity and disapproval were sensations which she entertained in about equal proportion until she met their object in person. It was late on the next afternoon that Dr. Manners signified his intention to call on his hostess, and when the message came, the nurse was somewhat unprepared for the feminine flutter which she perceived in her patient. Jane wanted a fresh blue linen robe; she also wanted a hand glass when she arranged her hair, although, since it was short and waved softly, she usually ran a comb through it without inspecting the results. Now she was studying her reflection, and shook her head as she surveyed herself.

"He'll find me changed."

Wilfreda saw the flush of excitement and the brightness of eyes which were extremely becoming to the invalid, but which indicated a stimulation which might be followed by exhaustion, and she began to urge that the first interview be made short. To this counsel of prudence Jane turned a deaf ear, and was impulsively willful. She was going to enjoy herself for once, she declared. Refugee living was not the whole of living in China. Barry Manners and she had a range of experience and interests which was far from the weariness and poverty and destruction and anguish of war. With him to talk to she would tolerate no intrusion of nursing routine.

"In short, Freda, dear, I'm not in a mood of sweet reasonableness."

"You are in a mood which I have not seen before."

Jane put down her glass and looked up at the anxious eyes above her.

"I see what you are wondering, what you don't quite dare suggest, my very dear. Don't you think that romance and Brother Ass can hardly be associated under present circumstances? Isn't the notion even ludicrous? Now expand your understanding a little, and grasp the fact that there is an enormous range of relationships between human beings, and between men and women, which does not appear in current fiction, nor, I might add, very often in our one-track missionary world. Well then! When Barry was in Peking, Miriam Fairchild and I were young. He had a fancy for Miriam, but he never touched that woman wrapped up in grief and remorse. I do not know why, but I have always been sure that there was remorse in Miriam's sorrow. Barry never touched her because he never was as devoted to anything human as he was and is and always will be to the pursuit of whatever it is that scholars pursue. In my limited and lesser way, I shared some of his interests, and I also shared his interest in Miriam. If I had my own loneliness, my own heart hungers, I was aware that they were of a sort which Barry's esthetics and antiquities could not satisfy. And so it was friendship with us from the start . . . and you do not blame me, do you, for wanting it to be friendship at this time of finishing?"

Wilfreda bent over and kissed her.

"I do not blame you," she said.

"Ah . . . here he is," breathed Jane.

The man who came into the *lang-tse* was, as Wilfreda had seen the night before, very tall. He was dark and, in spite of his scholar stoop, bore himself with distinction. He had an elaborate manner, more like Europe than America, the nurse thought, and approached his old friend as if she were a great lady to whom the most exacting courtesy was due. Wilfreda almost expected to see him kiss the hand which Jane was putting out so eagerly, but he did not. He took it in his own, which she noted were finely formed and well cared for, and regarded Jane with a frank pleasure which was an interesting contrast to his formality.

"And so, my dear, we meet after so long."

"Too long, Barry. This is Wilfreda Grayson, who is staying with me."

The nurse found herself included in the atmosphere of elaborate consideration.

"You and I, Miss Grayson, are fortunate to be staying with Jane."

"Do sit down, Barry. Wilfreda will forgive us if we talk our own talk."

"I must have a good long look at you to begin with," said Manners, accepting the invitation to sit down. "I see the years have not dealt hardly with you. There is increased fineness; the exquisite, in short, appears as a signal quality."

"Always the courtly Barry. And shall I respond that the gray in your temples becomes you? But it wouldn't matter to me if you looked like a Hottentot, my dear professor of gardens. I have been as eager for your arrival as the poet you once introduced to me . . . do you remember? He sang:

> I have swept the dry leaves from my doorstep
> For the coming of my friend."

"The professor forgets what the student remembers," said Manners. "But you were always a very apt pupil, Jane. And there is an especial quality in our friendship for that reason."

"I have felt it. But Barry, tell me, are you comfortably established in the River Garden? Which room have you chosen for your own? Quiet Mind? Or Tranquil Heart?"

The scholar balanced his long frame upon the stool which had been provided for him, and Wilfreda became aware that some magic was working upon her since she now had lost all her annoyance, and was feeling apologetic that no more comfortable seat could be offered.

"My dear," he was saying to Jane, "you might know me well enough to be sure I have taken possession of both. While I may, I shall live in the grand style. I shall sleep in Tranquil Heart. In Quiet Mind the servant will have his domain. In the Main Hall for Inviting the Pleasures I shall eat and read and meet my guests. I received Master Yuan there this morning."

"And how did you two get on?"

The visitor noticed the Englishwoman's expression.

"I see that Miss Grayson is astonished that we did not meet through your introduction, Jane. You were charmingly present in our thoughts, I am sure, although I had friends in Chungking who commended me to Master Yuan, and he came as a result of some letters from them."

"Wilfreda will understand that scholar folk get on rather better the world over when they are not bothered with women. But do tell me what you talked about?"

Barry Manners did have a charming smile, Wilfreda noted, as he turned to her.

"Isn't she like a spoiled child, Miss Grayson? As if the concerns of two bookish men were candy, and she a greedy little girl! But Jane, I imagine Miss Grayson would be more interested if you and I did a bit of gossiping. You know we are gossips as well as connoisseurs—in fact the two tastes go together."

"And are you full of Chungking gossip, Barry?"

Wilfreda felt that this conversation developed like a minuet; the lady sweeping curtsies, the gentleman bowing, and Jane following whatever lead she was offered.

"I'm full of memories of Peking days. I think of Miriam Fairchild. Did you ever know her, Miss Grayson?"

"I have been hearing . . ." Wilfreda was beginning but Jane was guilty of interruption.

"Of course, Stephen Purcell has been here and has been talking about Daisy, so Freda has heard me reminiscing."

"Ah. Stephen Purcell. I see, Jane, that you and Miss Grayson may have some gossip of your own. Purcell, I have gathered, is quite hopelessly in love with Miriam's Daisy?"

"Have you met him?" Wilfreda wanted to know.

"I have not yet performed that duty."

"Duty?" Wilfreda was now drawn into the conversation.

"I regard it as my duty to become acquainted with any young man who falls in love with the daughter of Miriam Fairchild."

"It must keep you busy," Jane remarked somewhat scathingly.

"It does. When I first found Daisy in Chungking, and she renewed my title of Uncle Barry, given me years ago, as you may recall, Jane, I told her I should be keeping an eye on her, and when I disapproved of any young man in her . . . ah . . . orbit, she and he . . . would hear from me."

"Dear me, Barry," said Jane, "you must be simply bulging with gossip. I now understand your need of a holiday in the River Garden of Pure Repose."

"Only," Wilfreda pointed out, "it isn't really a holiday. Stephen Purcell is still here, you know."

"I believe," Manners bowed deferentially in Wilfreda's direction, "that in his case, duty will be a pleasure?"

"It certainly will," the nurse announced, and then wished she had not spoken so emphatically.

"But tell us about Daisy." Jane leaned forward. "I hear of her but it is hard to feel that I have a fair picture. What is she like now?"

Manners reflected.

"I believe," he began, "that the word for her is 'fascinating.' Yes. The child we knew in Peking has become a woman with a most intriguing quality. I do not care for social functions, as you know, Jane, but I cannot avoid a certain number of them; and wherever I go, I meet Miriam's daughter, gowned with an artistry which makes whatever she wears a perfect frame for Daisy herself."

"That must take money," Wilfreda observed.

"It must, indeed. Daisy has confided to me that the money is supplied by the government. When I have admired her clothes, she has called them by an extraordinary new term. She says they are 'operational equipment,' and she brought eighteen evening dresses in her air luggage when she flew to Chungking."

This information was given with such profound gravity that the two women exchanged amused glances, and Jane protested.

"Barry, I was talking about Daisy, and you turn into a sort of man milliner and talk about her clothes. I positively draw the line on gossip about evening gowns!"

"Clothes," said the scholar, with continuing seriousness, "are a part of civilization and therefore an important manifestation of mores. They are also a part of personality. My interest in costume does not merit your rebuke, my dear pupil. But to resume about Daisy herself —I am always wondering what her quality is—why one cannot seem to get rid of her, so to speak."

"Is it . . . beauty?" breathed Wilfreda.

Manners threw her a swift glance and said to himself that beauty would always be a painful mystery to her.

"Beauty? No, I shouldn't say she had beauty, at least not what is beauty to me—not any traditional type. Beauty is curiously a question of current taste, of environment . . . it's extraordinary how the great beauties of one time and place in human history—"

"Yes, isn't it?" said Jane, averting a flood of scholarly reflections. "You know, I'm sure the Yang Kwei Fei who held her emperor enslaved for years would never be able to get a job in Hollywood today. She was far too plump. Daisy was an adorable little girl and a piquant adolescent. And now?"

"Now she is twenty-eight and has endured strain and hardship. She has the taut streamlined body of modern life; her admirers speak of her grin and her snub nose and her freckles, because it appears to be a species of compliment to refer to such things, and I suppose she has them. But the fact is that when she is present one pays no attention to anything else in the room. She has a vitality—a flashing sort of quality—which is enthralling."

"Enthralling to whom?" Jane wanted to know. "To an old friend like you and to a young unfortunate like Stephen?"

"To a good many kinds of people. I see her in the company of the most important, sometimes American, sometimes British, but often Chinese. Her Mandarin is excellent."

"And what does she do in addition to dressing well and going to parties with celebrities?"

"She, quite understandably, hasn't a great deal of time for uncles," Manners admitted. "And there's a good deal I'd like to know that hasn't been confided to me. Her chief is your cousin, Robert Trent, Jane. He, by the way, cultivates my acquaintance."

"Yes," said Jane. "I told him to go and see you."

"He has an intelligent interest in China—in the China of the past. I find conversation with him a refreshing change from the daily rumors. But about Daisy, I have gathered from Trent that her job is to pick up bits of information and fit them together with other bits. Sometimes important secrets emerge if the right items are fitted together. I notice how welcome she is among Chinese of importance. I observe that if there is a new arrival or a quiet departure—such matters are of significance—Daisy is likely to know about it sooner than anyone else."

"I wonder," Jane broke in abruptly, "what Daisy makes of life? What values do you suppose survive the violence in which her generation is immersed?"

"I wonder, too," Manners pondered. "Of course she has moved far, very far, from the missionary world in which she was brought up. You and I saw the beginnings of her revolt, and you are too wise to suppose that she could again be confined within narrow limits. But this I can say: utterly as she has broken with her early environment, the integrity of Miriam Fairchild is in her. Dear, dear I am ruminating like an old man whose taste for living has turned into a taste for gossip. Miss Grayson, I wonder if you have such a thing as a cough drop? My throat is suddenly congested."

Wilfreda slipped away, glad of an excuse to search for a cough drop, and Jane reverted to other matters.

"Did Master Yuan give you any information about the garden?"

"But my dear, we talked of nothing else."

"What does he take to be the oldest part of it?"

"Oh, the grotto was probably here before the walls were built. It may have been an ancient place of worship. By the time the Wangs came, the walls and water system and the general design must have been in existence. There is a court in the northwest section, which we are to visit tomorrow, which was the original dwelling space."

"I know its name," said Jane. "But as yet Freda hasn't let me go there. It is called 'All Past Wishes Come True.'"

"Ah," said Manners reflectively, "that name has a Taoist flavor. Dear me, my throat is extraordinarily dry."

"Would a Glic-Lic Tablet be of any service to you, sir?"

Stephen had found the two so absorbed that his arrival had been unnoticed. He stood before them holding out to Manners the product he had mentioned.

"Stephen! Thee should meet Dr. Manners. How does thee happen to be here so conveniently?"

"Met Wilfreda. She told me what was wanted. This looks nasty but is something I am never without. It's made of glycerine and licorice. Good for all sorts of things."

Manners gazed rather doubtfully at the remedy, but after Jane's introductions he sighed deeply and accepted the tablet which was so large and sticky that it made remarks from him temporarily impossible. Jane carried on.

"Dr. Manners is a very old friend. Daisy calls him 'Uncle Barry.' "

"I remember. There was an incident at the Peking Hotel in which you were concerned, wasn't there, sir?"

"And now," pursued Jane, "he is staying in the front court for a few days."

"I understand you are interested in the garden." Stephen again addressed himself to an inarticulate Manners who found his teeth fairly stuck together. "And I also understand you have an interest in me, which is reciprocated, I can assure you. So what about coming along for a look at the garden guesthouse which I occupy? No, Jane, thee can't be invited. The orders are for thee to rest. I hope you are finding some relief, sir?"

Jane saw that Stephen's eyes were amused at something. Manners, with his hand at his throat and his jaw still immobile, made a pantomime of his adieu and then an embarrassed retreat with the young man solicitously escorting him, while Jane lay back in her chair divided between irritation, relief, and amusement. Here were Stephen and Wilfreda setting up conspiracies and getting their own way with her. However, she had begun to feel tired, and when she thought of the fastidious Barry with his mouth full of Glic-Lic she was obliged to chuckle. She wondered how he would like Stephen.

The two men reached the grotto before Manners was able to speak, and his first remark was most natural.

"Good God, what sort of stuff have you been feeding me?"

"An old-fashioned country remedy, sir. Would you like another? Or is your throat better?"

Manners hastily said it was better, and Stephen returned the cardboard box of Glic-Lic to his pocket and asked when his new acquaintance had last seen Daisy. This topic of conversation was continued until they had crossed the footbridge beyond the Water Mirror Pavilion. But as they came in sight of the Studio of Clear Sounds, the older man's attention flagged, and Stephen, sensing the change in his mood, walked silently beside him. It was late in the afternoon, and the stillness which precedes the pageant of sunset had spread throughout the garden. The Pool for Reflecting the Clouds lay a blue mirror without a ripple upon its surface. Fish and bird and insect life seemed suspended as in a golden haze, and in all the peace of pool and grove they two were the only moving things. High above the brooding trees a single cloud was hanging in unchanging shape awaiting the tinges of sunset.

"Please come in."

Stephen led the way into the Studio, which was arranged with a main room in the center extending out on piles driven into the bed of the water basin, with two smaller apartments on either side which clung to the bank under the shade of great willow trees.

Manners established himself in a comfortable armchair and looked across at the Library of Four Delights, which, with its bamboo *lientses* down over windows and door, seemed a house which had shut its eyes.

"A perfect separation for maintaining a perfect friendship," he remarked.

"I hadn't thought of friendship as needing separation," said the young man. "But I suppose it may be an advantage."

"I heard this morning the history of this little structure," Manners told him. "It was built by Wang Ch'eng-Hsin, the grandfather of the present owner, to accommodate a friend who came to visit him and who stayed fifteen years."

"I think Jane mentioned that he was an artist?"

"He painted bamboos. He knew Wang Ch'eng-Hsin when the two were young men at Peking waiting to take the imperial examinations. Wang Ch'eng-Hsin was a gentle, confiding sort of person, quite out of his element in official life, so, although he passed brilliantly in the examination and was awarded a post, he soon retired in disillusionment, and Wu Mei-Sun came here to give him consolation and companionship. And you see—Wang spent his time in the Library—Wu was independent in the Studio—they could see each other's lights but they could not hear each other's voices. A perfect arrangement, as I remarked. And, of course, the sentiment connected with a Chinese garden is friendship. It is, in fact, the culminating experience for a scholar. His most intimate poetry is the poetry of friendship—not of love, as with us in the West."

"Then the Chinese man of letters loses out. I should expect his poetry would be tepid stuff," Stephen suggested, trying not to yawn.

"I suppose you wouldn't agree," said Manners with his charming smile, "but the Chinese sometimes hint that we in the West load the notion of love with more importance than human nature can support, and so it is continually breaking down because we expect too much. Passion burns—it is for the young. Friendship warms—it is the mature experience that does not demand but rather exchanges."

Stephen was silent, and Manners turned again to the windows which were open over the water on three sides. The cloud above the pool was turning clear gold in the sunset light, and the miniature scene made by the hand of man was sinking into shadow.

"But after all," the scholar murmured, "there is nothing like the burning."

Chapter Eleven

From Stephen Purcell to Daisy Fairchild

. . . Where in God's name are those letters you told me you were going to write to me? I'm still in Jane's garden and the planes are flying regularly between here and Chungking with plenty of your buddies winging back and forth who would bring me word . . . but you'll be bored if I plague you. You can't be different from what you are . . . and it's you I love. Perhaps I've said that often enough.

I'm sure you want to hear about Jane. She isn't at all well. She's just had a mysterious time when nobody could see her but Wilfreda Grayson and Dr. Hartshorn from Huai Yuen. Also, no questions were answered. She herself told me quite frankly that she hasn't been well for some time, but she prefers not to be asked about it . . . did I mind? I told her I minded very much not knowing what to do for her. Wilfreda Grayson has helped out on that point, however. It seems that one factor in Jane's trouble is malnutrition. I've been waiting for the next consignments for my truck, and have taken considerable satisfaction in negotiating an arrangement to add milk and eggs to Jane's diet. We have made out a little budget like this:

2 goats	CNC 15,000	
12 hens (& rooster)	2,400	
2 milk pails	1,000	
milk cloths, whatever they are	500	
1 goatherd for 1 year	12,000	(he comes cheaper than the goats)
1 milking uniform	1,000	
1 padded quilt	1,300	(for repose of goatherd)

Miscellaneous	10,000
Feed for goats at	
figure unknown	X
TOTAL	CNC 43,200 plus X

With a rate of 750 CNC to one American dollar, you can see that my investment is not very heavy. I do not itemize to outrage modesty but just to give you an idea of what is going on.

I haven't told you much about this place where I want you to come and visit Jane the next time I'm able to be here. (She is writing to you.) Since you were born in China, I suppose you have a general idea of what my present surroundings are like; but I wasn't to such gardens born, and I'm fairly bowled over by the size, the queerness, and most of all by the beauty of the place. The central garden layout, complete with lake and island, has a court to the east where Jane is secluded and one to the west where I am, besides some others where nobody in particular is. My house is built out over the water to get the coolness of evaporation in summer. Its name "Clear Sounds" is written up over the entrance, but evidently the sounds were sometimes convivial, because inside there's an intriguing notice which says "Don't go home till you're drunk"—at least that's the way Miss Grayson translates it. I don't believe Jane has discovered that one, bless her heart!

By the by, your uncle Barry Manners has been looking me over. He indicates I have made the grade with him. Wish I could be surer I had made it with you.

S.P.

From the Journal of Wilfreda Grayson

Jane has had another attack as a result of trying to entertain two visitors at a time. Dr. Manners, as soon as he understood that she could not be seen, fled (I am sure this is the proper word) back to Chungking. He was delighted to find such a vacation spot as this garden, but the mention of sickness alarmed him, and off he went. Stephen was here longer, waiting for his load to be made up for his next trip; but now he has gone, too, and the garden seems much emptier than when he was here.

Of course, Jane has had to miss a large part of his visit. This has turned out a fortunate thing for me since I have seen a good bit more of him than otherwise would have been the case, and he is a most delightful young man. I seldom meet persons of his ilk, and his society is something to write home about, as the Americans say. Only, I have no one to whom to write—no home, except this job in China.

On the day Dr. Manners left, I remember how Stephen came stooping through the doorway of our *lang-tse*, in time for our evening meal. He saw the square table set with only two little plates, two bowls, and two pairs of chopsticks. And then he saw me, and no Jane.

"What's this?" he wanted to know.

"I'm sorry; Jane sends regrets. She can't join us tonight."

He stood looking his questions, and, as I went on, I thought how out of scale he appeared in the small proportions of our San Yu Chai. "You remember Jane doesn't want people to bother about her; she sends word that she hopes you will enjoy your holiday in the garden; and you will have a daily message from her through me, until you can see her again."

He was more cheerful when I mentioned seeing Jane again, and sat down at the table just as Shang Ma brought in a plate of steaming dumplings (they were cooked with meat which his generosity made possible).

"Orders are orders," he remarked. "And since Jane has good reasons for all she does, I submit. Only, you will tell me if I can be of service in any way?"

I joined him at the table, wondering what I should find to talk to him about. He would not discuss his Daisy with me—it seems to be his only topic with Jane just now—and neither of us, I was sure, wanted to go over the very weary round of local conditions and global war, which most of our West China conversation dwells upon. But I need not have worried. He began at once to ask me about myself. It is seldom that anyone does that. Our guest was not inquisitive at all, but soon he knew most of my simple history: how I was born in Australia, how my parents died when I was still a child, how I was sent back to England and lived in boarding schools until my nurse's training was begun. And then how I heard R Square talk about his diocese in China, and had one interview with him—just one—and lived on it all through the succeeding years until I was accepted for service in the Far East—but not under R Square. It was the war which swept me into the Southwest, and brought me to him again. And I told Stephen how I had met Jane when we were both trying to rest after our year's work and were crowded into a small house with a number of other people trying to do the same thing, and getting very much in each other's way. I told him about our tramps on the hills, and how Jane did me good by making me feel that I was of some use to her—only, dear me, I didn't really say that to him either, but it is the kind of thing that is so constantly in my mind it slips off my pen here. However, he seemed to understand at once what Jane is to me, and he made me feel that since I was of importance to her I was of importance to him. He did this with a gentleness and deference that completely won my heart—and put me at my ease, although I had felt very shy when we sat down.

When he saw that I had come pretty well to the end of myself as a topic of conversation, he did a still more gracious thing, and began to talk about himself. He remarked that we had an experience in common, a bond in addition to Jane, because R Square had been the cause of his coming to China. He had met him in Washington when he (Stephen) had recently returned from living in Europe for several years.

"I'd been drifting about, you see, trying to decide what to do with myself, and in the meantime experimenting to discover what part of the world would, all things considered, be the pleasantest to live in."

This sounded strangely in my ears. I had never before talked with anyone who led that sort of life. All the people I have ever known have been obliged to earn a living; they have been trying to be faithful to a duty of some sort. I said so, and felt I had been very blunt. But Stephen was not put out.

"I know," he said. "That's been true of most of my people ever since we came to America with William Penn, and bought our land from the Indians. Oh, yes, we still have the same land. We have always been farmers and Quakers and we are Quakers still. But two generations ago, we became seed growers, a rather special sort of farming. We have had enough money all along, but the seed growing brought in more than usual farming does. So, when my father died, I had my own income and didn't need any more."

"You didn't want to be a seed grower?"

"It takes something of a scientific bent," Stephen explained. "And I'm not scientific. I have a cousin about my age who is a whiz at it; it is only sensible to have him manage that end. My mother's the best businessman I ever met, and she runs the commercial part. So where did that leave me? I was free to wander around and try to find out what I did like."

"I suppose you're artistic," I said.

Stephen laughed. "The truck driver is much obliged, but you do him too much honor. He's quite happy—the truck driver, I mean—at a symphony concert, but he never has wanted to wear his hair long and scrape a fiddle. If he has well-fitting easy shoes, and there's a good restaurant nearby, he likes to spend time in picture galleries. But he has no yearnings toward ruining good canvas. He likes other things besides music and pictures and books—such as taking a chance on getting himself killed on mountain climbs. But he isn't interested in making money; he isn't good enough at anything to want to make his taste into a profession; he doesn't want to reform the world; he doesn't even want to raise hell. Driving a truck seems exactly what suits him."

And so he talked on. I haven't put in the pictures he gave me—of the rolling country around his home, of his horses and the pets he had grown up with. And he included fascinating glimpses of his travels; he told me about one evening in Paris when he sat at a café and a poor violinist made the rounds of the tables, playing anything the guests asked for, and how he collapsed at Stephen's table and when Stephen talked to him and said he would see that he was looked after, the man replied, "I think you better." And Stephen, instead of being annoyed at the impudence, thought so, too, and did. And he told me how it felt to lie in a meadow full of wild flowers after a mountain climb, looking up at the peak where he had been the day before, shining like a silver needle against the sky. But it did seem clear that nothing very important had happened to him until he met Daisy. Meeting her had resulted in meeting China and poverty and war. And instead of being a carefree preson, he was now deeply and not very hopefully in love. It seemed to me that the man who had driven trucks for four years over the terrible, tragic roads of West China must be a very different person from the prewar Stephen Purcell. I realize now, as I write this, that it was only the prewar person he talked about.

Robert Trent to Jane Breasted

I've been to see your great friend Dr. Manners, and I find him rather high-hat. He's got a servant at his door, and a secretary in an anteroom to his office, and is trying to be seen only by appointment. This is not the way we Americans do things and he makes people mad. No ambassador would dream of remaining so unapproachable.

However, he is very cordial to me, although he is so formal that I keep wondering if my tie is straight and my ears clean—you understand—he makes me feel like a small boy. But when we get to our talk, I am fascinated. He certainly knows his stuff—must be very valuable in his job. I'd rather listen to him than do most of the things there are to do in Chungking.

No, I can't reciprocate and tell you how I put in my time. Security and the censorship are good reasons why not. But there is a better one. Necessary as my work is, and interesting, it sometimes makes me physically sick. There's a good deal I want to forget. Now you write about things which are good to remember, and I live on that goodness in your letters, so get busy on the next. And don't tell me about your gardens or your friends. I prefer to hear about you. Begin with your first birthday and come down the years, the whole forty-seven of them, please?

Jane Breasted to Robert Trent

You certainly are something like a holdup man in your stand-and-deliver directions for this writing game. I have been thinking of you, my dear Robert, as my warwork, the cheering up of the lonely GI, you understand. I don't see that the short and simple annals of JB are especially cheering, but since you say "please," a concession from a man in authority which I find quite touching, I will comply. However, I'll be brief and topical:

Parentage Quakers in very moderate circumstances. Father a city librarian, hence my immersion in books, which we never lacked in our house though they didn't belong to us. Mother all quietness and goodness. Neither parent now living.

Education Grade schools and the city high school. Then a small college you never heard of. Academic standing of deponent always mediocre except for English and history.

Deviation from the Normal   Decided at the age of twelve to go to China. This took some doing, as the Quakers had no work in China, and, as a matter of fact, I have been passed around to serve in various missions and institutions as will hereinafter appear. But among Friends, if one has what we call a "concern" for a course of action, one can get a hearing and sometimes support. This was my experience, and at the age of twenty-two I sailed for China.

Subsequent Career   First I studied language for one year (and have been studying it ever since). I chose to take a teacher, a woman trained to instruct foreigners, and go into the country near Peking to live with a family of farmers to whom a local mission commended me. I did this in order to share the life of the rural majority of people in China. I expected to be homesick and uncomfortable; instead, I enjoyed myself hugely. Next there came a demand for a teacher of Elementary-Subjects-Mixed in a school managed by the Irish Protestants in Harbin, Manchuria. Three years. Following this I was quite overwhelmed to be invited to teach English in Ying Ta in Peking. This was a newly organized university, supported by a combination of missions, and it had a phenomenal growth during the ten years I was there. It was then I knew Daisy Fairchild and her mother, and Dr. Barry Manners, my Professor of Gardens, and other scholars and cosmopolites. Most important, I came to know about one thousand young Chinese who were in my classes.

In addition to my teaching, I kept on reading—philosophy and theology were now added to my first loves of literature and history—and I talked whenever I could with my really learned colleagues both Western and Chinese. The next thing that happened was a demand that I join a training school for religious workers in the country, and the training school was in Nanking. It was an unwelcome demand, I admit. I loved the richness and the privilege of my university work. But then, I had never forgotten my first year in the country, and I knew that on the campus which had been the pleasure ground of an imperial prince (you see, I cannot leave my gardens out entirely!), I was far away from the life which most Chinese have to live. The Quaker concern rose up again, and I went to Nanking. There I taught a part of the time, but I spent weeks with my students in mule carts and Chinese inns. I let the village women handle my clothes and speculate as to whether I was really like them underneath—or did I have a tail?—while I tried to get their attention for other matters. All this came to an end when the Japanese started their East Asia Co-prosperity Program, and the trek of the schools to West China began. Our little institute was among the first to arrive in the hinterland. We found a temple in an isolated village and settled down under the eyes of the placid gods who watched us as we tried to carry on our own work. One day a bombing plane which had been over Chungking flew by and (I suppose) jettisoned its last stick of bombs. Several of us were wounded, and no temple was left. This experience made us one with the plight of China. Our books were burned, our teaching staff reduced to one person, myself, and our support for the future was precarious. We decided to stop the bookwork and offer ourselves to the human need all around us. One by one, my students got employment, and when the last was gone, I walked across a few miles of countryside to a small orphanage for children which was supported from Chungking. I was provided for, of course, since my Mission still got funds to me, and I just went to work washing and feeding and nursing and fending for these children. I forgot to say that one of my Ying Ta girls was head of the orphanage so she was willing to use me. After three years, I am taking a little holiday, as I have explained.

So (I've left out the years at home which I spent in study to make my teaching more respectable) you see I have put in my years in this country in a very nondescript manner. You might call me an academic nursemaid. This isn't very amusing, is it? I think my gardens and my friends—and certainly you yourself—much more interesting. If you can't tell me about your life in Chungking, you have some fifty years of pre-World War II, to account for. I think you might begin on them.

Wang Wei-Chou to Jane Breasted
Dear Teacher Jane,

Miss Grayson has sent me an account of you, some of which is very encouraging, and some of it revealing your need to conserve your strength. Be very careful, I beg of you, so that the next report will be all good.

The occasion for writing you now is to forward the enclosed. It is curious that you mentioned my old friend just as I was leaving you, because although I had known nothing about her for years, I began to get tidings again as soon as I reached Chungking.

I have not seen her, and I do not know the details of her situation. I hope she is telling you these herself. I understand, however, that it is imperative for her to leave, and I suppose she is asking your advice. I dread any anxiety for you, but I know that if I do not send you her letter, you will be very displeased with me. If you write to me enclosing your answer, I can make sure she receives it.

I am not at present in Chungking, but I am not very far away. You are never out of my thoughts.

I am, with deepest respect and affection,

Your student,
Wei-Chou

The enclosure:

I write you in English. It is less likely to be read by rotten eyes. I do not use your language much, so I forget and make mistake, but you will not care of that.

You and I have a long and queer friendship. It is a firm one, I believe. Always our ideas are different, but always our friendship remains. Perhaps you like to know what has happened me?

I always work and work. Sometimes I am very dangerous, but I never mind it. I never want to marry. Marriage is prison to me. I think you know that. But I do not escape love. Certainly life is a mystery. I have been suffered and fighting for the people, but now life plays me a trick.

That man urged me to marry, but I refused again and again. Then I knew a child would come to the world. I wanted abortion, of course. How can I care a baby? But he wanted that child. And I thought at least he should have a descendant if he wants, though I do not see how he can care it either. So we argue, and I carry the child, and do not get rid of it.

Now he is died. He was outside a bomb shelter when a raid came. I am going to give birth, and I am alone, and have no place to go. My Teacher, can you help me? Do not be angry at my foolish letter.

Chapter Twelve

Sylvester Fuchs, medical officer of the air base, was finishing his conference with Lloyd Osborne of Intelligence, and with the commanding officer, Colonel Harley Smith. The case of Captain John Fernald had been presented, and the question of the relations of air-base personnel with the Quaker missionary in the Wang Family Garden was being debated.

"When we first came here," said Osborne, "we checked that place. The only people in it were an old Chinese who is some sort of friend of the owner, and four servants. The owner is a doctor with the national army. He has made one visit recently. The old Chinese is a refugee from Peking, been in the place three years already. He never comes out, nobody goes to see him, he gets no mail. The servants are the caretaker and his wife and the two coolies. They go to the nearest village to buy food and once in a while they go to Huai Yuen."

"Any suspicion of a radio on the premises?" Smith wanted to know.

"There's no radio," said Osborne, looking at his notes. "Some weeks ago, this Quaker missionary moved in. An Englishwoman, Miss Wilfreda Grayson, a member of the Anglican Mission, is with her. She came up from Kweichow after the Japs bombed the hospital where she was working."

"Sounds harmless."

"Dr. Hartshorn of the Huai Yuen Medical Center visits the Quaker professionally."

"Of course Dr. Manners of our Embassy has been over and gone back. Anybody else?"

"A driver from the Friends Service Section has turned up. Name is Stephen Purcell."

114

"A damned CO," was the comment, with the added remark, "safe enough, I suppose."

"Then some Chinese."

"That's what we've got to watch. The Tokyo Rose broadcasts are getting our men down. No inkling yet, Osborne, how she gets her information?"

The Intelligence officer bit his lip.

"Not yet, sir."

"It's hard to see how the Japanese broadcasts can link up with anything in that garden," Fuchs put in. "Still, it's better to check everything."

"Everything," said Smith grimly. "We'd hardly got to this isolated base before Tokyo was sending us regular messages. You remember we got congratulated upon opening a new base; Rose had my name and number and promised she'd recite the names and numbers of everybody else in the outfit within ten days. She did, too. . . . Well, what about the Chinese visitors?"

"Several have come out from Huai Yuen just for an hour or two. We haven't reports on all of them. They're mostly former students of the missionary."

"Check up on 'em. Now," the colonel turned to Fuchs, "you say Fernald has been okay since that one break of his?"

"Yes, sir."

"And you've been approving of his visits to that Quaker woman?"

"Yes, sir. She seems to keep him quiet. He's even cheerful."

"A good thing he is. He won't have a hell of a lot to be cheerful about in the near future. But I want to know more about this woman he sees. What's her name?"

"Jane Breasted, sir," said Osborne.

"No Quaker would support the war. Get a line on her, Osborne— what she talks about, whom she writes to, and especially what about the Chinese she sees."

"Yes, sir."

The conference was over, and as the two subordinates walked away, Fuchs made a suggestion.

"Want to take me on your staff, Osborne?"

"What's the big idea?"

"How about letting me report on the Quaker? I'm interested in her for my own reasons. These single women scattered around China, doing missionary jobs in isolated places, must be full of frustrations and neuroses. I can get an idea of this one from the medical angle while checking on your security points."

"Go ahead," said Osborne.

"You seem to have come out of your tail spin very well, Fernald," Fuchs told Jack later in the day. "Miss Breasted must be an interesting person."

The pilot did not reply.

"I wonder," Fuchs went on, "if you would take me along when you get your next pass to go over? I'd like to meet your girl friend."

"This isn't just a request, I know," the pilot answered. "I've been expecting to be assigned a buddy. You are better luck than I thought I'd have. You can come, of course. Only you may be wasting your time. We're not certain to see Miss Breasted."

Fuchs gathered that it would be better not to repeat the reference to the 'girl friend.' He pricked up his ears at the final words.

"Not see her? Why not?"

"She rests a lot."

The medical officer nodded. His surmises might prove correct.

Two afternoons later, Shang Shih opened the gate to admit Benny Li, who was by this time a familiar figure. The Shih Mu, the gateman explained, would be resting for another hour. There were two American flying officers also waiting to see her. Since Li Hsien Sheng spoke their language, he might enjoy talking with them.

Benny stopped, reflecting rapidly. He might be walking straight into trouble if he became known to such guests. On the other hand, Shang Shih might easily wonder why he turned back upon hearing of the presence of the Americans; he might even mention it to someone who would do more than wonder. And American Intelligence could have nothing on him as yet. The boldest course would be the safest—as usual—said Benny to himself as he walked into the gate with his pulse quickening its beat and with the nervous twitching in the pit of his stomach which accompanied his professional activities all too frequently.

He followed Shang Shih along the path to the east, and when he came out on the strand of the lake, he saw an easel set up beside the double-roofed round pavilion. A uniformed figure minus its coat was working away with brushes and canvas, while another lounged on the low steps smoking a cigarette.

Shang Shih turned back to the gate, and Benny advanced with casual deliberation. As he came within speaking distance, the artist stopped his work, and he and the second American surveyed the Eurasian in silence.

"I hope I'm not interrupting," said Benny.

Jack looked relieved.

"Thank God you speak English. I was afraid we'd have to try and dig up our two words of Chinese and then fall back on sign language."

"Not necessary," said Benny, seating himself on the steps but careful not to be too near the other American who had not yet addressed him. "As a matter of fact, I'm partly Scotch, and I was educated in an American school—a good way from the States, of course—I speak Scotch, English, and American. Take your choice."

"I suppose you know Miss Breasted," said Fuchs civilly.

"Oh, yes. I was her student at the American school I mentioned. That was years ago in the north. My name is Li."

Neither American responded to this self-introduction, and Jack went on with his sketch. Presently he began copying the Chinese characters on the nameboard over their heads. Benny made another effort.

"Can you read what you are writing?" he asked Jack.

The artist smiled and shook his head.

"The Ch'in T'ing. You might translate it 'Lute House,'" explained Benny.

Jack stared at the little building.

"Lute House," he repeated. "It certainly beats me."

"What beats you?" Benny asked, pleased that a conversation seemed started at last.

Jack waved his brush.

"Look at it," he said. "Mighty pretty. Round stone plinth, slender pillars, delicate grille, and a fluted double roof so light it's ready to float off into space. And under the top roof, laid out on a table in plain sight, is the *ch'in*—all complete except for one thing."

Fuchs got up from the step as if to verify Jack's items, and then said, "Except what?"

"Don't you see? There aren't any stairs to the second level, and there never were. There isn't any way to play that lute. There it is. You can see it. But nobody ever touches it."

"Damn queer," said Fuchs, and sat down again.

"Teacher Jane can explain," Benny chimed in. "But Chinese gardens are really foolish. They are old stuff, anyhow. We moderns don't build such things as *ch'in t'ing-tses*. We don't like them."

At this point, Shang Shih returned with a basket of small tea bowls which he arranged on the table in the *t'ing-tse* behind Fuchs. The Shih Mu had been spending the heat of the day in the Joy of Bamboos, he explained, and was coming to join them for tea. She apologized for keeping them waiting. Benny was somewhat uncomfortable in his present company and grasped at an opportunity to escape, after translating what Shang Shih had said.

"I will go and meet her," he said. He rose and walked away with what he hoped was an air of proprietorship, indicating his superior familiarity with the garden. A bend of the shore soon screened him from the two Americans, and as he went toward the bridge which Jane must cross on her way, the mouth of the grotto yawned invitingly beneath its pile of jagged rock. The day was oppressive, and Benny turned toward the coolness of the underground chamber.

I've never been in there, he reflected. I can hear Jane as she passes along. . . . Might have a look around.

Over the entrance there was a smooth surface with the words "Tu Yun"—"Cave of Clouds"—but Benny gave only a rapid glance at the name and plunged into the tunnel stretching directly from the opening into the heart of the mound. At a depth of twelve feet he found a transverse passage, cunningly supplied with faint light and a draft of air from blocks of stone tilted to admit them. The coolness of the earth rose pleasantly around his heated body. There were niches, contrived for seats, and in one place Benny found a recess so deep that one could lie down at full length. The back of this recess was not faced with rock. It was simply a thin coating of plaster that kept the earth from crumbling into the cave, and Benny found himself staring at it with open mouth.

We've got to move, he was thinking. My God, we've got to keep moving. And of course they could work out the location after one or two broadcasts . . . but couldn't everything be hidden behind there . . . and a facing of rock put in . . . ? And the aerial . . . the rocks and the trees growing on top of the grotto mound . . . they'd have a hunt. They'd never get it first time trying. . . . I'd better not be seen coming out. I'll get on, to the bridge. But this is an idea.

He started for the entrance, but as he came into the tunnel he heard Jane speaking to Wilfreda on the lakeside path. He waited until she was out of sight, and then circled the lake in the opposite direction. She was pouring tea when he returned to the lute *t'ing-tse*, and she introduced him to the others so that now he had learned the names of the two men from the air base—which was something. When she inquired how he had missed her, he had his excuse ready.

"I took a walk around the lake," he said, "to make an inspection of that little island. I got interested in examining it—or rather, Teacher Jane, I knew you'd be interested in what I could find out. The bushes and the trees have grown over the edges, but it's got a very unusual shape. I finally made out what it's supposed to be."

Jane was all attention. "What?"

"It's a bat. It lies with wings outstretched and the head is just suggested by two rocks laid together here on the south side."

The two Americans and Wilfreda looked blank, but Jane followed Benny's pointing finger and made out the wing shapes and their ribbed points, as he showed them to her in the overgrown earth mass which sent long green shadows into the water in the late afternoon light.

"Of course, of course," she said. "Master Yuan says the name of the lake is the 'Happy Sea.' Now the bat is '*fu*' and happiness is '*fu*,' so here is the bat flying happiness into the garden—a fantastic pun— and a poetic idea! Garden landscapes are full of fantasy, but I've never before come across a bat island."

"Do you mean that the water basin is entirely artificial and the island was blueprinted as a bat to start with?" inquired Fuchs.

"Oh, yes. The whole garden was made by coolies with wicker baskets, just as they are making your air base now. And some Chinese scholar thought out the plan for their work."

"It's out of this world," said Jack, "with islands turning into bats and lutes stuck up where nobody can play them. Now go ahead and explain that, Jane."

Benny drank his tea, satisfied that he had created a diversion which took attention from him. He was concentrating upon the details of his new scheme, and considering how he could manage a way to enter and leave the garden unobserved. In spite of the callousness which had grown up in him through his years under Japanese tutelage, he wished it had not turned out to be Jane's garden which was about to prove so extremely useful. The results for her might be a little awkward. But after all, nothing much could happen to her. She might be required to go back to Huai Yuen—that would be the worst. There was a good chance no one would do anything at all—if no evidence could be discovered. Benny hoped he could compass that. He caught scraps of her talk with Fernald.

". . . did you ever hear of the Seven Garden Arts? Playing the table lute is one of them."

"Then why do they put it where no one can possibly play?"

"The idea of music is rather better than the reality, when the performer is unskilled. . . . I'm afraid I don't make myself clear."

Benny put in his contribution. "Don't you remember, Teacher Jane, the proverb, 'Don't play your harp to the cows'? Don't try to put Chinese ideas into Western heads."

Wilfreda spoke up quickly.

"We have that idea in the West. You get it in Keats:

> Heard melodies are sweet but those unheard
> Are sweeter"

"Anyone who has to listen to his neighbor's radio should be able to sympathize with the idea of leaving the other fellow's program to the imagination," said Fuchs. "But this garden is full of surprises. I wonder why this little sheet of water should be called a 'sea.'"

"I suppose it may be from the idea of the unity of all experience," answered Jane. "The large is implicit in the small, and the small in the large."

"You are a student of Oriental philosophy?"

"Only as I find it in the gardens."

Jane felt a little restive under the eyes of this man who had come with Jack. She led the talk back to the garden as a subject which would not involve her own acquirements. "I said, a moment ago, that the design was made by a scholar-artist in the first place; but the original plan couldn't have included what we see today. The Wang family has been here for generations and each master has added something according to his own interests and tastes—and financial ability."

Shang Ma came up the steps and began to collect the tea bowls. Wilfreda handed her the teapot to put first into her basket and added an observation.

"It's not entirely the masters," she said. "I came across a new thing which I hadn't ever seen before, on my early walk this morning. It is Shang Shih's contribution."

"What did you find?" asked Jack.

The servant looked at him and then at Wilfreda as she made a gesture.

"Do you see that rise of hills? It screens off the southeast corner of the walled area. I've been in the other three corners. One is Shang Ma's," and as she pronounced the name the woman's eyes were upon her. "One has the sleeping quarters for the men, and one the outlet for the water system. But I'd never been in the fourth, so I strolled over. I found the gateman in the act of burning incense before a miniature temple. It is not more than three feet high, but every detail is perfect. It seemed new; and the man told me he had built it when his wife began to have her hysterical seizures. It's a fox-fairy temple."

Wilfreda had been careful to use only English, but Benny struck in with the Chinese equivalent.

"Oh, a *hu hsien miao*. They're nonsense, but very common, of course."

"My God, look at the woman," said Jack suddenly.

Shang Ma had her basket ready to take away, but she had not yet lifted it. She stood beside it, shivering, her eyes strange. As the others turned their attention to her, she cried out, an unnatural animal cry. Fuchs, sitting on a lower step, sprang to his feet, and Wilfreda, who was standing at the other side of the table, started around it, but Jane was before her. She took the woman firmly by both arms, which were beginning to twitch as the hands curled up into a close shape with bent fingers like paws, and spoke to her in a low insistent tone.

"Shang Ma! Shang Ma, look at me."

The woman was shuddering more noticeably. She yielded so that she half lay on Jane's breast, while the latter's hands still confined the movements of her upper arms. Her eyes rolled, then narrowed to slits. She crooked her neck; an expression of stealthy cunning spread over her face as she said in a high whining tone:

"My name is not Shang; my name is Fox."

Benny, perfectly ashen, took precipitate steps backward, and Fuchs, after a glance at him, experienced an unpleasant thrill. In spite of his profession and ignorance of Chinese, he became aware of a perfectly new and completely unscientific sensation. Jack was staring in amazement, but he was evidently not affected as were Benny and Fuchs. Wilfreda passed to Jane's side, but the latter motioned her to be quiet. She spoke again to the half-grinning lips and the squinting eyes.

"Since your name is Fox, go away to your own temple behind the hills, and let Shang Ma come back."

The cunning of the leering face intensified.

"Why should I go to a small temple, when in Hunan I have a great one with many rooms, and rich treasures?"

"All the better," said Jane. "Go far away to Hunan, and don't ever come back."

The woman shook from head to foot. Jane nodded to Wilfreda, and the two stood controlling and supporting the shuddering figure. The eyes closed. There was a deep sigh, and the trembling ceased; a moment later, the grin relaxed, and the hands unflexed and dropped to the sides. The little group outside the Lute House stood in perfect silence until the eyes opened again. They were dazed but their expression was natural.

"Finished," said Jane gently. Then she spoke to Shang Shih, who had evidently heard the cry and had come to stand immobile with the others.

"I think she can walk now. Lead her to her bed. Let her lie down and do not allow her to get up for an hour or two. Slowly, slowly, Shang Ma. You feel tired and must rest."

The gateman received his wife from Jane and Wilfreda, who helped her down the steps. She stood leaning against her husband, looking vacantly at Jane for a moment or two; then he plucked her sleeve, and she turned obediently and followed him slowly and uncertainly until both were out of sight. Jane wavered down on a step and spoke to Wilfreda.

"Well, Wei-Chou warned us, but that's the first time we've seen it."

Benny came forward hastily.

"I'll have to be going now, Teacher Jane. Thanks for the tea."

"You'll be coming again before long?" Jane suggested, but Benny made a precipitate retreat without responding. She followed him with a look of surprise, as Fuchs addressed her insistently.

"You handled that woman in a very remarkable manner, if you'll pardon a doctor for saying so. May I ask what it was you said to her?"

"Oh . . . I . . . I just told her to come out of it," said Jane. "Using Chinese expressions of course."

Wilfreda intervened.

"You will both forgive me for pointing out that this has been very tiring. And perhaps you will excuse Miss Breasted now?"

Fuchs was loath to give up at this juncture, and while Jack was putting away his brushes and packing up his easel, he attempted to go on.

"I wish I understood your technique with hysteria."

Jane was guilty of an impatient look.

"I'm not medically trained as you are, Dr. Fuchs," she said. "I haven't any idea of technique. Of course I have seen hysterical school-girls and hysterical village women, and have dealt with them from time to time."

"Yes, that's what I'm asking. How do you deal with them?"

"But you saw," said Jane. "It's just common sense. And one never does the same thing twice—each person is different. But you must know so much more than I do, that I—I'm afraid you are laughing at me. And—and—good-by now."

She hesitated for a moment, looking at Jack.

"You'll come back to finish your picture? And," recollecting herself, "you too, Dr. Fuchs?"

"Sure thing," Jack spoke for them both, adding in an undertone, "see you again, Box of Tricks."

As he followed the medical officer to the jeep, Fernald was in a broad grin. Jane had certainly put on a show.

"Say," said Fuchs abruptly, "that Eurasian fellow was a bad color. I've heard about the belief that foxes possess human beings, and I bet he thought he saw it happening."

"You weren't too cheerful, yourself," commented Jack, aware that liberties would be permitted.

"I admit it," was the answer. "It was clear enough that the woman herself felt possessed. Was there ever a human face which suggested an animal face so strongly? Weren't you a bit upset yourself? Come now."

"Who, me?" said Jack, starting the motor. "Hell no. Why would I be? Wasn't Jane in charge?"

"Well," said Osborne, when he met his emissary after the latter returned to the base, "what have you got to report?"

As Fuchs attempted to give an account of the afternoon, the other's stare of comtemptuous incredulity brought him up short.

"Oh, I know," he said with an embarrassed laugh, "it sounds as if I was making it up, but I'm not."

"Look here," Osborne pointed out, "I've got a report to write. Can you see me beginning with a statement that there's this dame who drives fox spirits out of a she-slopey? What's that got to do with security? Get down to brass tacks. Who was there, besides the fox spirits?"

"There was a Eurasian, name of Li. Miss Breasted called him Benny. She's known him a good many years—taught him in a school up north. I heard her ask him if his paper wanted him back in Chungking. Seems he's a newspaperman. He said no, they wanted him to stay on in Huai Yuen. Then Miss Grayson—"

"Oh, the nurse . . ."

"That's right. She asked Li what paper he was on, and he said the *New People's Journal*, but that he wasn't their regular staff. He free-lances most of the time."

"I'll have him looked up. What else did you talk about?"

Fuchs reflected, and then began to laugh.

"It's hard to remember the small talk, on account of the end of the afternoon, but if you want to take it down, it was something like this: Chinese garden design—including an island made like a bat—and lutes stuck up under a garden house roof—um—the poet Keats—now how did he come in? Oh yes, he came after a Chinese proverb about harps and cows. . . ."

Osborne put down his pencil.

"Have you gone completely haywire? What did the Quaker woman say about the war?"

"Nothing. Subject didn't come up."

Osborne glared.

"Why the devil didn't you bring it up? Didn't she talk pacifism?"

"Not a word."

"You thought she might be a mental case. What about that?"

"Oh—ah—I doubt if she is."

"Your whole story sounds crazy to me. Might get your own head examined. What did you make of the woman?"

"I find myself wondering what she makes of me."

"Do I put that in my report?"

The withering accents were sobering, and Fuchs shrugged.

"I have one suggestion."

"What's that?"

"You and the old man better go over there yourselves," said Fuchs.

Chapter Thirteen

"Daisy will be arriving very soon," said Jane. "Is everything here ready?"

The Porch of the Fan stood to the west of the Happy Sea, somewhat higher than the other garden buildings. It was set on the slope of the hills which rose sharply behind it, and it was at the center of its own deep indentation of the irregular shore. Before it, steps of natural rock led down to the water, and from its windows no other dwellings were visible. Even the Water Mirror Pavilion, its nearest neighbor, was screened by a stand of *wu t'ung* trees. The spread of the lake water, the outline of the Island of the Bat, and in the distance the perfect arch of the moon bridge made up its prospect and created for it an atmosphere at once open and secluded.

"I wonder," Jane went on thoughtfully, "if Daisy won't think this is too lonely a place to sleep? We could have her in our court, you know. We could put her in the East House."

"No," Wilfreda disagreed. "We couldn't. I don't like this sudden descent upon you without a by-your-leave. I'm not going to have your peace and quiet destroyed. If she doesn't like this place, she must be hard to please."

"It's the most remarkable bit of fantasy in all the garden. Master Yuan says it was copied from the pleasure grounds of a Ming princess, with changes to meet sumptuary legislation," answered Jane.

The two women were standing by the path at lake level, looking up at a triangular platform which supported a building, with a spread of many-cornered roof over rooms set in the shape of a lady's folding fan opened out to its fullest extent. Lying close to the steps which led up to it, and all about the space before its door, were the vague forms of

126

grayish-yellow porous rocks which half concealed, half accented the conscious elegance of the toy dwelling. The rocks in front had sinuous, curling surfaces, but behind, they rose in sharp peaks and jagged tooth-like forms.

"Daisy's very good-humored, and not hard to please," said Jane, going up the steps as she spoke. "But I'm not sure her pleasure will be increased by the subtleties of garden building. Do you see how the architect has played with his medium? Here, on the terrace, are the sticks of the fan done in pale stone embedded in the darker local brick. It's plane geometry up to the rise of the rooms, which are solid geometry—three rhomboids for the body of the fan."

The doors of the central section were open, and Wilfreda stepped in with housewifely preoccupations.

"I see our visitor is to be entertained in state," she remarked. "Here is a formal placing of table and chairs in the middle room; the cot and the stool are in the one to the north, and the washing arrangements in the one to the south. It's all swept and clean, and the young woman should be able to camp out quite comfortably."

"Still, it doesn't seem very cordial to put her so far away."

"She will come to us to eat," Wilfreda reminded her patient. "She has no idea how ill you have been?"

"Oh, no," was the hasty reply. "And, Freda, I very much hope she needn't know. There's nothing about me now to . . . make her inquisitive, is there?"

She faced about inviting scrutiny. Wilfreda looked her over carefully.

"You are so much better since that last attack," she admitted, "that I can hardly believe my eyes. Still, you aren't exactly hearty, you know. How long is it since Daisy has seen you?"

"Five years," was the reply. "The year her mother died, she went back to the States. And met Stephen Purcell," she added.

"She should have written asking if her visit would be convenient," said Freda with some severity.

"Oh, Daisy is a young modern," said Jane. "She doesn't write, she wires; she doesn't travel on wheels, she flies."

"And she doesn't ask. She demands."

Jane did not comment, but went down the steps and turned in the direction of the Water Mirror. Wilfreda followed her, pursuing a rebellious train of thought. . . . Daisy would put an end to all their tranquillity . . . would probably upset Jack Fernald, just as Jane had got him steadied and quiet, and would force Jane to overexert herself.

"Well," said Jane over her shoulder, "if she does upset Jack, we'll just have to try to quiet him again; and you needn't worry about me."

Wilfreda gasped and came to the other's side. "Jane! I didn't say anything. I didn't."

"No, but I could feel what you were thinking. It was natural for you to consider consequences for Jack and me, after seeing what she has done to Stephen Purcell. It will be all right. The only thing is, I would very much rather Daisy should not be concerned about Brother Ass. Let us keep our own counsel, Freda."

"And our routine."

"Oh, you will find me very obedient."

"At present, I find you positively uncanny."

"Never mind. I'm uncanny only by fits and starts. It's not often I can tell what goes through people's minds. Usually I'm consumed with curiosity. For instance, what money dealings have you had with Stephen, you unprincipled woman? How much has he spent on goats and chickens and wages and getting our possessions out of the hock shop?"

"I'll keep you in the dark as long as I can. Tell me some more about Daisy."

They had reached the Water Mirror and Wilfreda sat on the steps and drew Jane down beside her.

"Haven't I chattered enough? I think you know the main points."

"I gather Daisy has rebelled completely against the missionary world in which she was brought up."

"You remember Barry Manners said that she could not be expected to do anything else."

"But she's still fond of you?"

"Aunt Jane!"

Wilfreda saw a fluffy-haired girl in uniform running along the path by the rock screen, calling out as she came. In another moment, Jane appeared completely mixed up with the shining brown of the flying hair and the dingy brown of the khaki clothes of the newly arrived guest.

"Aunt Jane, you're exactly the same as ever, aren't you?"

"Exactly," said Jane, emerging from the embrace. "I've come to that age, Daisy, when a woman is a species of pickle, and goes on for some time just as if she were in a bottle on a shelf."

"You and your pickle bottle!" said Daisy, holding Jane at arm's length. "You're too thin. What do you mean by it?"

"Everybody in West China gets thin," said Jane. "Just look at Wilfreda Grayson, here, who is staying with me."

"I'm looking," said Daisy, shaking hands. "I hope you don't mind, Miss Grayson, if I say that I think neither you nor Aunt Jane should be encouraged in thinness. Here's the coolie with my bag."

"Not a young officer from the air base? Dear me, Daisy, you aren't losing your grip, or anything, are you?" inquired Jane.

"There were only two who brought me over in a jeep. I sent them off, of course. Where do I go?"

Jane rose from the step.

"Suppose you show her, Freda. I'll be waiting for you at the Chai, Daisy. It is nearly time for lunch." And somewhat to her nurse's astonishment Jane turned smilingly away and took the path toward her own quarters. Her young guest stood looking after her. Then she glanced at Wilfreda.

"She's been sick, hasn't she?"

"Yes. She still needs a good deal of rest. Did she write you?"

"No. But Stephen Purcell did."

"We go this way," said Wilfreda.

Daisy fell into step beside her and Lao Pa brought up the rear.

"It's a fine old garden, isn't it?" Daisy offered politely.

. . . Not going to ask me about Jane . . . considers me an outsider . . . all the better, Wilfreda thought, and then said aloud:

"I suppose you have seen finer, in the north?"

"The great Ch'ien Lung gardens are all around Peking. I've seen them, but I've never lived in one. Is this where I'm to be? What a dream!"

Wilfreda paused outside the door, and Daisy, remarking that she would have a wash and be only a moment, left her without ceremony. The barefooted coolie went down the path and Wilfreda settled on the steps with her chin in her hands. She was aware that she was not only disliking the fact of Daisy's arrival but was guilty of considerable antagonism to the young woman herself.

"What about tooth water?" said Daisy's voice from the south room. "Do I dip from the lake?"

"Mercy, no!" Freda was professional at once. "You'd get typhoid. Didn't Shang Ma put some boiled water on your table? But perhaps she had nothing to pour it into. I'm sorry I didn't notice."

"Ah!" said Daisy. "I expect you and Aunt Jane haven't finished your quart of Gordon's Gin. That's what it probably is."

She came out the door and met the other's blank stare with a chuckle.

"You haven't been living in Peking and environs, Miss Grayson, or you would know that all the good missionaries equip their guest bedrooms with quart bottles which have 'Gordon's Gin' blown in the glass. If the unregenerate didn't drink, I don't see how the elect would ever brush their teeth."

"We don't have Gordon's Gin here," said Wilfreda, trying not to be stiff, "but I'll find some kind of bottle. And don't use lake water, please, for anything."

"Can't I have an early-morning plunge? Stephen says he does. He's described his house—the one where he stops when he's here. Where is it?"

"It's not far from your Fan Hsuan," said Wilfreda quickening her pace. "Do you expect him soon?"

"I've come to spend two days' leave with him," said Daisy, "so I suppose he'll be turning up. But he wasn't at the base to meet me. We're going into Huai Yuen for dinner tonight. He asked me to dress, but I'll feel silly riding a truck in an evening gown."

. . . One of her eighteen, thought Freda, but bit her lips tight over the words.

They were standing at the door of the Chai and the Englishwoman hurried on to the kitchen for the food which Shang Ma had ready. The menu was vastly improved. There was a small wooden bucket of rice, a plate of green vegetable cooked with scraps of pork and egg, and a covered bowl of cucumber soup. When she returned to the room where Jane had set the table, she found Daisy talking eagerly. She stopped for a second as Wilfreda came in, and the latter was aware that she changed the subject when she resumed the flow of conversation which seemed characteristic of her.

"I often think," said she when they were seated, "what a lot of bother we'd save in the West if we only served food as the Chinese do. And why not? You can be delicate about your eating, and sanitary, when you use two pairs of chopsticks instead of quantities of silver things which need cleaning and are such a temptation to burglars. And then think of the dishwashing you'd save, when each person needs only one bowl and one tiny plate. And no table linen, either; and hot cloths at the end of each meal are much the most pleasant sort of napkins."

"But how," said Jane, "would you serve a nice juicy beefsteak with only a pair of chopsticks and a tiny plate?"

"Beefsteak," returned Daisy, "would not be served. It's barbarous to bring a great piece of flesh and blood on the table. Beef would be served, of course, but it would be cut into small bits in the kitchen."

"Then I'm afraid you'd be too elegant for the American man," Jane pointed out. "I remember reading the lament of an Englishman who came to China with Lord Macartney's Embassy. He says in his diary that Chinese food consists only of hashes and stews, and he didn't like it."

"He was an undisciplined Britisher of the eighteenth century," said Daisy. "The housebroken American of the twentieth knows better than to complain about his food. He will eat out of a can and say, 'Darling, how wonderful, did you make this all yourself?' "

Wilfreda was miserably conscious of being in the way. As soon as she could, she gathered up the empty plates and bowls, thinking only of leaving the other two free to talk of their intimate interests which it was obvious Daisy had no intention of sharing with her. But as she started out with the heavy wooden tray, she turned to remind Jane that it was time for her rest. She could not help hearing Daisy's clear voice floating over the wall as she walked off: "For goodness' sake, Aunt Jane, am I never going to have you to myself?"

As she came back from the kitchen, planning to snatch a book and her writing materials from her room and then decamp to some remote spot in the garden distance, she met Stephen hurrying toward the Chai. He gave her a preoccupied nod and disappeared into the court, and she realized that it would be unnecessary for her to leave. She lingered about until she saw the two young people departing through the vase gate to the north. Jane was putting on her loose dark robe when the nurse went into her room.

"So you are going to get your rest after all. I felt awkward about reminding you of it, but I couldn't see that Daisy intended to move if I didn't—even when I did."

She drew the cot out from the wall, and after Jane had stretched herself upon it, with a practiced hand tucked the net under the thin pad which served as the mattress.

"Poor Stephen," said Jane.

"Why poor Stephen? He was beaming a moment ago as he went off with his guest."

"He will have less time with her than he expected. There will be this afternoon in the garden, and tonight he takes her into Huai Yuen to dinner, and then they will drive back here. But before noon to-morrow, he must leave on his next trip to Chungking, so he loses his second afternoon and evening, which he was counting on."

"Then why doesn't Daisy go back to Chungking in his truck?"

"She hasn't time, of course. She will fly in forty-five minutes. The truck will be on the road three days. However," Jane continued, "I'm not entirely sorry things have worked out like this. It will give me some opportunity to talk with my young woman and get a little idea of the years which have passed since we were in Peking together."

Wilfreda turned to leave the room but was called back.

"Stephen's going to Chungking reminds me that he can take my reply to Wilson's last letter—and the note he enclosed. It will be safer to have it go by hand than to put it in the post."

"What are you going to say?"

"That depends on you."

"On me?"

"My dear," said Jane, "since Willow is going 'to add,' as the Chinese say, and since I'm a broken reed, the question is are you prepared to superintend the addition? I know I ought not to ask you—and yet I do."

Wilfreda looked amused.

"And I ought to forbid you to bring a political fugitive into the garden—and yet I don't," she answered. "Of course I'll look after her, if you are determined to have her come."

"I'm so grateful," said Jane. "My plan is to have Stephen get her away and bring her to us. I must speak to him about it before he goes. But it is good of you Freda, good of you."

"We came to the garden to be quiet," Wilfreda observed. "First you furnish a holiday for Dr. Manners. Now here you are entertaining a pair of lovers and miscellaneous company from the air base and proposing to undertake a dangerous character and a baby into the bargain. I don't know why I encourage you in such mad performances."

Jane settled her head comfortably on her pillow, and looked up gratefully.

"The reason is that you are a blessed person and pay attention to things which are of more importance than Brother Ass. You understand so completely what I really need."

"Which is your afternoon rest," and Wilfreda again turned to leave the room. But as she lifted the bamboo screen she heard a final remark.

"I think," said Jane drowsily, "that the one thing I need most now is a baby. It's wonderful of you, Wilfreda, not to object to my having one."

Chapter Fourteen

Shang Shih considered that life in the Wang Family Garden was becoming complicated. Since the Shih Mu had arrived, he had been constantly opening his gate, and his shrewd old head was busy deciding just what the circumstances and business of these several visitors might be. The first to arrive had been the young man from the air base. He had come in over the wall, an intolerably scandalous proceeding; but Shang Shih had gathered that on that occasion he had not been himself and the offense had never been repeated. Now he came with curious things which he used for the making of garish pictures of the garden. Shang Shih had not lived fifty years in a great scholarly family for nothing. While he regarded the fine arts as above his proper sphere, he knew that pictures which are strong in color and sharp in outline and look as if you could walk into them are curiosities rather than true paintings. However, this young man was pleasant enough; he had always a smile for the gatekeeper and a few words of greeting which he evidently supposed were Chinese. Furthermore, his devotion to the Shih Mu was unmistakable. He almost always had a tin can or two to furnish variety for her table, and the tins themselves were invaluable for all sorts of uses in the Shang kitchen. His largess to the gatekeeper himself was all that could be desired.

Stephen Purcell, known to the Chinese as P'u Hsien Sheng, seemed to have a fabulous amount of money, although he worked like a coolie and dirtied himself driving and servicing the great trucks which everyone knew carried precious medicines and other supplies over the West China roads. He arrived at the garden as grimy and evil-smelling as it was possible for a foreigner to be, many degrees smellier than any Chinese laborer. But he was always ready with a generous tip for

134

a good supply of hot water, and he had brought shirts and shorts to the Studio of Clear Sounds which were unnecessarily numerous and of very fine quality, so Shang Ma reported. He, like the young pilot, concerned himself for the Shih Mu. He was the patron of the chickens and goats now domiciled in the service corner of the garden, where Shang Ma took good care to see that they contributed to the income of the Shang family as well as to the nourishment of the Shih Mu. Shang had also learned that Stephen belonged to the same *hui*, or religious organization, as the Shih Mu, a *hui* which, while Christian, would have no truck with war. All Chinese know that the waging of wars is fit for the gross and inferior orders of humanity only. It may at times be necessary to fight, as under the present circumstances when the dwarf-monkey people were on the rampage. But the object of fighting is to maneuver the enemy into a position where he will negotiate, and, if that can be done, the Chinese advantage will always result because the Chinese are the superiors in brains to all men within the four seas. Therefore, Shang Shih had a particular respect for the intelligence of the *hui* to which the Shih Mu and Stephen belonged. It must be the most enlightened of all the foreign *hui* which pursued their many activities in wartime China.

As to Christianity in general, Shang Shih was not enthusiastic. He knew that in the Court of Retirement, the hall now called "All Past Wishes Come True," had originally been an ancestral temple containing the family tablets. No tablet now remained, and for four generations no incense to the ancestors had been burned there. This state of affairs was due to the conversion to the foreign religion of Wang Wen-Hao, the father of the young master's grandfather. He had returned from Canton where the family fortunes had been laid in trade, full of fervor for the outlandish superstition, and had committed several extravagances, the worst of which had been the removal and destruction of the family records. This tale Shang Shih had heard from his own grandfather, who told him that Wang Wen-Hao had wept for three nights before he perpetrated the outrage and had put all the ancestral names into a book of remembrance so that they might not be entirely lost. This he kept in his own possession. But when his time came to die, he burned even the book, realizing that in no other way could he destroy all possibility of the revival of ancestral rites.

This deed had been a great scandal in its day. No other stately landed family was in such a position, and many awkward situations had resulted. However, the son of Wang Wen-Hao, although in his turn professing the strange religion which fortunately had few followers in the vicinity, had cared much more for the civilized pursuits of scholarship and had been of a gentle, unaggressive nature; the difference, therefore, from his neighbors had been minimized, although certain Christian customs had remained characteristic of the family. From the time of the conversion of Wang Wen-Hao to the maturity of the young master's father, Wang Tsung-Tao, no concubines had been taken. Then, because no child had been born to the first wife, there came the abortive attempt to make Wang Tsung-Tao accept the Little Mistress for whom the secluded Joy of Bamboos had been added to the garden retreats. But the scheme had not worked; the Little Mistress had been married off to somebody else, and in due course the first wife produced the young master Wang Wei-Chou. Was he, too, of this Jesus cult? His reverence for the Shih Mu would argue that he was; and Shang Shih had once found a large book in Wei-Chou's belongings upon his return from the north, which the local letter writer had pronounced to be the Christian sacred writings. But the young master had displayed so many un-Chinese traits in his dress, his food, his habits, and above all in his delay about marriage, that the old servant felt great difficulty in understanding much about him. His benevolence to his servants and his tenants was unfailing, but his doctor's occupation did not seem scholarly, and now he was actually a soldier. This, at least, proved that he had not joined the *hui* of the Shih Mu . . . and of P'u Hsien Sheng. After this mental excursion into family history, Shang Shih returned to the problem of Stephen—why he found it necessary to drive trucks was truly mysterious. Perhaps the young man was trying to acquire merit, and in the West, driving trucks was the way you did it. The Shih Mu was set apart from the evil of desire; P'u Hsien Sheng might be attempting to become equally purified when he should have attained to her age and wisdom.

At this point, his pipe went out, and Shang Shih replenished the tobacco in the tiny bowl, shaking his head as he did so. The theory that P'u Hsien Sheng was trying to rid himself of the earth taint of desire

would not agree with his attendance upon this young woman who
had arrived the day before. Foreign women, in Shang Shih's opinion,
were as a rule so fierce that any civilized man would shun their society.
Now the outlanders had gone so far as to drag their women into their
war. This person who had just come had worn a uniform something
like that of the young pilot, and Shang Ma had reported a gun in her
bag. But last night she had appeared at Shang Shih's gate in a thin
cloud of something rosy, with golden shoes, gold at her waist and
throat and in her ears, and a little gold bag twinkling in her hand.
P'u Hsien Sheng had been like a man bewitched, he himself clad in
the garments Shang Shih had seen foreign men wear on formal occasions. And these two had gone off in the unspeakable truck to Huai
Yuen, and had not returned until the moon was low. What doings
were these? To be sure, the Shih Mu had mentioned that they would
return late, indicating that this behavior had her countenance. But it
certainly did not seem that P'u Hsien Sheng was avoiding earthly
concerns.

A knock at the gate interrupted the smoke and the pondering.
Shang Shih opened to Li Pei-Ni and informed him that the Shih Mu
was expecting him in the Water Mirror, and Benny, nodding, strolled
off without waiting for the old man to announce him. The servant
did not much approve of the Eurasian in spite of tips that were not
inconsiderable. He watched him out of sight and remembered that
several callers who were, he suspected, emissaries from the air base
had wanted to know about the Eurasian, while Li himself wanted to
know all about everything which went on in the garden. P'u Hsien
Sheng was courteous to this visitor who came very often, but he never
sought his company; the American officers avoided him. Only the
Shih Mu received him without reservation, but the English nurse
prevented Li from seeing her too often, so that he spent hours wandering alone in the garden and pretending that he enjoyed it, but upon
that point not deceiving Shang Shih in the least. Today, however, the
arrival had been preceded by a note, and the orders were to send him
to the Shih Mu when he came.

Summer had begun in the garden, and the early freshness of the
morning was already gone. The intense heat which brooded over the
plain was lessened by the garden waters and trees, but in the short walk

from the gate to the Water Mirror, Benny found himself perspiring. The sunlight had penetrated the shelter of the Pavilion and lay upon a large portion of the floor, and he saw that Jane had retreated into the shadiest corner and sat cooling herself with a paper fan which raised quite a pleasant breeze.

"I'm here to say good-by, Teacher Jane," he said as he took his place beside her. "It's been good of you to let me come and see you, but now I'm leaving."

"Oh? Is your paper recalling you?"

Benny assumed an attitude of dejection, leaning on his elbows and staring at the floor. The fact was that he had established a private means of entering the garden, and had already installed a radio and its necessary equipment in the grotto, with the purpose of "going underground" and in the future making visits to the premises only at night. It had been ridiculously simple. He had never in all his experience found a place where suspicion was completely absent. It was only with the air-base personnel that he had needed to be on his guard.

"My assignment is finished," he said in answer to Jane.

"And so you go back to Chungking?"

"On the postal truck tomorrow."

He would, in fact, begin that journey in order to make an unnoticed return.

"And what will your paper want you for next?"

"Nothing. I told you I wasn't their regular staff. I'm out of a job."

Jane looked at his good clothes and his startling jade ring.

"Then I hope you have a little money put away to carry you until you get another."

Benny shrugged—it was a particular mannerism of his.

"I wouldn't want you to worry about me. I've always managed to get along." Then he added after a moment's pause, "If you could give me an introduction to somebody in the American services in Chungking, I'd make a fairly useful secretary."

Jane looked thoughtful. Getting jobs for useful Chinese had been a function of hers ever since she had arrived in China. Benny continued his dejected attitude.

"I don't suppose that wonderful-looking Miss Fairchild would need a handy man, would she?" he suggested.

"Daisy? Where have you run into her?"

"Oh, I saw her as she arrived at the Huai Yuen Club with Purcell last night," said Benny. "I was with another party at the same place, and everybody knew her. She's quite famous in this part of the world."

"Benny," said Jane. "I don't entirely like the way you say that. What, exactly, do you mean?"

"Nothing out of the way," said Benny hastily. "It's only that she's with the American OSS and has done a lot of exciting things. She's known for her wits and her courage—that's what I meant. But you might ask her if there's any vacancy in her office, mightn't you?"

"I doubt if she's the person to ask," said Jane. "I think her superior, Major Trent, does all that sort of thing."

This was really too easy. If Jane could be induced to send him to her cousin, Benny's number two would have to take over the fag and the danger of the nightly broadcasts, and Benny's superiors would be mightily pleased with him. He scarcely dared to breathe.

"I might write a note to Robert Trent," said Jane. "He's a distant cousin of mine."

"I'd certainly appreciate it," said Benny in his best American idiom.

Jane suddenly stood up.

"If I write a note for you," she said, "you should do something for me. Let's get out of this heat, and go into the grotto. It will be cooler there and there's something I want to investigate."

Benny's face and manner betrayed nothing as he walked beside her, but he was furiously wondering if getting the radio installed and hidden had not been as successful as he had supposed, if Jane was suspecting something and wanting to uncover his treachery. He paid close attention to her as they walked together, but to follow her remarks and his own thoughts at the same time was something of a strain.

"You and Daisy and Jack Fernald" (now why was she dragging the pilot in?) "come out of the war world and find Wilfreda and me living away from all the confusion and poverty and terror of it, and you must feel that we are not living at all. I suppose you have been through so much suffering yourself Benny—and have seen so much—that you can't think of anything except war and what war does."

"I don't think about it if I don't have to," said Benny. "And I've got used to a lot, Teacher Jane."

She stopped in the mouth of the grotto.

"What I'm trying to do," she said, "is to apologize for myself."

"For yourself?" Benny stared.

"Yes. In the midst of all the misery and wickedness—that you know so much better than I do"—a muscle in the Eurasian's cheek twitched —"in the midst of it, I remember that it can't last. By its nature, violence is brief. And there are things that do last. I'm interested in them."

Nothing in all this seemed to connect with his agony of suspense. Jane turned, went down the tunnel which opened into the central chamber from which the transverse passages led east and west, and came to a halt before the north wall of the cave where, shoulder high, two wooden leaves were shut together and secured by a wooden bar.

"Would you mind lifting that bar away?" she asked. "It's too heavy for me to manage."

Could she possibly know that he had been opening those doors two nights ago? Still, even when they were open, there would be no trace of his visit unless . . . unless . . .

Benny fumbled at the bar, and took it away. Jane herself opened the wooden leaves which pivoted in stone sockets.

"Here is something that has lasted," she said.

In the broad day, the light from the mouth of the cave diffused itself within the chamber where they stood, and showed clearly the life-size figure carved in white stone which sat on its lotus pedestal looking serenely down at them. It appeared swaying from the waist, and the garment flowed in lines of the utmost beauty; the face was so dimly touched by the light that its features were hardly visible, but that was scarcely needed to convey more than was given in the attitude of the leaning head.

"The Goddess Kuan Yin listening to the earth cries," said Jane.

(That was all she wanted . . . all she knew. The secret of the other sounds to which the Kuan Yin was soon to listen was still safe.)

"It is cooler in here," said Benny, clearing his throat.

"You haven't an atom of curiosity, have you?" said Jane. "You don't ask me why this lovely thing is sealed up in a grotto—you haven't a guess of your own?"

"Maybe to keep it safe from bombing," Benny hazarded.

"It was put here before the wickedness of bombs began." Jane shook her head. "Sit down on that seat cut in the stone and smoke if you want to. I must have a good look at this now I've got the doors opened."

"It's not unusual to set up shrines in grottoes," said Benny indifferently. "West China is full of caves with figures in 'em. I've never bothered about them. I'm always too busy to run around like a tourist. But I do remember what the gateman said about this grotto. He told me, one of the days when Miss Grayson wouldn't let me see you, that it was here before the rest of the garden was built. Seems there was a temple not far away that's tumbled down now, and one of the monks from there turned hermit and came to live in this cave. He hollowed it out a good deal, I expect. That hermit must have been here more than three hundred years ago, and still the people around here remember he was a holy man and regard this as a sacred place."

"You see," said Jane, "the memory of that man lasts. People in Asia seem able to remember goodness better than the restless folks in the West. But Kuan Yin wasn't here when the hermit was. She stood originally on a pedestal on the Island of the Bat. Imagine her long whiteness reflected in the green lake water."

"Then why isn't she reflected there now?"

"Such a story," said Jane. "I refuse to tell it to a listener who is as bored as you are—at least I'll spare you the frills and just mention the fact. The Wang who owned the garden between 1800 and 1870 was named Wang Wen-Hao. He was one of the earliest converts to Christianity in Canton, and when he returned here he felt he must take away all the signs of other religions. But he couldn't bear to have Kuan Yin broken up, so he just put her here and had a niche made for her and closed her in as she is now."

Benny looked at his watch, and Jane reluctantly closed the doors.

"I suppose you must go," she said. "Your note mentioned you couldn't stop for lunch."

"I'm sorry. I should be starting back."

Benny put the bar in place, and as he did so Jane turned toward the entrance.

"Come with me to the Chai," she said, "and I'll give you that note to Robert Trent."

Chapter Fifteen

"Well," said Daisy, "Stephen's almost ready to leave. I'm going to walk with him as far as the great road where his truck will pick him up. Then I'm coming back to the garden to pack, and the people at the air base have promised to send a jeep for me, so I'll catch the last plane going to Chungking tonight. I'll be back in the war world by eight o'clock. The idyl is over."

"Has it been a good idyl?"

"Aren't you a bit mixed, Aunt Jane? How can an idyl be anything but idyllic, if you catch what I mean? But I haven't seen nearly enough of you."

"Nor I of you."

They were walking slowly up and down the length of the *lang-tse* which curved along the Pool of the Rock and Pine. The afternoon sky was high and cloudless above them.

"But," continued Daisy, "you now understand the kind of person I am; you can note the differences between myself when sixteen and myself at present. All the details can wait. Don't you think I have been nice to Stephen?"

"He seems happy. Are you going to allow him to remain so?"

"How can I tell?" said Daisy. "I've given him a day and a half which is more than any other man in the whole of the CBI theater can boast. I must point out to you that I have sense enough to grasp the fact that Stephen is a much better matrimonial bet than anyone else I happen to know, even though he is a CO and a truck driver. I respect him for sticking to his own line, which is very far from my line. I do suppose we've got a chance of making a go of things when it comes time to talk about renting a flat and buying chops for me

142

to cook—although I don't think of that far-off event as at all romantic, and Stephen, poor fellow is much too serious about it. But
now we have finished exchanging views on chops and flats; he re-
turns to his job, and I to mine. Nobody can tell what may happen
from one half-second to another. So why ask me if Stephen will continue to be happy? I don't run the universe."

"I think you run a good deal of Stephen's universe," said Jane. "But
there doesn't seem much point in talking about it. When you get
back to Chungking, remember me to Barry Manners and Robert
Trent."

"Of course. And that reminds me," said Daisy, "Uncle Barry wanted
me to say he hopes to come over again within the next ten days if
it's convenient, but will write before he turns up. I've already reported on you to Major Trent."

"Reported on me?"

"Oh yes. I had my orders. So as soon as I had seen you, I sent off
a memo: Attention Major Trent. Subject: Health of JB."

"And what did you tell him?"

"I said you had been working too hard and eating too little, like
everybody in West China, but that nothing much is the matter. Just
what you would like me to say, wasn't it? Stephen has been scaring us
to death. He's been seeing too much of your nurse, Aunt Jane. I fear
she scatters gloom instead of sunshine in this naughty world."

"Daisy, hush!"

The younger woman was startled by the quality in Jane's voice, but
she defended her first remark.

"Oh, I suppose you are fond of her as you are of everybody, but
really she is on the dried-up and long-faced side, and she can't be very
good for you. It's clear she can't bear me. I don't mind a scrap, of
course, but I'd like you to have more cheerful society."

"Daisy, you don't know what you are talking about, and you'd just
better keep quiet."

"Why, Aunt Jane! What a pepper pot you are. It shows you've
got plenty of energy, anyhow. There, don't get mad at me. I won't
breathe another word against your Wilfreda. She's devoted to you,
I suppose, which is something in her favor."

"Yes," said Jane, who had recovered her mildness. "There's quite a lot in her favor that you don't know about. So refrain from further nonsense, Daisy, my dear, and I'll get over being mad at you—which I certainly was for the moment."

"That's normal; people are always getting mad at me and getting over it. I suppose it's inevitable that there's a lot that we can't know about each other. I couldn't help wondering when I found that Eurasian here this noon, what on earth you had been talking to him about all the morning."

"Chiefly about himself. He's out of a job now, so I've given him a letter to Robert Trent," Jane answered.

"Oh!" said Daisy. "Aunt Jane, you are an innocent. What do you actually know about that young man?"

"He needs work. I am not acquainted with many people in Chung-king who can help about jobs."

"I saw him for only a few minutes, but I'd give him a wide berth instead of a job, myself," Daisy commented shrewdly. "Do you really like him, Aunt Jane?"

"My personal feelings about him don't matter."

"But do you?" Daisy persisted.

"There is such a thing as compassion."

"Which is not the same thing as liking or trusting a person," Daisy pointed out. "And nobody wants to be pitied."

"I can imagine circumstances when I shouldn't mind it, myself," said Jane meekly.

Daisy was pursuing her own thoughts.

" 'Compassion'—I don't believe I have heard the word since I came back to China. It isn't in current talk. There are a lot of words like that. I remember being rather shocked when I found 'immodesty' on a page of Henry James. Nobody now says it or writes it—"

"What's that about Henry James?" said Stephen's voice.

He appeared at the door of the Chai as the two women paused near it, and looked at them with appreciation. Daisy and Jane made a combination which summed up for him the desired elements in life.

"I'm impressing Jane with my ability to talk about something besides myself or the war," Daisy told him. "And now, Aunt Jane, I shall go walking with this young man in his truck-driving clothes.

"Good-by, Jane," said Stephen. "I'll do what I can about the passenger you want me to bring back. With luck she'll be here in a week. Coming, Daisy?"

"Good-by, Stephen. Daisy, when you want me, I'll be in the Court of Retirement, across the garden. Shang Shih will show you," Jane called as the two were moving away.

The girl hung back for a moment.

"What are you going to be doing there?"

"I have an errand in the hall called 'All Past Wishes Come True.'"

"Sounds good. I wish you'd change the name hung up over your bedroom. The Nameless Room—it gives me the creeps."

"Daisy!" Stephen's voice was impatient.

"All right, then; I'll be seeing you, Aunt Jane, where All Past Wishes Come True." And then she was gone.

At the hour when the tree shadows were long over the water basins, Jane went musing on her way toward the courtyard in the northwest corner of the garden which Shang Shih had, at her request, unlocked. The heat of the day was abating; there were drafts of coolness from the evaporation of the streams, and the garden cup rimmed by its hills was filled with a golden stillness by the westering sun. The peace of her surroundings sank deeply into her mood. The elements of "creaturely activity," with their stress and strain, were now diminished. Benny was gone. As Jack had not appeared during Daisy's brief stay, there were no complications on that score. Wilfreda had betaken herself to Huai Yuen, so that even the shadow of friction between her and the young guest, to which Daisy had so frankly if blunderingly referred, was eliminated. It was after five, and that day she had not heard the thunder of the B-29s going off on their errands of destruction. All the earth cries, Jane thought, were muted and taken up into the tender serenity of the declining day.

Her way lay between the Island of the Bat and the Temple to the Flowers, and she pondered the legacy of the past. It seemed strange that in the midst of the warm young life around her she was yet so acutely aware of people who had sunk away from this garden living into a distance of time. But as she walked, she felt that the personality of Wang Ch'eng-Hsin, Wei-Chou's grandfather, was almost as clear to her as that of her student himself. She had only to look across the lake to see the exquisite Porch of the Fan, built for the bride he never

saw and later the scene of his happiness with the beloved to whom he
had been faithful. She passed the Chess Pavilion which, with the
Lute House, had been added to the garden during the fifteen years
when the artist Wu Mei-Sun was resident in the Studio of Clear
Sounds which, in its turn, was Wang Ch'eng-Hsin's offering to a
great scholar friendship. Late in his life he had brought the secluded
Joy of Bamboos into existence. There was some mystery about that
retreat, and neither Shang Ma nor Master Yuan had much to say
about it, except that when it was constructed, Wang Ch'eng-Hsin's
wife had been dead some years, and the master had been very much
under the influence of an old relative called Wang Ku Ku who was,
Jane gathered, a good deal of a tartar. Yes, the grandfather was so
definite in her mind that she could almost fancy she saw sometimes
in the garden distance a slender elegant figure with a sensitive gentle
face accompanied by his artist companion Wu Mei-Sun.

But now she was reaching further back and trying to evoke the shade
of the gentle scholar's father, the convert Wang Wen-Hao, who must
have known an experience of struggle in complete contrast to the
serene detachment of his bookish son. She stood at the steps leading
to the Temple to the Flowers, and looked from them to the Island
of the Bat just below her. These were the scenes which his conscience
had despoiled of their traditional beauty and significance. She knew so
little about him. She had only a guarded reference or two from Master
Yuan, and anecdotes passed down by word of mouth among the
servants . . . and yet, as she stood looking at the island and trying
to make out where the pedestal of the Kuan Yin had once stood,
Wang Wen-Hao seemed present to her and in spirit she saluted him.

How overwhelming the experience must have been, she thought,
when the young believer came to his garden, gazed upon the graceful figures and charming faces of the Taoist flower maidens in the
Temple which overlooked his home, and upon the surpassing serenity
and beauty of the Kuan Yin who had been the refuge and hope of
devout Buddhist forebears, and had felt that he must take away the
maidens and hide the Goddess of Mercy from the light of the sun.
Wang Wen-Hao had been a sincere and earnest monotheist, but
surely not a fanatic or he would have razed the Temple walls and
smashed the Kuan Yin. He was faithful to his God and inexorable

with himself, but he had been as gentle with the feelings of others
as his sincerity would allow.

And after the putting away of all objects of Taoist and Buddhist
worship, it had been some time before he had taken the final step
with his ancestral tablets, in the Court of Retirement to which she
was directing her steps. During this interval he had built the Chai
of the Three Friends and had doubtless known many hours of prayer
and meditation there. He had greatly enlarged the Library, and he
had not interfered with the family collections of poetry and Confucian
texts, although Taoist and Buddhist material had been eliminated.
But of course his supreme sacrifice had been the destruction of the
ancestral tablets. And so she came to the place where they had once
been kept.

She passed into a courtyard of greater proportions and more somber
dignity than any other within the garden walls. Its southern boundary
was a *lang-tse*, with its outer wall pierced by lantern windows of many
shapes. This ran along all four sides within the enclosure and linked
the side houses with the main hall rising steeply to the north from its
high stone plinth. The shadows of evergreen and bamboo were thick
on the pavement, and the double doors stood open into interior darkness which had once sheltered the tablets of the family. To the Chinese mind, these represented the continuity of Heaven and Earth,
of past, present, and future. To Wang Wen-Hao, Jane reflected, passing from such a notion of his own blood inheritance to an awareness
of the whole family of God in time and in eternity must have been
something like passing from preoccupation with the straight line
to a comprehension of the nature of the sphere. And there had been
no Christian community to sustain him in his new illumination. The
man had set his face like a flint and had ordained that as for him and
his house, they would serve the Lord. But what had his womenfolk
and his sons and his servants made of it? There was no way to enter
into their experiences. The son and the grandson had, at least, not
reversed the decisions of Wang Wen-Hao. The tablets had never been
restored; the Temple to the Flowers had continued empty; the Kuan
Yin had remained in the grotto. Moreover, certain Christian char-
acteristics had emerged in family life. Since the days of Wang Wen-
Hao, there had been no taking of secondary wives. Wang Wei-Chou

held his Christian ancestor in reverence, she knew. How much of the Inner Light had survived three generations apart from religious fellowship? Had it been the Christian heritage that had sent Wei-Chou for his education to Ying Ta? And how much did the Person and teachings of Jesus mean to that young scientist? Modern life was perhaps no better climate for spiritual awareness than the isolation of a garden in West China.

A brisk step sounded on the path outside the open gate, and she turned to look out from the shadow into the sunlight where Jack was coming toward her. She felt the splendor of his youth with a pride for which she rebuked herself, but which persisted in her as he hailed her gaily.

"Hello, Jane."

"Jack! I thought you were off somewhere."

"Have been. Got back an hour ago. Hear you have a guest who is taking the plane to Chungking tonight. I'm to drive her back to the field. Who is she?"

With Jack's question, Jane's pride and joy turned into an anxiety which was watchful and tense. She drew a deep breath and answered as easily as she could.

"A girl I knew in North China. Her mother was an intimate friend."

The young man dismissed the subject. He came to Jane, took both her hands and scrutinized her searchingly.

"What about you? I've found out you've been keeping mighty busy. Sure you're not doing too much?"

"Sure. I'm on the upswing. And you seem very fit."

"Thanks to you."

He stood looking down at her. Then it happened.

Jane heard a rustle, a little sighing of air in the trees. She glanced up and saw that Daisy had stepped into the court. As she started toward her, she realized that the girl's cool glance had encountered something unusual. Her lashes swept her cheeks; she seemed suddenly shy. This was so totally uncharacteristic that Jane avoided turning her eyes upon the man at her side but went straight forward and made introductions with formality. Then she saw the two of them together. Jack had a look which dwelt upon and drank in the whole of the girl before him. It seemed he was taking possession of her, body and soul, at that one point in time and space. It seemed that she was aware of a power over her, and knew herself defenseless against it.

Neither of the young people made any acknowledgment of being named to each other. To Jane, it was an eternity before Jack broke the silence.

"I'm driving you to the base."

"Oh," said Daisy, "yes . . . my . . . my bag is . . . in my room."

"At the Fan Hsuan," added Jane. "We'll walk there with you."

Outside the Court of Retirement, Daisy pressed close to the older woman, and Jane thought the hand on her arm was trembling until fingers were dug into her flesh. Jack walked beside them until the path by the water grew narrow, when he fell back and allowed them to go in front. At this, Daisy dropped Jane's arm, murmuring, "I won't be long . . . I won't be long . . ." and fled down the lakeside track and up the stone steps of the *hsuan* like a hunted creature. The other two halted to wait for her, and Jane felt a great need to sit down. For an interval, Jack was perfectly unaware of her; but then she saw a smile beginning in his eyes and lips and knew that he was returning from timelessness to the here and now.

"Well!" he said, as if he were recognizing a strange and wonderful thing. "And she belongs to you."

He looked at his watch. "She's certainly taking too long. They won't hold that plane for her." He called into the space above them, "Are you coming?" and Jane noted the absence of any conventional phrase. This—whatever it was—reduced words and actions to lowest terms.

Daisy's voice answered him faintly, and in a moment she did appear. She handed over her bag, and on the way to the gate she hazarded a few very brief and pointless remarks, which Jane picked up and elaborated but to which the young man made no reply. He was in a great hurry and swung along at a pace which left Jane breathless.

"Please . . . Aunt Jane can't go so fast," Daisy remonstrated.

"Beg pardon. But we'll have to step on it to make the field in time."

"Oh," echoed Daisy, "to make the field in time."

Daisy reduced to an echo . . . Jane felt a wild desire to laugh. Then the thought of Stephen intruded, bringing compassion and dismay.

You couldn't tell, Daisy had said, what the next half-second would bring forth. You certainly could not.

When they came out the gate, the jeep was standing on the near side of the stone footbridge. As her bag was thrown into the back of the car, Daisy murmured something indistinct about her gratitude, and then hastily climbed into her place. The motor whirred, the jeep bounced across the bridge, and buzzed away toward the base. When it was gone, Jane backed up against the gate and sat down on the broad stone block in which its leaves pivoted. She felt utterly spent. She closed her eyes and tried to relax, her mind refusing to cope with the situation presented by her intuition. But almost at once she was roused by Shang Shih who stood immediately before her with an expression of perturbation which she had not seen in him before.

"The Shih Mu must get up," he said with insistence. "The Shih Mu must go inside."

She looked at him without stirring.

"Quickly."

In the garden one never had to do anything quickly. What was the matter? The countryside stretched in waves and folds of green under the high blue; there was no sound at all, now that the motor had whirred off into silence. And no one was about. . . . Then she realized that Shang Shih was standing close in front of her in order to block her view. She rose, and in spite of all his efforts, she saw. Lying under a scrub willow, in a spot which had been covered by the jeep, was somebody . . . somebody the color of earth with only an earth-stained loincloth . . . somebody lying on his face.

"The Shih Mu must not look," said the gateman, still trying to get in her way.

"Is he dead?" Somebody was very still.

"I do not know. Better if he is. We must go inside and shut the gate at once."

"But why? Who is he? How did he come to be here?"

Shang Shih looked anxiously down the track leading to the highway. If only the Hu Shih would come and make the Shih Mu listen to reason.

"I do not know. I myself have only just noticed. It is probably a *t'ao ping*—a deserter. I think he was brought here by others who were afraid to have him found on their land. When the American came, he was not here, but I have been inside the gate since then until now and did not see him, how he came. Let us go in and shut the gate."

Jane had forgotten her exhaustion. If the man was regarded as dangerous, he must still be alive. In spite of Shang Shih, she went nearer, and what she saw stopped her like a blow. He had been flogged. He lay on his face with his back cut to ribbons, and the dried blood mingled with the dark loam of the fields.

And now Shang Shih was before her again. This time he dropped to his knees, spread out his arms, and knocked his head on the ground.

"I implore the Shih Mu, do not bring this man inside the garden."

"Shang Shih, get up!" But Jane dragged at the supplicating old body in vain.

"The Shih Mu does not understand. If this man is found inside the gate, if we Chinese have anything to do with him, our punishment will be like his." And the old man beat his head at her feet again.

"Get up!" Jane repeated. "I will not ask you to bring him inside our walls."

Then she went over and made herself look closely. One emaciated arm lay free of the body. She thought she could detect a pulse. The head was turned to one side and she saw the sharpness of the nose. The end must be near.

"I must shut the gate," Shang Shih insisted. "We can have nothing to do with this."

Jane's course became clearer to her. Wilfreda would be returning in the early evening and they two would consult without involving the Chinese servants. In the meantime, there was one little thing which remained.

"Go in and shut the gate," she said.

"But the Shih Mu?"

"If anyone comes," said Jane, "I shall explain that you have nothing to do with this."

The man was lying by the channel of water where a strip of grass was green and fresh. She sat down, dipped her handkerchief into the stream, and moistened the swollen lips. Shang Shih, after a horrified but understanding appraisal of what she meant to do, turned toward his gate.

"When the Hu Shih gets back," said Jane, "I will speak with her and we will decide something."

The gateman withdrew inside the door, and the leaves swung slowly together. The shadow of the wall lengthened and deepened. No one came. After a little while, Jane found it easier to reach both the water and the mouth if she took the head in her lap. She was glad of her long training in sitting cross-legged on country *k'angs* which made the position possible for her. The sun was out of sight behind her, but she knew when it sank from the intense flush which suffused the eastern sky. Low on the horizon before her, a pool of light began to spread, and then came the lift of the yellow moon. She did not notice Daisy's plane when it went on its way. She did not sense the passing of time. She sat still and dipped and bathed, and dipped and bathed, until she heard the sound of Wilfreda returning.

Chapter Sixteen

From the Journal of Wilfreda Grayson

Daisy is gone and Jane is prostrated. She has just avoided a severe attack, but, thank God, I believe it actually has been avoided. If she has several days of complete rest, so that her relaxation becomes profound, she may once more pull up to the place where she can enjoy her garden and the people who come to her. I wish I could expect the next arrival to be less of a strain than the last, but I know I cannot. Jane's days are numbered, and if she chooses to fill them— or even to shorten them—with the exigencies of other people, I shall not attempt to thwart her. I did resent the incursion of Daisy Fairchild, but that was out of "pure cussedness," as Stephen would say, not out of pure concern for Jane.

The fact is that I was, and still am, jealous of Daisy. I dreaded her coming, and when she got here found myself disliking the young woman herself, although I can't deny that she is charming. It is perfectly ridiculous for me to resent the renewal of an old tie which connects with precious memories for Jane—Jane, a soul poised for flight. Of course Daisy has no inkling of this, and if she had she could not take my place. I know that Jane turns to me because I see death as she does—not as a pit of darkness but as an opening into Light. This makes it possible for my dear one to show her inmost self to me, and yet, here I am getting stiff over the child of an old friend and indulging in mental meanness about youth and charm. I notice with satisfaction that the girl isn't beautiful; her eyes are too pale, and her skin not too good. I grudgingly admit her power—the disturbing power of aliveness. Having admitted that, a passion of bitterness wells up in me, although she is almost a stranger and has certainly never done me any harm. But she keeps Stephen in trouble—now is that what is the matter with me?

Well, the day she arrived I realized that I am an unregenerate on the subject of Daisy. Since she was to stay only until the last plane of the second day, I decided to remove myself until she should have flown away. I was terrified lest that Fuchs man should appear and understand how I feel. He is a keen observer, and very inquisitive about Jane and me, and I dread having him gloat over what I might betray. Jack Fernald has been away, so we have been spared complications on his account. Stephen admits to Jane that Daisy lets numbers of men in Chungking think she is in love—or just going to be—and Jack would probably join the procession of the deluded. Stephen doesn't seem to expect Daisy to love him; he says it will be enough if she lets him love her, and marries him after the war. I wonder just how much his money has to do with her willingness to marry after the excitement of OSS has come to an end? Spiteful of me, but I can't help it. Anyhow, I didn't want to watch Stephen and Daisy together, so I went off to Huai Yuen at daybreak and didn't get back until two hours after moonrise. I returned to an amazing and dreadful manifestation of the war world which Jane and I had thought to escape for a little while.

I had no parcels, so I took a ricksha only to the point on the highway where the track turns off to the garden. I paid off my puller, and walked on, enjoying the night. The stream which feeds our pond turns a very ancient mill wheel midway of the path; the trees of the garden some distance ahead made a superb mass against the sky in the flood of light. I went along to the bridge outside our walls in a rather dreamy frame of mind. But as I came near and looked across, I saw someone sitting down on the ground, on the further bank of the stream. It came as a shock when I realized that the vague figure and the pale face were Jane's; and then I was close enough to see that she was sitting by a man, lying on the ground, but she had his head in her lap. I was right beside her before I made out the bare flesh of the body—a raw mass which stank. As I got to her side, Jane looked up at me, and said, "Freda, is he dead?"

I knelt down and tried to find a pulse, but couldn't be sure; other signs of death were lacking, so after I had had a look, I could only say I didn't know. But I told her he wasn't conscious—and it seemed unlikely he would ever recover consciousness. I said there was nothing we could do for him and she must be sensible and go to her bed.

To this she paid no attention; she did not even appear to hear me. After a little, she told me how terrified Shang Shih was of having anything to do with the man, and from experiences of my own I knew well enough that he had reason for his dread. The saddest sight in all West China is that of the farmer-boy conscripts ragged, hungry, and terrified, driven in gangs along the roads to frightful camps where they are held, and from which if they attempt to escape they meet the fate of the poor fellow outside our gate. As we talked, I began to have an uneasy feeling that Jane and I were being watched. There was open ground around us, but there are little rises here and there, and scrub willow grows a short distance down the stream. It was quite possible that the shadows of the bushes or of the walls contained eyes which we could not see.

"You can do nothing more," I urged. "The cruelty and suffering are both over. And you have no strength to spare."

Again she withdrew into herself and seemed not to hear me. I saw she was sustained by the demands of the moment—the demands as she felt them. I knew she would remain until she was satisfied, but what she was waiting for I did not understand. I said no more, and sat down at the feet of the man to keep vigil with her. The moon rolled high, and it seemed the shadow of the wall, creeping toward us, was the only movement in the night. Jane ceased to stir and as she sat cross-legged and motionless, she was like an image without its temple pedestal. We remained for hours, and at last the presence of death was unmistakable. Then Jane bade me get the gate open and go fetch one of her few sheets. When I had brought it, we wrapped the poor dishonored flesh away from sight, while Shang Shih watched us anxiously. After all was done, Jane turned herself and spoke into the night.

"You can come and get him now," she said in Chinese, but she did not wait. She came inside with me and in the morning Shang Shih reported that the body was gone.

Jane was almost gone, too. I had my hands full in the hours that followed, and all the time I was caring for her, I was asking myself why she had indulged this strange behavior. I understood her well enough to be sure that she had been obeying a deep-seated impulse. I knew better than to question her then or later.

When Shang Ma brought in the morning porridge, I learned more of the significance of the night's doings. The amah had heard from her relations in the village that terrible floggings took place yesterday morning in the conscript camp, which is just beyond the nearest foothill to the west. These floggings are routine and the victims often die. The man we saw had suffered and been left for dead, but had recovered consciousness and crawled away to a ditch, where he was found by the son of a farmer who is some kin to our servant. To assist the escape of a conscript is to court a fearful penalty, but goodhearted countryfolk are loath to turn such a man back into cruel hands. A family conclave took place, since the discovery was made on family land, and one of the older women spoke of Jane's dealings with Shang Ma's hallucinations, of which there has been very exaggerated reporting. It was decided to try to enlist her sympathy in this case. The utmost caution was required. No one dared to be known as taking action in the matter. The farmer and his oldest son who had discovered the conscript improvised a litter, which they slung to a carrying pole, and the man was carefully covered before he was removed. They were prepared to tell anyone who questioned them as they trotted off with him that they were conveying a sick relative to the Huai Yuen Hospital, but they met no one in the side paths they followed to the garden gate. Once there, they watched their chance to deposit their burden at the time when the jeep made a screen for them. The farmer took his pole and his ropes away with him, and left the young boy to hide in the scrub willows and see what would happen. (I was right that eyes were upon us during our vigil.) Of course it was the merest chance that Jane ever saw the poor fellow, and what the boy would have done in case she had not, Shang Ma did not say, but I gather an appeal might have been made through her. And it dawned on me as she talked how the village folk regarded an action which to my Western mind was entirely futile. The man was moribund before Jane found him. She did him no good and herself harm. But to our village neighbors, Jane's hours of tending such wretchedness were not a waste of energy but rather a deed of great significance. These people have cherished the legend of the hermit who lived in our grotto. They once saw his holiness, and they have remembered. Now they have seen compassion, and they will not forget.

But this is something Jane does not discuss. Since she has been able to sit in her peacock chair, we have been concerned with other matters. We have had reports about our last visitor since her return to Chungking. Major Trent writes Jane at great length these days, and I have objected to the way she consumes her energy in writing to him. When a fat envelope arrived this morning, I began to scold, so Jane endeavored to soothe me by reading out his remarks on the subject of Miss Daisy. He wanted to know what had happened to create a change in her. He said, if I remember correctly, that she was something like a collar with the starch out of it, and told Jane he could not have her ruining the morale of his staff. As if Daisy's tricks were any fault of Jane's! I began to bristle again.

"Oh, Freda, don't you see he's joking? I know you don't like me to write long letters, but now I'll tell you why, in Robert's case, they are so voluminous."

This was clever of her, for I was curious. I stopped fuming to listen.

"Freda, did you ever write to anyone you had never seen and knew you would never see?"

"Of course not; this cannot apply to you and Major Trent. You've told me several times he has mentioned coming to the garden."

"So he has. But in this he explains that he is not coming. He sees no slightest chance of getting away from Chungking for several months, and that means, we are not meeting. Well," Jane went on in her usual placid manner, "the fact that I hadn't met him made, I found, a curious difference in the way I wrote to him. When I write to someone I know, I am influenced by his ideas and emotions. I adapt myself to what he will understand; I avoid what I think he won't like. In Robert Trent's case, I was in the dark on those points, so I found a certain freedom to give rein to my ideas and my own likes and dislikes. I enjoyed it, and it appears he did, too. Now that I am sure that I am not to be limited by any meeting at all, I may become rash. I shall astonish him, if I want to, but I don't believe I shall bore him."

"I am sure you won't." I looked at the pages in her lap. "But what does he write about at such length?"

"Oh, about himself. There is a great deal to say about yourself once you get started, Freda. He feels free, too."

"Then you must be getting to know each other, and what becomes of your freedom?"

"Having begun with it, we shall probably continue in it. But this letter isn't entirely like that. He speaks of meeting Wei-Chou and Benny Li."

"And what about them?"

Jane read out more of Major Trent's remarks. He admired Wei-Chou and found an unusual attitude in him. He wanted to know what Jane's connection was with the Chinese—why he was so fond of her.

"Well, what shall you tell him about that?" I inquired.

"That I haven't the least idea. I've never done anything for Wei-Chou except teach him. Not many students respond to the little one can do, as Wei-Chou has responded. Benny isn't like Wei-Chou, you notice."

"How did Major Trent happen to meet Benny?"

Jane laughed and read the bit about that. It interested me so I remember it. It went something like this:

"Another young product of yours breezed in here with a note from you, and I got some amusement from the encounter. You certainly have experience in writing letters of recommendation—if that is what you call the document Li Pei-Ni brought me. I never read anything so sweetly noncommittal, and I promptly gave the young man a note to the Friends of the Wounded Soldiers and advised him to ask them for a job. He thanked me profusely, but I had a feeling this was not exactly what he had hoped for. I suppose you wanted to help him out, but you were not vouching for him—am I right?" Jane remarked that he was.

I told her I hadn't liked the Eurasian.

"People usually don't," she said, "which tends to make them untrustworthy—that's part of the pity of them. But, you see, Robert understood my note correctly. He doesn't take me for a fool."

"Who does?" I demanded, and Jane smiled and said Daisy had been impressed by her unworldly innocence.

"Oh," I flared, "don't talk to me about Daisy!"

Jane turned back to her fat letter. "I won't," she told me. "I see I'd much better not."

Chapter Seventeen

It was all over for him, Jack reflected as he stood inside the gate to the grounds surrounding the foreign-style house where Daisy and several other young women who were waging the war from Chungking offices were billeted. He knew exactly what had happened to him in the brief encounter with Daisy Fairchild, and he had managed only forty-eight hours later to get a pass to Chungking where he proposed to discover what their meeting had meant to her. She had given him reason to suppose it had meant something. She had certainly seemed conscious of the storm which had mounted in him. If she had been putting on an act, it was a new one, thought up especially for his benefit . . . and that again might mean something. But whatever it meant, he was going to find out about it. When he had spoken with her on the telephone, she had said she would meet him at this gate. Was she coming . . . or would she stand him up?

There was a step on the path, and the pilot turned. Daisy was approaching with a certain, if somewhat unconvincing, airiness.

"Nice to see you," said she, looking away, not seeing Jack at all.

"It's nice of you to let me come on short notice."

"Nice of you to turn up. Now we've about exhausted what's nice, haven't we?" she smiled.

"Exhausted, nothing," said Jack. "We've a lot of niceness before us. But we haven't too much time. The jeep will have to call for me at one-thirty tonight, so I can be at the airfield for the take-off back to Huai Yuen. I've got the hours till then all planned out for us."

"Hours!" exclaimed Daisy. "I didn't promise hours. I—"

"We're taking rickshas into the city. They're waiting. We're going to an extra-special restaurant for Chinese chow."

"I'm awfully sorry," the girl said hurriedly. "But I can't possibly. . . ."

Jack had been walking her out of her gate, and she saw the two rickshas in the road. He laughed softly at her "can't possibly," picked her up, and put her in the one nearest him.

"Oh, I think you can," said he, standing over her so that she could not get out.

He had the satisfaction of a look into her eyes as she glanced swiftly from Jack to the blank-faced pullers, and back to Jack again.

"Of course," he went on, "you can try to get loose. I don't think you can. But unless you raise an awful racket, you won't get out of going to have Chinese chow with me. I decided that's what we would do, because it's the best bet for getting you all to myself."

He stopped. She did not seem very angry.

"Please, Daisy."

And then she was laughing.

"All right, young Lochinvar. I'm not going to kick and scream for the benefit of the coolies."

"You promise?"

"I . . . yes."

"Until my last minute?"

"Do I get a ride home?"

"In the jeep," said Lochinvar, leaping into his own ricksha and giving the signal to start. The pullers trotted off, keeping evenly abreast.

"We're blocking the road," the girl pointed out. "Did you tell them to?"

"No. But it's intelligent of them."

"Well," said Daisy, "they can't keep it up long. There are motorcars out here and in the city the traffic's a mess."

"In the city," Jack told her, "most of our way is going down steps under our own power. Did you ever eat at this restaurant? Its name is 'Pillowing on the River,' believe it or not."

"I never have. I've heard of it from the Chinese who are gourmets. How did you know about it? And who translated the name for you?"

"Dr. Manners. He has chosen our menu. Wrote it out in Chinese and sent it to the joint ahead of us. Said he would supply the towels and also the tea."

"So you've been to see Uncle Barry?"

"Is that what you call him?"

"He was my mother's dear friend, and Aunt Jane's, in Peking when I was a child."

"I'd certainly like to hear about your mother and Jane in Peking. But not tonight."

"Why not tonight?"

"We've got other things to talk about—or rather, one important one."

"What?"

"Us," said Jack. "There's an awful lot to go into. Don't you think so?"

Daisy fastened her eyes on the head of the puller bobbing in front of her and did not reply.

"Don't you think so?" persisted the pilot.

She made a visible effort.

"What I think is that you'd better snap out of all this. Since I've promised you the evening, we'll have it; but stay off the young Lochinvar stunts and this sort of talk."

"Yes?" said Jack amiably. "Now what sort of talk do you mean?"

"Oh you have a good direct approach. I suppose it usually goes over fast. But you should get one thing firmly in mind—nothing is going to go over tonight. Nothing at all."

She had managed a fairly collected manner, but now she tried to meet his eyes and that attempt was not a success. The young man decided that things were not going badly and leaned back in his ricksha. He changed the subject.

"I went to see your Uncle Barry to deliver a present from Jane."

"How is she?"

"I didn't see her when I went to the garden this morning. Sometimes she isn't seeable, you know."

"I know she has her ups and downs. Uncle Barry was worried about her at first, but when he saw her he realized she was just worn out with refugee living. She should be getting rested now. What was she sending Uncle Barry?"

"A map of the garden. In fact," said Jack, "it was more or less my present, too. Master Yuan had a queer old thing done by a Chinese hand long ago, and I made a copy for Jane. Then she wanted Dr. Manners to have one, so I did another. I'm fascinated by that place— it's a dream world where things change into other things—walls turning into roofs, and rocks turning into faces or animals or mountain heights, and a girl you meet turning into the girl you can't forget."

He leaned out of his ricksha toward hers to see what effect this had, and his puller looked back and spoke sharply. Daisy continued to contemplate the bobbing head before her.

"I . . . didn't know you were interested in such things," she said.

"There's a lot about me that you don't know, and that you are going to find out."

A passing motor forced his ricksha back and no more talk was possible until they got out. They had reached the spot on the spine of rock which is Chungking, from which they could see the junction of the two rivers which embrace it, far below. The evening shadow from the mountains behind them was already over the city where ruinous low buildings clung to the precipitous slant down to the racing waters. The moist suffocation of the day's heat still lingered in the air, but the shadow was a grateful change from the searing of the sun.

Jack stopped the rickshas and paid them.

"We go this way," he told Daisy, and his hand was under her arm as they turned into the twilight of a byway which had broken surfaces under foot. Every now and then there were black gashes in buildings and hillsides where bombs had crashed and fire had gutted everything. The streets and alleys which ran in tangled belts along the spine of rock dipped lower and lower until they ended in flights of jagged steps. When Daisy stumbled as they threaded their way downward, her companion drew her closer, and the two fell silent as the dimness grew, although here and there it was jabbed by unexpected street lights. They walked on and on, and as they went their hands wove themselves together. At last they came to a steep descent of almost two hundred steps, which brought them to water level. On one side, the river snatched at the narrow track on its edge; on the other, the lofty walls of the ancient and famous restaurant Pillowing on the River obstructed all other objects. There was an entrance through the mass of masonry, and as Daisy paused before it she made the first remark since they had begun the descent.

"It's close in under the rock, isn't it? I suppose that is why it has escaped the bombs."

"Daisy!" There was urgency in the tone.

"What?"

"Please don't talk about the war. Not tonight. Let's skip it, shall we?"

"All right. If you think it can be skipped that way."

It was the first point she had scored and she stepped through the entrance feeling better. She found herself in a courtyard full of irregular shapes which, in the vague half-light cluttered the spaces without declaring their use or nature. A few feet away there was an opening into stronger illumination and here she could see greasy tables loaded with soiled dishes, buckets on the floor, and half-clad bodies passing to and fro against the ruddy flare of cooking fires somewhere inside. The breathless Chungking air was burdened with heat and smells, and altogether it seemed a most unattractive approach for a famous place of entertainment. Under a small electric light bulb sat an extraordinarily fat man who appeared to be gloating over the abacus before him. He looked up as the two Americans came in and made a gesture toward a passage at his left. Here a thin man in a worn gown received them with a courtesy which was a contrast to the apathy of the fat one, and ushered them up a flight of rickety stairs and along a passageway filled with booths which were screened with dingy half-curtains that concealed from the waist up the customers sitting within. At the end of this row of booths, he turned right and passed through a heavy door. The smells, the noise of screaming waiters and convivial patrons, and the grime which had covered everything became nonexistent. Before them, latticed shutters were swung open to the night air, and through their frames the guests overlooked the wide black sweep of the river. Across the current, the opposite bank, brilliant with lights, rose distantly and unevenly against the stars.

"Not as bad a joint as it looked to be," Jack commented over Daisy's shoulder.

The girl nodded. The room was large. Its walls were panels with carved borders, within which there were paintings of birds and flowers, mountain views, and garden scenes. At one side there was a heavy table of fine wood, with chairs correspondingly heavy and fine, drawn up to it close together under a light which was pleasantly subdued by a painted lantern. There was another much smaller table with chairs opposite each other, already prepared with dishes of seeds and sweets.

"Looks like we begin here." The host invited his guest to sit down while the waiter brought in cups and a pot of tea. He rinsed the cups, threw the water out the window, poured tea, and disappeared.

"It's plain that Uncle Barry is a valued patron," said Daisy. "You are getting all proper attention without having to say a word. Isn't this marvelous tea?"

"Is it?" Jack sipped dubiously. "I wouldn't know. Tea is not my idea of something to drink on a hot night."

"You'd rather have a cocktail with ice in it. But after you've had your tea you'll feel cooler. This must be from Fukien; it's a great treat."

The waiter was back again with a wooden tray on which small towels lay steaming fragrantly.

Daisy accepted one promptly, and Jack, following her example, comforted his sticky face and hands with the hot folds while the waiter brought in a large porcelain bowl filled with steaming water, which he placed upon the other table. Daisy went over to take charge of the scalding of every utensil to be used during the meal. Tiny plates, black chopsticks, silver spoons with round bowls and long handles, porcelain scoops with turned-up edges and short handles were ranged at each place with a generous supply of sheets of thin yellow paper which, Daisy remarked, had uses too numerous to mention. When the first dish was brought in, Jack chose a porcelain scoop and served his guest with a generosity which she explained was incorrect.

"You mustn't make me look like a glutton," she objected. "The idea of a Chinese meal is a succession of delicious tidbits; you taste, and taste, and reflect upon what you are enjoying. You don't crowd down the whole of the first dish like a coolie who eats to fill his stomach."

Jack obediently revised his ideas of the duty of a host and put three small pink shrimps and seven green peas on Daisy's plate. He served himself a little more liberally but found he had slight inclination to eat, and Daisy was not doing justice to her three shrimps. The two chairs were very near together and Jack leaned forward with a question which had been tormenting him for two days.

"Daisy, I want to know something."

"What?"

It was difficult for him to speak and the words came out slowly.

"What makes you so lovely . . . so lovely that I can't think of anything else?"

"Even when I'm eating shrimp and peas?" she replied, making an attempt at being matter-of-fact, and succeeding too well, he admitted to himself as she drew away from him and made an ostentatious attack upon the food. She now began to talk at a great rate, and it was his turn to be silent and uneasy. She explained the dishes as they were brought in, and told him about the restaurants in the north which Barry Manners had frequented with Miriam Fairchild and Jane Breasted when Daisy, as a child, went "tagging along." The shrimp was followed by duck livers broiled over charcoal, and there was a dish of sweet ground pepper into which Daisy dipped her morsels for perfect seasoning. Jack experimented with his chopsticks and blundered so steadily that Daisy finally took them away from him and fed him the duck livers until they were gone. Then a pewter platter shaped like a fish was borne in with especial pride by the waiter, and on it, laid out in state, was a golden carp in sweet-sour sauce. Daisy exhibited the supreme degree of chopstick virtuosity as she competently tore the fish to pieces, and while Jack scooped up his portion with a spoon she launched into a long anecdote about watching cormorants sent out from fishing craft with rings around their throats to catch their prey and bring it back in their beaks to their masters. She had seen them one misty morning when they were abroad in a country district far away from Chungking.

"Were you alone . . . off in Szechuan, somewhere?" Jack demanded.

"As it happened, there was an OSS man with me. But are you getting protective?"

"We'll be coming to that," the pilot grunted.

The next concoction looked to him like a stew. It was dark and sticky and full of meat and vegetables in small pieces.

"Beef and bamboo shoots," said Daisy. "And wine to cut the richness of the sauce."

The wine was hot. Jack lifted his bowl, which was the size of a walnut. "To the remainder of our evening together," was his toast, and he added one of the few Chinese phrases he had picked up: "*Kan pei.*"

They were served bean curd with red peppers, followed by large mushrooms stuffed with chopped delicacies, which Daisy said she could not identify, so she began a dissertation upon the contrast of textures in the mouth between the smooth bean curd and the plump body of the mushroom. The table was getting well covered, since no dishes of food were removed as others were added, and by the time a whole duck, floating in a bath of clear soup with his head curled dreamily about his side, was placed before them, there were ten courses on the board, and very little had been eaten.

"Don't you like your Uncle Barry's menu?" Jack inquired.

"It's a heavy atmosphere tonight," Daisy answered. "And I've really been waiting for the almond soup, which I call the 'poetry of eating.'" She chattered on anxiously while she spooned a milky confection into little bowls. But the almond soup didn't disappear very fast either, and when hot towels came on again, Jack called for his bill.

Daisy rose. "It's been awfully . . . nice," she said. "But I really think I must be getting back to the billet now. Suppose I wait for you in the passage outside?"

She was edging toward the door, but Jack was across her path. The two stood face to face for a moment, and then the girl turned away and went over to the window. The bill was paid, and the waiter departed announcing the tip in a professional shriek. Jack faced toward the window.

"We're not going to put it off any longer. You are going to listen to me before you go anywhere. You know what's happened. I love you."

There was no answer. Jack reached up to the electric light and put it out. Then he was across the room and Daisy was in his arms. The body he held was rigid. He turned the face into the shaft of light from the lopsided moon rising far down the river, and it seemed something closed and shut away from him. His lips were on her hair, her eyes, her mouth. He talked incoherently.

"It happened like a stroke of lightning . . . it can never stop."

She was stiff and still. His passion could not reach her.

"Daisy, you've got to tell me how you feel . . . I can't go back like this."

She made a sudden move away from him, but he held her.

"No! Since I saw you two days ago, I've been living in a world where nothing has been real but you and me . . . do you get that? Only you and me . . . the two of us. What's it been like for you since two days ago? Tell me. You've got to tell me."

He was demanding her response with every power in him, and now she came alive. Her arms were wrapped around his neck and she was straining against him, and she was speaking to him. Her tears were rolling out with her broken words. "There isn't me any more . . . only you."

The lopsided moon was well on her heavenly way when the waiter coughed outside the room and remarked as if into space:

"*Yu i-ko jen shuo jeep-i-ch'ê teng-chiao.*"

It was Daisy who took notice of the interruption. She translated anxiously. "Jack, he says the jeep is waiting. What time is it?"

"Who cares what time it is? Tell him to go away."

But Daisy was looking at her watch in the moonlight.

"Jack, it's ten minutes to two."

With that the world of war and air raids, of AWOL penalties and OSS office routines came back into their two heads. They raced for the entrance court where a messenger was lounging with the information that the jeep had been at its appointed station for some time, but that it would not be there much longer. There was a scramble up the two hundred steps, with Jack muttering in Daisy's ear that he must take her back to her billet, and her gasping replies that he must not be an idiot; and then the rush along the tortuous ways until in a main thoroughfare they found the jeep in charge of a driver who turned an accusing torch on his wrist watch as Jack came up.

"Two seven, Captain."

"Can you make it?"

The answer was the roll of the engine. Daisy pushed Jack into his seat.

"Do get going." The jeep shot away and was out of sight.

Daisy did not remember much about her movements through Chungking that night. She recalled walking, walking through black ruins in sticky moonlight, through the night life of the city in the glare of electric bulbs . . . walking as if she could never tire. Finally she found herself standing at the point in the road where Jack had put her into her ricksha. She got to her room and sat down on the edge of her bed. It seemed to her that the distorted moon was high . . . very high. Probably Jack was already at his own base, if he had made his plane. If . . . there were a thousand ifs. The dawn was beginning before it occurred to her to lie down.

Chapter Eighteen

"I had the lantern windows lighted in your honor," said Jane.

Barry Manners stood at her side in the Water Mirror Pavilion, gazing across the Happy Sea toward the Court of Retirement. Twilight was dim over the water and the tree-bordered shore; the Porch of the Fan was indistinguishable in its niche of rock and hill, but beyond it, shining in the violet air, was a line of little glowing shapes cut in the wall which stretched on either side of the roofed gate.

"Let me look." Manners narrowed his eyes. "I see a fan; a leaf of the persimmon; its fruit, which is the symbol of fertility . . . the lights are taking on clear outlines with the deepening of dusk. My dear Jane, no one but you would think of such a welcome to a war-weary spirit."

"Enjoy them while you may," said his hostess. "We lighted them with the short native candles which will burn only a little while. Like much of this garden beauty, the windows show their charm for the transient moment."

"Ah, when the beautiful thing perishes, the beauty itself does not die, but passes to some other manifestation. Let us walk toward the *lang-tse*," Manners suggested. "These shapes were made to beckon through the night on occasions of high festival, I suppose."

"It is high festival with us when you are paying the garden a visit," Jane told him, as they started slowly along the shore.

"Consider that I have made my best bow. My dear, Daisy brought me an encouraging report of your health. I am delighted your difficulties are behind you. This Szechuan climate is known for its treachery, and I thought Daisy seemed a bit off color when she returned from her two days with you. Never in my life have I been so afflicted with what

169

the darkies call 'miseries.' And still, of course, I must get on with my work. War waits for no man."

"Oh, I am sorry you are feeling the heat. What was the matter with Daisy?"

"Nothing very definite . . . nothing one could put one's finger on . . . or so I thought at first. An absence of her usual sparkle. This is the Fan Hsuan where she stayed? She told me its touching history. Which reminds me—it may be possible for me to remain with you longer this time than I had expected, if entirely convenient?"

"Entirely," Jane assured him. "You will want to spend hours with Master Yuan. I learn through Shang Shih that he contemplates a little feast. He can afford it since Stephen bought his album at the price you suggested. I was quite abashed to discover how little I understand its money value. It's a good thing I consulted you—good for Master Yuan, I mean."

"A very good thing if I am getting a feast out of the transaction. And you should have your cumshaw as middleman, so you are invited I hope."

"Master Yuan did suggest it. But Wilfreda says positively no evening engagements. You can tell me about it afterward. To go back to Daisy, can't you explain a little?"

"Your Stephen seems desperate about her, but in Chungking on this last trip, he didn't see her—at least, he hadn't the last I knew. He took it too much to heart; he is in love in a somewhat old-fashioned way, I should say. What did come over Daisy while she was with you?"

He heard the breath of a sigh, and Jane stopped as they came in full view of the row of lantern windows.

"You think there was something?"

"Something quite unprecedented. She made me a small scene, Jane . . . I should never have expected it of our self-possessed young woman. Ah . . . do let me drink in your lantern show for a moment, and then, as we go on, I must tell you about it."

He counted the little windows before which they were standing, and again enumerated the shapes, each different from its neighbor and all making a harmony of pattern which began to fade away as the lights sank low one after the other.

"They are going out; but I shall long remember the gentle unmechanized loveliness you have given me on this first evening. . . . About Daisy . . . no one could be more her own mistress than she, more equal to any exigency. Three days ago she came to see me—to have tiffin, to be exact. I was flattered that she took the time for me; they say she is dated three weeks in advance—'dated'—an odd thing to have our scholar word seized upon by the young vulgarians who now make free with its twisted meaning. Don't you agree? Ah, where was I . . . what was I telling you?"

"That you were flattered when Daisy came to tiffin," prompted Jane.

"To be sure. So I was. On that occasion it was extremely hot. The supply of ice is entirely insufficient, and my establishment is not equipped with an electric refrigerator—something should be done about that. Daisy and I talked about various matters. She was distrait, and I took an uncle's privilege to remark upon it. Suddenly she threw her arms around my neck and burst into tears. My dear Jane, I could not have been more amazed if I had found Niagara Falls upon my shoulder."

"She must have been overwrought. I'm told she does very—very dangerous work at times," said Jane hastily.

"The last candle has gone out," Manners sounded a melancholy note. "For some reason, Jane, I feel you are not saying exactly what you are thinking."

They walked slowly eastward as he continued. "Daisy threw some unintentional light upon the cause of her *crise de nerfs*. She asked if I had ever been completely upset . . . torn away from my own plans for myself . . . made to feel overwhelmed and uncertain about everything. This admitted of only one interpretation, and I believe I murmured that I have been young . . . have had my own *affaires de coeur* . . . while I was soothing her as she lay on my shoulder. But at the suggestion of a love affair, she got up hastily and said would I forgive her foolishness and forget all about it? She tried to change the subject."

"And you didn't allow her to change it?"

"You must understand that I felt I had some right—as Miriam Fairchild's old friend—even some responsibility. I intended, if possible, to learn what man was at the bottom of all this. And, do you know, my dear, the person who popped into my head was Trent. He has remained noticeably unattached ever since we have had him in Chung-king; but of course he sees a great deal of Daisy, who seems irresistible. I took the liberty of putting it to her . . . it might be embarrassing to find a superior in the role of a suitor. But with catastrophic results."

"Catastrophic?"

"The word is deliberately chosen. I was appalled. My dear Jane, she began laughing in a perfectly uncontrolled manner—it was more alarming than her tears. There is nothing to do about hysterical laughter, you see. One cannot apply a fresh handkerchief, and so on. Really, really . . . well, she saw that I was startled and succeeded in stopping herself, saying, 'Uncle Barry, let me tell you something about the view of my boss on the subject of yours truly. When I first met him, I was so impertinent as to ask him one day whether he liked me, and he said he did. So then I went a step further, and said I, 'Then why do you never do what everybody else does . . . I mean, every-body who likes me?' Said he, 'Do what?' Said I, 'Take me out of course.' He looked at me and asked a little question in a very gentle voice. He wanted to know who was boss in our outfit, and I told him that of course he was. And said he, 'Exactly; and Daisy, I propose to continue in that capacity.' A little disconcerting she thought it was. Anyhow, that ended my notion that possibly it was Trent who was upsetting our young woman."

They had reached the steps of the Temple to the Flowers by this time, and here they found Wilfreda, who had an air of suppressed excitement although she spoke quietly enough.

"Jane, I think it's time for your bath. Excuse me, Dr. Manners, but a bath in a tub is not very easy to arrange in the Garden of Pure Repose and Jane ordered hers to be ready at this time, so I must re-mind her that the water is getting cold."

"Then I must go," said Jane. "Forgive such domestic details, Barry."

"Of course," said Manners. "Have a good bath, Jane. I shall be having a delightful evening with some old books I bought in a dark little shop today, while I smoke my pipe in the Hall for Inviting the Pleasures. And we can go on with our gossiping some other time. And so—until tomorrow, my dear hostess."

He left them at the bridge and the two women turned in the direction of the Chai. As soon as the tall figure was out of earshot, Jane made an eager demand.

"Has Stephen got back?"

"Yes. He drove the truck in at the back gate and parked it as usual in the coolie service court. He asked me to get rid of Lao Ch'i and Lao Pa, so I sent them off to prepare your bath as we arranged, and then he took off the canvas cover of the truck so that she can come out. I don't know how she has ever borne the journey in the stuffiness under that cover, but Stephen has got her here safely and not even our own servants know she has come into the garden."

Jane quickened her pace and led the way through the bamboo grove and around the low hills to the open space where the truck was standing dimly outlined in the starlight. No one was visible. Jane went straight into the dense shadow of the big car, and Wilfreda heard her say, "Willow, my dear, my dear."

There was no audible word spoken in reply, but as Wilfreda came near enough, she saw the shadowy outline of a woman taller than Jane holding the little figure away from her with her hands on the slender shoulders. After a long moment, Jane spoke to Wilfreda again. "Stephen has gone to his own room, hasn't he?"

"Yes."

"Then, Wilfreda, please go ahead of us. We will follow at a distance and wait for your signal that the coolies are out of the Chai, and everything is safe."

Wilfreda returned to Jane's quarters and found the big lacquer tub full of steaming water waiting in the east room. She made sure that the servants were out of the way and then went to fetch the two who were waiting in the protection of the bamboo grove. A moment more and the three women were within the Chai.

"Close both gates and fasten the south door," said Jane. "Thank goodness for the paper lattice which will make it unlikely that anyone will look in on us."

"Yes," said Wilfreda, "and then shall I help Willow with her bath?"

The newcomer had gone into the east room, and by the light of the lamp burning there, Wilfreda saw that she was far along in pregnancy. She was dressed in the poor black cotton of the Szechuan peasant. Her legs were bare and the feet thrust into rough straw sandals. Every detail was characteristic of the worst poverty, but the poise of the head, which seemed shapely under its load of soiled white cloth wound turbanwise, and something in the set of the shoulders and bearing of the body, distorted as it was, did not agree with the coolie clothing.

"Wilfreda," said Jane, "I want to do a few of the first things myself. Stephen has managed very well about food, so she isn't hungry. But Willow is so exhausted that she has scarcely said two words to me, only she warned me to keep away because she says she has lice. Please get that yellow tin which Jack Fernald produced the other day. I'm going to start by giving her a Flit shampoo. It's going to be a serious job to get her cleaned up, and I think I would like the wooden foot tub to soak off the crust of filth on the extremities before we put her into the bath."

"You can't put a woman in her condition into a hot bath," the nurse objected.

"You can't? But how are we ever to get her respectable, then?"

Jane was as disappointed as a child deprived of a special treat. It was plain that she had anticipated the scrubbing up.

"We must be satisfied with sponging off for the present. I'll get the Flit; and the foot tub is an excellent idea."

Wilfreda brought the insecticide and the small, round firkin from her own room. She found Willow sitting in the straight chair opposite the door and Jane removing the soiled head rag.

"Put the foot tub down by her, please, Freda, and we'll have some of the bath water in it; and give me the tin, and the clean towel and safety pins which are on the table."

Jane soaked one end of the towel with the Flit; she also rubbed it through the rough black locks which were cut short and stuck out when the turban was removed. The saturated cloth was plastered over the head, and then the dry part was wound firmly around and fastened with the safety pin.

"Now," said Jane, talking softly, as she worked, "by morning you will find all those wretched little crawlers have become perfectly quiet and then we'll get rid of them with soap and water. I know how to give a Flit shampoo. I'll never forget the time I needed it myself. Don't try to talk. You'll soon be going to rest."

Wilfreda brought a heavy clay jug; she dipped up some bath water and poured it into the foot tub. Willow made an effort to prevent Jane from going forward with the washing of her feet, but she was too exhausted to make much objection to anything.

"Let me do this for you," Jane said gently, kneeling down with soap dish and brush. "No, Wilfreda, I want to do it myself. Your turn is coming."

The nurse stood watching while Jane soaked and scrubbed, taking her time over a condition which required more than usual attention. The steam from the bath water floated through the room and made the air oppressive. When the washing of the feet was finished, Willow stirred and spoke. "Now, Teacher Jane, you have done too much for me; and I can manage the rest. Please both of you go out and let me bathe alone."

Jane had risen to her feet and was looking rather doubtful, but seemed to understand the reason for the request.

"Very well, then. Miss Grayson and I will wait in the court, and if you want anything, you can speak to us."

When they were out of the heated room, Jane murmured to the nurse, "I'm afraid there are marks on her body that she doesn't want us to see. She has been in prison, you know."

"Recently?" Wilfreda asked.

"I think not. She hasn't had time to say very much, but I judge she has been drifting from one miserable warren to another in Chungking to keep out of the hands of the Tai Li police. Did you ever see anyone so done up?"

"Yes," said Wilfreda, "I think you were done up yourself the other night after our little session outside the garden gate. And I want you in bed now as soon as possible. Here, get into your peacock chair while you wait."

"It's too bad she can't stay the night in the east room near us," commented Jane. "The name is so appropriate, 'A Little Nap.' But Shang Ma might find her in the morning. By the way, we must dirty the bath water a little before the coolies carry it away. We can pour some from the foot tub into it, but not too much, Freda. I wouldn't want anybody to suppose I was as dirty as that, after living here for weeks." And she chuckled softly.

The scrubbing and splashing behind the lighted lattice did not go on very long. A clean garment of Wilfreda's was ready when Willow asked for it, and the things she had worn were placed in the pile of laundry, which the nurse would attend to the next morning at the washing stones before any curious eyes were open. It was nearly eleven o'clock when the three women stole through the paths leading to the Joy of Bamboos.

"Ever since I knew you would come," Jane breathed in Willow's ear, "I have been using this isolated house so that no one will be surprised that Wilfreda and I often visit it. But no one else has any errands here. You will not be disturbed. Now, go peacefully to sleep on the cool mats and get a good rest."

"It is long since I have rested," was the answer.

"I think you are safe in using a torch as soon as you are inside," said Jane, feeling for the bamboo screen that hung over the door. "Wilfreda and I know the garden so well that we can find our way by starlight, and we didn't want to risk a coolie noticing us, although, as I told you, the servants are accustomed to my visits here."

She raised the screen, and switched on her torch just as she was about to step inside. Willow reached over and put it out.

"Listen!" she whispered.

The three stood perfectly still and the night silence flowed all around them, except for a little tree creature cheeping somewhere in the bamboos. Jane could not detect another sound.

"What was it?" she asked finally, speaking under her breath.

"I heard a rustling near the house . . . I thought."

"The wind?" murmured Wilfreda in her turn.

"No."

Again they were still. Again there was only the small voice squeaking faintly. At last Willow moved into the house. She felt her way to the east wall as Jane guided her, found the bed of mats under the net. She slipped off her shoes and lay down. Then she whispered, "It was nothing. Go to your own rest, Teacher Jane."

Wilfreda drew her patient away, and the two women did not speak until they were once more in the Chai. As the nurse put away the torch, with its costly battery, and lighted the saucer lamp, she found Jane looking troubled.

"Shouldn't we have stayed with her, Freda?"

"Surely there was no need of it. She was only nervous at being in a strange place."

"Remember, she is a hunted creature. But she is certainly safe with us?" Jane seemed to be asking a question rather than making a statement.

"Of course she is safe. And she is brave and sensible, and said herself that it was nothing. She went to bed, and so must you."

In the bamboo grove barely three paces from the door of the house where Willow lay, Benny Li was standing as if he had grown roots like the tall stems around him. He had been in the garden on an errand of his own, and on his way out heard footsteps behind him. He had stepped off the path, and had been just outside the circle of light when Jane's torch went on. He saw her with Wilfreda, and the stranger to whom she was speaking. When the light was snapped off, he knew the scrape of the bamboo leaves had been heard, and he dared not move again. But when the two women went away, he felt sure that they had abandoned suspicion, and he was left in possession of a valuable piece of information. The arrival of the newcomer, who was Chinese as he had been able to see, might prove extremely convenient for him. His own activities could be laid at another person's door, perhaps, and in any case, he could curry favor with local authorities by reporting a secret visitor to the Wang Family Garden—in case she turned out to be a mystery, of which he had little doubt. However, there was no hurry. He would wait before he decided how this discovery could best be turned to his own advantage.

Chapter Nineteen

The morning after Willow's arrival, Wilfreda was up early. It was the pleasantest part of the garden day, she thought, as she followed her custom of a plunge in the Pool of the Rock and Pine. The mysterious freshening of the air which came at dawn lifted the sense of heaviness from her lungs, and for an hour or two she felt no physical discomforts whatever, which, she reflected was not a normal state for anyone in summer on the Szechuan plain.

She busied herself with preparing the day's ration of food for the refugee. Jane and she had decided that since the nurse occasionally lighted a small charcoal stove to prepare special nourishment for her patient, Shang Ma's curiosity would not be aroused if they used it once a day for Willow. Wilfreda cooked a generous portion of a good quality of rice which Jane had taken special pains to select, and carried it over the paths to the Joy of Bamboos where she found that Willow was already up. The latter smiled at her visitor, but she made no reply when she was asked if she had slept well, and neither did she comment when the good hot food was placed before her.

"Here is fruit; here are eggs which have been boiled. Teacher Jane wishes you to eat heartily and increase your strength."

"You are up very early," said Willow. She did not offer to touch her breakfast.

"I am always up at this time."

Wilfreda decided that if China chose to be laconic, England could match the effort. She went toward the door, marveling at the absence of the usual polite expressions of interest and thanks which are as natural to the Chinese as the drawing of breath. The refugee addressed her abruptly.

178

"I heard last night that you are a nurse."

"I am a midwife."

"Do you think my child will come soon?"

Wilfreda turned around.

"Are you willing to let me make an examination?"

Willow nodded. "Now."

"But your rice is getting cold."

To this there was no reply, and Wilfreda took swift advantage of the opportunity unexpectedly given her. When she had finished, she asked one question. "This is your first child?"

"And my last." The reply came with startling intensity.

"Why do you say that?"

The nurse had decided to give no indication of any knowledge of Willow's history.

"There are plenty of children in China already."

The tone had changed completely. Was there humor in it? Wilfreda felt baffled and took refuge in becoming professional.

"Your baby may be born at any time. I am glad you are here where we are ready to take care of you."

She opened the door to the inner room and pointed to the preparations she had made there. A table was stacked with rough brown paper which was absorbent. There was a tall jar full of water, a brazier with charcoal and a kettle beside it. Her nurse's bag was on the floor. "Perhaps," she went on, "you would like me to stay with you at night until your labor starts. We shall visit you often during the daytimes, and keep track of you."

"Let Teacher Jane decide what is to be done. Tell me, how is she?"

The demand was very sudden, but Wilfreda considered that she met it smoothly.

"She is as usual. Didn't you think so?"

"I saw very little of her last night; but I did see that she has a nurse."

"We are old friends. I am her guest because my hospital was bombed and it takes time to reorganize. Before long I shall be going back to work in Kweichow."

Willow met this with a very level glance.

"I am not a fool," she said.

Wilfreda went back to the Chai and told Jane she had never in her life talked with a Chinese who was so curt. "Her rough behavior isn't really convincing," she complained. "It doesn't go with her physical type. Her hands are exquisite, and her mouth, in repose, has beautiful sensitive curves. She must adopt this manner as part of her disguise, but why keep it up in private?"

"I haven't seen her for years." Jane was thoughtful. "I'm glad you have given me some warning of what to expect. You say the child is to come soon?"

"Stephen was in luck to get her here in time. By the way, there's one thing you haven't made clear to him or to me," added Wilfreda. "He was asking me last night how you expect to keep Willow's presence a secret after the child is born?"

"Oh, the servants will have to know; but I don't see that it concerns Barry or Master Yuan."

"Won't they wonder why they weren't told before—the Shangs, I mean?"

"Of course. I shall explain that it was because of the Szechuan superstition that it is bad luck to have strange children born under the family roof. I shall give them to understand that because of this idea I kept my own counsel. And I shall say that it is my own student who asked me for help, so what else could I do?"

"All very well," commented Wilfreda. "But Stephen pointed out that Shang Shih is responsible for reporting to the police as people enter and leave this garden. So when he finds we have a mother and child mysteriously added to our midst, what is he to do?"

"Report." Jane rose from her breakfast.

"Then the police will come to register Willow, find out who she is, and arrest her."

"No," said Jane. "They won't."

"But—"

"They will come, but they will not see Willow."

"Why not?"

"They will see me instead," said Jane. "I will deal with them. And now, Freda, I am going to the Joy of Bamboos so that I may get reacquainted with my old student before the sun is high and before

Barry emerges from his morning leisure and possibly wants to see me."

She greeted Willow with the conventional words, "Have you eaten?" and as the guest answered that she had, Jane's eye was on the table which was bare of a single scrap of food. This was one point gained. Seeing her bathed and in clean clothes was another. Jane sat down on the stool by the table while the refugee stood leaning against the doorframe where the light sifted through the bamboo screen upon her heavy distorted figure. It seemed she was choosing to be uncomfortable.

"I look at you, Willow, and you look at me. It is years since we have talked together."

"You are thin, very thin," said the Chinese.

"And so are you."

"You have eaten bitterness in this war. You have worked too hard."

"And so have you."

Willow turned a very searching gaze upon her teacher and Jane held her breath, but the comment which came did not touch her secret.

"I think you are quiet in your mind."

"And I see that you are not."

The younger woman clenched her hands. "How can I be quiet? How can I bear the fate of the Chinese people and be quiet?"

"My dear," said Jane, "are you going to talk to me about the Chinese people and not about yourself?"

"What do I matter? What does one person matter? When you know what I know, you do not think about one person."

"Even one person who has lost her man, who is going to give birth, who is wanted by the police? Willow, have you become careless of your life?"

Jane was almost stern. The girl bowed her head, and then came and sat on the edge of the bed near her.

"You are right. I am going to give birth; I should think about that."

Jane took the long slender hands in hers and there was silence for an intimate moment. Then she put the obvious question.

"What are your plans for the child?"

"I have thought of leaving it with some woman to nurse; but I have no money."

"You do not see any way to keep it with you while you should be feeding it yourself?"

"Of course you think that would be a good thing for me," the words came almost savagely. "It would cure me of my wild ways; I would have to settle down and be a respectable job holder and mother, if not wife and mother. That's what you think."

"Well," said Jane mildly, "it doesn't matter much what I think, does it? The question is what do you think?"

Her tone was in such contrast to the roughness of the previous speech that it seemed to give Willow pause. She sat brooding, and Jane waited. Finally her question was answered.

"I think I have no way but to ask you to take my child."

"I hoped you were going to say that."

The two sat looking at each other, and there were tears in the eyes of the Chinese. She drew a long breath.

"But I have to ask you . . . what conditions will you make with me about taking it?"

"Conditions?" Jane was puzzled.

"I am a Communist. I believe in the revolution. You are a Christian. You do not."

"Oh," said Jane. "Are you thinking that my reason for welcoming the responsibility for your child is that this will give me a chance to take it away from you? Because you are a Communist, and I am a Christian? Willow, you should know me better!"

"Do you mean that you make no conditions at all?"

"The sensible conditions would be, I should think, that I may do for and with the baby all that my best love and wisdom suggest, as long as you leave it in my care. Obviously, I cannot be you, Willow. If the baby is with me it has to have my best wisdom, not the wisdom of anybody else."

"But the child's future remains in my hands?"

Jane smiled. "Ah, that is where you and I disagree. The child's future belongs to neither of us. You have a philosophy which makes you think you control the future. I know very well that I do not. And neither, my dear, do you."

"Let us not argue." The voice had again a sharp edge. "You have one set of ideas, I have another. But if you take my child and care for it until I can get it back again, I do not see your reason. You give too much for too little."

"So?" said Jane. "I do not feel that between you and me there can be a question of too much or too little. If you will trust me with your baby, I will care for it as well as I can—and with great joy. But there is one point we haven't considered. Suppose I . . . I have to leave China?"

Willow pondered. "Of course. You are a foreigner. Any number of things might happen which would force you to leave and go back to your own country."

"But in that case," Jane suggested, "I could probably make some arrangement. For instance, Wei-Chou would help me. He has helped you, hasn't he?"

Willow's underlip was thrust out at this reminder and she looked positively forbidding. Jane put out her hand and touched the frowning face. "Now you look exactly as you did the day I would not let you out of my house to march in a street parade. Do you remember?"

"And many students were arrested that day, so I was glad you listened to me, that one time. Now I am glad you have accepted Wei-Chou's help and have come to me."

"I have no other way. But I shall go as soon as I can; and I shall send for my child. It must grow up with the revolution. And you will see whether the future is ours or not!" The assertion was passionate. Again Jane countered with an increase of quietness.

"I am glad you do look to a future, Willow. The past has been so bitter that I half-feared I should find you a broken thing."

"Do you mean you feared I might die in childbirth?"

"I feared you might have too little will to live."

"I am strong. I shall not die. I have thought of death for myself and the child, but that is past."

"Thank God for that." Jane stopped and her eyes dwelt long upon the brooding face which now was turned away from her. Then she took her resolution. "Can you tell me, Willow, what has been happening to you since we were together in the north? I am not asking you to speak of matters which are secret; I do not want you to go into details which will be painful. But there are years of your life which are blanks to me, and which have made you what you are now."

To her great relief, Willow left brooding and looked at her frankly.

"There is a little that I cannot tell you; there is more that I will not. But you want to know me as I am . . . ? You are my old teacher and you are my friend always. Now, I will be, as much as I can, like a child that speaks to its mother."

She paused.

"I do not want to hurt you. But if you are to understand me, you must see that my life has found its meaning in working for the revolution. I do not believe in God, but I have a god—the Chinese people who have suffered for thousands of years with no hope until now. And now, we have a hope that nothing can take away from us, and it gives us a strength that no terror and no rottenness can stop. We shall get the mountains and the rivers back from the Japanese, and then we shall take them away from the warlords and the landlords, the money-lenders and the proud foreigners and from their running dogs—" She stopped suddenly. "I do not want to hurt you," she repeated.

Jane did not speak and Willow became a little anxious. "You are not hurt? You are not angry?"

"I am a little of both, perhaps," said the other slowly. "But it does not matter because you are making me understand. I think I grasp as well as I ever shall what the revolution means to you; what I want to know is what it has done to you—to you, one of the bravest and most honest people I have ever known."

And then she heard the story. She heard how Willow's first encounter with the discipline of the Communist party had resulted in her revolt. She had broken with the organization and attempted to find her place in the world of young poets and writers who adopted various courses of romantic self-dramatization or else attempted to follow in the footsteps of the great Lu Hsün who began a new approach in literature to the life of the people. She had picked up a precarious living by doing various types of literary hack work. Then came an opportunity to visit Russia. She had undertaken the care of two children in a family returning to Moscow from Shanghai, and she rather shamefacedly joined in Jane's amusement over the notion of her firebrand turned nursemaid. She had not kept her job very long but had made other contacts among Chinese radicals who were students in the Soviet capital. While she was there, her desire to be once more in the ranks of the party returned; but she was not regarded as trustworthy. She turned her face toward China, and managed to find her way back to Peking, only to land in jail on suspicion of being what she longed to be and was not. With the assistance of the man who became her lover, she made her escape, and the two made the dangerous journey through Japanese-occupied Shanghai to Hongkong which was the asylum of a large number of Chinese radicals. There, for a time, she tasted an intense, if secret, happiness. Her lover had been of one mind with her, and through him she became again established in the party. But when Hongkong was threatened, they left for the mainland, and it became necessary to separate. His fate had been to die in a bombing raid, and hers to pass from one hiding place to another, just one jump ahead of the Tai Li police. In Chungking, she had made a connection with a former University classmate and heard of Jane's presence in West China. The services of this same classmate had been enlisted in making the contact with Wei-Chou.

"And so you see," Willow finished, "I have been wandering and living in jails and in holes and corners. I have been dirty and hungry most of the time, and I have come to know that such things do not matter. One person's sufferings cannot be regarded in the comradeship I know . . . in the world we have to live in."

"And when you heard that your lover was dead," said Jane softly, "was that also of no importance?"

Willow did not answer at once, but she gave no sign of breaking down.

"When I heard," she said finally, "I thought of death. But I was given work to do. I put death away until afterward."

"And the work is not done yet?"

"My work will never be finished. I know that now."

"Nor mine," said Jane. "There we stand on common ground."

Willow looked at her doubtfully. "But you may have to leave China."

Jane rose. "I will not go until I must. Now, let us be practical. You have nothing prepared for this child, I know, because you didn't bring even a bundle of necessities for yourself."

"I have nothing. And I hate sewing."

"Fortunately, I don't. Well, Wilfreda says we may not have much time, and I must see what can be done. Do you want something to read to pass the time?"

"I don't wish to read."

"What shall you do with yourself?"

For the first time in their interview, Jane saw a look of affection in Willow's eyes.

"Do not worry about me, Teacher Jane. Here, I am under your shadow and I can let my sorrow lie quietly in my heart, and clear my mind of all thinking, and rest, and be empty for a while."

"Rest and be empty," repeated Jane. "That is right. That is what you need. But," she added curiously, "can you actually stop the succession of thoughts that are constantly shaping themselves in the mind—and be empty, as you say?"

Willow nodded. "In prison I learned to do this. It is more refreshing than sleep."

"Rest, then. The garden is a better place to practice emptiness than a prison."

And Jane went away.

Chapter Twenty

"And so," said Stephen to Wilfreda, "Jane has imported an expectant mamma and you are going to take charge of the passenger I have delivered safely into your hands."

He was leaning against a pillar of the *lang-tse* of the San Yu Chai. The moist heat of the drowsy summer day permeated everything, and the young man, although fresh from his plunge in the pool by his quarters, was aware that his clothes were sticking to his body and his forehead was beaded with sweat. But he forgot his discomfort as he saw the pleasure with which Wilfreda was greeting him.

"Yes. I suppose my turn comes next. I always expect to do whatever Jane wants. Sometimes she bewilders me, but in this case I understand what we are about."

Stephen looked up with a whimsical smile.

"Did it ever occur to you that where there is a Mary there always has to be a Martha?" he asked. "In the case of Jane, there is so much Mary that she needs a perfect regiment of Marthas. I consider I was on a Martha job myself when I brought Willow from Chungking."

Wilfreda looked at him.

"You don't seem refreshed," she remarked, "even after a long night and your morning plunge. What kind of a trip did you have?"

Stephen avoided her eye.

"Not so bad; but I was scared to death all the time, since I don't possess a certificate in midwifery. I'll never race the stork over West China roads again, even to please Jane."

"You did well to get here in time. Jane is with Willow now, listening to her account of herself, so far as she will condescend to give one. Please tell me how you managed on the journey. I'm curious about all the details."

Wilfreda sat down at the Table of the Eight Immortals which had been moved into the *lang-tse* for the morning meal, and drew a pair of shears from beneath a pile of white material. Stephen took a stool opposite her and watched as she went to work.

"Preparations for the blessed event?" he inquired.

"Yes. Willow had nothing with her, absolutely nothing."

"So I noticed."

"These are some old Canton flannel night things of Jane's which she says she won't need again."

Wilfreda's shears clipped busily as she spoke. "See how worn and thin the material is! But it will make soft little shirts and blankets, and so on. Now you are forgetting my curiosity."

"Well, I sent Jane's note to Colonel Wang according to instructions and mentioned the day and hour I expected to be leaving from the Service Section Hostel. Four days went by and absolutely nothing happened. Then the night before the day I had set for departure, I went over the truck to check it myself, as I always do, and found Willow sitting in the cab. Somehow, she had found out my routine and knew when I would work on the load alone. How she got into the hostel compound I haven't the least idea. She has less to say than any woman I ever met, and she has cultivated a rather abrupt manner, which isn't encouraging. It's not a bit like the behavior of educated Chinese I have known."

"Jane says she comes of a great landowner family, and had to beg the life of her own father when her comrades got into his part of the country," Wilfreda remarked.

"I can't imagine her begging for anything," said Stephen. "She suggested when I found her, that I make a place in the middle of my load of crates, and so on, where she could be hidden, because of course she had no travel permit, or papers of any sort. I objected that it would be fearfully hot, but she said she could take it. I shifted my load, and got a mattress for her."

"She told us last night you had given her plenty of food. That was another problem, wasn't it?"

"Yes, it was. And Hot Dog, my mechanic, was still another. Willow didn't want him to know I had a passenger."

"Hot Dog? What an odd name."

"He was the Bishop's devoted henchman," Stephen explained. "We FSS guys took him over, and he was so fond of American eats —the food we had before the Burma Road was closed—that we named him in honor of his favorite refreshment—which is a thing you'd call a bun with a sausage and mustard stuck into it. He is very proud of his English name, I can tell you, and he's an awfully good scout. But Willow said it would be terrible for him if she was caught and he was implicated, so the thing to do was to keep him in ignorance of her presence on the truck."

"And you succeeded?"

"I think so. Hot Dog is nobody's fool, and he must have thought my arrangements pretty queer on occasions; however, this is not my first journey with something to hide, and Hot Dog doesn't ask questions, or answer them."

"What about the trip?"

"We got away from Chungking all right, because the police there know me—but don't know too much about me, as yet. When we were out on the road, I began driving harder than I usually do, because although Willow said nothing about herself, I figured that time was of the essence. The speed, of course, made the going harder for her, and Hot Dog opened his eyes at the way I was stepping on it. I wanted to check on how she was standing the pace, so after two hours I stopped and sent him off to beg some water for the radiator. I consulted Willow and asked if I'd better go carefully or just light out for the River Garden of Pure Repose. She said she could take anything, so that was that.

"The road that day was all up and down and I knew she had to brace herself, so I was sure she was getting mighty tired—best I could do. I made the inn I was aiming for, just at dark, and I told Hot Dog to go into the house and bring out a lot of hot food. Told him I was extra hungry, though why anyone should crave the kind of food you get at a house by the side of a Szechuan road undoubtedly struck him as queer. I got enough to feed Willow. There was coming and going in the inn yard, but very little light and so we managed."

"And where did you sleep?" asked Wilfreda.

"On the truck, of course."

"In the driver's seat for three nights?"

"It wasn't such a good idea, in one way," Stephen explained, "because it made the traveling public curious. Also Hot Dog warned me that there were bandits reported ahead on our road. Consequently, we got away the next day at dawn. It's my theory that bandits are seldom very rampageous at four in the morning."

Wilfreda had cut two little blankets from the back breadth of one nightdress. She now slit the side seams and said:

"Stephen, lend me your handkerchief."

He pulled out a square of fresh linen.

"Why my hanky?"

"It's about the size of a baby's diaper," said Wilfreda. "It will do for a pattern. Dear me, Stephen, you do have elegant handkerchiefs."

"Relics of better days."

Wilfreda's shears clipped around the edges of his contribution.

"Thank you," she said. "Now I have the size. Do go on."

"The second day," pursued Stephen, "the road was bad. We had to ford streams and there were always people trying to get on at such places."

"I know," Wilfreda remarked. "What are called 'yellow fish' on West China roads—the ones who ride without paying."

The young man nodded.

"I wasn't taking any yellow fish. Sometimes I had to push them off the load, and once the only way was to drop a wad of money in the dust and get going while my would-be passengers scrambled for it. It was hot as blazes, but in spite of that I kept having cold chills up and down my spine.

"We didn't stop at an inn the second night. Hot Dog said we were attracting too much interest; best I could do. We got to a mission station and how I thanked God when their big gates swung shut on the crowd, and when I got to the cleanliness and peace which I always find in such places. But even there, Willow wouldn't come out. She said it might be dangerous for the preacher. She certainly worried about danger for others more than about danger for herself. She must be political dynamite. But here is the archconspirator."

He rose as Jane came into the *lang-tse*. She looked very sober, but she smiled when she saw Stephen and the work upon which Wilfreda was engaged.

"Willow had a fairly good night, I think," she reported, "although I believe she is so accustomd to sudden alarms that she didn't let herself sleep really deeply."

She came over to the table and looked at Wilfreda's work. "It's a good thing you have started the layette," she observed. "Freda, I have an idea for some little trousers—with a slit up the back—the kind that Chinese mothers use even for the newborn. I remember hearing them called the 'step-into-sit-out-of pattern'! If you wouldn't mind going through the chest in my room, I think you will find some odd pieces of colored cotton. It will be nice if there is a bit of red."

Freda rose at once, and Jane slipped into her place and picked up the shears.

"I can go on with this," she said, and the nurse, nodding, went in search of more material for the work in hand.

Before beginning her task, Jane paused a moment to drink in the prospect before her. The morning light was a glory upon the face of the pool. The flat top of the dwarf pine which stood over the Mi Fei rock filtered the sunshine upon the gray mass beneath it. On the banks, the sharp green of the bamboos hung in bladed shapes, and on the surface of the water a single lotus was opening its rosy cup in the shade of the eastern shore. She turned her eyes from the peace of the garden scene to look at Stephen and remark:

"Willow was born to this but she doesn't like me to remind her of it. She says she has no heart for the enjoyment of gardens now."

"Thee told me of her tragedy—the death of her lover," said Stephen.

"It's not only her personal grief. It's her whole revolutionary outlook. While the people suffer, Willow knows little rest—or peace."

"Tell me more about her. I don't understand her sort at all," said Stephen.

"Willow hasn't given thee any account of herself?"

"Not a word." And he settled himself to listen.

"She belonged to one of the important clans in her district, and there were several concubines so the children were numerous. An old-style scholar was invited to teach them, and Willow was well grounded

in the Chinese classics. But it was decided to give her a modern education as well, and she was sent to a mission school."

"Was that when thee first knew her?"

"No. That school was in the south, and Willow became a Communist while she was still preparing for the university where I taught
her. She is a born rebel and experimenter, and at that time the student
Communist movement was beginning. She met a young organizer who
made a great impression on her. He was dying of TB but he lived in
poverty and jeopardy. She contrasted him with the missionaries in
the school. They had security; they lived comfortably; they seemed
to her very busy exercising authority over others, instead of doing
dangerous and arduous things for the masses. Willow cast in her lot
with peril and hard work, and she was already an underground agent
when she entered the university in the north."

Stephen whistled softly.

"Did thee know it?" he asked.

"Not for some time after my friendship with her had begun. In
her sophomore year, she was arrested. At first she was kept at police headquarters, but later she was moved to a military prison,
which alarmed all her friends. We went into action, and got her
out."

"Got her out? Can schoolteachers open jails in China?"

"Sometimes. We saw influential people, and the University agreed
to readmit her if she were released. It was shortly after she returned
to the campus that she and I became really intimate."

"Thee chooses thy intimates for unusual reasons, I must say,"
Stephen commented.

Jane reflected. "I was a propagandist—and Willow was one, too;
she was prepared to make sacrifices which were not required of me.
I shared her passionate desire that the Chinese people should have
a better life; I had a deep respect for her courage and devotion."

"And had she respect for thy capacity for the same things?"

This question made the dimple peep out.

"I'm afraid not. We used to have arguments in which Willow
maintained that Christians are no longer brave and devoted. I remember pointing out to her that in China we had died for our faith as late
as the Boxer year, which was 1900. I thought that if we were tried

again we might not be found wanting. However, I was all untried, and not disposed to make rash claims for myself."

"Thee might have pointed out something else, I should think, namely that Christianity and communism are not the same things and should not be equated. One is a religion, the other is a political system."

"Isn't thee being academic, Stephen? The pattern of human behavior does appear so full of repetition! I can't see that in two thousand years Christianity has managed to separate itself entirely from political systems; and I do see that in communism there is now a fervor which is building a religious content into its political system. But of course, I know very little about these things. As I was telling thee, Willow and I became friends, dear friends."

"That began, then, years ago. What has happened since?"

"I know very little about it, and I am not likely to know much more. It is enough for me that now she needs me."

"I found out for myself that Willow is uncommunicative. But Jane," Stephen brought his eyes away from the pool to her face, "I wish thee would be a little more open with me about thy health. Don't I deserve to be trusted after bringing thy revolutionist all the way from Chungking?"

Jane laid down her shears, and the young man saw in the look she bent on him something which he knew he did not fathom. She was grave, but there was in her a joy which was so intense that it communicated itself through his puzzling.

"Stephen," she said, "Brother Ass is behaving himself in a seemly manner at present. And whether he behaves or not, all is well with me. That is what I want my friends to know, and remember."

The water stood in the young man's eyes . . . he could not tell why. He looked away across the pool where the round lily pads were green on the gray surface. Jane continued her work, and changed the subject with her next question.

"Tell me about Daisy."

"I didn't see her."

"But why didn't thee?"

"It's the pattern I'm familiar with." Stephen got up and prowled about uneasily. "One day, it's all right; the next, I don't know where

I am. I told thee I'd take anything she handed out, but I . . . I wasn't looking for this. She just didn't want to see me . . . and didn't."

"What did thee hear about her?"

"Oh . . . as usual, she's having fun. Three men at least think they've got her signed up for keeps. I believe the time will come when she'll be tired of playing around. That'll be after the war, of course."

"What does thee intend doing after the war?"

"Most young Americans in West China are gambling with their lives; they don't see a future. I have no right to plan for one either . . . and just at present, Jane, I don't feel greatly interested."

"The blight of war!" said Jane. "But in spite of it, there is a future. And the future is of the greatest interest to me."

Chapter Twenty-one

Evening came softly into the garden on the night of the feast to which Barry Manners had been bidden by Master Yuan. The guest left his own court through the moon gate to the west and strolled in the direction of the Library of Four Delights, full of appreciation of his surroundings. There were no stirrings of air on the Szechuan plain which was, Barry remembered, the basin of an ancient lake; but there was moderation of the heat, now that the sun was down. The moving waters cooled the earth surfaces with their exhalations, and the scents of growing things merged into one faint fragrance. The night shadow had come over the gray-green garden, and the stars were looking into its pools. It would be early morning before the waning moon would be high enough to shine under its trees.

The peace of it . . . in what did it consist? Barry asked himself. Not a pipe . . . not a wire within the old walls, to carry the irritation and strain of mechanized living . . . was that it? Or was the closeness to the ground of the dwellings, where the low roofs seemed to brood over the houses, the reason why he, as a garden dweller, felt all his being quieted, in spite of the woe, the frustrations, the horrors of the war? He turned the corner of the path where the Studio and the Library were both in view. A Chinese house lighted up, was just like a paper lantern, he thought, enjoying the pattern of a wooden grille against an illuminated wall; or rather, he corrected himself, like a child's plaything, so small, so low, so dim were these structures compared to the geometrical masses in which the building of the West was done, with their glare of electricity. Here he found the dream charm of insubstantiality; the physical form could not survive the least contact with furious modern ways, and yet it had within its frail shapes

195

the quality which answered to man's need for rest, for sanity, for beauty. This embodiment of those healing things must perish, but they would manifest themselves again, in happier days . . . in happier days.

Master Yuan was waiting to greet him, with all proper apologies for the repast which was certainly in contrast to the feasts of forty courses in Peking restaurants or to the elaborate eating which even in war days went on in official Chungking. But the *pièce de résistance* of steamed crabs was in true scholar tradition, and Manners was able to quote the ancient poets in appreciation of the dish. The soup was served in exquisite Ming bowls, of paper-thin porcelain most delicate to touch, and decorated with the characteristic blue in the beautiful clearness of line and sureness of execution which satisfied a fastidious eye. And the wine was a comfort to the palate and a relaxing of the tongue. Manners was not loath to meet the challenge to empty his tiny bowl again and again.

Master Yuan was a gracious and meticulous host, but it was soon clear that the postprandial part of the evening was to be the most important. The Library where the table was laid was lighted with great horn globes in which large candles were burning, and the narrow table often used for the display of paintings was now covered with a single scroll of calligraphy. It had been unrolled, and two weights of glass held it open.

"I see you have something to show me," Manners said when he knew the proper time had arrived to introduce a subject which must be approached with attention and deliberation.

It appeared that the writing was that of the artist who had lived in the Studio of Clear Sounds in the time of Wang Wei-Chou's grandfather, and that there was still in existence a sort of garden day-book in which Wang Ch'eng-Hsin had narrated the circumstances under which this particular piece of calligraphy had been written. And there was an entry—the old scholar dropped his voice—which mentioned that Wu Mei-Sun had also brought with him certain documents which had been handed down from his famous Yuan dynasty ancestor Wu Chen. There had been one of Szechuan's periodical upheavals due to the blood lust and greed of a warlord, and the daybook hinted that these precious things had been hidden somewhere in the garden.

"What year would that have been?" Manners asked with interest; and from the data given in terms of a Ch'ing dynasty reign year he computed that the treasure had last been seen in 1879.

"Has the present owner never made a search for this?" he wanted to know.

The old scholar replied that Wang Wei-Chou was very seldom at home and had become so *mo tun* (modern) in his interests, that the recovery of the work from the brush of Wu Chen had not concerned him as much as it should have—the last was hinted rather than directly stated. But he had given Master Yuan leave to hunt about himself, and had ordered Shang Shih to open the strong room behind the Court of Retirement for the purpose.

"And you have never found any trace?"

"I have made an inventory of the items still in the strong room," said Master Yuan. "And there is no trace. I have examined the grotto, as a likely hiding place, and one possibility has occurred to me."

Manners looked his interest, and the low voice became a whisper.

"I have considered the statue of Kuan Yin."

"Of course," said Manners. "There would be a hollow place near the heart where writings—if they were small enough—might be deposited, along with a jewel or some such thing. But wouldn't marauders think of that? Was the garden entered, in fact, in those troubled years?"

"It was. And I have examined the heart chamber of the statue and found nothing. However . . ."

At this moment, the two heard heavy footsteps and unfamiliar voices approaching the Library, and as the scholars exchanged glances, Lloyd Osborne appeared in the open door, and spoke abruptly.

"Hello, Manners. Please tell the old man we must come in. Sorry to disturb him and you."

"What is the matter?" said Manners, as two Americans in uniform came in behind the young officer.

"Search party. We heard a radio last night and pin-pointed it in this garden. When it started up again tonight we came over."

"A radio!" said Manners. This time he did not translate. "Well, you certainly won't find it here."

"We'll have a look around."

"I've spent a good bit of time in this room," Manners told him, "and I know there's no space where a radio could be hidden. I've examined the bookcases and the curio cabinets. They are all shallow, and nothing is locked. You can see for yourself."

Osborne glanced around and noticed a doorway, covered by a screen of split bamboo, over which hung the usual board inscribed with Chinese characters.

"What's that?" he asked, pointing.

"That?" Manners adjusted his pince-nez. "That door, according to the name over it, leads to the Chamber for Relaxation after the Fatigue of Labor."

"For God's sake! You don't imagine I care what it's called? I mean, what's in there? Tell the old man we're going in."

Manners said a few apologetic words to his host. The distress which the latter attempted to conceal aroused his sympathy and Osborne's suspicion. The officer lifted the screen and turned on his powerful electric torch.

"Well," he said, "There's plenty here that seems to be locked. Tell him to open up."

The room was very small. Under the window to the north, there was a carved bed, and beside it, a stand with a brass washbasin. The wall space was crowded with chests stacked on top of each other, all, as Osborne had stated, displaying imposing padlocks. Master Yuan produced his keys in silence, but as Osborne was about to take them, Manners interfered.

"See here," he said. "Don't let your men begin throwing things around. I'll do the searching under your supervision. These boxes are probably full of paintings and other valuable things. Let me handle them."

"Okay. I don't want to upset the old man any more than is necessary."

One by one, the chests were lifted out into the larger room, and Manners unpacked and repacked, until it was clear that nothing remained concealed. The best of the old man's collections had been taken out for the visitor's benefit and what remained in the chests was rather pathetic evidence of the care with which every vestige of scholarly treasure trove was lovingly hoarded. The last box to be opened had his supply of fur-lined garments for winter.

"You see? Nothing here." Manners closed the lid and snapped the padlock in its place.

Osborne stood frowning.

"We've been through every other building in the place. And we worked over that grotto. I thought it was queer that white stone figure was shut in behind doors, but we went into the niche and all around— drew blank. Manners, I'd like some talk with you."

"By all means."

The scholar feast had come to an unexpected conclusion, and Master Yuan accepted his guest's acknowledgments and farewells with expressions of his own gratitude for help in the protection of his belongings. Then he vanished from the doorway while the Americans went down the path, and Manners looked back to find his silhouette over the table where the scroll of calligraphy lay. For him the rude interruption was at an end. He had retired once more into his own world.

Osborne told his men to wait for him in the jeep outside the gate and followed Manners into his quarters where the two men could talk at leisure after the servant from Quiet Mind had supplied them with drinks.

"I want to get your help," the Intelligence Officer began. "You are the only one in this garden who is one of us—really, you see. You are in the war effort; but the others are all queer in one way or another. And now we have certain knowledge that there's a radio here which we can't find, it's time we took drastic action. I'm inclined to order everybody out of the place—and—"

Order everyone out of the place—wreck his vacation—Manners cleared his throat.

"Have you suggested this to Miss Breasted?"

"Not yet. She's a Quaker and a pacifist and all that, but we've come to have a great respect for her. I don't want to upset her. But what else can I do?"

"Well," said Manners, lighting his cigarette, "I think I can make a suggestion. I am, as you point out, in the war effort, and I understand how important security is. It seems to me that having me here to keep an eye on what goes on is a fortunate thing for you. I have a rather specialized knowledge of Chinese ways, and it may be that in a day or two I shall pick up a clue which wouldn't mean much to you, or any other American new to this country. Do you want me to see what I can find out?"

"I'm not sure I can wait. And there are peculiar things happening here all the time. I found something very peculiar tonight."

"Possibly it is something I could explain."

"Have you been all over this garden?"

"I believe there are several of the buildings I haven't seen."

"There's one little one, very far out of the way, in the bamboo grove to the northeast. Have you been there?"

"No."

"We were there this evening. Found a table all full of paper and jugs. Also a hot-water bottle. Who wants that, this weather? And under the table a black bag. Turned out to be a doctor's bag with sterile dressings and instruments."

Manners laughed.

"I can't see anything peculiar so far."

Osborne sulked. "Can you explain it?"

"Of course. Miss Grayson is a nurse. The bag is hers. Miss Breasted has recently been in the hospital—is just recovered from an illness. That bag and the equipment of the little room are no business of ours. It certainly doesn't suggest any connection with your radio. By the way, is this the first time you have heard a radio talking?"

"No. We've been hearing it off and on ever since we got to this base. It is a will-o'-the-wisp affair. We hear it, locate it, make a raid—and it isn't to be found, but it keeps quiet then for a bit. I'm getting desperate."

"I can see you need help, and you are going to get it," said Manners. "I am pretty sure I can find out a thing or two before long. By the way, did you tell Miss Breasted what you were after?"

"I told Miss Grayson. She met us and took us all around the place where she and the Quaker live, but she said Miss Breasted was off with a servant and we didn't bother to hunt her up. Do you think you can do more than we have done?"

"I can try," said Manners.

In the San Yu Chai, Stephen was with Jane.

"I hope this unexpected visit hasn't upset thee?" he said to her as she lay back in her peacock chair looking at the reflections of stars in the Pool of the Rock and Pine. "I got Willow into the truck and they didn't search that. They know I don't operate enemy radios, and they were busy going through the garden buildings. I made myself a job with a tire and stayed with it until they went off. So that's that."

"Yes," said Jane thoughtfully. "But since they couldn't find that radio tonight, they will be coming again. And if a radio is being played in the garden, somebody is here secretly, so the problem of keeping Willow hidden remains."

Wilfreda came to the door of the Chai.

"Jane, I think Willow's labor has begun. I ought to stay with her tonight. But I don't like having you alone in this court. Stephen, you are the only one in the secret. Could you sleep here?"

"Of course. What do I do if Jane needs you?"

"Come and tell me," said Wilfreda.

"I shan't need anyone," Jane insisted. "Although of course, Stephen, I shall appreciate it, if thee will ease Wilfreda's mind by being within call."

"We can set up my cot on the *lang-tse*," Freda suggested. "Please help me bring it out. I have sometimes chosen to sleep here, so Shang Ma won't be surprised if she sees it."

The arrangements were swiftly made, and then Wilfreda took her candle lantern and went away to the Joy of Bamboos. Stephen sat down on the steps of the Chai.

"Sleepy, Jane?"

She suddenly straightened in her chair. "Listen!"

There was a confusion of footsteps on the path outside, and the sound of voices talking in Szechuanese, with Shang Shih audible above the others. Jane heard him distinctly: "The Americans have been all over this *yuan-tse* tonight, I tell you, and they have found no one but the people I have reported."

"Ah." She rose. "The Chinese police."

"Good God," said Stephen. "And Willow in labor."

His tone carried so much alarm that Jane leaned toward him.

"Don't worry," she said swiftly. "Just follow my lead."

Behind Shang Shih there was a crowd of shadowy figures who seemed in the gloom to be more numerous than they actually were. Jane rose, faced about, and confronted them with an air which Stephen had never seen before. There was very little light, but her silhouette showed her head high, and there was no mistaking the cold authority in her voice.

"And what is the meaning of this?"

A figure detached itself from the crowd of shadows, pushed Shang Shih aside, and made a speech to which Jane listened unmoved. Stephen could understand only her brief reply:

"The hour is late."

Then Shang Shih broke in with a flood of aggrieved oratory. Again Stephen could not follow the Chinese but was clear about Jane's answer:

"It is quite true. Here is Pu Hsien Sheng. He will tell you that he brought my old student to me only last night."

She turned in his direction and made an elaborate translation, after which Stephen used one of his few Chinese phrases.

"*Twei-liao*—correct."

The leader of the police now put forward a demand which Jane met without hesitation.

"Her name is Fang. Her age is thirty-three. I told you before that she is a former student of mine, so I know all about her. Do you wish to see her?"

Stephen choked. Was Jane crazy? The shadow with the authority obviously did wish to see the former student. At this, there was a curt, "Wait a moment," and the missionary disappeared into the Chai. While she was gone, Shang Shih fidgeted with his lantern, and the assembly of dark forms shifted its feet and muttered with heads together. When she came back, she was carrying a torch which Stephen recognized as a recent present from Jack Fernald. She grasped it so that its beam was focused on some white things she had draped over her left arm. These were the articles which she and Wilfreda had been working on that morning, and spread out on top of them like a splash of blood was the tiniest pair of red cotton trousers that Stephen had ever seen.

The squad of police had come forward as Jane reappeared, but now stopped short.

"Well," she said acidly, "you wish to see Fang T'ai T'ai? It will not be convenient, but you observe neither custom nor courtesy. This way," and she moved toward the door.

No one followed. There was a hurried consultation. Then a question that Stephen could get: Had the Americans seen Fang T'ai T'ai?

Jane's voice had a cutting edge. American men, she said, did not intrude upon women about "to add." This produced a decided effect. The muttering and the shuffling were resumed. All at once the dark figures made profound bows which brought the guns on their backs into sharp relief in the torchlight, and the court was cleared as suddenly as it had been invaded. Shang Shih lagged behind, but a short "I will see you tomorrow" sent him after the others.

Stephen was conscious of an unmanly weakness in his knees, and he collapsed on the step of the *lang-tse*. Jane shut off her torch, disposed of her baby clothes, and came back to her own chair.

"And now," said Stephen feebly, "will thee be good enough to explain what has happened? Also, which is more to the point, what is going to happen next?"

"Oh," Jane began, "they had got information from somewhere— they didn't say where—that we have a new guest in the garden."

"Do you think they have been informed from Chungking?"

"No. It was quite obvious they didn't know her identity. Neither did they know why there was an American search party here tonight. They assumed it was for the same errand. I took the line with them which I have been expecting to take."

"Thee expected them?"

"I was prepared."

"I saw thee shame them by saying they had no manners. They took that hard. But won't they be back?"

"Not for a day or two."

"What makes thee so sure?"

"Stephen, I think I heard that thee has confessed to being unhappy about traveling with a pregnant woman?"

"I was scared to death."

"These men are scareder, if one may use the expression. Here in Szechuan we are very close to the ancient and primitive mind. There is universal dread of contact with a woman in Willow's condition, which turns up even in thy modern self. With Szechuanese, it is a powerful taboo. I intended to make use of it, and I have."

Stephen found himself laughing helplessly.

"And they believed thee! Of course thee does have a reputation for telling the truth, which comes in handy at times. Also, a baby that yells will be proof positive. But since they know Willow is here, although they don't know who she is—what next?"

"She must leave. I hope, Stephen, thee will not be as plagued by masculine fright on the way to Pao Chi with Willow as thee was when thee brought her from Chungking."

"What? Did I hear something about me . . . and Willow . . . and going to Pao Chi?"

"Certainly. Thee told me that day after tomorrow thee leaves for the north. Willow can go underground there until she is entirely strong and able to do the mountain trails to Yennan. She will lie on her mattress in thy truck and make the journey comfortably, since the land rises and it will be much cooler than it was coming from Chungking. I can keep the local police away for two days, I'm sure."

Stephen held his head and groaned.

"Jane, thee is a sort of witch woman. I don't fancy this assignment at all."

"But thee will undertake it?" she asked very gently.

"In my part of the world I never heard of a woman who can make the exertions thee assumes Willow can make. Wouldn't it be all right to let Hot Dog drive to Pao Chi?"

"This is a matter of life and death," Jane reminded him.

Stephen was silent. "The baby goes, too?" he finally asked.

"No. Willow could never get the child along with her. Besides, I need the baby."

"Thee needs the baby?"

"Yes." There was laughter now in her voice. "I've never had one, and I think it's high time I did."

"What thee is really doing is wishing a baby on Wilfreda," Stephen burst out. "Thee certainly asks a great deal of her, Jane."

"Oh, I know, I know. She is everything to me; there is no end to her goodness. But if thee will help me in one thing more, the baby won't be a burden to her—only a joy to us both."

"I'm beginning to be afraid of thy need of help, Jane. What's this idea?"

"If thee can spare some money, we can find a good wet nurse in the village," said Jane briskly. "That is really all I want, Stephen, and I promise no further demands are to be made upon thee, poor boy."

"Oh, the money is easy. Thee may always command that. But can't thee think of any other way to get Willow to safety?"

"Can thee?"

There was a long silence this time. Then Jane began speaking softly.

"When she has talked with me, it has appeared that in spite of her personal tragedy, in spite of her condition, all she really wants to discuss is her belief in the revolution, of which the war of resistance, she says, is just a minor interlude."

"Didn't she take time out from propaganda to thank thee for giving her asylum?"

"Did she thank thee for driving her from Chungking?"

"No. It makes me wonder whether if thee or I got into a jam with her crowd she would help us."

"She is ruthless with herself. No matter what her private feelings might be—and she has affection and gratitude for us who befriend her —she would probably be guided by what she felt was politically expedient. That's the difference between Willow and you and me."

"Thee means," supplied Stephen, "that our Christian view embraces the good of the whole of humanity. Hers embraces . . . just the good of Communists."

"She envisages the whole of humanity as Communist in the end," said Jane. "And there is a tremendous drive and energy in her and her comrades. It is a force we must all reckon with."

"And how are we going to cope with it?" The question was almost desperate.

"We have been meeting it in our way ever since she came to us. Is thee prepared to continue—or has thee had enough?"

It was not usual for Jane to speak like this, but Stephen accepted the rebuke.

"I guess I deserved that. All right. I will drive Willow to Pao Chi."

Chapter Twenty-two

Jane's interview with Shang Shih took place the next morning, and it was quite clear that he felt the Shih Mu had now gone too far in the use she had been making of his master's hospitality. The guests who had so persistently appeared since the two foreign women had taken up their residence in the garden had been a strange collection. He had done his best to carry out his instructions with regard to them all, deriving comfort from the circumstance that the Shang family income had benefited in no small degree. But to be subjected to a police raid on account of a strange woman, and to have her child born in the precincts of the Wang Family Garden without even the knowledge of the servant who was its appointed guardian, produced in him the stiffness of offended dignity which Jane had anticipated.

"I know," she said as he stood before her while Shang Ma cleared the breakfast table and kept a sharp ear out for all details, "I know that it is not the custom in the Province of the Four Rivers to receive strangers at the time of adding. But the war has driven many good people far from their homes down the river, and this guest is one of my own old students. How could I refuse to help her?"

"What will my master say when he knows the police have been here?"

Jane was tempted to tell the gateman that Willow had been received through the good offices of Wang Wei-Chou himself, but she refrained. It would be best to assume all the responsibility and leave Chinese, of whatever description, entirely free of it. Instead of making explanations of her proceedings, she assured the gateman that she would be answerable to his master, and she administered what comfort she could to his offended loyalty by praising his faithfulness and hinting that he need not fear any further attention from the yamen. Then she turned to Shang Ma.

"Did you not tell me a short time ago about a young relative of yours who has recently given birth? I wish to find a good nurse for this child. You must understand that I am the baby's dry mother."

This opened pleasant prospects for the young relative and Shang Ma was not too offended to miss the proffered olive branch. Shang Shih departed, but his wife was eager for more information.

"And when was the baby born? Only three hours ago? Ah, the Hu Shih has been up all night? Mother and child—how are they? It was a first child? Has the Shih Mu seen it?"

"Not yet, Shang Ma. I want you now to go to the Joy of Bamboos and, if Miss Grayson will allow you, stay there with Fang T'ai T'ai so that the Hu Shih may bring my dry daughter and show her to me. I have her little clothes waiting for her in my room. I made them myself."

"I noticed the Shih Mu's sewing." Shang Ma wagged her head. "But I thought it was for some foreign woman in Huai Yuen. The Shih Mu is very clever."

Jane was glad to have so much conceded her. She waited impatiently for Wilfreda, and when the nurse came, she was carrying a small white bundle with a tiny black head at one end of it.

"Just give her to me!" was Jane's demand.

Wilfreda smilingly stooped and laid the baby in her arms.

"Keep the flap of the blanket over her eyes as the Chinese do," she said. "There is bright sunshine this morning."

"Her eyes are nothing but little creases in her face," said Jane, looking very carefully. "She's fast asleep. Well, little one, you aren't as poor and thin as I was afraid you would be. Oh, Wilfreda, how soft she is . . . and how sweetly she draws her breath."

"She draws it just like any baby," Wilfreda remarked, and as her friend looked up, the two women laughed.

"Of course I shall make an idiot of myself over this child," Jane said. "But it's time I took some thought for you. Can you leave Willow with Shang Ma now?"

"Yes, she should sleep for a while."

"Then you should sleep too. And Stephen says I may hire a wet nurse, so there will be plenty of help as soon as you can let Shang Ma go off to get her. Isn't Stephen a dear?"

"Indeed he is. After you went to bed last night, he came up to the Joy of Bamboos and helped me. I had provided a little clay stove and a basket of charcoal, and a big jar of water. I could have managed myself, with luck, but I was thankful for another pair of hands for a bit."

"I should think so! He has reminded me that I am asking a great deal of you. I don't ever forget it, Freda."

"Oh, this is what I am in China for," the other answered. "Only, of course, as a rule one doesn't have to work alone. It was a responsibility, but everything has turned out well. It's amazing what these Chinese women can stand."

"Then go to your own rest. Little Hope and I are going to be perfectly happy for hours and hours," said Jane. "She can sleep in my arms just as well as anywhere else, can't she?"

"I suppose so, though it isn't according to the books," Freda answered. "Do you mean you've picked out a name for her already?"

"Yes. Willow was sure it would be a girl and chose her Chinese name. But she asked me to give an English one, and that's what it is —Hope."

Barry Manners had a leisurely early morning in the Court for Inviting the Pleasures. He had decided that the threat to security, which was also a threat to his arrangements for a week away from Chungking, was more important than any other matters, and he spent the first freshness of the day in considering possible courses of action. If a radio had been on the air, then someone was operating it. Lloyd Osborne had not mentioned his investigations of garden residents, though of course he had made them. Manners decided upon a little conversation with Shang Shih.

The old man presented himself with alacrity when he was sent for. A guest who brought his own servant and discussed bronzes and paintings with Master Yuan was possessed of learning and wealth, and deserved respect on both accounts. When Manners introduced the subject of the raid of the night before, the servant opened his heart.

How, he demanded, could he be responsible for what went on now in the Wang Family Garden? His mind was seven parts tumbled up and eight parts tumbled down! Certainly he had heard no suspicious sounds of a without-wires machine, but he could not be in all parts of the place at once. He had enough to do in tending the gate, and looking after Master Yuan, and now everyone had become suspicious and was asking questions of him, Shang Shih. The Shih Mu allowed too many strangers to come and go. Could he be called to account for what she did? The air-base officer had behaved as if the Chinese of the Wang Family Garden were doing something wrong. He had left men to watch; they walked around the walls all night. Had the officer questioned the Shih Mu about her friends? Did the officer know that a strange woman was hidden in the garden, and was giving birth to a child into the bargain on that very night? This Shang Shih had learned from the Shih Mu's own lips when the Chinese police had come the night before.

Manners raised an eyebrow as he listened to the outburst. So the bag with the instruments was in the little garden house for this pur- pose—and the woman had remained hidden. Osborne hadn't seen her or heard of her. Well, it was doubtless one of Jane's philanthropic performances, and had no connection with the immediate problem. But Osborne would not be pleased to learn that his information about the inmates of the garden had been incomplete, and he might con- sider that if one person had been kept out of his way, there were others, bent on less innocent business than that of giving birth to yet another Celestial. It would be well to move as rapidly as possible. The next thing to do was to see whether Master Yuan had anything interesting to add to what he was saying when he had been interrupted the night before.

Late that afternoon, Lieutenant Osborne again made his appearance in the garden, this time alone, and in response to a message. He found Manners waiting for him.

"You have something important to tell me?" he demanded.

"Of the greatest importance. But I want one assurance from you before I proceed any further."

Osborne looked his question.

"You remember the old scholar whose room you searched last night?"

The young American nodded.

"He has been of the greatest assistance," said Manners. "And what I want you to promise is that you will let me handle anything which comes up concerning him."

"That might be tying my hands, mightn't it? I mean—it's a blank check you are asking for."

"Well," said Manners, "I understand what I'm dealing with, and it's because I understand these matters that I'm able to help you. And I'm not unacquainted with your security headaches. How about it?"

Osborne hesitated. Manners had an obstinate air, and, after all, he wasn't a fool.

"Okay."

He found himself escorted very rapidly through the garden to the grotto which he and his men had searched the night before, and there he met Stephen and the old Chinese who were waiting for him at the mouth of the cave.

"I thought you'd like to see your radio *in situ*," said Manners. "We haven't touched it as yet. Come in and make your own observations."

The wooden doors which ordinarily enclosed the Kuan Yin were now wide open, and the goddess sat immovable and beautiful before them. But just under her feet there was blackness instead of her lotus leaves. The block of stone upon which they were carved had been taken away and was now in the passage at one side. The pedestal, he saw, as he switched on his torch, was not solid as it had appeared, but was made of stones, hollowed and set together without cement. Inside, under the serene figure was quite a space, and in it was what he had been searching for.

"How did you find out this was hollow?" he demanded of Manners.

"We are indebted to the learning of Master Yuan," was the reply. "He made the suggestion, and Mr. Purcell was good enough to help us investigate. We found the piece which has been removed not too heavy for one person to handle once it was identified."

"So the old fellow knew about this?" said Osborne. "Maybe he knows the operator, too?"

"You are leaving that to me," Manners reminded him.

The Chinese scholar had been standing apart from the three Americans waiting until their conversation should be finished. Osborne had looked toward him, and now he moved forward.

"Please tell the American officer," said Master Yuan, "that caution should be used in investigating the interior of the pedestal. Something of the greatest value and importance might be injured by injudicious haste."

Manners translated, and added a word of explanation which made Osborne stare.

"But if he thought the junk he's interested in was here, why did he wait until now to look for it?"

"Chinese scholars," Manners replied, "are not very good at dealing with such matters as the identification of movable stones in what seems a solid substance. Nor am I, myself. We both found Mr. Purcell's practical skills most essential."

Osborne proceeded to remove the radio from its hiding place, and then handed his torch to Master Yuan.

"Please tell him I'm much obliged—and if he'd like to look for his stuff, this will be useful."

The Intelligence Officer busied himself with the inspection of the radio while the old man approached the hole and played the beam around the dusty interior. Nothing was there so far as he could see. But Stephen took the torch and after a moment or two noticed that some loam had been pushed into a little ridge at the back when the radio was shoved in. He reached a long arm into the space and felt in the dirt. He brought out a scroll, tightly rolled, its dark-brocade mounting stained with the damp soil.

"Is that all?" asked Osborne, as Master Yuan received the find in trembling fingers.

Further search produced nothing more, and the Chinese, after asking Manners to express his gratitude, bowed slightly and retired to the Library of Four Delights where he could examine his scroll at his leisure.

"Now," said Manners to Osborne, "are you satisfied that this is what you have been looking for? If you are, what do you propose to do next?"

"Leave it where it is, of course," said Osborne, "and watch for the operator. But I'm afraid too many persons know we've found it. And why did you let the old fellow go off by himself? He may be warning some slopey at this moment."

"I'll answer for Master Yuan. You would never have found your radio without his help. And you must have observed that he did not take the slightest interest in it. I'll go after him as soon as we have finished here and make sure he doesn't mention our explorations of Kuan Yin's pedestal—but it will be quite unnecessary. Chinese scholars do not chatter."

"Well, then," said Osborne, "I'll call my men off their beat around the garden, and we'll let the operator suppose that we have given up the search here. Next time we hear him, we can nab him. But what about you, Purcell? Will you keep quiet?"

"Of course," said Stephen curtly. "I don't nab, but I don't blab either."

He replaced the movable stone, as soon as Osborne had restored the radio to the spot where it had been found, and then the three separated as Stephen escaped to his own quarters, and Osborne and Manners strolled back to the Hall for Inviting the Pleasures.

"You say," Osborne remarked, "that it was this old fellow's learning which gave you the idea of an empty place under the statue. What sort of learning do you mean?"

"He knows the whole story of Buddhism in China," was the answer, "and in particular he knows about the art which arose with Buddhism. He knows the customs connected with the idols—as you would call them. It is not very usual to leave a pedestal hollow, but it is sometimes done, as you saw in this case, and he suspected that we might find it so."

"Is he a Buddhist?" Osborne wanted to know.

Manners betrayed a slight degree of shock.

"Oh, my dear fellow! Of course not. He is a scholar."

"Well, he can't be very rich. What makes you so sure he isn't taking a little cash from the Japanese in connection with this business?"

"If he were, it would be rather strange to lead you to evidence of his complicity, wouldn't it?"

Osborne agreed.

"Still," he said, "I'd certainly like to know what it was he grabbed up so anxiously. I should have had it opened on the spot."

"Suppose I go over and have a look?" Manners suggested.

"Well?" the young man demanded when the Sinologue returned from doing his errand. "Did you see the thing yourself?"

"Yes."

"Could you read it, yourself?"

"Easily."

"What is it?"

"It's not the text that is important. It's the handwriting—the calligraphy. That makes it very precious."

"The handwriting!" said Osborne. "But what's the text?"

"It is the Diamond Sutra," said Manners, "from the brush of the great calligraphist of the Yuan dynasty, Wu Chen."

Chapter Twenty-three

From the Journal of Wilfreda Grayson

Last night Stephen left for Pao Chi with Willow comfortable on her mattress behind a screen of boxes and crates. She has been with us exactly four nights, on the second of which I delivered her of a little girl. That was an evening stuffed with events. A search party came over from the air base hunting for a radio they had heard broadcasting to Japan, and we had a business keeping our guest out of the way. (The radio was not found.) Then when Willow was back in the Joy of Bamboos after that intrusion, she confessed that her pains had begun, and I went on duty with her. It was one o'clock in the morning when Stephen Purcell called me out into the grove to tell me that the Chinese police had been in the garden because information about Willow's arrival had somehow reached them. Jane had let them understand she was in labor and that had sent them scurrying. He thought Jane had been wonderful in getting them to go, but I told him that the Japanese, even when drunk, are equally bashful about entering premises devoted to midwifery. Stephen said he could fully sympathize with the Japanese in this matter, and so it surprised and touched me when he awkwardly asked if he could be of any help. I did need an extra pair of hands, and was thankful to have him fire the charcoal stove for me and get the boiling water ready. Willow took her ordeal in silence, and the labor was short, so we managed very nicely, but of course we were up all night. When I carried little Hope to Jane in the morning, she simply took possession of the child and before night had a wet nurse, introduced by Shang Ma and paid for by Stephen, all installed in our court, with a routine proceeding like clockwork. Willow has seen the baby only once, and that apparently was just in order to make sure that the little thing was physically sound! We did not tell her about the police raid until the morning of the third day, and when we did, she agreed that it was best for her to leave with Stephen. She told us that she can go underground on the road to Pao Chi, and I hope she is already in safety, out of Stephen's truck and off his hands. I also have reason to believe that not much more attention will be paid us by the local police. They lost face in their encounter with Jane, and there is no way in which they can call her to account for her actions. She has told Shang Shih to report the departure, and we expect no further trouble.

Willow is gone, but I find myself thinking about her most of the time. She seems a new type of Chinese—very different, so far as I know, from anything this ancient race and culture has produced before. Jane says, by the way, that "Willow" isn't a translation of any Chinese words at all, but is a nickname used by a few friends in the University where she was Jane's student. It was chosen because of her slenderness and grace, and this connects with what I started to write. She has deliberately destroyed the grace, the gentle speech, the good manners of her bringing up. I suppose her rough behavior has sometimes served as a protection or a disguise, but it seems it has become an integral part of her when she is short with Jane who is devoted to her.

This new type not only disregards courtesy but actually appears to be trying to root out family feeling. I do wonder whether it is going to be possible for Willow to choke her maternal instinct as she seems bent on doing, and I also wonder whether Chinese women in any numbers will follow such an example. About the tragedy of her love affair she has never said a word in my hearing, although I suppose she has talked to Jane. About her child, she has kept me gasping. As I wrote above, she has seen her baby only once. She is leaving the little thing with Jane and me for the time being, but on the other hand, she has no idea of permitting her daughter to grow up among Christian people. No. She regards this helpless mite as a potential revolutionist. There are institutions, it seems, in the Yennan territory where Communist parents leave their children to be reared. I remember the English letter which Willow sent Jane (of course all our talk is in her own language) in which she observed that "marriage is prison," so I have heard with interest how in the party, family life is discouraged and men and women live in dormitories when they are not moving from place to place. I understand that there really is a program to break down the Chinese family system, which is called "feudal," and which any modern-minded person would like to see modified in some ways. But with all its drawbacks, Chinese village life, based on the Chinese family system, is one of the most stable institutions human society has managed to produce, and what will happen if it is destroyed is beyond me to imagine. But to return to Willow. I do not suppose it is fair to say she has no natural feeling for her baby, but she is certainly not allowing the brooding, tender instinct to take possession of her.

Another characteristic which is harder to get rid of than any other, at least for Willow, is humor. I don't have very much myself, I know, but I recognize it as part of the Chinese (and I must add, the American) make-up. Of course there is plenty of British humor, but some of us in our stratified society lack the lighter touch, and I'm one. (Mr. Punch is often a mystery to me!) However, I enjoy people who do have this saving grace, and I have learned to recognize that its complete absence is one mark of the fanatic. The Japanese military have no ability to see a joke, and the remorseless philosophy which Willow has embraced would rule out humor from its adherents, if it could! But as Willow parted from us, I noticed that grimness can't always prevail.

When it was time for her to leave, Stephen and Hot Dog brought a carrying pole with rope to the Joy of Bamboos, to use in making slings in which her mattress could be moved. I saw Jane looking down at her beloved student with her gaze which seeks and dwells—I have no exact words for it—and in the face of the younger woman there was a response which showed that between these two utterly different people affection is deep.

"I remember," said Willow, "how, when I was a student, the soldiers raided our campus looking for me, and you warned me, and got me away. Now I have this to remember."

"Well," said Jane, "and please keep another thing in mind, too, Willow. When you Communists get into power, don't you come to arrest political suspects in my house, or in Stephen's, or in Wilfreda's."

Willow went stiff for a moment, which was her attempt to be the new kind of Chinese. But then a slow smile began in her eyes, and finally curled the corners of her lovely mouth. She promised nothing, but she got the point.

And so she was spirited away, and Jane has inherited the joys of vicarious motherhood. She has the most touching delight in little Hope. We have had some talk about the arrangements which must be made, if Willow cannot send for the baby before Brother Ass stops carrying Jane around, and she is not entirely clear what is to be done. But she is serenely confident that a way will open and makes me share this confidence so that I do not worry. I suppose it is the knowledge that Stephen's big heart and deep purse will be close at hand which makes me easy.

It was amusing to watch Dr. Manners the afternoon when he came to visit us and found little Hope in Jane's lap. She had discovered that the child has her mother's hands, with long delicately shaped fingers, and that she keeps these hands most of the time spread out like little fans, and doesn't want us to change their position. Jane tried to interest the learned one in this bit of baby behavior, but soon realized that in spite of his elaborate courtesy he was not charmed. (I can see that a scholar bored by a baby is quite funny!) She called Sun Nai Nai to take Hope away, and then gave her complete attention to her friend's researches in the garden. He wanted to explain his theory about the three highest points in the range of artificial hills at the center of our northern wall. (These hills interest me because on one there is a stone table with seats where Jane sometimes goes.) He called them the "Fairy Peaks" and said they are often found in Chinese art, and that he believes they are the result of some glimpse of the volcanic heights of Japan looming through the mists on the view of a Chinese voyager long centuries ago before there was much active intercourse between the islands and the continent. He also discoursed with learning and enthusiasm upon the origin of the Mi Fei rock. He thinks it must have been a gift from an important personage in the north, and he explained to Jane how it was made into a great ball of clay so that it could be rolled to some waterway, and then how it must have come up the river to this distant spot and what delicate technique it took to chip the clay away from the wonderful mass itself. To all this, Jane gave the closest attention—or appeared to do so. She enters the worlds of the people around her; her friends usually take it for granted that their preoccupations are what interest her the most. I have tried to get into her garden world, but I still don't like the Mi Fei rock.

Jane Breasted to Robert Trent

. . . So much for my comments upon the things you tell me about yourself in your long letter written in the heat of the Chungking night. It is amazing to me, that you should care for the observations of a woman who has lived far from the world of affairs and can know very little about the America which is your proper element. I suppose our various spheres of activity come closer together under the pressure of the war—and so what a Quaker missionary thinks can be of some concern to an officer in OSS. And conversely, what he thinks—and what he needs—are of importance to her.

I sense something in the way you write—something you make no mention of. Your wistfulness is what I mean. I hope that does not annoy you? You have settled your way of living. The people around you accept your mastery of yourself and your situation. But is it enough? I have the impression that you are looking for something more. Now, are you afraid I am going to talk religion and are you planning to skip what comes next? Let me tell you about one of my own causes for wistfulness. I wish that our words for religious values could be renewed. The present stock of expressions associated with the things of the spirit is shopworn. I make a statement, and what my hearer gets is a false, or at best a dingy, meaning. And so I have not very much to say in these words which have lost their freshness and power. But all the same, I have a little more to say, and please, Robert, do not skip!

You write that I did not tell you very much about the Jane who went to the places and did the things I summarized for you in an earlier letter. Now you are demanding, in your usual way, some information about that inner Jane. I should like to oblige, but how to do it in the language which has gone stale is my problem. However, I will say that as I have moved through recent years of chaos and war, I have been conscious of an acute contrast between the outer and the inner phases of my experience. I will open before you one concrete example of that.

You know that I have space here in the garden for visitors, and you have met at least four of the people who have been here—five, if we include Daisy. But my most recent guest you are not likely to meet. She is an old student, very dear to me, who has identified herself with the Yennan faction. I believe I need not say any more than that to give you a rather clear understanding of her connections and ideas. She has now finished her stay with me, and is gone, but while she was here I spent hours with her, and most of that time I felt like a tree lashed by a storm. I heard her savage anger at the iniquities of our time, for which I have no defense. I marked the ruthlessness which these wrongs have bred in her and her comrades; I was conscious that her dynamic self was always on the stretch of some tension, and that she seldom knows any peace and never reaches an equilibrium. And while I was battered by her wrath I began to find a pattern of words arising in my thoughts which cooled and stilled me as a stream of water refreshes the growing things on its banks. This pattern of words came again and again, as a strain of music runs through the head.

Now I do not know whether these words will convey anything to you. They would mean nothing to my angry guest. But since you have some knowledge of your mother's faith and practice in Friends, I will tell you about them.

The words come from a powerful impression which I received in childhood. My family, when I was little, always went in summer to a Quaker settlement in the Allegheny Mountains, of which perhaps you have heard. It is a child's paradise, with bathing in a mountain lake, ranging the woods for the treasures little folks bring home in grimy hands, going to sleep at night by the glow of the campfire always burning before one's tent—a good-smelling, good-tasting, good-feeling holiday! On First Day, we had Meeting in a grove of pines a little way from camp, so that the sounds and silences of the forest were with us as we sat on the thickness of the needles on the ground. Most of what I heard there, of course, was quite over my head, but one utterance sank deep into me.

In those Meetings there was one old Friend who gave me the words I have spoken of. He preserved the mysticism which we Friends had more generally in the seventeenth century than now. When he rose, he began speaking as the rest did, but soon his sentences became rhythmical, his voice rose to a chant, and his body rocked to and fro. He seemed to experience a great happiness and peace; his old face shone, and his eyes looked far away. I liked the feeling of his joy, and one phrase, which he repeated over and over, remained in my ears. It is that which comes back to haunt me so beautifully now:

We . . . shall be satisfied . . . with the brightness . . . of His rising.

I have never had an experience of God quite like that of the old Quaker who chanted First Day after First Day about the satisfying he had in the brightness of His rising. Neither, I suppose, have you. We experience God in the way of our own time, which is not favorable to ecstasies. For some of us, that sense of wistfulness, which I find in you, is as far as we go. But in these years in West China, it has become clear to me that there is no satisfying to be had out of the sorry scheme of things in my external world, while that inner brightness does not fail me.

J.B.

Chapter Twenty-four

The night had been very long. The flickering of the nerves which twitched at arms and thighs and feet and took away rest had been increasing for hours. Jane tried to control her unruly body and sometimes held it rigid for a moment; but the instant she relaxed, the hot writhing began again, and the flesh which panted for rest was forced back into its unremitting exertion.

At intervals through the night she had risen and paced the floor. She was thankful for the room to herself where she need disturb nobody. She was glad there was stone under her feet which bore her silently while the exhaustion within her contended with the stretching nerve threads, the carriers of misery. When would collapse release her? She thought there had never before been so many hours, consecutively, of this ordeal; and she knew it presaged an attack which would carry her far toward the end. When that took place her consciousness would become like a hand holding a searing iron—reduced to pain alone. But now, her mind was clear and tranquil above the body fret.

It must be long after midnight. She thought of the coming of the light with inexpressible longing, and remembered that for her there would not be many more dawns. She felt an inner compulsion to go abroad into the open air as night drew to its end.

She went over to her basin and pitcher standing on the table by the little saucer of oil with its floating wick. It always gave her a sense of intimacy with the Bible world when she used one of these archaic lamps—a sense which disappeared when she began the attempt to get a light from the box of locally made matches, which had perhaps one

222

in forty capable of igniting. Jane scratched and threw away, counting the number of useless sticks, until a little jet of flame appeared.
She applied it to the clumsy, stinking wick and it caught and burned.
Then she took off her nightdress, and sprinkled her shoulders and
arms with cool water. The fresh drops gave her momentary relief;
but it seemed to her that she was also making a gesture of ceremonial
purification before going out to find the light.

She put on a fresh gown, and over it her loose dark robe. Her straw
sandals had cost her three hundred dollars the first summer she had
been in Huai Yuen, and she never wore them without remembering
that item in her cash account. With this mundane thought twisting
her mouth in a wry smile, she extinguished her light and stepped softly
into the court.

It was a well of shadows. The roof ridges of the four little buildings
cut delicately against the sky where stars were dim. The great old
pine in the corner, and the thickets of bamboo under the windows
where Wilfreda slept had differing densities of the dark; and darkest
of all lay the earth under the steppingstones which led to the door in
the wall. Jane put out her hands to try by sense of touch this thing
which was absence of light. She examined with her fingers the indistinguishable leaves, the rugged tree bark, the vaguely rising wall.
Last of all, she laid flat palms on the stones and the soil and it seemed
that from them a coolness and quiet flowed through her. She thought
without dread that soon they would cool and quiet forever the vagaries
of Brother Ass, while she herself would go free.

She had come out with no definite object in mind, but as she went
on she realized that she was not on her way to any of the garden sites.
The exquisite little scenes conceived by the artist mind and brought
into existence by the laborer's toil, did not call her now. She would
not now be aware of man—man the cunning and evil, and ruthless,
nor even of man the creator of beauty and lover of goodness. She
was in the hand of her Creator, which would soon close over her little
existence in space and time, and the works of man were a trifle and
a burden to her. Her mood was for the planets and the heights—the
great things of God.

She turned from the path, and managed to find the steps of the
eastern ridge, cut in the packed earth. She would circle the garden on

the wooded rise from which she could look over the plain and up to
the stars. At the highest point she could reach, there was a slab table
with stone seats where she would watch for the sun.

She did not see the path as she went slowly northward, but her
feet knew when they trod on hard earth and when they strayed from it.
At first the growth between her and the wall made a complete screen,
and she could see no distance. She lost the freshness that rose into
the garden air from the stream, and passed a remote corner where she
knew there were hothouses, sheds for garden tools, and the sleeping
quarters of Lao Ch'i and Lao Pa. Then she was near the rear gate.
Here the growth fell away so that the uneven terrain to the north
glimmered vaguely under the dim heavens. It was a world of undefined
forms, drained of all color. It was vast. It stretched above the
Himalayas themselves, the towering peaks now shrouded in night
and blotted out in the thick air. Jane shuddered. She was a living pulse
in a spreading suffocation, a miasma, without form or light, a great
void.

She put her hands before her and touched a tree. It was rough,
definite, comforting, and she leaned against it. As she did so, a tiny
point of light flashed out of the dimness to the west, low down on the
plain. It pricked the thick air and was gone. Then it pricked again. It
was coming nearer.

The watcher stood very still. There was only one thing that behaved like that, the bulb of an electric torch; this one must be held
in the hand of someone approaching the garden wall. As the pin-
pricks of light came nearer, she lost them, and realized that they
were too close in for her line of vision. Presently there were steps, and
a figure outlined for a moment in the glow of the torch passed directly
beneath her. Then the scent of a good cigarette became noticeable.
Jane sniffed. She had an association with that particular smell. She
decided to speak.

The sound of her voice in the night was startling to her own ears
and she could sense that to the visitor it was an uncanny interruption. There was no answer, but a complete cessation of movement.

"Don't be troubled," said Jane. "It must be surprising to hear me
talking to you, but I have had a restless night, so I have come out to

try to walk myself quiet. I was surprised by your light as I came along the hills here inside the wall."

There was no answer.

"Benny," said Jane, "if you won't speak to me I shall be very suspicious. You told me you were returning to Chungking. What are you doing here?"

"Teacher Jane!"

The voice was hoarse but plainly Benny's.

"Teacher Jane, you won't get me into trouble?"

"I suspect," said Jane dryly, "that you've already got yourself into trouble."

"What do you mean?" The tone was sullen.

Jane slid to the ground and sat on her heels, with one arm clasping the base of the tree.

"If you won't give me a frank account of yourself, you must be here for no good reason. We had visitors not many days ago. Maybe they were looking for you."

"Listen, Teacher Jane. These are bad times. I've seen and done bad things since you were good to Mother in Manchuria. I couldn't help myself. But I'm trying to get out of the mess. I'm trying to get away. A word from you to anyone about finding me tonight will trap me."

"You appeal to my compassion, Benny. But you don't tell me what you are doing. You must consider whether I have the right to risk danger and distress for other people in order to shield you."

"Teacher Jane, do you believe I would hurt you?"

"Benny I have some common sense. You could gain nothing by hurting me; but when I ask myself what you could gain by certain very hurtful activities which are too general here in West China, the answer is easy."

"What gain do you mean?" Benny spoke too hastily.

"Money!"

"I'm hurting no one. I swear it! But I tell you again one word from you will—do you know what they do to a poor fellow like me when they even suspect what you are hinting? And to be turned over to torture by—by you. Oh, I can't believe you will do it."

Jane could not answer. Of all the monstrous, meaningless violence of war, torture was the evil which held the greatest horror. She did know as much as she could bear to know, what Benny feared. Yet, he must be a spy. His terror was evidence enough. And there had been the raid.

"Promise me to be silent."

His speech was indistinct. His tongue was thick in his mouth.

"Benny, speak the truth and I'll hide you, I'll help you get away. You have only to stop what you're doing. . . ."

"I tell you I'm hurting no one. You wouldn't believe what I said if I talked. You can't hide me. You can only keep quiet."

"Benny, is it because of you that Tokyo Rose seems to know so much? But no. Don't answer. Perhaps you will tell me this: Why did you pretend to go away?"

"I have nothing more to say. I tell you I'm not doing any harm. What are you going to do?"

"Benny, I don't know. I don't know."

"Then there's only one thing left for me. You remember my brother? He knew what the score was, and now, so do I."

Suddenly Jane realized that he had gone. She struggled to her feet, intending to call him back, and then checked herself. An outcry might wake the coolies sleeping in their huts not far distant. She sat down again, trembling and chilled. The violence against which she had borne witness all her life had snaked out a tentacle of its octopus strength and caught her in its grip. To betray Benny was unthinkable, and even at that moment she was sure he knew it. To be responsible for his treachery was impossible. She must stop him without injuring him. Surely he knew her too well to mean his parting threat. She went over it as coolly as she could, but she had almost lost physical control of herself, and became aware that she must deal with the mounting nerve storm. Perhaps she had mastery enough to exercise the shivering flesh and make it obedient to her bidding. She began crawling along the path, forcing her shaking hands and feet to push against the steady ground, and gradually she stilled herself enough so that she stood up. She fell after a step or two; but she persisted, and in the end did walk uncertainly forward. Through her racing, anguished mind a familiar rhythm began to assert itself, first as a beating with no meaning. Then gradually its sense came in the midst of her tumult:

We . . . shall be satisfied . . . with the brightness . . . of His rising.

The words flowed in repetition as she went on. She was following the hill path as she had at first intended, and the stifling sense of the chaos within and the void without produced one blind instinct. Light. She must get to the light.

She reached the highest point on the hill chain, and groped to a stone seat by the slab table. She was facing the east, but the thick dark was still on the horizon. Exhaustion set in; her bodily energy was at an end. But it seemed her thought was clearing and was independent of the inert flesh which, prone upon the stone slab, gasped and turned dim eyes upward. The flow of the word pattern continued and anxiety receded. There came a great compassion for Benny and for all sufferers, guilty and innocent alike.

The rhythm broadened until it seemed the rhythm of life itself which was focusing her attention in intense concentration. The compassion grew into a strange sweetness which embraced all living creatures, and yearned toward the heart of God whence it had descended upon her. As dawn began, the sweetness passed into a thrilling heat, an element not only within her but one in which she existed, clarified, exalted. She had knowledge anew of her being and of all being. There was the night and the dawn; the cold and the heat; the suffering and the surcease from pain; the turning from God which was evil; the turning toward Him which was good. All things were in balance and God was in the midst.

The body slipped to its knees, the arms still across the stone slab. The first sweetness and the second heat were taken up into an ineffable light, in which time ceased.

When the sun rose, flaring red, pouring its blaze upon the plain, Wilfreda looked into the Nameless Room and found it empty. She waited some time and then went out on a search. It was long before she thought of taking the hill path, but at last she found her friend, scarcely able to speak, and unable to rise. Lao Ch'i and Lao Pa carried the Shih Mu to the San Yu Chai and laid her upon her cot. Wilfreda took off the nightdress with an eye for the earth stains from Jane's falling and crawling. She brought the basin and water and bathed her without comment.

"Forgive me," whispered Jane. "I did not mean to make a fuss and . . . so much washing."

"You had better not try to talk now," said Wilfreda. "But can you tell me in a word what happened? Did you have an attack?"

"Not an attack. Later . . . I will try to tell you."

"You must be very quiet now, if we are to avoid one."

"Yes. I must not be sick now. I have things to do."

Chapter Twenty-five

The Szechuan world was gray with mist. Dawn was beginning to lighten on the plain which lay filled with clouded air. No outline of mountain rise or branching tree or low house roof could emerge from the drifting vapors which filled eye and throat with a stifling, if impalpable, density. Sound had become as vague as shape. Solidity seemed a vanished thing.

Wang Wei-Chou strained his eyes for a sign of his garden wall, for a shade of the tree masses rising lofty within it. He was traveling the narrow track from the main highway in a sedan chair carried by two bearers. The little box was very confining for his tall body, and the mist condensed in large drops on his curtains and dripped upon his knees unless he hugged them uncomfortably close to his chest. Before him a gang of coolies tramped rhythmically, bearing on their shoulders the lacquered poles which distributed the weight of a burden, long and narrow, covered with strips of coarse oiled cloth. He could not make out the figures of the men in the lead. The dark shape they carried loomed and swayed and melted into the unearthly dimness.

He took out his pocket flash and looked at his watch. Half-past four. It was an unusual time to be on the road, and he had already been out two hours, but he had his reasons for an arrival at dawn at the River Garden. It was time he was there. The coolies with their load could not go as fast as a ricksha, but they knew their way. Hsu Lao Pan, the man in charge of them, was walking ahead sounding his signals on his wooden clapper for the shift of the load from aching shoulders to those unburdened who waited to take their turn. The Wang family had dealt with the Lao Pan for many years, and it was only the strength of the long-standing connection which had made possible such an errand at such an hour.

Ah . . . the sound of the full current of water gliding in the channel outside his walls. Wang spoke to his men who set down his chair. He stepped out with relief.

"Hsu Lao Pan," he called.

The clapper gave a signal and progress was halted.

"We have arrived." He addressed the outline of a figure which emerged in the grayness. "Let the men set down and rest. I shall go inside."

"We will sit a sit and wait a wait," was the reply.

Wang had stopped at a little distance from his gate. He went forward alone, sensing a dawn freshness in the wet air and drawing the moisture deeply into his lungs. He accompanied his knock with his own voice so that Shang Shih might not be troubled by the early summons. Presently the dark leaf of the gate swung ajar and Wang stood beside his old servant, who had his hand under his arm to fasten his gown even as he made his respectful bow.

"The master is unexpected."

"I have been on the way all night," was the answer. "Who is now here with the Shih Mu?"

Shang Shih launched into an account which threatened to go on indefinitely. His master listened until he realized the number of items to be communicated, and then interrupted.

"Enough. I will hear it all later. Let us go now to the Court of Retirement. Take the keys."

They moved into the garden. The trees rose up into clouds that hid their higher branches. The path led now not to charming glimpses of slender columns under sloping roofs reflected in clear water, but into mists which began to move a little in the strengthening light. Step by step, they passed where low stones marked the ascent to buildings themselves yet out of sight; they heard fish leap in the hidden lake and early bird words from invisible trees. They came to the dim walls pierced with the lantern windows, and Shang Shih undid the oblong lock and gave entrance.

The eaves dripped upon the flagging. Deep shade was in the narrow covered galleries. Wang Wei-Chou went directly to the door of the main hall and paused before the tall carved panels.

"This place is not now in use?" he asked.

"It has not been used since the removal of my old mistress."

"Open the doors."

It was gloomy inside the great room, gloomy and damp. Wang Wei-Chou took out his flash and its thin beam fell on the wide stone slabs of the floor, and on the intricately patterned lattice. It was a tiny thread of light when it was directed upward into the open-timbered roof, but even by such feeble rays, the impression of the fine proportions and stately dignity of the pillared hall gave satisfaction. There was a large screen fronting the open doors, made, he remembered, of a precious deep-red wood, with ivory inlay of little figures of old men and sleek donkeys traveling along mountain roads where delicious little buildings were perched on cliffs, and garden flowers and rocks appeared in the most unlikely places. He recalled the details of this family possession as he turned his light on it. The red of the wood was vague even under the beams of the torch, and the inlay appeared as little patches of pallor; but he satisfied himself that the screen was in good order, and then crossed to the west end where there was a ponderous table and, on either side of it, narrow benches like trestles. These he inspected carefully. They were dark with mold which in the damp could hardly be called dust; and their paint was flaking away, but they were sturdily made and would serve his purpose.

"Sweep out now, and place these *pan teng* before the screen within the doors. Leave all entrances open. I have a certain thing to bring here. I shall go and return soon."

Shang Shih fetched a broom of straws, bound together but minus a handle, and busied himself with breaking down cobwebs and cleaning corners, sills, and lattice, while his master returned to the men outside the garden.

"We will go in," he said to old Hsu. "There is only my gateman awake and others must not be disturbed. If I find there has been no chattering about my errand, after a certain time I will give each of your men a silver *tael*."

Hsu Lao Pan received these instructions impassively, and the gentle

taps of his clapper got his coolies through the routine of the movements which raised their load again upon their shoulders. Then the
signal was given to go forward. The shuffling feet and the tapping clapper were the only sounds as they went through the paths to the Court
of Retirement. There was delicate shifting and balancing to be done
when it came to getting through the entrance to the Court and into the
open doors. But once inside, the burden was eased down upon the
trestles and the stiff oiled covering stripped away. A black-lacquer
coffin, its lines picked out in gold leaf, stood massively in the Hall
Where All Past Wishes Come True.

"Examine it well," said Hsu Lao Pan. "There has been no damage
in the carrying."

The other went over the whole surface methodically with his
torch.

"I see it is as you have said. Your money, you have. Let the men
know that in addition to the wine money I distribute now, there will
be the other of which I have spoken."

He said a word to each carrier as he distributed the tips, and then
they gathered up their poles, their ropes, and cloths, and followed
Shang Shih, whom he had motioned to see them out of the garden.
He himself lingered in the Court. The mists were waving now, as if
the plain were breathing out and drawing in their tenuous shapes. The
walls and rooms and galleries, crowded upon by the dripping pines
and the drenched bamboo, shut him away from the glow of sunrise
which came to him there as shafts of intenser light aloft in the shining
vapor. He walked the low-roofed *lang-tse*, passing from the elevation
of the main hall down the shallow steps to the level of the Fragrance
of Bamboo, on to the south wall by the lantern windows, then back
again past the Shadow of Pines, up four steps to the open doors where
he looked in upon the lacquer and gold which now was clear in outline, ponderous and shining. It had possession of his thoughts as
he walked . . . it was inevitable that Jane must die. From his knowledge of her history, he had believed that she had more time to live
than Dr. Hartshorn had anticipated. The Chinese had also been
confident that the garden would give her some refreshment, perhaps
a surcease before the final suffering shut in upon her. It had been a
satisfaction to provide for her last days the surroundings which were

her heart's desire, but he had not been content to stop with that. It was for his satisfaction that he had now taken a further step. She had no near relative in China; she had no member of her own Mission close at hand. The community at Huai Yuen would do all they could when death took place, but he had been unwilling to leave matters in their hands. They were put to it for money; their arrangements would be, from his point of view, exceedingly crude. He had therefore during his last leave gone straight from establishing Jane in the garden to Hsu Lao Pan and his coffin shop, and had given his orders. He knew that a Japanese offensive was in the making and that soon he would be on duty at the front far away from his old friend, and it would not be possible to be with her at the end. But he had been able to get a brief leave at the moment when word came that his orders had been carried out, and the coffin containing fine-textured and exquisitely wrought Chinese grave clothes was in readiness for the time when Jane might be "invited" to occupy its state. The thing was done, and well done. The question remained as to who could take charge of the final arrangements when he himself could not stand as he wished to do, in the place of the son by the side of the casket. . . . Strange how matters of life and death claimed simultaneously a man's attention. In his days with the army he was absorbed in the fortunes of war, constantly occupied with his work, and yet underneath his public and professional life were the personal matters which he never relinquished. His mother, his son, in their distant retreat, were safe and provided for; this foreign woman who had touched him deeply in his youth had need of him now.

Shang Shih came back with a kettle of hot water and his master's bags, which he deposited at the gate of the court in order to accomplish the locking of the Hall Where All Past Wishes Come True. He joined Wang Wei-Chou by the open doors and together they surveyed the fine workmanship and precious materials of the new purchase.

"This magnificent coffin," said the old servant, "has cost a great deal."

Wang mentioned the exact price.

"For whom is this prepared?" Shang Shih demanded with the freedom born of his long service. "It is too small for you." He dropped the ceremonial third person of address. "The Lao T'ai T'ai, your mother, has her coffin already, the exact mate of your honorable father's. She took it with her when she went to our other estate."

"This matter," was the answer, "is not now to be talked of. But you and your wife may hear and be silent. The coffin is prepared for the Teacher Mother."

In Shang Shih's eyes, as Wang Wei-Chou knew, this would appear a very benevolent, if extravagant, proceeding. It did not suggest any immediate anticipation of death. It was simply an addition to a sense of security to know that one's body would be protected and housed in dignity; and the only peculiarity in the whole affair was that his master had brought his noble gift to the garden at a time when all possible admirers were asleep, and evidently did not intend to give the Shih Mu the pleasure of seeing it. Wang observed the old man's perplexity and as the doors were locked he said:

"Take care to obey me. The thoughts of outside country people are very different from Chinese thoughts. Some might imagine that I had an evil purpose in buying the Shih Mu's coffin."

"The thoughts of the outside country people are often very queer," Shang Shih agreed. "I will obey. Where shall I take the bags and bring the morning rice?"

"I will stay in the Fragrance of Bamboo," said his master. "Make ready there, and I will hear the account of the guests while I eat. Let Shang Ma tell the Shih Mu as soon as she is awake that I am here and bring me word when I may see her."

It was Wilfreda who received him when he presented himself at the San Yu Chai in response to the eager note received from Jane later in the still-foggy morning. The nurse met him at the gate, and with a gesture which asked for silence, led the way into the empty Chai and closed the door communicating with the court, before she turned to him.

"Jane is lying down in the room you chose for her. I will take you in presently. But first, I think you would like to understand what her condition is now."

"Please tell me."

Neither sat down. They stood and spoke in low tones as Wilfreda gave a nurse-to-doctor report up to the morning when Jane was missing. The other followed it closely.

"That brings us, you say, to day before yesterday. Is there anything more?"

"There is, but—"

"But what?"

"I don't know how to tell you. I . . . I wonder if you will understand."

"You can tell me and see."

He stood looking down at her, waiting.

"There was an . . . an experience . . . which was very exhausting. It sapped her strength. You'll see it at once. But the others don't notice. It's amazing how blind people can be."

"You mean she keeps so steady that her condition is not understood?"

"Not understood at all."

"She's been rather full up with Willow, I judge, as well as with her own affairs."

"Oh, so you know about Willow?"

"Shang Shih told me. He considered she took a great liberty to have a child in the Wang Family Garden. But Willow, as I remember her in college, was always taking liberties." And he smiled. "What exactly was the thing that sapped Teacher Jane's strength?"

"A mystical experience . . . it is not a thing to put into words."

Wilfreda brought it out at last and then looked anxiously to see what such a communication would mean to a modern-minded scientist. Wang stood intent.

"Surely you can give me some details?"

She told him what she could. "It left her very weak. Now she summons energy for an especial occasion. Of course she insists she must see you."

"I confess to complete ignorance about matters of this sort. But I do understand some things. I understand that you have carried Teacher Jane from day to day—and done it alone."

"I give her my poor washing and mending and fetching and tending," answered Wilfreda. "That is all I can do."

She turned sharply away, and opened the door.

"Jane is in the room, over there." When she had left him, he crossed the court.

"Come in, Wei-Chou."

Jane was lying on her cot under the lattice through which a pale light fell on her. The mountain mist swirled in at the door as he entered it and hung in the spaces under the roof so that the little house shared in the strangeness and insubstantiality of the outside world. But in Jane's eyes and smile there was warmth and light, although he was quick to see that she made an even smaller bundle in her white sheet than she had when he brought her in her litter to the garden.

"Never mind about looking at Brother Ass professionally," she said. "From you I have no secrets and you will see how it is with him and me; but he matters very little now, just so he will take me a short way further. Sit down and let us talk about something else."

He pulled up a stool to her side and she went on.

"You come at an auspicious moment. Have you heard about Willow?"

"I have. And about her baby. And about your other friends. Shang Shih has made a full report."

"There's very little that escapes Shang Shih," Jane commented. "I must apologize for filling your garden so full of people. I haven't been able to help it." And she looked up a little comically.

"I knew what would happen when I invited you," he assured her. "I am honored and pleased about everything you have done."

He took her hand, let a finger rest on her pulse.

"You should see Willow's baby," Jane began again. "This garden is a place where everything goes blessedly . . . birth, and also, I believe, death."

She waited a moment.

"It is good to be with you and Wilfreda," she continued as he made no reply. "You both know that Brother Ass is not good for much more work, but neither of you confuse me with Brother Ass. At least Wilfreda certainly doesn't, and I hope you don't, Wei-Chou, in spite of your attention to that pulse."

"I suppose I am very far from being as clear about life and death, and body and spirit as my teacher," he answered, "and I'm a doctor. Brother Ass is my business. But I am also your student, you know. I hope to become clearer as I go on."

Jane nodded. "You will."

He laid down her hand.

"Brother Ass is not doing badly. I shall not interfere with you, if that is what you mean. Is there anything I can do for you while I am here?"

Her face lighted up.

"Oh, yes; yes, there is. Wei-Chou, I hope you will not feel that I have been prying and impertinent, but during my days in your garden, I have asked Scholar Yuan to tell me about the people who have lived here, and from him, and the testimony of the place itself, I've an acquaintance now with your great-grandfather, Wang Wen-Hao . . . and your grandfather Wang Ch'eng-Hsin, and with his artist friend Wu Mei-Sun. I can feel their personalities, it seems to me."

"You probably feel them more intimately than I do," said the Chinese, a little sadly. "You know how I have been absorbed in very different interests and how the whole tendency of my generation has been away from the beauty of the past. Since I was sixteen years old I have spent very little time in this place. But what is it that I can do for you?"

"I am coming to that. I have learned which buildings here were erected by your forebears, and I am told that the Joy of Bamboos was built at your grandfather's orders. But neither Shang Shih nor Master Yuan appear to know for what purpose it was intended. Now, if you don't mind, I should like you to tell me."

"I shall tell you with pleasure. It will be good for you to be quiet for a little now, so close your eyes, while you listen and forgive me if I am clumsy at storytelling, which isn't my usual occupation, you know."

Jane drew a breath of contentment and lay relaxed, he noted, as he began.

"I am touched and also a little amused by the discretion of my servant and my old tutor. They both know the story perfectly well, but it is one which is as near a skeleton in a chest—is that the correct expression?—as we have in our immediate past, and so they haven't talked about it."

"But you really don't mind?"

"From my point of view," was the answer, "it reflects credit upon all concerned. So here are the facts. You have heard about my grand-father's romance and its connection with the Porch of the Fan. When his son, Wang Tsung-Tao, became of marriageable age, a bride was chosen for him with a little more attention to his own wishes than had been the case in the preceding generation. In fact, he and the lady—who is my mother, of course—were actually allowed to see each other. This was an ordeal for my mother—she has sometimes men-tioned how very trying she found it—but the young couple were pleased with each other and the marriage took place. Then followed four years during which they became deeply devoted to each other."

"Ah," said Jane, "I have heard of many Chinese marriages which produced romance after the wedding."

"We Chinese say that in the West, people let their water grow cold, while we in China begin with cold water and let it grow hot," was the comment. "But while my parents were happy in each other, the family was very much dissatisfied, because during these four years there were no children. My mother was heartbroken, of course. There came a time when my father was away from home for almost a year, on busi-ness connected with our interests in Canton. When he came back, he paid his respects to his parents in the Court of Retirement, and my mother was also present; but their first meeting was formal—you understand our ways. My father observed that there was a young woman perhaps above the position of a servant, who assisted in offer-ing tea with an almost exaggerated modesty. When he was alone with my grandfather in the Library of Four Delights, he inquired who this addition to the household might be, and was told she was his newly purchased concubine. It seems there was a most energetic aunt who more or less ruled my gentle grandfather after his wife died, and she decreed that there should be no more nonsense in the Wang family about following the requirements of a foreign religion. It was neces-sary to have another generation of Wangs, and for that purpose a concubine must be taken. She chose the girl herself and induced my grandfather to build the Joy of Bamboos for her use."

"And what did your father do?"

"He made no objections when he was first informed of the family decree. He knew quite well that it was his aunt rather than my grand-father with whom he would have to reckon. My father was not as brilliant as my grandfather, but he had considerably more will power. When he was finally alone with my mother, he reproached her for agreeing to the business, though of course he knew that it was almost impossible for her to do anything else. But he made his own solution. A friend of his was thinking of getting married, and my father coolly arranged to send the girl out of the garden at an early opportunity. Then he offered her to his friend. He had a battle with my aunt, of course, but, from what I have heard, I think he really enjoyed telling the old lady where to get off—do I say that correctly?—and it was not very long after all this that I put in an appearance, and my old aunt had to be quiet. In consequence, the Joy of Bamboos never has had much use."

"Willow stayed there," said Jane.

"I know. And she is safe by this time?"

"Yes; we have had word. I'm afraid Shang Shih was very uneasy about that whole affair, but I did try to safeguard him and the other servants."

"Everything you have done was as it should be. I have explained to Shang that Willow was here with my knowledge. That is enough for him. And now your old student is turning into your doctor and ordering you to be quiet, Teacher Jane."

"I always obey orders. It was a nice story. And as you go out, you'd better drop into the Joy of Bamboos, and see the baby."

Chapter Twenty-six

The west windows of Tranquil Heart opened on a little space between the house and the wall enclosing the Court for Inviting the Pleasures. Outside was the path leading from the gate into the garden, and voices on that path were audible one morning at an hour which Barry Manners considered unseasonable as he was awakened from sleep. He lay rather stupidly in his bed, without paying much attention, until a phrase startled him.

". . . have provided her coffin."

The voice was that of Colonel Wang, whom he had met the night before in the company of Master Yuan and had found very silent, in spite of obvious good breeding and the intention to be a courteous host. He was speaking in English to some man who was not easy to identify as he replied:

"But removal will be impossible until after the war."

"I hope you will make clear to Major Trent, who I am told is the only relative in West China, that as long as my roof stands, there will be shelter for Teacher Jane's coffin."

Manners sat up in bed, and then he got the name of the other speaker. "Dr. Hartshorn, I am leaving for the front where an offensive is beginning. I know I shall not see Miss Breasted again. Is there anything more I can do for her?"

So it was the little doctor from the Huai Yuen Hospital who was talking with Wang in this extraordinary manner . . . and breaking into a man's morning rest.

"There's nothing any of us can do, Wilson. Another attack, and the end will come. And from what you and Wilfreda Grayson have to say,

I should judge the attack to be imminent. I suppose you agree with me since you have prepared the coffin already."

"You know our Chinese ways, sir, and I trust you are not shocked."

"Of course I'm not shocked. You have made kind arrangements for what would otherwise be a difficult situation. I'll see that Wilfreda and Major Trent understand your wishes, when the time comes."

"I thank you, sir. I am leaving at once."

The voices had lingered as if the two speakers had come to a halt, but now he heard steps.

"Then good-by, my boy. And God bless you."

The steps turned the corner of the wall in the direction of the gate, but as Manners sat still, the short light tread of the little doctor came back, and Manners heard him sighing and clearing his throat as he came.

God, what a shock. What an incredible thing. Jane, so ill she was expected to die, so ill that the coffin was all ready and waiting for her. Gruesome . . . unbelievable . . . but he could not doubt his own ears. Two doctors had been talking, two men devoted to Jane. And what was he to do?

He got out of bed, hunted for a flask, and poured himself a drink as the first action required in this shattering situation. He looked at his watch. Only six o'clock. Wang was making an early start and Hartshorn must have been spending the night in the garden, though Manners had not been aware of it. But now he recalled that he had seen Hartshorn with Wilfreda Grayson once before, and she had remarked that he came out often from Huai Yuen to visit them. Of course. He was looking after Jane professionally—but Manners had never thought much about that; Jane did not seem ill. She was small and thin, but then the climate wore everyone down—he himself had lost thirty pounds and was frequently off color. He must not neglect his health. He must see a doctor at once upon his return to Chungking—and Jane was always so gay, so full of their common interests—how could a dying woman be as cheerful and as intelligent as Jane? Incredible . . . but the fact . . . indubitable. . . . Perhaps she did not know how serious matters were . . . he had heard nothing about her own view of herself . . . ah, he had hit the right understanding . . . she did not know she was ill, and therefore she did not give the impression of illness to others. But was he entirely correct in saying she was always cheerful? What about their last talk, three mornings ago? Come to think of it, he had been in Huai Yuen all day on Thursday, Friday, Saturday. He had not tried to see Jane—perhaps he should have inquired about her, but she understood him perfectly. She was never offended when he went his own way; she had left him on purpose to do as he pleased with his time in the garden. He had been tired and more interested in seeking out Master Yuan than the little missionary. Still, perhaps three days was too long, perhaps she had been ill while he had been oblivious. And now . . . what was he to do? Illness and death always upset him. Even in the war, he had been a long way from them—though his own health was far from robust—he must really be careful.

That last talk with Jane . . . she had reverted to the subject of the raid. She said she was worried for fear something was going on in the garden and appealed to him to see if he could find out what it was, and prevent it from happening again. Of course she knew nothing about the finds in the grotto. Manners had soothed her, and said he would look around. Actually, he had kept his ear out for a night broadcast, but Osborne told him the instrument had not been heard again. What was he to do? He could go to the grotto and see if there was anything there—it would be a way to interrupt this disturbing flow of thought.

He dressed and went on his errand, to the astonishment of the servant in Quiet Mind who found his master addicted to informal costume and great privacy in his morning hours. Manners discovered nothing to see and nothing to do when he got to the grotto, and he fretted aimlessly about until he decided to open the wooden doors and have a look at the Kuan Yin. The mouth of the cave was to the south and the sun was nowhere near it, so that when he had done this there was not enough light to make it any pleasure to view the statue. But another idea occurred to him. Suppose he removed the block and looked at the radio again? Perhaps he could notice that it had been moved, or something of the sort. He remembered how Purcell had drawn the block out—could he do it himself? Yes. The stone came away easily. He looked. The radio was gone.

Manners sat down in the niche where Benny had smoked and

listened to Jane, and tried to collect himself. Possibly he was mistaken; possibly the dimness of the light accounted for his not being able to see; maybe the radio had been pushed deeper into the space—in which case it had certainly been moved. He broke a long branch from a bush outside and worked it around within the pedestal. It encountered no obstacle. The radio was certainly gone.

Manners replaced the stone and felt suddenly clear. He must go to the air base immediately and report this to Lloyd Osborne. Of course. And once at the air base, would it not be sensible to return to Chungking? He need not see Jane again. Surely, that was best. He could do nothing for her, and he might be badly in the way . . . yes, in the way. He might betray what he knew. Jane would not mind his sudden departure. He could write her a letter and say he had been obliged to leave on some hush-hush errand. She would think nothing of it. She had never objected to any of his whims. And he could write her a letter . . . yes, surely that would be best. The sooner he was off, the better. Possibly he might drop by and bid Master Yuan farewell. But no; it would be unfriendly to see Master Yuan and not go near Jane. Dear Jane. How could this be true . . . this cruel thing? Should he get hold of Hartshorn and find out more about it? But already he knew too much. No. He would go to the air base without delay. He could walk. And the servant could pack up and follow.

There was one thing he could do for his old friend before he went. When he returned to his room he wrote a hasty note:

Dear Jane.

Most unexpectedly I find myself leaving your beautiful garden and your gracious self. I am returning to Chungking where I shall write my thanks for all your kind hospitality. I feel it is yours as much as the hospitality of Colonel Wang whom I enjoyed meeting last night. One thing I want you to know before I go: you need not fear that any more visits in search of a radio will be made. I assure you, that business has come to an end. Do not give it another thought. Ever yours. . . .

He stared at it. Was there anything which betrayed his grievously disturbed frame of mind? The note was so inadequate—years of friendship—but perhaps he would hear from her once again. And she from him. After all, the doctors had not pretended to set a definite time. He hesitated for a moment, underscored the word "ever," and then folded his paper and wrote her name.

The little missive was handed to Jane later in the morning as she sat in the peacock chair where she could look out on her pool and rock. Wilfreda and Dr. Hartshorn were with her, and also Stephen who had that morning returned from his trip to the north. She glanced over the few words and paused as she read what Manners had meant to be a comforting message. But did it mean that Benny had been caught? She was grave.

"Here's Barry gone off in a hurry," she announced. "He had almost finished the visit he intended." She looked at Stephen. "Did thee hear anything at the air base as thee came by?" she asked.

"Hear anything?"

"Have they ever found the radio they were hunting for the night thee hid Willow?"

"I heard nothing about that. But did thee know that they have opened a sort of Red Cross Club at the base with a hostess so that the men can have guests, and that Daisy is there this week end?"

"No," said Jane. "I didn't know that."

She did not ask if Stephen had seen Daisy, fearing that it would humiliate him to say before the others that he had not, and there was a silence. Then he spoke again.

"Jane, has thee forgotten what day this is?"

"What day? Thee means it is First Day?"

"Yes," said Stephen. "Why shouldn't thee hold Meeting for us?"

Wilfreda's eyes sought Dr. Hartshorn, but he gave no sign of objection.

Jane glanced swiftly from face to face. Stephen's need she knew; it seemed that the tired lines of Dr. Hartshorn's forehead betrayed a burden of spirit; and of Wilfreda's cares she was never unmindful. They were all weary and sorrowful. She folded her hands in her lap.

"Let us enter into silence," said Jane.

The mists were in the garden that morning, curling over the hill rises and the *lang-tse* roofs, wreathing the dark trees, moving on the face of the pool. They drifted over the small hushed group. The moments passed. Gradually a concentration began to spread among them. The peace of their mood became heightened, transmuted into something which stirred, which cleansed, which lifted.

Jane's voice was heard:

What shall we render unto the Lord for all His benefits toward us?
All our fresh springs are in Him.

What shall we say in the face of the sufferings of our time?
All our woes and our despairings are from His hand.

What shall we do with ourselves in a world of violence and war?
All the labor of our bodies, all the efforts of our souls, can be wiped out by one bomb.

How shall we meet our secret griefs and terrors?
In the nights, in the days, which one of us escapes being afraid?

How shall we bear the joys which come to us and are denied to our fellows?
How have we dared to taste of loving kindness and tender mercy?

And the benefits and destructions, the terrors and the joys
Will not submit themselves to our understanding.
His ways are all unsearchable.
His paths past finding out.

From His strange and terrible and glorious acts
Our only refuge is Himself.
For He only is our hope
And in Him only is there any promise of life.

The voice had begun calmly enough in the opening sentences, but it rose in a cadence of anguish; at the end, it sank into quiet affirmation and the silence closed over it. The water, lapping on the stones of the pool, came soothingly to ears filled with words which were but dimly comprehended. Gradually, as it had come, the concentration lifted. They did not know how long they had been sitting together when Jane unfolded her hands and laid them on the arms of her chair. As she did so, Daisy came in at the door opposite. Her eyes were fixed on Jane, and she was swaying toward her—swaying and stumbling.

"Aunt Jane . . . Jack went out on mission last night, and he didn't come back."

Stephen caught her in his arms as she collapsed.

Chapter Twenty-seven

To Shang Ma the arrival of Sun Nai Nai, now the proud nurse of Willow's child, was a great boon. Conversation, in the form of an extended monologue on her own part, punctuated by brief and respectful answers indicative of the closest attention on the part of her auditor, was her greatest delight; and it was a pleasure which did not often come her way. Shang Shih and Master Yuan, being men, could not be expected to take any notice of the chatter of a woman. The Hu Shih was always very busy and tired; the Shih Mu had, on several occasions listened with flattering absorption to various matters connected with the history of the Wang family; but for a week now, the Shih Mu had been ill. Sun Nai Nai and the baby, who was known to the servants as Hsiao Mei Mei—Little Sister, had been moved to the Joy of Bamboos, far away from the Court of the Three Friends, where the Englishwoman had taken charge, shutting out all visitors. Even Shang Ma herself was permitted only in the *lang-tse* where the nurse ate hurried meals. It was an odd and sinister idea with outside country people that the sick should be isolated. Chinese flock in upon their indisposed friends, and comfort them with their attention and concern, and benefit them with their combined medical wisdom. But these strangers always behaved as if an invalid were already sealed in a coffin. The poor thing was allowed only the barest necessities of food and tending, and was inhumanly left alone much of the time. And, of course, foreign ideas of medicine were very rudimentary. Master Yuan, being a scholar, had read the Chinese works dealing with herbs and with the art of acupuncture; Shang Ma had no doubt that if he were invited to use a few needles, the Shih Mu would soon be entirely well. She had, indeed, ventured to express this opinion to the Hu Shih, who had

246

then changed the subject. Nothing had come of her effort to be useful, and Shang Ma was not surprised that the atmosphere of the Court of the Three Friends grew less and less healthful.

Things had, in fact, been going from bad to worse, ever since the night the Americans had raided the Wang Family Garden—that night when Master Yuan had his feast of steamed crabs. But Shang Ma had been enjoying herself in spite of the misfortunes of others. Sun Nai Nai she regarded as under her supervision. For many hours of the day, Sun Nai Nai could not only be ordered about but she could be talked to indefinitely. She had been summoned now, to spend the morning in Shang Ma's own corner of the garden. Hsiao Mei Mei had been fed until she slept, and was reposing on the bamboo bed of the inner room. Shang Ma had found a pile of discarded linen in P'u Hsien Sheng's quarters and was busy cutting it into shapes for shoe soles. These pieces were to be treated with an application of flour paste, plastered on a long board, and then left to dry in the sun as a first step in the task of making Shang Shih's winter footgear. The pasting and plastering was assigned to the young wet nurse, who worked at it contentedly as the older woman's talk flowed on.

The doctor from Huai Yuen had been in the garden that morning. Shang Shih had inquired about the young foreign woman who a week ago had walked into his gate without seeing its guardian at all; a little later she had been brought out in P'u Hsien Sheng's arms, and been taken away to the foreign hospital. It seemed the doctor had only shaken his head in response to the inquiry, and had hurried on to visit the invisible Shih Mu. When he had emerged from her guarded doors, Shang Shih had again asked for news, and again all he could report was a shake of the head. Master Yuan was appealed to after the doctor had conferred briefly with him, but he could throw very little light upon the condition of the Shih Mu. It was evident to the gate-man that the old scholar was disturbed. However, the Shih Mu had several times before been invisible, and had emerged her blithe self, so Shang Ma summed up the domestic news for Sun Nai Nai with a note of optimism, and told her that with the change of the moon and the setting up of autumn, which was imminent in the Chinese calendar, improvement might be expected in that quarter.

Sun Nai Nai said that so much sickness made her feel afraid some bad influence was at work in the place, and it was a pity the Hu Shih had refused to buy a silver lucky lock to hang around the baby's neck. The mention of Hsiao Mei Mei produced an air of condescension in Shang Ma.

That child was certainly not properly provided for. Look at its clothes—mostly depressing white. To be sure, there was the one pair of red trousers, and cloth was too expensive to buy; but the foreign women might have found some more old bits of colored cloth to make the little thing's appearance cheerful in some slight degree. Naturally, the children of the Wang family had all had amazingly fine outfits—with red satin for state occasions; but this child belonged to no family at all, and had been born under the Wang roof through the mistaken benevolence of the Shih Mu and the young master.

Sun Nai Nai had seen the young master only at the time when he had come to look at the baby. She had taken the child to the Joy of Bamboos to be out of the way, and she said the young master had come up the path very slowly to the low door, where he had bent his head in order to enter. He had looked at the baby for a moment or two, but then he had seemed to go into a sort of daydream. He had walked about the two little rooms, and had gone to the window of the inner one and remained gazing out into the green stillness of the bamboo grove for a long time. Then he had come back, spoken kindly to the wet nurse, and. . . .

"He gave you money, of course," said Shang Ma. "He always does. How much?"

Sun Nai Nai had not intended to confess to this part of the interview, but she stood in too much awe of Shang Ma to refuse the information.

"Eight hundred yuan."

Shang Ma held out her hand.

"Two hundred," she said briskly.

Sun Nai Nai did not dare to delay or even to pout. She took a packet of oiled paper from some hiding place inside her coat, opened it, counted out the sum required from the wad of paper currency, folded up the remainder, and stowed it away before she returned to her work. Shang Ma rippled on.

"Ah, and so the young master had thoughts in the Joy of Bamboos?

I can well believe it. There he spent his wedding night, and it was not as such nights usually are. I remember the time myself because of a great trouble which happened to me. Do not fray the edges of the cloth as you paste it on the board—pay heed to what you are doing. . . . Ah well, you have never seen a great occasion in a fine family; how should you? You are only a country girl, and when a bride is carried to such a house as ours, all you know about is the procession with the red chair. But I was born in the Wang family service; I was brought up to understand good manners, and I was sometimes allowed to wait upon the old mistress herself in the days just before our young master received his bride. Ah, in those days we did such things in the grand style. For weeks beforehand, everyone was busy with preparations. Everyone had new clothes, and my old mistress was so pleased with me that she gave me silver earrings and hair ornaments which, as you see, I wear to this day. I embroidered my shoes myself; but of course they are worn out. I must say, the young master seemed to have less interest in the wedding than anyone else. My old mistress began by consulting him about the food and the plans for entertainment, but all he would say was that she must please herself and the old master, so finally she stopped talking to him. The only thing he did was to insist that the bridal chamber must be the Joy of Bamboos. This was not at all convenient. The room where Mao Hsien Sheng lived just now—Tranquil Heart—was the proper place. Guests, upon arrival, would be conducted to the Hall for Inviting the Pleasures for the old master and mistress and the young master to receive them before a great Double Happiness Character embroidered upon red satin. Then they would naturally be invited into the bridal chamber, which would be just at hand, and there the bride would be seated on the bed with all her red-satin quilts folded in piles behind her, and the beautiful hangings making her dark head with the pearl and jade look so charming. I expect the family still has the wonderful ornaments I saw our little Young Mistress wear that day. . . . But, as I was saying, she did not sit in Tranquil Heart, but away off in the Joy of Bamboos, and so, perhaps some of the guests did not go to see her. The young master had the notion that the less his bride was teased, the better, and he was quite angry about our customs of plaguing young people during their bridal night. He was so moody about the whole thing that Old Master and Mistress did not want to dispute any minor points with him. When the approach of the red chair was announced and the firecrackers were actually going off outside the gate, he behaved as if he were ill, and it was all the Old Mistress could do to drag him to the entrance court in time to receive the bride. Then he did go through the rest of the day with politeness to everybody, but when night came . . . ah . . . well, no wonder he had thoughts in the Joy of Bamboos."

Sun Nai Nai looked up sideways with appreciation of Shang Ma's relish of a juicy bit of gossip. The older woman paused with an excellent sense of dramatic suspense, and wagged her head knowingly.

"Never shall I forget those hours after the bride had been left in her room and the Young Master had gone in to her, for I was in the worst trouble of my life, and I hope never to be so frightened again. Of course, we had all the family connections at the wedding. Many of them came from a great distance and had to be accommodated with beds after the feasting was at an end. They came with their children and servants and we were put to it to house them all. The younger sister of my Old Mistress had a daughter whose son was ten years old. She had brought an amah for him, of course, a great cow of a woman, and what did that pig of a creature do after she got here but fall ill with some sort of fever and vomiting. And so my Old Mistress commanded me to take over the care of that ten-year-old boy, who had never seen me before and who never listened to anybody, anyway. As soon as he saw me, he started to plague me by running off and hiding. All day I followed, and my only comfort was that at least the walls were high and he could not get out of the garden. When the feast took place, I felt I knew where he was for a time. The guests were seated in the houses around the Happy Sea. The Old Master and Mistress, with the most honorable of their friends and relatives, were in the Water Mirror Pavilion. The children were in the Orchid and Plum Blossom *t'ing-tses* so that the older people could enjoy their pretty faces and amusing antics. Young unmarried ladies had their tables in the Porch of the Fan, and young men were served in the Lute House. There were lanterns and tall cresset lights all around the lake, and as the guests feasted, the bridal pair went from table to table to thank them for their good wishes. Of course the bride was not supposed to drink nor to eat, and hung down her head when she was urged; the Young Master carried all this off very well, I must say. He was attentive to everyone, but he did not allow himself to get drunk, as some of them intended. They knew the customs of our family are a little different, and so the young men made allowances and were not offended with him. But all this time, I was trying to keep my eye on that ten-year-old boy. He would slip out of his place in the Orchid *t'ing-tse* and follow the bridal couple when he was not supposed to; he would join the older guests and make them laugh with his pert answers to their questions; and they liked to make him drink more than was good for him, too. I found he was very curious about the bridal room and the young people, and so were all the other children, only he was unmanageable. At last I thought I had him safe. A dish he was very greedy about was being served, and I supposed he would stay put for a moment with his bowl and chopsticks. I myself was worn out with him, and had not had a bit of fun. And I was young and giddy, too, and . . . well," said Shang Ma evidently changing her mind about giving a complete account of the evening, "I was away from the *t'ing-tse* a little while—for a few moments only, you understand—and when I came back, that wretch of a guest child was nowhere in sight!

"Oh what a panic I was in! I hunted over the whole garden. In the Hall for Inviting the Pleasures, the red-satin Double Happiness Character was being taken down, and the theatrical troupe which was going to give plays on the *t'ai* the next day, was moving in their properties and making places for sleeping. I was young and pretty then," Shang Ma simpered, "and I had no business in the quarters of the players, as you may imagine, but I thought the boy might have gone to watch what they were doing. Once in their court, they teased me and they would not let me go, until I made a great fuss; so when I got out by the lake again, the lights had all burned down and the guests had separated. The men from the restaurants who came to help with the feast were taking away the tables and cleaning up; never a one of them had laid eyes on my naughty boy. I was distracted, for I was supposed to sleep with him. I knew his mother would not give him a thought

until morning, and what would become of me when she found I had
not put him to bed I was terrified to think. I went to every single
garden building. The Old Mistress had her sisters with her in the
Studio of Clear Sounds and I listened outside the window until I was
sure they knew nothing about the runaway. The Old Master was still
up in the Library of Four Delights with Master Yuan, and I heard
them say that weddings were for the young and were fatiguing at
their time of life. Then they began to talk about their books, which
I thought was much more tiring than anything a person could do at
a wedding, but of course scholars are not like other people. I ran on to
the Court of Retirement. Here were the beds for the young women
and the children with their amahs. I hoped my little rascal had found
his own place—but it was empty. I did not dare tell anyone I had lost
him—that would be for the last when I had given up all hope, but I
knew I could not go to the Chai of the Three Friends where the young
men were accommodated. I decided to get Shang Shih to help me;
we were not then married, but he was a friend of mine and would do
me a good turn if he could. So back I went to the gate and told him
my predicament. It was now getting on to three o'clock in the morning. Even the young men were quieting down when Shang Shih went
to hunt for my Ti Ti in their quarters. He came back saying nobody
had seen the boy, and I remember I broke down and began to cry and
wring my hands and wail. We were standing by the Moon Bridge, and
I had some crazy idea of beating my head on the stone rail or jumping
over into the water, when I heard the Young Master's voice.

" 'Here is your nurse, Ti Ti. Now go with her back to your own bed
and be a good child.'

"And there in the dark of the night was Wang Shao Yeh's tall
figure—and he was still in his silk wedding clothes, as Shang Shih and
I could both see. He put the boy's hand in mine and then went away.
Of course you understand what the small rascal had done. He had
gone and hidden under the bridal bed, and waited to see what would
happen."

Sun Nai Nai again slid her eyes expressively in Shang Ma's direction,
and the latter again wagged her head and paused for dramatic effect.

"Of course I got the whole story out of him," she said. "Just a little after he hid himself, the bride was seated on the bed. The women took off her ornaments but did not undress her; they went away leaving her alone. Not long after that, the Young Master came. The boy lifted the embroidered hanging and peeked, and he says our Shao Yeh took no notice of his bride, but went over to the open window and stood staring out of it. After he had been there a few minutes, the New Wife began to cry. She put her little hands over her face and sat in her place swaying and weeping. When she did that, the Young Master turned around and spoke pityingly to her. The little boy did not understand all he heard, but it was something about the two of them suffering. Then the bride asked the Young Master what it was that made him sad, and he told her a long story, and the little boy was not interested and felt sleepy. And then the New Wife said to her bridegroom, 'Since it is so, and you cannot love me, at least let me serve you and comfort you, and let us not grieve our parents who do what they do for our good, as they suppose.'

"And then the boy said the Young Master sat by his bride and they two wept, and some dust got up the boy's nose and he sneezed and they heard him. So they pulled him out from under the bed, and the Shao Yeh came out with him looking for his nurse. The next morning when the Old Mistress and all the guests heard the story, they were very much amused and made him repeat it over and over again so he thought he had done something to be proud of. But the Old Master put his foot down that nothing was to be said about it in the presence of the young couple, and Old Mistress smiled and told the boy's mother that perhaps it was a good omen for the young people's future after all. But she spoke severely to me and I was in disgrace a long time. However, the Young Master's son was born within twelve months, and about the same time it was decided that I should marry Shang Shih, so no evil results came of that night's work. Now, as you see, the Young Master had good reason to look about in the Joy of Bamboos and to be lost in thoughts of the past."

"I have heard the Young Mistress died when her son was born," said Sun Nai Nai sadly.

"Ah, yes," said Shang Ma, "but she did not die in the garden. She was in our city house when that happened, and he was not here. So he was not thinking of the death bed when he went again to the Joy of Bamboos; it must have been the wedding night that came back to him."

"I have filled this board full of shoe shapes," said Sun Nai Nai. "No more can be put to dry at this time."

"And the child is crying," observed Shang Ma in gracious dismissal. "It is time for you to give the breast."

Chapter Twenty-eight

Dr. Hartshorn to Wang Wei-Chou

Jane Breasted died early Monday morning, ten days after you left her. The immediate cause of death was heart failure. Your wishes were carried out. At noon on Tuesday, she "ascended into the coffin," as you Chinese say.

The Friends do not use the burial service common to the rest of our churches; they do not approve of ritual. But the scene in your Ancestral Hall on Tuesday noon was something like your Chinese ceremony of encoffining, and this seemed right to me.

Wilfreda Grayson used the garments you provided; we put the satin footrests, and the headrest in place. We wrapped our friend in the great quilt which fills all the space. There were present only Wilfreda Grayson, Stephen Purcell, and myself. Stephen and I closed the coffin and he sealed the lid. Then we three remained there together in silence until it was time to go.

Purcell has asked me about Jane's finances. I have had to confess that there is no money in hand with which to meet this emergency. Of course, we missionaries in Huai Yuen would have done our best, if you had not stepped in. Purcell would have helped. But none of us, not even Purcell, could have made matters go so simply, so swiftly, so beautifully.

We three send our gratitude to you.

Daniel Hartshorn

I enclose a note from Miss Grayson.

Wilfreda Grayson to Wang Wei-Chou

It is not possible to write at length just now, since I have a good deal

255

to do in making final arrangements, but I think I should tell you what has been decided about little Hope. None of us knows how to communicate with Willow; as I look through Jane's papers, I have come to the conclusion that her only method of reaching her old student was to send word through you. It seems therefore necessary to ask for your protection of the child and her nurse until Willow arranges to have her taken north—which I understand is her intention.

Hope is well, and the woman Shang Ma got for her has been taught a few simple things about hygienic care. We called in Scholar Yuan to ask if he could help us with suggestions, and he thinks it perfectly simple to leave the baby with the nurse in the garden. He even volunteers to inspect the two at stated intervals himself, though what he knows about babies and nurses I can't imagine.

A word about Jane. The end came after she sank into a coma. I was with her. And let me add my own wonder at the exquisite grave clothes we found ready folded in the coffin. She never, in life, was as delicately dressed as she is in death.

I do not know what Jane has meant to you, but I know what your goodness meant to her in the weeks you gave her in your garden. Later, I can write more about it. But that must be for another time.

W.G.

From the Journal of Wilfreda Grayson

Everything is over. Jane had only a week of the agony we dreaded for her. She went into a coma and died when her heart mercifully failed.

That was two nights ago. I have been so occupied ever since that I have had no time to myself. Now, before I leave the garden, which is emptied of everyone but me and Master Yuan, I must set down for myself, and for Michael Chambers, and for a few others who will want to know, some account of these final hours. Events have taken place which concern more than Jane, but there is nothing which is not concerned with her.

Why do little things related to the end of a life seem charged with significance? For Jane herself, there was no sense of coming to an end as she approached death. She felt like one about to pass through a door which was open into light. "Light" was a great word with Jane. The illumination of the doorway was all she needed to know about the other side. So, she had no fear.

Bodily pain she did fear. She supposed, as we all did, that she must endure its very worst a long time before she was done with Brother Ass. And yet, I remember that when I came to her in the spring just after her bad attack, she was not anxious. She was letting herself lie quietly in the hand of God, and said she would be braver the next time. I do not believe she brooded over the frightful prospect before her while she was here in the garden. Now, she will not be hurt any more.

It may be that the shock given Jane by Daisy Fairchild was the beginning of the end. Stephen Purcell, Dr. Hartshorn, and I were with her in the San Yu Chai and she had been holding Quaker Meeting. Of course this is not my way of worship, but I have heard from R Square about the "Covered Meeting" as the Friends call it, when there is a communal experience of the presence of God. This is what happened that morning, and Jane spoke to us in words which I try to remember. R Square will understand them better than I can.

The mood of worship (that seems the wrong word, but I can't think of another) had hardly lifted, when Daisy Fairchild appeared. She took no notice of anyone but Jane. She said Jack Fernald had been lost on mission, and then she fell unconscious and Stephen Purcell caught her in his arms. Dr. Hartshorn went to work over her at once and found that she had a high fever. We thought her bad news might be only delirium, but we found out from the air base that it was true. Daisy had flown over from Chungking to be with young Fernald, and when she arrived, Fuchs noticed that she was not well; but she would allow him to do nothing; she said she was a "tough gal," and she and Jack were to have this time together, and she could not afford to be sick. When he proved to be missing, her one idea was to get to Jane. That accomplished, she fainted.

Stephen got her away to the Huai Yuen Hospital, and there she still is, in a critical condition. No one puts a name on the infection. It is one of those myriad diseases that war against us here in Szechuan. I suspect she was careless about taking precautions—I remember I had to warn her not to use lake water to brush her teeth. Anyhow, her arrival and collapse put the finishing touch to the strain on Jane's strength. Wang Wei-Chou had left her that morning. His good-by had been as gentle and quiet as possible, but still it was good-by for them both. And now young Fernald had been blotted out—they told us later, he went down in flames. As soon as Stephen and Dr. Hartshorn had taken charge of Daisy, Jane let me put her to bed.

The day had been filled with rolling mists, and while I undressed her, the light was growing dim. When she stretched herself upon her cot, she looked up as we heard the first showering on the roof.

"Hush," she said. "The rain."

I was obediently quiet, and she lay listening, as the downpour came steadily, filling our ears, filling the Nameless Room, filling the garden, filling all space in the Szechuan world. She laid her hand under her cheek. I came to sit beside her, and when I took her pulse, it betrayed the exhaustion I expected.

After this, she said a little more. She spoke of Jack Fernald in a sentence or two about his death, and I perceived that she had known about him and Daisy, although just what she knew she did not tell me. She did not say anything about her own shock from the way the news came to her, or of grief for a young life horribly cut off in its prime. She seemed to be dwelling upon something they had discussed, for I heard her whisper, "but he had it," several times. However, she was too withdrawn to say much about the events which had crowded upon her that day. She did not seem to worry about Daisy.

Soon, I thought she slept, but I did not leave her. I sat trying again to call up the words she had used that morning in Meeting, while deep twilight came in at the lattice below which she lay, and at last the dark. After a time, I discovered that her condition was not sleep, and sent Lao Pa through the rain to Huai Yuen to let Dr. Hartshorn know. He could not get back before early morning the next day.

She had a week of suffering, but we were able to keep her under morphine most of the time. When the end came, Dr. Hartshorn told me about the extraordinary forethought of Colonel Wang. He took Stephen and me to the Court of Retirement, and when I saw the great coffin of costly cedarwood, with its ornament of lacquer and gold leaf, I said that I felt Jane would not have chosen such a splendid accommodation for Brother Ass could she have been consulted.

Stephen, although he is a Friend, did not agree.

"She would have understood that it was necessary for Wang Wei-Chou to do this service for her in his own way, according to his own tradition. Jane would not have preached Quaker plainness to him any more than Jesus rebuked the woman with the alabaster box of ointment."

"I know she would have been understanding," I answered. "And I think she would like Brother Ass to stay in the garden as long as possible."

Shang Shih had come with us to unlock the doors, and now he spoke to Dr. Hartshorn.

"The master prepared the grave clothes. Shall I get them for the Hu Shih?"

I had forgotten this part of Chinese custom. At a sign from the doctor, the old servant approached to take away the coffin lid. It is a ponderous thing, and Stephen finally helped him swing it to the floor. Inside we found coat and trousers of white Szechuan crepe, embroidered with the pale-pink plum blossom which is called in Chinese the *meihua*. It is the symbol of spring, I remember Jane once told me. I have never handled such exquisite garments.

That noon, Stephen, Dr. Hartshorn, and I returned to the Hall Where All Past Wishes Come True, and there we three did what was to be done. Then we stood together near the open doors and in the silence of our hearts gave thanks to God for Jane and for her entering into peace. While we were there, two golden butterflies were playing in the shaft of sunlight that touched her resting place. As we left the court, we found the servants waiting at the gate. Shang Ma says they went in and bowed before the coffin. I believe Master Yuan went at another time. I have asked Shang Shih to let the doors stand open so that garden light and air may flow in, as long as I am here.

That was Tuesday. The two men returned to Huai Yuen, where Daisy occupies Stephen completely. Dr. Hartshorn lets him do some of the sitting up with her because they are so desperately short of staff, and Stephen is so desperately anxious to be of use. For me, after the others were gone, rest was imperative and yet I could not rest.

On Wednesday, I set about the packing up. As I was busy in our quarters I heard Shang Shih's familiar shuffle, followed by an unfamiliar step, and then I saw a tall man with heavy shoulders and thinning hair coming into the *lang-tse* where I had taken Jane's letters and books for a final looking over. The thing I noticed about him was the very penetrating quality of his level glance.

"Miss Grayson?" he asked, coming toward me. "I am Robert Trent."

I invited him to sit down, and as he did so, he saw what I was doing and recognized his own letters on the table before me. We looked at each other, and I saw he was laboring under a burden of shock and grief which brought us very near together.

"I heard in Chungking," he said. "She never gave me a hint of this."

"There were very few who knew," I answered. "She preferred to have it so. She felt it was best in view of everything."

"Can you explain a little to me now? Her letters were so gay, so outgoing, so carefree . . . it is impossible to imagine they were written in the shadow of death."

"To Jane, death was not especially shadowy. And hers came much more mercifully than she expected." I found myself telling him more than I had told anyone before—even Stephen Purcell. Perhaps I thought her cousin had a right to such intimate knowledge. He listened in wonder, and he had a great sympathy for me in the midst of his own sense of loss, which was deep. It was extraordinary how we two strangers drew together in those first moments of our talk of Jane. Finally he lifted a letter from the pile before me.

"This is my last to her. It's of no importance now. It refers to one of her old students who was picked up by our Intelligence. His name was Li."

"Oh, Benny? Did you say his name *was* Li?"

"He has committed suicide," said Trent. "He thought he was going to be turned over to the Chinese police and took that way out. I don't blame him."

I found nothing to say. Trent stared at his letter and then tore it slowly to pieces.

"That Eurasian was a queer sort to be a pal of Jane's. But she evidently had all kinds. He had a little money, and he sent word to me that he wanted Jane to use it. Told me how to get hold of it for her. In his message he said another thing. He wanted Jane to understand that he knew she had never done him any harm—it was he who had hurt himself. I wonder what that meant. Do you know?"

I didn't. I had never liked Benny. But this message touched a tenderness in me. Of a sudden my head was down on my arms, and I was weeping—weeping the tears held back so long; they were crowding now, and not to be denied. Robert Trent let me cry for some time, comforting me as if I had been a child, producing his big handkerchief for me to mop up with. At last, I was quiet, and we had a long talk about all sorts of little things which it relieved me to tell and pleased him to hear. At last, he got up and said with authority:

"You had better put all this away, now. I can see that you are quite worn out."

"I got some sleep last night."

His level glance was on me.

"I should think not much. And I have been keeping you too long. I go back to Chungking within a few hours. What are you going to do?"

I said I must finish disposing of Jane's effects if he, as next of kin, gave me permission. He smiled at that.

"One favor before I leave you. Could you let me have something of Jane's to keep—a book perhaps?"

A copy of the writings of Meister Eckhart, a German mystic, full of her notes and marks was lying with her papers. I gave it to him.

"We shall meet again," he said. "But now, I must go back to the air base and you must give yourself a break."

He went away, and I obeyed him and lay down on my cot. The good tears had made sleep possible.

Wilfreda Grayson to Michael Chambers

Tomorrow I shall be leaving Huai Yuen on the postal truck, and should be in Chungking in two days' time. From there I will get whatever transportation I can to Kweichow. I shall go by air if possible. In any case, I shall be on hand soon after, if not before, the date of the reopening of the hospital.

Stephen Purcell will not make the trip south this month with the FSS trucks. Daisy Fairchild's serious illness has not yet reached the point where we can be sure she will recover; but she is young and strong and there seems good hope that she will live. Dr. Hartshorn tells Stephen that her war work is finished; she will require a long convalescence, and should be flown back to the States as soon as she can stand the journey. Stephen has been such a picture of woe that I have been worried about him, and Dr. Hartshorn has undertaken to cheer me up. He says that when Daisy comes out of this illness, it is probable that all the events just before it will seem very remote to her —as if they had happened to somebody else. He thinks there is a good chance that in the end Stephen and Daisy may come together, and he has given this encouragement to Stephen himself.

Expect me in Kweichow by the end of the month.

W.G.

Chapter Twenty-nine

The autumn fogs had begun in the Wang Family Garden. They were not like the mists of summer, for they billowed over the plain in a dark density which did not weave and lift. The days became dim and chill, and there was scant visiting of the sun. The gray of the waters and the rocks was the gray of icy currents and an age-old dankness. The green of the foliage was not entirely stripped away, but the camphor trees dropped old leaves all over the garden walks, and the bamboo blades in the grove grew pale and sifted in yellow leafmeal upon the ground. The coolies put on their padded clothes. Shang Shih got out the brass charcoal container, with its perforated cover, and filled it with glowing fuel. When this was placed under the hem of his heavy quilted gown, it produced a pleasant coziness as he sat smoking his long-stemmed pipe. It was not now necessary to open his doors very often, and he approved of a quiet life. The two women and their baby charge kept to their own quarters in the San Yu Chai. Hsiao Mei Mei sucked and slept, smiled and blinked, kicked and cuddled, and disturbed no one as she grew heavier and livelier—these last were the only changes which Shang Shih observed in her, although Shang Ma was full of reports of remarkable progress which were not of much interest to a man.

Master Yuan, in the Library of Four Delights, had opened his cedar chest and chosen the robe lined with unborn lambskins as best suited to the beginning of the cold. He had, moreover, ordered a supply of charcoal to use in his potbellied stove, which Lao Pa kindled out-of-doors, and, after waiting for noxious gases to burn off, carried by its two handles into the Library. This luxury the old scholar permitted himself late in the day; but even with fur-lined garments, the good fire, and an extra measure of wine, his blood moved sluggishly and his hands were often too stiff for proper handling of his writing brush. However, this was in the nature of things for the learned; since remote antiquity, scholars had suffered from cold hands and feet, which could therefore be regarded as accompaniments of erudition.

Every morning when it did not rain, he took a deliberate promenade in the garden. His route never varied. He crossed the footbridge to the north of his own quarters, rounded the spur of hillocks enclosing the Pond for Reflecting the Clouds, passed the Court of Retirement, and went around the lake, returning along the path to the south of the Library. When he went by the wall with the lantern windows, he usually paused, but the doors which guarded Jane's rest were now never opened. Once every few days he ordered Sun Nai Nai to produce the baby for his inspection. Since he was very capricious about the matter and made the demand at most unlikely intervals, the nurse was obliged to keep little Hope neat and clean at all times, since she never knew when she would be summoned and the heavy spectacles of the old man would be bent upon her and her charge. But there were no intrusions into the room which served as the nursery. Shang Ma was the only visitor there. The women looked after domestic matters while Shang Shih smoked in peace and Master Yuan busied himself with the pursuits of his age and calling.

He had, in fact, his regular routine, which varied ever so slightly, but which kept him constantly occupied. After his morning constitutional, he used the best hours for the exercise of his writing brush. He had made up his mind that something in the nature of his memoirs would be a re-creation of the scholar world to which he belonged, and which, he was aware, was now upon the point of disappearing from the face of the earth. He would enshrine this legacy to posterity in his most painstaking square character. His calligraphy, he knew, did not have the power and the distinction of a master, but it was good in its style. He did not fail to keep the two walnuts which ensured flexibility of finger muscles rolling in his right hand in moments when he permitted himself a little leisure.

One morning when the fog was particularly dense, he found his desk so dark that he decided to burn a lamp in order to aid his brush strokes. In his writing he had come to the greatest experience of his life, and he must do justice to it. For he, Yuan Hsü-Feng, had taken the Palace Examination which had made him a member of the Han Lin Academy and had after the customary lapse of time been presented to the Emperor himself.

His memories carried him into profound revery. The dark Szechuan world, with its somber trees dripping upon the decaying leaves at their roots, and the chill which pinched his fingers and feet with the warning of declining vigor, was no longer present to him. He was standing under the brilliant blue of Peking skies, with a royal sun blazing over the pageantry of which he, young and highhearted, was a part.

He was with the other candidates for the last of the long series of examinations which had weeded out thousands of competitors. He had passed within rose walls, through the Flowery West Gate of the Purple Forbidden City . . . now he was going along the white-marble canal, the River of Golden Waters, to the Gate of Supreme Harmony, which was giving him entrance to the innermost shrine of imperial majesty.

At a noble distance, across the spaces crowded with princes and court officials in splendid attire, he sees the golden-roofed Hall of Supreme Harmony lifted before his eyes. It is high, high above him, supported on three white-marble terraces with five flights of steps opening ways of ascent through the encircling balustrades. On each of the three levels, bronze incense burners are smoking fragrantly into the sun-drenched air . . . and he, Yuan Hsü-Feng, is treading those cloudy steps, is rising into the sacred presence. He is in a grandly proportioned chamber under a roof coffered in green and blue, carried on pillars of smoky gold. He is at the steps of the dragon throne. . . . Finally, when all is done, he is prostrate before the Son of Heaven.

But as the old man in the distant Province of the Four Rivers recalled that triumph, it was not his own achievement which appeared most precious to him. It was rather the sense of a secure order of reasonable life which he had once taken for granted. While the Son of Heaven sat on his dragon throne facing southward over his vast dominions, there was stability and reason in life. The worship of the

Emperor had been the veneration of Order and Reason. Now, nothing was sure. Nothing was according to intelligence. He had lived through one upset after another, with things getting worse and worse, until the dwarf-monkey people had actually swarmed into the empire and were in Peking itself. The resistance of the Chinese was broken into two factions. There was bitter hostility, he knew, between Chungking and Yennan. To crown it all, the Western peoples had mixed in China's war.

His eyes had grown tired and he was beginning to write incorrectly. Master Yuan left his desk and resorted to his bronzes for a thoughtful and refreshing review, until Shang Shih arrived with the food basket. He used afternoons for less exacting work than his memoirs, and to-day he proposed to play with the composition of some antithetical couplets which must have exact balance of meanings, as well as all other attributes of proper verse. He selected a maxim for poetical treatment and made a list of words which were in balance.

man	world
autumn water	breezes of spring
stillness——	

But the balancing expression for stillness gave him a good deal of trouble, and he did not finish his couplets until the food basket was again brought to him. As night came on, he took out his *ch'in* for a pensive twanging, but the cold was penetrating. Outside, an icy drizzle was beginning, and he had thoughts of an early bedtime. But as he was contemplating this pleasant prospect, the grinding of airplane motors overhead disturbed him. Louder and closer, and then farther and fainter they sounded, only to return again and again. Once, when the American officers had been in the garden, this phenomenon had taken place, and the scholar had inquired why aircraft seemed to whir around and around overhead. "Some poor fellow trying to get down," he had been told. That was in the summer. Now that autumn had come, he heard the desperate circling more and more frequently.

On this night of rain, the poor fellow up aloft continued his grinding about for more than half an hour. The noise of the motors then came so low that Master Yuan felt uneasy. The roar increased until another noise, something he could not identify at all, burst all around him. It was an explosion, and dreadfully near. His first impression was that something had happened in the garden itself. Then the whole horizon to the southeast became a vast red glare.

With shaking hands, the old man kindled a lantern, and instead of waiting for Shang Shih to report to him, went out to the gate. He found the leaves of the door wide open and the guardian gone. Shang Ma and Sun Nai Nai, with little Hope in her arms, were in the gatehouse clinging to each other. The only information they could give was that one of the coolies had said the glare came from the neighboring Village of the Eight Families which now appeared to be on fire. It was not long before Shang Shih materialized out of the black rain. He had sent the two coolies to find out what had happened, since neither would stir a step alone. The glare was becoming a deeper flaring red.

Although it seemed an eternity to the group huddled in the gatehouse, it was not more than forty minutes before Lao Ch'i came running back. Lao Pa was behind him, and the two shouted their news in fragments. As Master Yuan pieced it together, he learned that one of the American planes had crashed and plowed through the main street of the village which was only a short distance across the fields. The terrible steel monster had ripped through twenty houses before it had turned over and burst into flames. Many villagers, trapped in their dwellings, had been killed; more had been hurt, and now the whole hamlet had been set on fire by the blazing plane. The coolies had learned this much and had come racing back.

They were only the first arrivals. In a short time, others swarmed out of the wet darkness. Shang Shih grasped that practically all the roofs of the Village of the Eight Families had been wrecked or were ablaze, and in the bitter downpour the people who could walk were fleeing to the garden. The gateman was appalled at his responsibility. Was he to admit the whole countryside? But Master Yuan now took charge of the situation. Many great families became blind and deaf to the suffering of the people in times of emergency, but since the days of Wang Wen-Hao, that had not been the way of this family. The tutor knew very well what orders Wang Wei-Chou would have issued had he been at his gate that night, and he proceeded to issue the same.

"Unlock the Court for Inviting the Pleasures," he said. "Let Lao Ch'i and Lao Pa at once prepare fires and lights. The women and children may go into Tranquil Heart and Quiet Mind; the men should be in the main hall."

The first refugees to arrive were routed to their places by Master Yuan himself, who stood in the center of the court, oblivious of the downpour and his own lack of protection, and gave dignified directions. Shang Shih produced an umbrella with the spread of a small tent, and induced the old man to make use of it before he was wet through, but by the time there was a steady stream of those who were arriving on foot, there were trucks from the air base outside the walls. These were driven by American soldiers and were filled with those who were wounded and burned.

Master Yuan returned to the main gate in time to meet Lloyd Osborne who had an army interpreter with him. Through this man he learned more of what had happened. The whole crew of the plane, which was a transport bringing in supplies from India, had been killed. No one yet knew how many of the villagers were dead. The trucks had been sent from the base with Osborne and Dr. Fuchs to contribute medical supplies and assistance in the transportation of the survivors, but there was no space sufficient for the work of the doctor except in the garden. The village was burning; the small huts and tents of the base would not accommodate such numbers. Could rooms here be used?

"It is permitted," said Master Yuan.

The interpreter told him there were forty injured in the trucks outside and there would be more to come. The scholar turned to Shang Shih.

"Open the Court of Retirement," was his order.

The gateman was reluctant. "Does the Venerable One remember—?" he hinted.

"Tell the American officer that the coffin of the Shih Mu has not yet been removed," said Master Yuan, "but that we have no other place large enough for forty injured people."

The interpreter did not translate the impatient and profane re-marks of Osborne and Fuchs who had joined the conversation, but he reported that the Americans saw no other possibility of shelter, and Master Yuan repeated his order.

"The Shih Mu did not injure people in life," he observed to the gateman. "There need be no fear of her in death."

The glare of the burning plane lighted the way for refugees and for trucks until two hours had gone by; when it sank into an uneasy flickering, the procession to the Wang Family Garden of the weep-ing and the wounded was finished. The outside country people worked with a feverish efficiency to which Master Yuan gave a somewhat reluctant admiration as he looked on.

The hall where Jane's coffin stood was provided with a huge white light strung up to one of the rafters. It spit and hummed but gave out a tremendous illumination, throwing into sharp relief the miser-able bundles of flesh, torn, crushed, or singed, over which the Amer-ican officers bent their taut faces. The most seriously injured were carried from the trucks and laid on the high, heavy tables rapidly collected from the formal rooms of the garden, and the American doctor, in a weird white costume which appeared from one of his leather cases, dealt with all, one after another, who were brought to him. Before very long, rice straw was carried in from somewhere, and as fast as a patient was bandaged and eased he was laid upon a pile on the floor. Osborne directed all these arrangements while Fuchs worked, both keeping an interpreter busy between them. Presently the latter came over to Master Yuan.

"Would you be willing to help?" he wanted to know.

"What help?"

"The Americans want the names of the people. They want them written down. There will be silver given to the families, but there must be a way to count it up. They want the names of the refugees in the other court as well as those of the injured here."

This was work for a scholar, and Master Yuan set about it. The Americans wanted more than the names, it appeared; they wanted information as well, and there were more than two hundred people concerned. The old man and the interpreter worked long hours among the terrified children, the weeping women, the sullen men, the incoherent sufferers while the arc light sputtered and the rain poured down.

Faint day began to dawn. Master Yuan was feeling dizzy from his protracted exertions, when, after a final trip to the Hall Where All Past Wishes Come True, he turned in the direction of his own quarters. He had paid no heed to the cold while he was occupied, but now he was aware that his body was a sliver of stiffness inside his sodden robe. He tottered uncertainly on the path under his huge umbrella which was suddenly too much for him to manage. He lost hold of it and was near falling, when a strong hand was slipped under his arm and a familiar voice was in his ears.

"My honored old teacher, you have wasted too much heart tonight."

He supposed he must be lightheaded and he could hardly frame his lips to his reply.

"Is it possible it is you, Wei-Chou?"

"It is I. I arrived at Huai Yuen last evening on government business. Because of the rain I intended to spend the night in the city, but on account of the accident I made haste to the garden."

Master Yuan was assisted into his own room, and there his fire was rekindled. His wet clothes were taken from him and his feet put into hot water produced by Shang Ma, who had been hovering behind her master, but who was allowed to do nothing but fetch and carry. All the personal service was offered by student to teacher in the old Chinese way, and Yuan Hsü-Feng had never felt so content in all his life as when he found himself given hot drinks and hot applications, topped by a dose of something which made him pleasantly drowsy.

"I hope now," said Wei-Chou while Shang Ma was taking away the discarded clothing and the various jugs and dishes and pails which had been used, "that you will not take cold. I beg you to remain indoors tomorrow and cherish your honorable body. I shall look anxiously for a letter from you to tell me about your health. You have done a good thing for the Wang family in opening our gates to the people."

"Shang Shih had some doubt," croaked the old man, not wishing to use his throat any more than he must.

"Shang Shih is faithful, but you are benevolent and wise. I am thankful to have our family helpful to the poor. I was about to send you a letter concerning the child who is being nursed by Shang Ma's young relative," he added. "I have received word that she will remain here for the present, probably as long as the war lasts."

"Will this be at your expense?"

"It seems she will be here at the expense of Teacher Jane. Major Trent, her relative in Chungking, has sent me a sum of money which he has received from the Eurasian who used to visit in this garden. He was the operator of the radio of which you have special knowledge. I desire to place the money in your hands. It should be enough for three years."

The old man nodded. He understood clearly, but he was disinclined to talk.

Wei-Chou saw him rolled in his covers, where he fell asleep before any further conversation could take place. The younger man reflected that this was well. He could leave his farewell messages with Shang Shih, and give instructions that Master Yuan was to be supplied with Wang family rice until further notice.

As he listened to his tutor's regular breathing, he knew his time for departure had arrived. He crossed the room to survey the weather from the window by the desk, and under his eyes was the section of the memoirs upon which Master Yuan had been at work. The fine, clear calligraphy communicated at a glance, and he read a few lines of the story which in his student days he had heard times without number. He sighed, and turned over the sheet, uncovering the poem with which the labor of the previous afternoon had closed:

> When a man is at peace with himself
> Like the stillness of autumn water,
> Then the world can receive
> The freshening breezes of spring.

Day had come and the deluge from the gray skies was not abating. The master of the Wang Family Garden stood looking out into the dreary cold of ice-rimmed waters and dripping pines, remembering the summer dawn when he had last returned. It was borne in upon him that he stood at the end of much that was familiar and dear. His young son, he knew, could not expect to rear another generation in the manner of former times. The family solidarity, and the practice of a great art of fine living, of which the Chinese scholar had been at once the root and the flower, had flourished worthily within these ancient walls; but now the scholar was old, and his code, his art, and his learning belonged to the past.

Wang Wei-Chou's thoughts turned to the child now sheltered within his walls, born of rebellion, and dedicated already to the revolt of the many against the few. Might there come a time when she would be returning with angry followers to drive him and his away?

The image of the child brought with it the memory of Jane, and over this he brooded. Her touch upon him had begun during his university career. It had proved a turning point for him, and had decided his choice of a profession. It seemed to him, now, that her illness and death had added something to her which had become her legacy to him. He groped for a formulation of it, aware as he did so that what was vague and difficult for him to grasp was probably supremely simple and clear to her. He could not see all that she saw, neither could he walk in all her ways. But something there was . . . something which drew him and steadied him. He was deeply aware of it. He would carry it with him all the rest of his life.

His life . . . his future. He was on his way to the front where the offensive had begun. He might not survive, but that possibility had been a commonplace with him for the last four years. Suppose he did come through the war? The young intellectuals he knew had glowing visions of the role they were to play in creating the new China, but he was not as confident as they. His mind turned insistently to Willow and the forces she symbolized, forces rooted deeply in the history and the experience of the Chinese people. The future as he saw it was one of menace as well as of hope; but for him and his son, the menace was much greater than the hopefulness. This he faced in that early morning hour, as he stood looking into the autumn rain. Then he went out to the gate.

Chapter Thirty

Robert Trent was clearing his desk. It was New Year's Eve, and in the smothering fog which filled the Chungking streets, there were noisy crowds; but in his small room it was very quiet. An unshaded electric bulb hung over his worktable, a crude unpainted stand with drawers that did not fit. He had before him letters and papers sorted into piles, and these he was bestowing in folders bearing the labels of his personal affairs for the year 1944.

His task was almost done. He took up the folder which was marked "Jane." The last papers were lying under a small black-bound book, and this he pushed aside in order to go through them. There were the letters from his cousin; there was the note Li Pei-Ni had sent him after his arrest, begging Trent to come to him; there were documents and correspondence with regard to the fund Li had transferred to him, which he had sent on to Wang Wei-Chou; there was a letter from Wilfreda Grayson reporting her arrival in Kweichow.

Trent placed Jane's letters in her folder, and transferred Wilfreda's to another marked "Current Correspondence." The rest he tore into bits which he dropped on the smoldering charcoal in the brazier standing on the floor at his side. The fragments flared briefly and then turned to ash, leaving threads of acrid smoke in the chilly room. This done, he picked up the book.

It opened easily of itself to one page. Here were penciled marks underscoring a passage at the end of a chapter, and in the blank space beneath, six lines in Jane's hand. Trent sat long over his reading:

God lies in wait for us with nothing so much as love. Love is like a fisherman's hook. Without the hook he could never catch a fish, but once the hook is taken, even though the fish twists hither and yon, still the fisherman is sure of him. And so, too, I speak of love: he who is held by it is held by the strongest of bonds, and yet the stress is pleasant. Moreover, he can sweetly bear all that happens to him. When one has found this bond, he looks for no other.

> *The hook of love*
> *Caught me, long since:*
> *And when strength failed*
> *And pain beset me*
> *Then, on that hook I felt*
> *The tug of God.*

The River Garden of Pure Repose

CENTRAL SECTION

1 Water System
  1a Pool of the Rock and Pine
  1b The Happy Sea
  1c The Pool for Reflecting
      the Clouds
2–2–2 The enclosing walls
3–3–3 The system of artificial hills
      3a, b, c The Celestial Peaks
      3d Stone seats and table
4 The Main Gate
5 The Gatehouse
6 The Turquoise Gates to the Court
  for Inviting the Pleasures
7 Tranquil Heart

8 Quiet Mind
9 Hall for Inviting the Pleasures
10–10 Moon Gates
11 The Water Mirror Pavilion
12 The Plum Blossom T'ing-Tse
13 The Orchid T'ing-Tse
14 The Lute House
15 The Chess T'ing-Tse
16 The Moon Bridge
17 The Temple to the Flowers
18 The T'ing-Tse for Awaiting
  the Moon
19 The Porch of the Fan
20 The Island of the Bat

EAST SECTION

21 The Garden Rockery
22 The Grotto
23 The Joy of Bamboos
24 The Rear Gate
25 Tool House
26 Coolie Quarters
27 The Nameless Room
28 The Cool Room
29 Room for a Little Nap
30 The Chai of the Three Friends
31–31 The Vase Gates
32 The Gallery for Placing
  the Hand upon the Pine
33 The Mi Fei Rock
34 Kitchen
35 Servants' Quarters

WEST SECTION

36 The Fox Fairy Temple
37 The Studio of Clear Sounds
38 The Library of Four Delights
39 The T'ing-Tse for Looking to the
  Snow Mountains
40 The Gate to the Court
  of Retirement
41–41 The Gallery of the Lantern
  Windows
42 The Shadow of Pine
43 The Fragrance of Bamboo
44 The Hall Where All Past
  Wishes Come True

The
River
Garden
of
Pure Repose